MISSING PIECES

MEREDITH TATE

OMNIFIC PUBLISHING
LOS ANGELES

Omnific Publishing
1901 Avenue of the Stars, 2nd floor
Los Angeles, CA 90067
www.omnificpublishing.com

First Omnific eBook edition, March 2015
First Omnific trade paperback edition, March 2015

Library of Congress Cataloguing-in-Publication Data

Tate, Meredith.
   Missing Pieces / Meredith Tate – 1st ed.
   ISBN: 978-1-623421-78-6
   1. Dystopian—Fiction. 2. Arranged Marriage—Fiction.
   3. Alternate History—Fiction. 4. Family Dynamics—Fiction. I. Title

10 9 8 7 6 5 4 3 2 1

Cover Design by Micha Stone and Amy Brokaw
Interior Book Design by Coreen Montagna

Printed in the United States of America

To my late mother, Jessica Ross Tate,
who encouraged me to keep writing and follow my dreams.
And to my two favorite men:
my father, Paul, and my husband, Vincent.
Thank you for believing in me

THE IRRESISTIBLE FORCE PARADOX

What happens when an unstoppable force meets an immovable object?

Friendship is a single soul
dwelling in two bodies.
Aristotle

FOURTEEN YEARS OLD
PART ONE

PIREN ALLSTON

I committed a felony on my thirteenth birthday.

My parents don't know. In fact, nobody does. If anyone learns, I'm screwed — a "fate worse than death," they call it.

I didn't murder anyone; what I did was far worse. The crime was quick, it was careless, and it happened entirely inside my head. A wandering mind is a dangerous place.

I was at the library studying for a history exam when it happened. A girl sat down beside me and pulled out her books, spilling highlighters and pens all over the table. I've known the girl a long time; she's been my best friend since childhood. She flashed her familiar smile, and an unexpected urge shot through me: I wanted to kiss her.

The forbidden thought flashed through my brain and vanished in seconds, but the intensity lingered behind, as if a magnetic force ripped through my whole body. My eyes grew wide. The pencil slid from my hand and landed on the table.

"What?" she asked.

I gaped at her.

She poked my arm. "Out with it."

My mouth opened, but no words came out. I shook my head, backing my chair away from the table. Heart thudding like a bass drum in my chest, I bolted from the library.

Lying in bed that night, my mind raced, struggling to recall the exact wording of the Law I just broke. They made us memorize it in fifth grade, but only pieces clung to me: *Only desire your Assigned Partner. Only kiss your Assigned Partner. Attraction to the Unassigned is forbidden, punishable by Banishment.*

Tracy Bailey is not my Assigned Partner; she's not even supposed to be my friend.

I hardly slept that night, but woke the next day relieved that my secret was safe. That's the good thing about thoughts; they only get you in trouble if you share them.

My Partner is a girl named Lara Goodren. I met her at the Assigning Ceremony eight years ago, when I was six.

"I love you, Lara Goodren," I said to her, when prompted by the Master of Ceremonies.

"I love you, Piren Allston," she replied.

The audience erupted, clapping and hooting their approval. Mom and Dad snapped a million pictures as I wobbled on the stage, staring at the ground. Then back to our seats, and on to the next couple. The whole exchange was awkward as hell, but I did it anyway, as expected and without question.

That was the first time I said "I love you" when I didn't mean it. It wouldn't be the last.

TRACY BAILEY

My Partner's name is Sam Macey. He's got chocolate-brown hair, dark eyes, and a shit-eating grin. Piren says he looks like a cartoon character when he's concentrating real hard. He says when I'm married to Sam, I'll sound like an idiot, because my name will be Tracy Macey. He calls me that when he's trying to piss me off. It works.

I remember at our Assigning Ceremony, Sam was picking his nose. He was probably the first person everyone noticed upon entering the Ceremony Hall, shamelessly digging for gold in the center of the room. The moment I saw him, I scrunched up my face in disgust.

Herded to the side of the stage, I stood among the throng of ribbon-clad, six-year-old girls. A couple of smug five-year-olds joined our group, added to our class to even up a slight gender disparity. Giggling and whispering, we speculated on the potential identities of our Assigned Partners. Tightly-suited boys fidgeted in anticipation across the room.

"Look at that one, with the red hair," one girl said, pointing.

"He's so cute!" said another.

"I want him."

"No, he's mine."

Hundreds of spectators took their seats, thrumming with excitement. There was so much noise in that damn room, it was like crowding inside a buzzing bees' nest.

"Ew, look at that one," a girl said, pointing at the nose picker.

We giggled until our cheeks ached. One fact became clear: no one wanted to Partner with the chubby kid with his finger wedged up his nose. The girl unlucky enough to land him as a prize would surely be ridiculed forever.

Much to my horror, an hour into the Ceremony, the unthinkable happened.

"Sam Macey," the announcer said into the microphone, "and Tracy Bailey."

My heart stopped.

Giggling rabidly, the other girls released a collective sigh of relief. I dredged my miserable feet up to the stage, fists clenched at my sides. Taking one for the team wasn't exactly what I pictured when I envisioned meeting my future husband.

"I love you, Tracy Bailey," Sam said, fiddling with his tie.

I could hear the other girls laughing behind me. My cheeks burned.

"And I love *you*, Sam Macey!" I said in the most hyperbolic, sarcastic chortle I could muster. They could force me to Partner with Sam, but they couldn't force me to be nice about it.

Sam waddled off the stage, and I followed, sinking into a curtsy for the crowd.

Even for a precocious six-year-old, sassing at the Assigning Ceremony was a bold move. Luckily, the announcer went straight to the next couple, oblivious to my contempt. I wasn't so lucky, however, when it came to my parents. The moment we got home, the lecture commenced: I had not *respected* my Partner, and if I don't *respect* my Partner, then I'm everything that's *wrong* with society. What an unthinkable *sin* I committed. I should pay *penance* for my attitude. *Blah blah blah.*

The chiding continued for days. One measly week of Assigned Partnered bliss and I already loathed the word "Partner." Every time I heard it, I wanted to vomit.

It took a week of smiling and nodding to smooth things over with my parents. I was almost in the clear when I opened my big mouth. I wondered aloud a question no one, no matter how audacious, is ever, ever, *ever* permitted to ask.

"What if I don't *want* to marry Sam Macey?"

My father backhanded me across the face. I stumbled backward into the coffee table and tumbled to the floor. Paralyzed with shock, I cowered on the carpet.

"How dare you!" he said, towering over me, half-empty scotch bottle dangling from his right hand.

Gripping my cheek, I floundered in a feeble attempt to stand. My father then delved into the next installment of his screaming lecture: the computers are *never* wrong. Never, ever, ever, and we *never* question our Assignments. How *dare* I get the nerve to ask such a stupid question? *Blah blah blah.* Sam Macey's my Partner, picked for me based on our genetic codes at birth, the *only* person in the entire *town* with whom I can produce strong offspring, and if I don't recognize the *sanctity* of this, then I'm a selfish bitch who doesn't *deserve* a Partner. *Blah blah blah.*

I learned a simple, albeit valuable, lesson that day: "Question the Assigning" equals "get beaten up." I needed to learn to keep my trap shut.

Mom sent me upstairs with no dinner. I sulked on my bed, racked with hunger, whipping a tennis ball at the ceiling. On each hit of the ball, I pictured Sam Macey's face.

PIREN ALLSTON

Tracy Bailey was the first girl to insult me. We were seven and standing in line for lunch at school. The cafeteria offered ample choices, and I couldn't make a decision to save my life. Behind me, Tracy tapped her foot while I weighed the pros and cons of a turkey sandwich.

She knocked into my arm. "Move it, Fat Head."

Everyone giggled. I could feel my face flush.

"Shut up!" I slammed my tray to the counter, sending my milk carton flying. Milk splattered in all directions, soaking the floor and drenching me.

The class nearly fell over themselves laughing as I pawed my wet shirt. My cheeks burned. I blinked back warm tears, determined not to let my classmates see me cry—that's the type of stuff that doesn't leave you till after high school. Head down, I sprinted from the cafeteria as fast as I could.

I spent the rest of the day fuming to myself at my desk until it was finally time to go home.

After school, Tracy Bailey's mother showed up at our house, dragging her daughter by her bushy ponytail. A smug grin spread across my face when I saw my enemy in such a humiliating position.

Tracy's family lived down the street from mine, and our mothers regularly swapped neighborhood gossip under the guise of friendly chit-chat.

Tracy slumped in the doorway, her blue eyes fixed on the floor. While I knew next to nothing about her, I recognized her overall broodiness; I'd seen her embody this posture at school toward various teachers and other authority figures.

I turned to leave her alone in the hallway with our mothers—listening to them blab for an hour seemed a suitable punishment for my curly-haired foe. But Mom grabbed the hood of my sweatshirt and yanked me back, holding me hostage in the doorway. I ground my teeth behind my lips and imagined Tracy vanishing into thin air.

Mrs. Bailey flicked her daughter's arm.

"I'm sorry I called you Fat Head," Tracy said, cheeks growing rosy.

I crossed my arms across my chest. "No you're not."

"Piren!" Mom jabbed me in the side. "Don't be rude."

Scowling, I shook my enemy's hand in atonement.

"There, isn't that better?" Mrs. Bailey asked, flipping through my mother's cellphone photos. Tracy and I nodded, glaring in opposite directions.

"Good. That's over," Mom said. "Piren, take Tracy out and play."

I clenched my fists tight as I could bear. Why would I want to play with Tracy Bailey?

"Now!"

I shoved past Tracy to get outside. I remember wishing I was a smidge older so playing alone with her wouldn't be an option. After all, she's not my Partner, and she's a girl. That day, however, I was stuck with her. As if it wasn't bad enough she ruined my morning, now she was ruining my afternoon.

Seeking an activity requiring the least contact with my nemesis, I dug my ancient sidewalk chalk out of the garage.

Tracy grinned, but I ignored her, spilling the chalk on the ground at our feet. I longed to tell her, in words more suited to a seven-year-old, to fuck off.

Crouching on the driveway, I rotated my back to her. I could hear her scribbling behind me, humming. The sound grated into my nerves. I drew a thick yellow line between us.

"This is my side. That's your side."

We colored in silence for several minutes, until my enemy's squeaky laughter caught my ears.

"This is you." She smirked at her monstrous stick-figure drawing. "Can't forget your big fat head."

Fury churned in my belly.

"Well, this is you." I added fangs to a stick figure of my own.

"You have horns!" She scribbled furiously.

"You have a big ugly tail!"

This went on for about fifteen minutes before we fell back to examine our masterpieces. Colorful chalk monsters, they were unrecognizable as ever resembling human beings. We simultaneously succumbed to giggles.

Tracy tapped my sneaker. "You don't really have a fat head."

"Well, you don't really have fangs."

We spent the next hour drawing cars and pets for our stick figure creations.

That was how Tracy Bailey became my best friend.

TRACY BAILEY

The clanging doorbell echoes from the entryway. My little sister charges past me to answer, primping her hair as she yanks open the door. It takes a herculean level of self-control for me not to groan.

"Good evening, Mr. and Mrs. Hughes," she says with a swoon. "I love you, Oliver Hughes."

A wide grin spreads across the face of her lanky Partner. "I love you, Veronica Bailey."

My sister and Oliver link arms. They traipse through the threshold, steps perfectly synchronized, eyes glued to one another. Oliver's parents trail behind, glowing with pride at their son and his eye candy—I mean, my sister. I follow them to the dining room.

Veronica Lynn Bailey is two years my junior. Her teachers describe her as "spunky," but everyone knows that's code for "obnoxious." She's a little brat, but she makes me laugh so hard I spit my water all over the floor. I've heard people describe her as the skinny version of me, except her hair doesn't curl. We've got the same cobalt eyes, same pale skin, same freckles on the bridge of our noses. Same dimples. She never knows when to shut the hell up, and if she's got an opinion, you're going to hear it. Fills me with pride when people compare me to her.

That being said, she's an enormous pain in my ass.

At their Assigning Ceremony, after the "I love you's," Oliver pecked her on the cheek, then sprinted off the stage to hide. The gooey-eyed crowd *awwed* and pouted, capturing it all on camera. I remember thinking it was weird they didn't lambaste Oliver for kissing my sister before their First Kiss Ceremony. I suppose the audience was so enthralled, they overlooked that little detail. Convenient. I'm guessing Veronica and Oliver could tag-team a murder, and everyone would gush about how cute it was.

Around her eleventh birthday, Veronica spent six hours hunched over a piece of poster board, mapping out the entire seating chart for their wedding. My parents hovered over her, goofy smiles plastered on their faces, adding guests to her already extensive list.

"At least we have *one* normal kid," and "at least *this one's* not a screw-up," are common catchphrases my parents love to use to differentiate me from my otherwise twin-personality sister. When the alcohol breaks out of the closet, so do the parental confessions. I bite my lip and keep my trap shut.

Nothing I can say, short of feigning affection for Sam Macey, could deter them, so why bother? What is there to admire about Sam anyway? His keen deodorant-forgetting skills? His ability to pick his nose in the middle of eighth-grade algebra lab? Sometimes I think it would be funny to idolize these wonderful qualities to my parents, but I can't take another black eye. Last time I showed up at school all bruised up, I got sent to the nurse's office. They handed me some lame pamphlet titled *Working Out Family Conflicts at Home*. The picture on the cover was some cheesy Photoshopped family, laughing and hugging. It was mortifying, and the brochure went right in the trash.

My mother kisses each of Mrs. Hughes' cheeks, and they chatter like a pair of hens, setting out our finest china. My father claps Mr. Hughes on the back, passing him a sweating beer can. We take our seats around the table.

Oliver and his parents come over for dinner at least once a week. Mr. Hughes and my dad are two peas in a pod. They can plow through a grocery cart's worth of six-packs in a matter of hours.

At least once a week, Mom harasses me to invite the Maceys for dinner too.

"Did you call Sam's mom yet?" my mother asks at breakfast.

I twirl my spoon through my cereal. "Um. Sure. I'll do it today."

"Promise?" She crosses her arms. "Because I feel like every time I ask, you say you'll do it, but you mysteriously forget."

I shove a spoonful of bran flakes into my mouth. *She's onto me.*

"Seriously, Tracy, I don't know what the big deal is. You've been Sam's Partner eight years, and we hardly know his family. You're fourteen, for God's sake. It's time."

"Sorry. I'll do it today, I swear."

Nope.

Mandated alone-time isn't Law until you graduate and cohabitate, so why rush? People swoon over their Partners at school all the frigging time. I swear, it takes the Jaws of Life to yank them apart. When I see people behave like that, I want to punch them in the face. I mean, I'm going to be married to Sam until I die. Isn't that more than enough?

PIREN ALLSTON

By our eighth birthdays, Trace and I were inseparable and didn't care who knew it. We'd clomp through Harker's Woods behind my house like we owned the whole forest. Trace's insatiable need for adventure rivaled that of my own. If an adventure didn't present itself to us, we'd invent one. We found all sorts of bugs to study, rocks to climb, and streams to wade through. The forest granted us unlimited access to the adventure we craved.

Our greatest forest discovery was an abandoned treehouse nestled in a sturdy oak tree. I'm guessing my neighbors constructed it years ago but left it behind as their kids aged. The tree itself grew at a slight angle, and it could easily be a hundred years old. While Harker's Woods is known for density, the treehouse tree stood alone in a wide clearing.

Whoever built the treehouse wasn't screwing around. A thick wooden ladder at least ten feet high led to the top. Four boarded walls sealed the fortress, parted by a single skinny opening for a door and two gaps in the sides. Coated in thick layers of pine needles and sap, the sticky floor appeared deceivingly unstable; however, it withstood our combined weight, even when jumping up and down. Carved into each wall, tiny porthole windows facilitated spying on the outside world. The best part, we agreed, was the fact that it was roofless. When we lay flat on our backs, the vast sky beckoned to us, inviting us to stay outside just a little bit longer.

From the moment we happened upon the treehouse, it became *our* treehouse — our sanctuary, our pirate ship, our castle, our hideaway, our place. We visited it every day after school.

Trace and I shared all our secrets lying on the floor of our treehouse, from the juicy to the mundane. I relished the chance to share my day's stories with her, and most afternoons I couldn't get up that ladder fast enough. She'd perch her chin on her hands and smile up at me, awaiting whatever news I wanted to tell. I knew she already accepted my secrets before I even opened my mouth. Her presence draped me in an overwhelming sense of comfort.

I told her everything: how my mom still tucked me in at night, how recurring nightmares wrecked my sleep, and how I'm jealous of my brother's dark hair. She told me about her parents' fights, and how she fell asleep at night to the sound of shouting. No topic was off-limits in our sanctuary.

One day, things changed.

"My parents said I can't see you anymore," Trace said, dangling her legs off the side of the treehouse.

My forehead crinkled. "Why?"

"You're not Sam." She rolled her eyes. "And my dad said if I hang out with you again, he'll smack me." She pitched a handful of stray leaves off the side with more force than necessary.

I leaned my head against the wood. "So, what do you want to do?"

"Nothing." She shrugged. "They don't know about this place."

"Aren't you scared they'll find out?"

"I won't tell if you don't."

From that day forward, the treehouse became our secret meeting place, far from prying eyes. Built too far into the woods to be seen from the road, it was the perfect cover for a forbidden friendship.

Sometimes, we imagined the treehouse was a castle we'd sworn an oath to protect. We dug a moat around the base of the tree and taped a paper flag to one of the portholes. Trace appointed herself Queen of the Castle and named me her trusty King: two royal friends leading a peaceful and fair kingdom.

Trace and I tied a collection of stuffed animals and action figures to plastic-bag parachutes. When enemies threatened the castle, we tossed our warriors over the side to fight. For a well-guarded castle, it regularly fell under siege.

One warm spring day, Trace and I marked our territory.

"P.A. and T.B. This tree is ours!" Trace said, slicing our initials into the bark with her father's pocket knife.

The whole kingdom went wild.

TRACY BAILEY

I pull on my shoes and slip out the back door.

Treehouse? I text Piren.

Some might say eighth graders are too old for treehouses, but they've obviously never had a treehouse. My phone buzzes.

Ya! One min.

Years of experience taught me to leave the house when my father drinks. The whiskey pops out, and so do I.

Hiking through Harker's Woods, I inhale the piney forest air. I climb to the top of the treehouse and hang my legs over the side. Soon, Piren's head pops into view below, his ruffled blond hair partially shrouded by his sweatshirt hood. He speeds up the ladder rungs and into the fort.

I point to his hood. "You look like an ax-murderer."

He tugs it lower over his forehead. "That's what I was going for, actually."

"Well, it's working. Candy?" I hold out a box of Junior Mints and pour some into his waiting hand.

He knocks it back in one swoop. "What's up?"

"Nothing. Bored."

He slides down beside me. "Your dad up to his usual antics?"

"Yep. As always."

Piren holds out his palm, and I press my hand to his. "Don't let him get to you."

We lean back against the treehouse wall, stretching our legs out in front of us. I stack a pile of twigs on the floor into a leaning tower. Those damn sticks always seem to accumulate during the night, as if the tree sheds a million little souvenirs for us while we sleep.

"I failed the algebra exam." Piren shuffles his red-sneakered feet. "Again."

"That sucks." I nudge his foot with mine. "But it's not the final. You've got time."

"Yeah, but I don't get it at all." His leg jiggles against the floorboards. "And Mr. Harvey's no freaking help."

"I'll help you. Bring it up here tomorrow. Don't worry."

He shrugs. "I'm not worried."

I raise my brows at his bouncing leg.

"Okay, maybe a little." He shoots me a sheepish grin.

I balance another stick on top of my pile. "Maybe Mr. Harvey can't teach you properly because he's too busy boning Mrs. Harvey in the copy room."

"No way!" His eyes grow wide. "At school?"

"Well, don't you think it's weird having Partners work in the same building? I mean, whose bright idea was that?"

He bursts out laughing.

Mission accomplished.

We sit in the tree for hours, and soon enough, our ribs ache from laughing. When my best friend laughs, his eyes light up, and I can't help but smile too.

Sometimes, watching the ground below, I feel invincible; it's Piren and me against the world. No one can find us, and no one can hurt us. Every time I climb those rungs, I feel like I'm crossing a barrier into the safe zone.

Our invincible moment is short-lived. Darkness descends on Harker's Woods, and Piren's phone buzzes.

"It's Mom. I gotta run," he says. "Pot roast for dinner."

I flick my stick-tower, scattering the twigs across the floor. "Does she know you're out with me?"

"Nope. Didn't wanna hear a lecture."

"Sorry." I rise to my feet and pat dirt off my pants. "If it's any consolation, my parents don't know either, but they'll still lecture me about something else anyway."

We say good night and walk back to our respective homes.

PIREN ALLSTON

Our elementary school boasted an enormous assembly room. It contained enough squishy red seats for the entire student body and an illuminated podium up front for speakers.

Only two occasions allowed students entry into the assembly room: the class graduation or someone got in trouble.

Trace and I always cheered when Principal Matthews announced assemblies. We knew it meant one thing: a troublemaking student had to get up in front of the whole school and admit whatever bad thing they did. Usually, the offense was stealing from the teacher's desk or mouthing off. Our principal called these "Atonement Exercises," and they were hilarious. Most kids stood on stage stuttering until a teacher finally grew merciful and let them leave.

Around age ten, Trace sassed our English teacher one too many times, and Mr. Matthews sentenced her to Atonement Exercises. He called a full assembly for Trace to state her sincere remorse to the school.

When he announced Trace's name over the intercom, I burst out laughing, right in the middle of class. Trace never has remorse for sassing anybody.

She took the stage with poise. Three hundred students watched as she gazed somberly toward the teacher she'd wronged.

"Mrs. Henkel," she said, laying a hand over her heart. "My dear, sweet Mrs. Henkel. I'm so incredibly, unbelievably sorry. My dark, dark world!" She threw her arms in the air. "It's a world of regret, Mrs. Henkel. It's a dark world of regret for what I've done. Have mercy on my poor, groveling soul."

She dragged it on for about twenty minutes, to growing giggles in the audience.

Finally, Trace threw herself on the ground in a heap of fake sobs at Mrs. Henkel's feet. Our teacher jumped back in alarm.

The entire student body rose to their feet in an eruption of laughter and applause. Trace stood and took a resounding bow.

Mr. Matthews ate up the whole act. He gave a longwinded speech congratulating Trace, saying, "That's how an apology should be done!" Trace's show became a running joke, not only between Trace and me, but the whole school.

For a good two months, anytime anyone remotely broke a rule, "It's a dark world of regret…" made a triumphant reappearance. Trace-impersonators lurked everywhere—the halls, the cafeteria, the library, everywhere. I admired her ability to inspire so many trouble-makers.

Following Trace's grand act, assemblies became a challenge. How would the next person top her performance? Students tripped over each other for a good seat. Trace even strived to outdo herself, scheming ways to get in more trouble and earn an encore production.

A few months after her show, we struggled to mask our enthusiasm when the principal announced another assembly. We bounded down the auditorium aisle like tigers, eager for the next contender.

But it was an administrator, not a student, who took the podium that particular day. The woman stepped up to the microphone, her lips pursed, eyelids heavy. Trace cocked her head at me from two rows down.

"Students," the administrator addressed, brushing her hands down her starchy gray dress. "I have to discuss something with you today. It isn't pleasant, but it's something you need to hear." She took a deep breath. "I was outside the other day, chaperoning recess, when I heard a student say something very…*disturbing.*"

Rigid teachers paced the aisles, inspecting the student audience for any signs of misbehavior. Fabric rustled throughout the auditorium as kids squirmed in their seats. This was not a normal assembly.

"This particular student," the speaker continued, "in some sort of perverse game, told another student—not their Partner—that they *loved* them."

Everyone in the audience gasped.

The woman pinched her forehead. "The student then proceeded to laugh, as if the crime was a *joke.* The words 'I love you' were said in blasphemy."

No one dared speak. Tension loomed over the student body like a thick shroud.

"Students." She closed her eyes. "I want to impress upon you the severity of this incident. In the adult world, this action would be a crime punishable by Banishment. That is not a fate I would wish upon *any of you.*"

Her stare bore into the crowd, meeting hundreds of trembling faces unable to break her gaze. "It is clear this student acted impulsively, as a child would. Therefore, the school administration has decided not to press charges or pursue expulsion at this time."

Relief washed over me, and I released the heavy breath I didn't realize I was holding. Sometimes when I'm anxious, I have this tick where I jiggle my leg. At this point, my knee bounced so fast, I worried it might launch into the air like a rocket.

"But know this." She thrust her index finger in the air. "If I, any time now or in the future, hear those words used illegally again, the student or students involved will be treated as informed adults, and punishment will be delivered as such."

I swallowed a lump down my dry throat.

"I do not wish to implore the Mayor to Banish a child. But do not put me into a situation that forces me to do what I don't want to." She scanned the tense crowd once more. "Good day."

The administrator swept off the stage, disappearing through a door in the back.

No one spoke a word as the assembly emptied. Not even Trace.

TRACY BAILEY

Today's Shaming Section of the newspaper boasts a juicy story on my childhood hairdresser, Sylvia Keyes. I liked Sylvia because she always handed out lemon drops after a haircut; it was the perfect bribery to make me chop my curls.

> Sylvia Keyes, 39, was found guilty three felony counts of adultery. Count one: physical and sexual intimacy with a non-Partner. Count two: attempt to conceive a child with a non-Partner. Count three: blasphemous use of "I love you" toward a non-Partner. Jack Archer, 45, was identified and charged as the non-Partner.

> Witnesses speculate Archer and Keyes met at Capstone Mall, where Keyes worked at Bridges Salon and Archer worked as mall custodian. Both Archer and Keyes had their allotted two children with their Partners, Rebecca Archer and Alexander Keyes. Rebecca and Alexander will immediately gain full custody of their children. The Mayor signed the Banishment Decree Friday evening, allowing Archer and Keyes a twenty-four-hour grace period to pack belongings before transport to Lornstown.

My dad finds the article before I do and slides it down the table to me. He knows I love reading the trashy stuff.

"Check out this one, Tracy. Big whore, fucking the mall custodian. Partner was a doctor, too. What an idiot she is." He sips his foaming beer, flipping to the next section of the paper.

I scan the article. "Wow, Sylvia Keyes. Who would've thought?"

Veronica slouches at the end of the table, reviewing her English homework. Her ears perk at our conversation.

"When are they sending her to Lornstown?" I ask. "Or is she already there?"

Dad swigs another gulp. "If the story's out today, I'd guess she's leaving soon. She can rot there with the bastard, catch all those sex diseases that place is crawling with." He swishes the liquid around in his glass. "Whole thing makes me sick."

"Says here she tried to get pregnant with this other guy," I muse, reading further. "Didn't think that was possible."

Veronica puts down her assignment. "A *third* child? And her Partner *isn't* the father?"

I shrug. "Guess not."

"Those people are animals." Dad sets his mug on the table. "You know what'll happen to that baby, Veronica? It'll come out sickly and defective. Someone should kick her in the belly, put it out of its misery."

"That's disgusting!"

"Yeah? You know what's disgusting? Sluts like this!" He slams his finger down on the paper. "Can't believe I let her cut you kids' hair with her filthy hands. Should get you both tested for diseases." He slugs back more beer, draining his glass.

Veronica swirls the water around her cup. "If she wanted to commit a crime, maybe she should've murdered someone instead of cheating."

"What?" My eyes narrow. "What the hell is wrong with you?"

"No, really, think about it. If you're gonna be a criminal anyway, just kill someone. If you're a murderer, you're stuck in a cell, but at least your family loves you. If you're an adulterer, all you get is a one-way ticket to Lornstown, and everyone hates you."

"That's stupid."

"Veronica's right." Dad cracks open another bottle and tips its fizzing contents into his glass. "I'd take killers over whores any day."

"Told you," Veronica says, and I stick out my tongue at her. "And Sylvia's kinda stupid," she continues. "I mean, an Unassigned relationship is gonna fail anyway, so why risk Banishment for some dumb guy?"

"I dunno."

Albeit unflattering, the article's photo of Sylvia captures her kind eyes. Her face was still beautiful when the picture was taken, not yet marred with the slash of Banishment. They'll mark her cheek before shipping her to Lornstown. Once she has that long, skinny, identifying scar, it's official; if she ever comes home or contacts anyone here, they'll execute her.

The further I read, the bigger the knots twisting in my stomach. I'll never see Sylvia again. Even in the grace period to pack her belongings, the town will avoid her like the plague. Adultery isn't contagious, but sometimes it feels that way.

"Do you think she loved him?" I ask.

My father rests his mug on the table and leans back in his chair.

"This man, this janitor—" he snorts "—she can't love him. She may call it love, but it's not. That's just a word to these people. They're like monkeys. They're sick; they don't know how to love. You can't just love any random person." He gulps his remaining beer and stumbles to a stance. "It's physically impossible."

Dad releases a growling beer-burp and struts from the room. Veronica taps her pencil on the table, turning attention back to her paper.

Sylvia's face burns in my brain. I flip the article over so she won't stare at me anymore. I hate to say it, but I almost wish she died; it's better than suffering in Lornstown. I shudder, pushing the paper away. *She did it to herself.*

Banishment sucks, but it's necessary. If home-wreckers ran around normal society, the whole place would go awry. It's a tough law, but it's better this way. I mean, who wants to stay in a place where everyone hates you?

PIREN ALLSTON

In third grade, the school added art classes to our schedules.

Despite her natural artistic ability, Trace hated art class. She threw her head back and groaned every time they handed her some markers and told her to draw. Her act made the whole room giggle. She invented all sorts of excuses to avoid doing any semblance of work.

"I have to go to the bathroom." Trace waved her hand in the air. For a few weeks, Mr. Wintle nodded to her and continued his lesson. When Trace's pee-breaks became half-hour disappearances, he grew wiser.

"Sit down, Ms. Bailey."

"But—"

"Now."

Trace slunk down in her seat, lips curled into a scowl. The moment Mr. Wintle turned his back, she made a face in his direction.

One morning, we came to class to discover Mr. Wintle moved our assigned seats. As always, he made everyone sit with their Partners, two Partnerships per table. But for the first time in history, he assigned Trace and Sam to the same table as Lara and me. My best friend and I high-fived when we saw our place tags.

"Do you have a full bladder today, Ms. Bailey?" Mr. Wintle asked as he walked by.

"Nope." She grinned. "Emptied it already."

From then on, every Wednesday at one p.m., we raced down the hall to art class. We jumped into our seats, eager to spend the next hour goofing off. I zipped through my assignments as fast as humanly possible.

Produces sloppy work, Mr. Wintle jotted on my progress report. I didn't care. The hour never felt long enough. Painting, sketching, collages, it didn't matter what we did; Trace was there, which made everything awesome.

"Today, I want you to draw your family portrait," Mr. Wintle said one day, scribbling notes on the whiteboard. "Don't forget the most important member of your family: your Partner."

He passed bins of sticky, decade-old markers around the room and gave us each a thick sheet of poster board.

For some reason, this assignment resonated with me. I meticulously mapped my entire drawing, shading and outlining when necessary. I squinted as I worked, determined to create a masterpiece.

As unartistic as I usually was, Sam Macey was one hundred times worse.

Sam's family portrait resembled a family of potatoes, the bulbous Trace potato the silliest of all. Trace glanced at her Partner's monstrosity and snorted.

"Is that me?" She pointed to the curly-haired potato.

Sam nodded, not averting his eyes from his work. Trace grabbed a purple marker, and scribbled all over his paper.

"Stop!" Sam groaned, slapping his hands over his poster board in a feeble attempt to protect it.

"There. It was already bad, why not add some purple?" Trace loathes purple.

Sam ripped his maimed drawing out from under her, face puffed into a pout.

"Looks real to me." I bloated my cheeks to resemble Potato Trace.

"Yeah?" Trace said. "Hey, Lara, don't forget your Partner's big fat head."

She flung her offending marker toward Lara's drawing, but my Partner held it out of Trace's reach.

I dragged my green marker across Trace's drawing. "How about some fangs for you?"

Our art war began. Trace and I practically fell off our chairs laughing, arms and markers flying all over the table as we graffitied on everything in sight.

Within minutes, the damage was done. Sam's picture, once akin to a family of potatoes, now resembled a family of scribbles. Likewise, every person on Trace's defaced drawing mirrored monsters familiar to our sidewalk chalk creations. Colorful specks dappled the formerly spotless table. We even managed to add a few smudges to Lara's family portrait, much to her dismay. She slid her chair away from us, pressing her paper to her chest.

Despite the fray, I managed to protect my masterpiece; after the battle, it remained the only unharmed drawing on the table.

Catlike, Mr. Wintle approached our rowdy group. "Hmm…"

I startled and darted my eyes to the table, still coughing down giggles.

I thought he planned to scream at me for disrupting the class and getting marker all over the table. Or conversely, maybe he wanted to compliment me on finally putting effort into my work.

But he had a different mission in mind.

Mr. Wintle gazed down at my masterpiece and stroked his chin. "Why is Ms. Bailey in your family portrait?"

What?

My eyebrows squished together as I studied my drawing. Seven carefully-sketched family members looked up at me from the page: me; my mom; my dad; my brother, Mason; Mason's Partner, Stephanie; Lara Goodren; and Trace. Blending shades of deep brown to achieve Trace's hair color was painstaking, and the result made my chest swell with pride. I labored on her eyes until they reached crystal blue perfection. To me, my artwork was flawless and worthy of admiration.

I shrugged. "She's my best friend."

The class fell silent.

Mr. Wintle's eyes narrowed into slits. "Excuse me?"

My lip trembled. *Did I say something wrong?*

"You're incorrect. Ms. Goodren, here—" he indicated Lara "—is your best friend."

Lara sank lower in her seat.

I could feel everyone's eyes on me. Blush crept across my cheeks.

"Class?" Mr. Wintle raised his voice. "Your family is the most important part of your life, which is why I gave you today's assignment. Your families are the people you love, and love is what separates us from scoundrels and criminals. It maintains order. Your parents, your sibling, and your Partner are the ones you love."

He strode around the room, hands clasped behind his back.

"There should never, ever, be anyone else who comes close to that bond. You have only one *best friend*—" he enunciated the words as if spitting poison "—and that is the person you'll be marrying someday. We must learn to differentiate the relationships in our lives: the people we love, and the ones we don't. It's inappropriate, it's foolish, and it's forbidden to think otherwise."

He locked eyes with each classmate as he spoke, circling back to me.

"Mr. Allston, give me your family portrait."

I froze. His gaze bore into me like a laser.

"Mr. Allston?" He snapped his fingers. "Now."

I took a deep breath and slid my paper across the table to him.

Mr. Wintle held it up for everyone to see.

"This drawing is an abomination."

He tore my masterpiece clean in half. I gasped as he made another rip, then another, until my artwork lay in shreds on the floor.

Sam smirked, clearly relishing every moment of my torture.

Mr. Wintle swept up the pieces in one swoosh of his broom and dumped them in the trash. Cramps dug through my stomach as I watched. I wanted to sock him in the face.

"Now, do it again. Correctly this time," he said. "And, I'm moving your seat. You and Ms. Goodren, come with me."

Glowering, I followed him to the opposite end of the room. Lara hung her head, towing closely behind.

"You go near Ms. Bailey and Mr. Macey's table one more time, and you'll be in Atonement Exercises, Mr. Allston," he snapped.

I clenched my teeth and nodded, plopping down in my new seat.

For the remainder of the period, Lara said nothing to me. I didn't care, I didn't want to look at her. Bitterness ate through me like termites on a log. Why couldn't I love Trace too? Why couldn't she be my family too? Why was our teacher such an asshole?

I threw together a new sketch to appease Mr. Wintle. It was quick and sloppy, as per my usual work. The drawing contained me, my parents, Mason and his Partner, and Lara. That's it.

The eyes held no emotion, and the drawing was, as it should be, without Trace.

TRACY BAILEY

Piren and I walk to the bus stop together every morning before school, and home together every afternoon. This daily tradition started when we were seven, and it continues seven years later. Sometimes, we sneak off the road to the treehouse. Other times, we meander the neighborhood streets together until we wind up back home.

It's a long walk, granting us legitimized time together not up for speculation by the entire world. We're neighbors; how can we not walk together? I mean, we share a bus stop. Should I be rude and walk ten feet in front of him so my parents can feel secure with themselves?

In some ways, I love it when my parents see us walking together. It pisses them off, but there's not a damn thing they can do, short of moving away. It's their fault for living here in the first place — I didn't choose this house.

On two occasions in the past year, Mom invited Sam over after school, precluding my walk with Piren. Both times were complete surprises for me; Sam followed me onto my bus home, insisting that my mom arranged his visit. I was irked she went behind my back, but what the hell could I do? I forced Sam to sit in a separate seat, across the aisle.

Walking home from the bus stop with Sam was a miserable affair. As we walked, he draped his arm over my shoulders.

"Stop it," I said for the bazillionth time, shoving him off me. Several paces in front of us, Piren shook his head.

"Come on." Sam laced his fingers with mine, but I ripped my hand away.

"Are you deaf? Keep your greasy paws to yourself."

My Partner thrust his hands in his pockets, grumbling as we traipsed the neighborhood streets toward my house. "You can't do this forever."

I flung a curly lock of hair behind my back. "Don't underestimate me."

Piren snickered, glancing at us over his shoulder.

"Turn around and shut up," Sam said. "This is none of your business."

Piren raised his hands, chuckling. We continued in silence, Piren in front, my Partner and I trudging along behind.

Sam inched closer to me until his arm brushed mine.

"Cut it!" I elbowed him in the side. "You're not sneaky at all. I know exactly what you're doing. I said no the first time."

He smirked. "When we're married, you'll have to touch me."

Over my dead body.

"Well, if that's what you think," I said, "you're in for a surprise."

Piren quickly morphed his roaring laugh into a phony cough.

"You keep walking," Sam said. "And keep your eyes up front."

My best friend shook his head but didn't reply.

"That's what I thought," Sam muttered. "Pussy."

I shoved my Partner's arm as hard as I could. "Don't talk to him like that!"

"Really?" Sam spun toward me. "You're gonna defend him over me?"

When I didn't respond, he growled something under his breath and pushed past me, speeding toward my house.

Piren stopped walking until I caught up to him.

"What's with him?" he mouthed, nodding at Sam's fading backpack in the distance.

I shrugged. *"No clue."*

Last week, Mom felt the need to address this with me.

"Tracy, I don't understand you sometimes. It's natural to want to touch your Partner."

I stirred my ice cream into a soupy mess.

"You should just go with it," she continued. "It's normal."

My arms fell onto the table with a thud. "If I ever have sex with Sam—" I leaned back in my chair "—I'll vomit all over the place—"

"Tracy!"

"—and then die. From puking all my guts out."

"You're impossible." Mom threw her dishtowel on the table in front of me. "It isn't a joke."

Oh. Did she think I was joking?

My mom attributes my attitude to my age, as contempt for sex in general. She's full of shit. There are lots of guys I'd love to bone. Just not Sam.

PIREN ALLSTON

Every February, the school torments us with another boring seminar about the Partner system. Each year's seminar takes a different theme, depending on your age. For example, the first year after the Assigning Ceremony, the seminar's theme was "Getting to know your Partner." We watched a video starring two newly-Assigned cartoon bears. They proceeded to ask each other stupid questions, like their favorite colors and best school subjects. The lady bear squealed with glee when she learned that she and her Partner shared an interest: a mutual love of forest berries. I doodled on my notepad in the back of the room.

At age twelve, the theme was "Understanding Urges." For this colorful seminar, the speaker handed out ridiculous pamphlets on sexuality, containing graphic and exaggerated drawings of naked people, with all the best parts blurred out. He rambled on about the dangers of lusting after non-Partners and the penalties of premarital relations.

"Waiting sucks," he said, slouching on a chair at the front of the class. Despite his graying hair, his backward ball cap and ripped jeans sent a clear message: *Listen to me, impressionable children! I'm one of you!*

"I went through it myself, not so long ago," the man continued. "I remember long nights in the dark, especially while cohabitating with my wife before the wedding. I wanted nothing more than to crawl into bed with her and consummate our love."

I had to clench my teeth together to keep from laughing. Whispers and muffled giggles drifted around the room.

My phone buzzed with a text from Trace: *Aren't u so glad u know all this about him?*

I typed back. *Yep. His sexual fantasies should b @ the top of our required curriculum.*

Buzz. *Oh man. Can u imagine the final exam 4 that class?*

Type. *I just hope it'd b written and not practical...*

"Ahem." The speaker cleared his throat, glaring at the rowdy class. "This is serious."

I straightened up, tossing my phone back in my bag.

"As I was saying," he said, "while you may wish to act out on those urges—especially you boys—it's important to remain celibate until your wedding night. Premarital sex leads to dangerous consequences, such as teen pregnancy, emotional distress, and of course, Banishment. But by all means, feel free to handle it yourself until then. Goodness knows, I did…"

That did it. Almost everyone exploded into hoots of laughter. Trace wrinkled her nose across the room as the disgruntled speaker raised his hands in a vain attempt to hush the masses.

Alan Carrey leaned toward me. "That's BS. Lots of people bone before the wedding."

My forehead scrunched. "Who?"

"People. Toni's older sister."

"How do you know?"

"I just do." He doodled a huge cock onto the censored part of his pamphlet. "It's kinda obvious."

I guess the speaker intended the seminar to provoke meaningful discussion; it only actually provoked crude jokes and piles of defiled pamphlets.

Last year for our age-thirteen seminar, a woman named Mrs. Prew visited our classroom. She wore her white hair pulled back in a pouf and suffocated us with her overbearing perfume. Old Mrs. Prew strutted up and down aisles of desks, spewing cliché metaphors about love.

"Think of yourselves as a puzzle piece," she said. "You're one solid item on your own, and you're very important by yourself, but you just aren't quite whole." Her eyes lit up, as if her stupid jigsaw analogy was a life-changing revelation.

"Now, imagine that as a puzzle piece, you're a certain color—let's say green." She paced between aisles of desks, brushing her fingers over the backs of our chairs. "You're looking around the room and seeing all sorts of other puzzle pieces. There are blue ones, orange ones, pink ones, but none that fit with you."

Trace stretched her mouth into an exaggerated yawn.

"Suddenly, in the back of the room, something catches your eye." Mrs. Prew flashed out her hands. "You see a big green puzzle piece, made to fit just with you."

By this point, most students' eyes glazed over. Some people texted under their desks, emitting little flares of light from their phones. However, a select group of idiots remained wide-eyed and enthralled with the presentation; Lara leaned forward in her chair, hands clasped under her chin, chomping at the bit to learn more.

"And, class, that's what Assigning is all about," Prew said. "We pair you to your correct puzzle piece—the only one who fits with you. We find the right Partner for you, so you don't have the burden yourself."

I couldn't look at Trace; every time she caught my eye, laughter boiled inside me.

"Now," Prew said, practically bouncing on her toes, "who wants to share how your Partner is your perfect puzzle piece fit?"

Several hands shot up.

"My Partner is perfect for me because he makes me happy every day. He's my soul mate, and I love him more than anything," one girl said. At the other end of the room, Trace silently pretended to gag.

One by one, my classmates shared their stories with Mrs. Prew and the class. The skill it took to re-word the same answer fifteen times astounded me. Everyone rambled how their Partner was their perfect soul mate, repeating the same damn thing. It was exactly what Mrs. Prew wanted to hear; she clapped and cheered, turning each mundane answer into an overt emotional display.

I leaned back in my chair, enjoying their washed-out answers.

A crumpled note plopped onto my desk. I unfolded it to find Trace's distinct handwriting:

Sam is a big green something,
but it's not a puzzle piece.

I choked on a sputtering laugh. Thirty sets of eyes fell on me.

Mrs. Prew lunged before I could hide the note. She snatched it from my hands and read it aloud.

Her brows lowered. "Who wrote this?"

Across the room, Trace stared at the ceiling. I could see in her tight mouth she was holding her breath, fighting back giggles.

"I asked you a question." Mrs. Prew's mouth thinned to a line.

"Uh...I...I did, I wrote it." I clamped my hand over my twitching leg.

"And who's Sam?"

I pointed to Trace's table, where Sam's face flushed red.

Prew's eyes flashed with fury. "Are you mocking my presentation?"

"N-No. Of course not."

"Well, then, who's the lucky lady who gets to be *your* Partner?" She showered me with spit.

I pointed a quivering finger across the table to Lara.

Mrs. Prew's frown morphed into a self-satisfied smile. She rested a hand on the back of Lara's chair. "Please tell us how your lovely Partner here is your ideal puzzle piece mate."

Lara's ears perked. Cheeks burning, I regurgitated the first answer that came to mind.

"Um, Lara is, uh, perfect for me." I scratched my neck.

"Why?"

"Because...she, um, completes me." I word-for-word ripped off Shelly Morrow, who said that exact statement moments ago.

Mrs. Prew beamed. "Perfect. Great answer."

Lara squeezed my hand under the table. Several tables down, Trace concealed her laugh under the guise of an unconvincing cough. Mrs. Prew whirled on her.

"Tracy Bailey! Maybe you'd like to share how your Partner is perfect for you?"

"Um, sure." Trace collected herself and held up a finger. "Sam is...He's really...um..."

She succumbed to laughter mid-thought.

Trace got more Atonement Exercises that week.

TRACY BAILEY

I retreat to my room after dinner and collapse onto my bed. Mom taps on my door and sidles in.

"Tracy, I pressed your uniform for tomorrow."

I scowl.

She lays the gray skirt and white button down across my comforter. I run my hand down the front, letting my fingers slide in the pleats in the fabric.

"I hate this stupid skirt."

Mom rests her hand on my knee. "You're a young lady. Ladies wear skirts to school. Pants aren't very professional for young women; they're for weekends and lounging around. Not for working."

"Is that their rule, or yours?"

"The school board *strongly encourages* it for all second semester eighth grade girls. And in case you've forgotten, that now includes you, my dear."

I stick out my tongue and wrinkle my nose.

"Oh, Tracy, come on. You used to like skirts!"

I blow out a gust of air. "I do like skirts—my own skirts, not this fugly one. My thighs rub together; it's gross. And I might accidentally-on-purpose flash someone."

"Oh, like you're doing to me right now?" Mom nudges my legs, spread wide open on the bed. "What am I going to do with you? Just keep your legs closed." She pushes my chin up with her fingers, forcing me to look her in the eyes. "Seriously. If the principal sends you home for being indecent, you're scrubbing all four bathrooms every day for a year."

"Fine." I wave out my hand in dismissal. "But don't expect me to like it."

She shoots me a sympathetic smile and brushes a strand of hair off my forehead. "You'll get used to it. Consider it practice for your future job." She rises and heads for the door.

I turn on my side and mumble into my pillow. "It's not fair."

"Oh, my darling daughter." Mom leans against my doorframe. "Life isn't fair."

PIREN ALLSTON

Vivid nightmares plagued my childhood, traumatizing me nightly for months. Every dream started the same: I stood on a pier, and the pier collapsed below me, thrusting me into open water. I gasped and gulped for oxygen, pumping my arms to swim, but was unable to move as the water engulfed me, draining the air from my lungs.

I'd jolt awake in the middle of the night, flailing and screaming until Mason or my parents came to calm me down. It reached the point where I hardly slept in my bed, but fell asleep face-down on my school desk instead. When I wasn't sleeping at school, I was yawning from exhaustion, and it pissed off all my teachers.

My parents brought me to psychiatrists, doctors, specialists, everyone. No one knew what to do.

"Your son has Generalized Anxiety Disorder," the shrink said to my parents, stroking his mangy salt-and-pepper beard.

My mother clapped her hand to her cheek. "What does that mean?"

The doctor jotted notes in his pad. "He's prone to anxiety."

I rolled my eyes. *No shit. Thanks for the bulletin, Sherlock.*

"We knew that already." Dad rubbed his forehead. "What do we do about the nightmares? It's ruining his grades."

"I'll write him a script; that'll help."

Seventy milligrams of anti-depressants and one whopping medical bill later, nothing changed. I awoke tangled in a sea of sheets, chest heaving, kicking and shouting. My mom sat at my bedside, eyes tearing, stroking my arm. It made me sick seeing her in pain.

One afternoon in the treehouse, I consulted Trace. She sat cross-legged and listened as I explained my dilemma.

"I can't shake these dreams." I slouched against the wood, clenching handfuls of my hair in fists. Legs stretched out in front, I had to bend my knees to keep my feet from reaching the opposing wall.

Trace tilted her head. "Is drowning your worst fear then?"

"Yeah, I guess. What's yours?"

"I don't know."

"You're not scared of anything?"

"I didn't say that. I said I didn't know."

She stacked a pile of sticks on the floorboards like she always did, balancing them in a leaning tower. Knee bouncing like a spring, I couldn't sit still.

"I'm such an idiot!" I kicked the side of the tree. "Why can't I just get over it?"

Trace pounced and grabbed my arms. "Don't you dare call yourself an idiot! That's my best friend you're talking about!"

I startled. She slid back to her twig tower.

"Well, thanks." I sunk down lower beside her, cheeks burning. "I wish I was like you, though. You're not afraid of anything."

She stopped stacking. "I'm afraid of my dad."

"What?"

"You heard me."

She piled more sticks as we sat in silence. Soon, the chilly evening air sent goose bumps down our arms; time to go home.

"Hey," she said, patting dirt off her pants. "Don't ever let me catch you calling yourself names again. No one badmouths my best friend and gets away with it."

She brushed past me down the ladder.

The next day, Trace invented a new game. We pretended the treehouse was a sinking ship, and we were drowning sailors. We threw stuff off the sides to conserve weight, grabbing neighboring branches for paddles, anything to save us from drowning. It became the best of our treehouse adventures. Trace called it "The Water Game."

Once it was only a game to me, the nightmares stopped.

TRACY BAILEY

"Sam's birthday's next month. What are we getting him?" Mom asks, ambushing me the moment I walk through the effing door.

"Ugh, I don't know." I dump my backpack on the floor. "Whatever you want."

"Tracy, this is serious."

I roll my eyes. "What do you get someone who doesn't do anything?"

She folds her arms across her chest. "We never have this problem with Oliver's gifts."

"That's because Oliver actually has interests." I kick my shoes into the closet. "Sam's only interest is pulling wings off insects and watching them writhe. Oliver's an actual human being."

Seriously. My parents and Veronica find the best presents for Oliver. I used to get jealous, because the gifts they bought for Oliver far exceeded the gifts they got me. One Christmas, my parents bought him a laptop. What did I receive that year? A book series called "Wedding Planning for Kids." Hooray. Thanks, Mom.

My mother collapses into the armchair and props her head up with her hand.

"Try to at least pretend to be grateful if the Maceys buy you something for your birthday this year. I don't want a repeat of last Christmas."

Last Christmas. How could I forget? Sam's parents bought me an expensive video game. Something with explosions, where you shoot things with grenade launchers and other assorted weaponry. The ad boasted it as "the hottest selling game this Christmas season!" so I suppose it was a well-intended gesture by the Maceys. Regardless, my family doesn't own a game console, so the gift was pointless for me. I think it was secretly a thinly-veiled ploy by the Maceys to get me to visit their house and play with Sam; he owns every console under the frigging sun.

I'm not interested in video games, or hanging out with Sam; both activities are equally repulsive. I brought the game to school after Christmas break and traded with Benny Roberts for two books in a mystery series I like. Benny lucked out, because the game cost twice as much as the books, but I didn't give a crap. I just wanted to get rid of it.

Lo and behold, my parents heard about my exchange and flipped their lids. Mom ratted me out to Sam's parents, who took it as a personal insult. They were aghast I didn't want to see their son and play the game. Mrs. Macey reamed my mother out on the phone for twenty minutes, saying she needed to "keep me in line."

Let's just say it's an event I'd rather not repeat.

PIREN ALLSTON

Toni Henders saunters past us in the hallway.

"Hey, boys…Hey, Alan." She winks at her Partner, brushing her fingers against his shoulder. "Good luck on your biology presentation later." She strides off, flipping her hair over her shoulder. Six different guys crane their necks for a closer look at her ass.

Real smooth.

Travis slams his locker and turns to Alan. "You're one lucky son of a bitch."

"I know," Alan says. "Take a gander, but keep your hands off. She's mine."

"What do you think, Allston?" Travis says. "Our friend, here, hands down —" he thumps Alan Carrey on the back "— has the hottest Partner in school."

I shimmy my backpack off my shoulders. "Toni's pretty. Not my type, though."

It's pointless to check out non-Partners anyway. Why bother?

"Hot with big tits?" Alan snorts. "How can that *not* be your type?"

Other than his one-track mind, Alan Carrey's built solid and plays quarterback for our middle school football team. I'd compare him to a gorilla, puffing his chest to parade his masculinity. He'd probably take his dick out and wave it around if he could.

"You jackass," Travis says to Alan. "As if we're all blind, right, Allston? We get it, Carrey. Your Partner has the biggest tits. Why don't you go put it on a billboard?"

I dig through my locker. "He needs to remind us, apparently."

"I swear, on Carrey's wedding night," Travis says, "I'm gonna get a text with the play-by-play."

"Nice." I grab my stack of notebooks. "Spare us the details, Alan. We all took sex-ed."

"Shut up." Alan knocks the books from his locker into his backpack with a single swipe.

"Well, if you don't want our commentary—" I slam my locker shut "—shut the hell up about it yourself. C'mon, we're gonna be late for gym." *And this topic is getting too awkward.*

Cracks about Alan and Toni's future wedding night are nothing new. It's a favorite topic around the guy's locker room before gym class. Alan feigns annoyance, but I know he loves it. He'll draw dirty pictures of Toni and put them in everyone's faces. Sometimes, other guys add sketches of their own to the drawings, involving male anatomy. I swear, they're more obsessed with cocks and balls than the girls are.

My dad says as a teenager, I'm supposed to be super attracted to Lara all the time. Like, get a hard-on every time someone says her name or something. Mason gets Dad's awkward lectures too. I think Dad's under the impression that my brother and I are like speeding hormone trains, ready to crush anything and everything cock-blocking our paths. And he wonders why I respond by stuttering into a new topic.

I try to force my brain to arouse when I see my Partner, but it's like forcing myself to read in another language; it feels foreign and uncomfortable. Visions of Lara prancing around naked don't cloud my mind when I sleep, despite what my dad thinks. Lara reminds me of pioneers in history books, as if she belongs in a different century. She's pretty, in the same way I consider my classy grandmother pretty.

Forbidden thoughts of other girls still haunt me, despite my efforts to eradicate them. Seriously, a dirty image will crop up in my mind, and I'll force myself to think of the least sexy thing I can, like wool sweaters, or eggplants, or giraffes, or anything other than girls. It doesn't work. The bad thoughts weasel into my brain and tunnel through my subconscious, like a song stuck on repeat. But how am I supposed to fight the thoughts when Trace and some other girls look so hot in shorts?

The sordid conversations always begin the same way: Alan instigates. Today, his crooked smile in the gym locker room warns that the lighthearted football discussion is about to take a turn for the dirty.

"Carmen Greene," Alan says, smearing on deodorant. "Alex, man, your Partner has some ass."

Alex spanks the air as the guys hoot their approval. "Gonna nail her on our wedding night."

"You'd so tap that now."

"I'd hit that so hard."

"And what about you, Parker? Kelly's got tits."

"Hell yeah. I'd like to squeeze them together. Just once."

I keep my head down, slipping into my running shoes.

Don't ask about Lara…Don't ask about Lara…What would I even say?

Jeers and whistles echo the room as they hash out each other's future exploits, all trying to one-up the other guys. The way they talk, you'd think getting laid is some sort of extreme sport. Like someone's gonna march up to Alan the morning after his wedding and hand him a gold medal. I can almost picture a reporter shoving a microphone in his face, asking, "Is it everything you hoped and dreamed it would be?" And Alan would churn out some stupid response: "Why, yes, Steve. I unlocked a lifelong achievement tonight: I got it in."

I shove my stuff in a locker and click my combination lock, only half listening to the guys' conversation.

Sam mopes alone on a bench in the corner, lacing his sneakers, emitting occasional grunts.

"Macey, man." Travis props his foot on the bench. "You got lucky too. Tracy Bailey. She's hot."

My ears perk.

Sam slams his locker shut. "Gonna fuck the shit outta her on our wedding night."

My stomach drops.

Everyone roars, laughing and hollering.

A sickening, violent reflex twists in my chest. My fists clench into balls. Paralyzed by a surge of unexplained hate, I wrestle back an urge to punch Sam in the face.

For some reason, the conversation isn't funny anymore.

"Does Toni know the guys talk about her like that?" I ask Trace, as we lean against the treehouse wall.

She snorts. "No, she's oblivious. At least, she's never said anything."

"It's kinda sad, if you think about it." I twiddle my fingers. "Alan leads the damn jokes, and she's stuck with him forever."

Trace shoots me a bemused grin. "Please. The girls are way worse. You should hear what they say about Alan."

I raise my brows. "What do they say?"

"Basically, we think he has a pea-sized pecker."

We snicker.

I pick at a loose thread in my shirt. "Do they…say anything about me?"

"Nope." She flicks my arm. "'Cause if they do, I'll smack 'em."

I return the flick.

We sit in silence for a moment, watching with bated breath as Trace precariously stacks twigs in one of her classic leaning towers.

"Oh, hey," I say, "I brought you a present."

I fish through my backpack and reveal one of Alan's dirty drawings. She bursts out laughing. Every time Trace laughs, her eyes crinkle at the sides. It's cute.

"Oh my gosh, you didn't." She rolls her head back. "You stole the boob drawing! Yes. I'm keeping this forever."

I shake my head. "You're so weird."

"Well, you're my best friend, so what does that say about you?"

TRACY BAILEY

Oliver lugs his stupid saxophone to our house tonight. The bulky case clunks into the doorframe, trailing a black scuff across the wood as he passes through.

Dumping his crap all over the living room, he bends over his sax, playing some God-awful rendition of "Jump, Jive an' Wail." Someone's wailing all right, but it's not the song.

Veronica sprawls out on the floor at his feet, mouth drawn up in a goofy grin. I lie on the couch behind them, clamping a pillow over my ears.

"How'd I do?"

Oliver stops playing every five frigging seconds to pose this question and scrounge for compliments.

"Oh, Ollie! That was *beautiful!*" Veronica breaks into furious applause.

Mom always says if you don't have anything nice to say, don't say anything at all.

So I don't.

He continues his assault on my ears, drowning the room in high-pitched squeaks. Teeth clenched, I flip on the TV at max volume. Oliver rips the instrument from his lips with a devastated gasp. Veronica jumps up and slams the power button off.

"Do you mind?" She huffs. "Ollie's trying to practice."

I snatch the remote from her greedy paws and flip it back on. She grabs to steal it back, but I slide it under a couch cushion beneath my weight.

"Just because your Partner isn't a musician—" she frantically paws at the cushions "—doesn't mean you have to ruin it for me."

I snort. "Musician? Is *that* what you call this?"

"Tracy! Stop!" She draws out her words into long, whiny syllables.

Oliver whirls around, facing his back to us. He clearly wants me to know he's offended. I really don't care.

In one final swipe, Veronica snatches the remote and clicks off the TV.

"That's right." She anchors her hand on her hip. "Maybe you should learn to play something for your Partner instead of squatting in front of the TV every night."

I leap to my feet. "Why? So I can spend my life kowtowing to someone like you do? No thanks."

"You're just jealous 'cause my Partner's better than your Partner."

"Really, Veronica?" I throw out my hands. "*Everyone* is better than my Partner! Okay?"

Nothing more to say, I stomp upstairs and fall face-down on my bed. Oliver's concert resumes downstairs, the distant squeaks drifting into my ears and making me cringe.

Somewhere in the house, my father's drunken hollering commences, adding to the already joyous array of sounds.

"What the hell is that noise?" He slurs his words into a jumble. "Sounds like tortured cats."

I smirk. For once in my life, I'm grateful for scotch.

PIREN ALLSTON

Only two blocks from our middle school, Under Five Café makes the best milkshakes. They have twenty different flavors.

Trace found the café by accident last year and insisted we try it. Always followed by an entourage, she led a group to the circular booth in the back, and we claimed it as our own. Thus, the daily tradition was born.

The Café Crowd, as we call ourselves, consists of Trace, me, Toni, Amanda, Josh, Alan, Travis, and a few others who filter in and out. I've invited Lara in the past, but she invents excuses about hating crowds. Truth is, I don't think she likes my friends. Her group hangs out at the bowling alley after school, which sounds horrendously boring.

I squish into the crowded booth between Josh and Alan.

Trace winks at me from across the table. "So, Piren, I hear they started construction at Laney Park." Everyone looks on, eagerly awaiting the oncoming story.

"Yeah? They finally tear down that hideous bridge?"

"Well, they weren't going to, if it wasn't for—"

"—the sinkhole, that totally—"

"—destroyed that old guy's yard—"

"—but who builds their home on a sinkhole?"

"Sounds like something Alan—" Trace whips her head toward our friend "—would do."

"Because he loves holes."

"Hey." Alan folds his arms over his chest. "Seriously? Why am I always the butt of you two assholes' stupid jokes?"

Within minutes, my best friend and I double over laughing. The rest of the table follows suit. I don't know if they're laughing because they understand our humor, or if they only do it to fit in, but they laugh regardless. The unamused waitress sets down our milkshakes, and we dig in. Toni, Amanda, and Alan chatter on about some television show.

My phone buzzes under the table. One new text message: Trace.

We r totes gonna write that story: Alan vs. Sink Hole.

I frantically type back. *Yes! I'm putting my $ on the sink hole.*

My phone buzzes. *It'll be a best seller. But u have to use ur pen name: Fat Head.*

I type back. *Duh. Fat Head & Fangs will b authors on the cover of every book in the library.*

Buzz. *Absolutely. And Alan is flexing again…I weep for humanity.*

I type back. *Lol. He is practicing 2 fight sink hole. 2morrow, back @ café after school?*

Buzz. *Of course, Fat Head! Under 5 = nothing w/o our stories. It's a proven fact.*

I race to Under Five after school and join a gaggle of the Café Crowd waiting at the counter. Peering around Alan, I keep my eyes on the door. Within minutes, Trace's curly-haired head bobs past the window. A grin erupts across my face.

She storms into the Café, arms tight at her sides. Sam lumbers in after her. My shoulders slouch back down.

Great.

Trace clomps toward the counter.

Sam wrings his hands. "Tracy, I'm sorry, I—"

"Please. Don't. Talk." She leans her elbows against the counter edge and scrubs her hands down her mottled face. Her Partner hovers four feet behind.

I bump against her shoulder. "You okay?"

"I'm gonna lose it. Sam's about two seconds from a face punch."

"Uh-oh. What now?"

Toni pivots toward us, banana milkshake in hand. "Oops! Somebody's in trouble." She wags her finger at Sam.

"Shut the hell up." He knocks her hand away. "Not your business."

"Oh-kay." She flicks her fingers out. "Someone's touchy."

Sam slams his fist on the counter.

"Hey!" Alan pushes between Sam and Toni. "Knock it off!"

Sam mumbles to himself, crossing his arms. If he could shoot fire from his eyes, flames would have engulfed the whole restaurant by now.

Alan takes Toni's hand, and they lead the others to claim our booth in the back. They step around Sam, leaving him a wide berth as they pass with their shakes, abandoning Trace, Sam, and me alone at the counter.

Trace sulks against the wall, mouth in a terse line, waiting to order. I stand by the register, mulling over milkshake options. Under Five recently updated their already extensive flavor offerings, throwing me for a loop. Mouth scrunched to the side, I scan the new menu.

Sam pushes past me to stand by Trace in line. Within moments, their heated bickering grows to the precipice of a screaming fight.

"Come on, Tracy. I said I was sorry."

"No, Sam. Just leave me alone."

"What can I do to make it up to you?"

"Um. Learn the meaning of the word no? Ingrain it into your thick skull?"

It's almost comical. From what I can gather, he tried to touch her yet again, and she told him—loudly and vulgarly—where to put his hands. Typical Trace.

Seven tense minutes later, I make my choice: the old but reliable strawberry milkshake. I approach the register to order. Trace shoves past her Partner, dropping her purse down on the counter beside me.

"I'm cutting you." She winks at me.

I release an exaggerated gasp. "How dare you."

She sticks out her tongue.

A twenty-something waitress with an eyebrow ring emerges from the kitchen, wiping her hands down her green apron. "What can I get for you?"

"Chocolate milkshake, please." Trace leans further over the counter and raises her voice. "And don't let Charlie skimp on the whipped cream."

The plump cook in the back peeks through the kitchen window and salutes her with his spatula. "You got it, Tracy."

Trace waves to him. "You're the best!" She lowers her voice so only I can hear. "Unlike a certain temperamental dude I know, who's about to get bitch-slapped."

I shake my head. "You guys are something else."

"Something else indeed."

I poke her arm. "And chocolate again? Boring." I blow out a theatrical sigh. "No variety at all, Bailey. What am I going to do with you?"

She returns the poke. "I know what I like."

Sam wedges his mass between Trace and me, squishing me between the metal counter and his sweaty back. I shudder and jerk away. That guy sweats more than anyone I know.

The cashier struts back from the kitchen, balancing Trace's chocolate milkshake on her wobbling plastic tray. She sets it down on the counter, whipped cream overflowing over the rim of the glass. Trace dips her finger in and pops it into her mouth.

The waitress punches some numbers into the register. "Four twenty-five, ma'am."

"You got it." Trace rummages in her wallet.

Scooting as far away as humanly possible from Sam's damp body, I place my order at the next cashier. Trace dumps a pile of coins on the counter and starts fishing through it. The cashier grumbles.

Sam's harsh gaze softens. "I'll get it for you."

"Shut up." Trace rifles pennies from a handful of paperclips. "I have enough."

"No, I really don't mind," he says. "I love you. I'm allowed to buy you —"

"Stop. Seriously. Just shut up."

The cashier clicks her claw-like fingernails on the counter. I imagine the Under Five employees aren't thrilled that a group of teenagers infests their restaurant every damn day. Trace scrapes a handful of dimes from her wallet and counts it in her palm.

"Tracy, I can just loan —"

"No, Sam!" Trace knocks his hand off her shoulder.

His grin fades to a frown. "What, my money's not good enough for you?"

She ignores him, pawing through her purse.

He snorts. "Never thought I'd see a rich girl counting pennies."

Trace whirls around. "Excuse me?"

"I just find it funny. Without Mommy and Daddy around, you're broke as shit like the rest of us."

"Don't you ever—"

"All right." The waitress cuts between them. "Are you taking this or not?" She pushes the milkshake toward Trace.

Pink flares across Trace's cheeks. "Just send it back." She grits her teeth. "I won't get one today."

She rips her purse off the counter and storms off empty-handed, abandoning her pile of coins. The cashier sweeps them into her tip jar. "Next."

Sam orders his own milkshake. Drink in hand, he proceeds back to the table after his Partner.

My knee jiggles as the waitress returns with my strawberry shake. I sway back and forth on the balls of my feet.

Trace is going to sit for two hours watching us enjoy our drinks?

I bend my knees, then straighten.

"Actually, ma'am, I'll take that chocolate one too."

"You got it." She rings it up and hands me both purchases.

I walk back to our booth with two shakes and conversation abruptly stops. Trace stares at me like I have three heads, her face frozen in a wide-eyed gape.

Shit.

"Uh, here, Trace." I shuffle my feet. "I…I got this for you."

I hold out my offering, stomach churning under eight accusing sets of eyes. Sam cracks his knuckles, curled lip baring his clenched teeth.

Is he going to punch me?

My hands tighten around the two glasses.

Damn it. Why'd I do it? No room for a brain in my fat head.

"Chocolate?" Trace reaches for the drink, dimples budding on her cheeks. "Extra whipped cream too. How'd you know?" She stabs her straw into the milkshake.

"Lucky guess," I mumble.

"Thanks, Fat Head."

"Anytime, Fangs."

"What the hell?" Sam balls his hands into quivering fists on the tabletop. Nobody responds. "Seriously, what the hell, Piren? She's *my* Partner."

"Oooh, watch out, Sam. An affair," Alan says.

Toni gasps. "Don't joke about that!"

"Would that even constitute an affair?"

"No, that's not it."

"Well, my mom says..."

The table erupts into heated debate. Trace leans back against the squishy booth wall, slurping her milkshake. I catch her eye, and she winks at me.

We're no strangers to affair jokes. After seven years of nontraditional friendship, we've heard them all, even the X-rated ones. We usually laugh it off.

Sam jumps out of the booth, shifting his eyes from Trace to me. Trace chatters on with Amanda, not giving her Partner another glance.

He mutters something incomprehensible under his breath, then storms from the café alone. The floor vibrates as he slams the door behind him, causing several patrons to look up. I slurp my milkshake, turning my attention back to the conversation.

Sam can hate me if he wants. Frankly, I couldn't care less.

TRACY BAILEY

I love to bake. I've been baking since I was a little kid. I make cookies, cakes, pies, cupcakes, you name it. If it requires sugar and an oven, I'm up for the challenge. I mean, who doesn't love a hobby where you can eat the finished product?

My mom and I bake together at least twice a week after school. Sometimes, Veronica joins us. Mom says baking is a great way to please your Partner because men love food. Personally, I don't think Sam needs any more sweets, but Mom disagrees. She always packs my homemade cookies into cute containers and ships them off to the Maceys, as if she's on a mission to give my Partner Type II Diabetes.

Today, we baked star-shaped sugar cookies. I squeeze dollops of pink frosting onto the tips, then sprinkle yellow sugar over the tops. Wiping my forehead, I examine my handiwork.

These stars are pretty damn cute. If I do say so myself.

I crack a point off one of the stars and toss it in my mouth.

Taste pretty damn good too.

Of course, Mom has to totally ruin the moment.

"Don't do that." She snaps her fingers from across the table. "They're for your Partner."

Forging my signature across a square Tupperware, she dapples the package with heart stickers. I unleash a pained moan.

"Oh, Tracy, come on." She ties it in a pink bow. "Sam will love it. It's sweet."

"Then why don't you put *your* name on it?"

"Don't get fresh."

I prop my cheek against my hand, leaving my half-eaten star cookie on the wax paper. When Mom's not looking, I steal another point.

Beside me, Veronica colors on a pink cookie tin for her Partner. She doodles "Mr. and Mrs. Oliver Hughes" across the top in her best attempt at calligraphy.

"Eager to buy Oliver's love with junk food, huh?"

"Shush." She sprinkles silver glitter around her container.

"You know," Mom says to me, putting the finishing touches on my farce-gift, "you'd make Sam a lot happier if you were more like your sister. You should be the one decorating this."

I grimace. "He's happy enough, thanks."

I'm so frigging sick of her packing my cookies, slapping my name on them, and sending them to Sam. What's it her business if I give them to Sam or not? What if I want to eat them all myself? I worked hard to bake them, why does Sam get to eat them? And he definitely doesn't need to think I slaved over an oven for hours, baking just for him. *Please.*

I slump back on my stool when an alternative plan pops into my head.

"Hey, Mom, before you pack those, I've got a better idea." I drum my fingers against the table. "I have geography with Sam tomorrow, how about I just give it to him in person?" I blink at her, parading my best doe-eyed innocence.

She presses her hand over her heart. "Really?"

"Yeah, it's more personal that way." Snort.

"What?" Her mouth stretches into a glowing smile. "You're going to start acting like a proper lady?"

"Yep." I keep my eyes down. "That's the plan."

She drops the container onto the countertop and wraps her arms around me. "I'm shocked and thrilled. I never thought I'd see the day you showed some initiative to please your Partner." She kisses my hair. "I'm proud of you."

I force a smile. "Thanks."

Barf.

I shove Piren's backpack as we traipse to the bus the next morning.

"I like your sweater vest today. Minimizes the look of your fat head."

"Well, thanks. Glad you think so."

"I wanted to sink my fangs into these, but in my abundant generosity, I thought we could share them instead." I whip out my surprise. "More fuel for your fat head."

"Sam-Cookies? For me? You shouldn't have." Piren's no stranger to my mother's antics. He tosses one up in the air and catches it in his mouth with a crunch. "Should I send your mom a thank you note?"

"Sure, just sign it from Sam Macey. And spell some words wrong so it's believable."

His mouth bulges with cookies. "Well, Ms. Bailey, these are excellent."

"Well, thanks, Mr. Allston. I aim to please." I grab a cookie for myself.

We demolish the entire batch walking to the bus stop.

At night, my mother flips on the TV and shoos me to the other end of the couch.

I groan. "Do we have to suffer through another stupid, sappy—"

"Shhh! It's starting." Mom watches with bated breath as opening credits roll across the screen to the sweet sounds of manufactured emotion.

Perched like an owl on the armchair beside me, Veronica catches my eye and chokes down a giggle. "Mom, you've seen these lame movies a bajillion times."

"Seriously," I say, "you must know all the dumb lines by memory at this point."

Mom waves out her hand in dismissal, her eyes glued to the screen.

I sink into the bolster pillow and grab my bag of chips off the coffee table.

"Stop crinkling that bag!" Mom hisses. "I'm trying to listen."

Great. Another night of pathetic characters bitching about their lives. Tonight, protagonist Rhonda's Assigned Partner is lost at sea, or the jungle, or wherever the hell else someone could possibly get lost. You'd think the guy's never used a frigging map before. Rhonda's all distressed, can't function without him, blah blah blah, until, spoiler alert! Her Partner Danny will turn up unharmed, with an enlightened sense of the world, and Rhonda's life will make sense again. It's the same plot. Every. Single. Time. And the sadder thing is, since the law requires actors playing Partners to be Partners in real life, their pathetic existence doesn't end on screen.

"Why doesn't Rhonda shut up and get a job?" I stuff a handful of chips in my mouth. "Quit complaining."

"Wouldn't it be funny if Danny actually drowned?" Veronica says.

"What will I do with myself?" I mimic Rhonda's squeaky voice. "My man up and ran away, and I can't breathe without him."

My sister pretends to faint. "I'm so sad and lonely, I'm going to die."

We snicker into our hands.

Mom mutes the TV. "That what you want? Your Partners to drown? Be alone the rest of your lives?"

Veronica's lip trembles as she shakes her head.

"You should be more respectful." Mom fuses her eyes back to the TV, and the volume recommences. "Be damn grateful you're not Rhonda."

I roll my eyes. "Oh, I am."

Veronica twists her watch around her wrist, her wide smile sunken into a heavy line across her face.

Way to go, Mom.

"Hey." I stroke V's arm. "Wanna bake some cookies?"

"Chocolate chip?" She leaps off the couch, and the light returns to her eyes.

"Keep it down in the kitchen." Mom toggles up the TV volume.

My twelve-year-old sister measures ingredients into a cup. A little flour poofs into the air, draping her in a thin sheet of powder. When V laughs, she reminds me of Piren in a way. They both give off this carefree ambience that fills me with warmth, like some sort of sedating drug.

Veronica plugs in the electric mixer, and it whirs to life. I crack an egg into the bowl and toss the shell across the room, where it plummets straight into the trash.

"Ten points," Veronica says. "And Mom would kill you if she saw that."

I take a bow, and V pretends to break into a round of applause, tapping her hand against the mixer.

She shoots me a mischievous grin. "Tell me a secret."

"You know all my secrets." I pluck a chocolate chip from her bag and toss it into my mouth. "You tell me one."

"I had a dream about my First Kiss Ceremony last night." She giggles into her hand, as if her confession is one, surprising, and two, a big scandal. It's neither.

I shake my head. "One track mind."

"I do not!" She shoves me in the arm, smudging flour all over my sleeve.

"Hey!" I fling a chocolate chip at her; she attempts to catch it in her mouth but fails miserably, and it deflects off her chin.

We ball mounds of dough onto a sheet of aluminum, sneaking gobs into our mouths.

I slide the cookie tray into the oven. "Tell me a real secret —"

"— I —"

"— not related to Oliver."

She clamps her mouth shut and juts out her bottom lip into a pout. "You suck."

"One track mind it is, then. Told you so."

"I want to be a dentist." Veronica claps her hand over her lips.

"What?" I scrunch my face. "Why?"

She shrugs, tilting her head to hide her flushing cheeks. "It looks interesting. And I wanna put braces on people." She runs her tongue across the shiny brackets on her own teeth.

"That's an orthodontist."

"Well, whatever. Something like that." She hunches her shoulders. "Don't tell Dad. He'd flip."

"Yeah, he would. Don't worry, I won't say anything." I swipe a few spare chocolate chips from the counter and pour them into my mouth. "You could totally do it, though, if you want. Go to medical school. Be a dentist, orthodontist, whatever gross tooth job strikes your fancy."

She tugs at her sleeve. "Really? You don't think it's stupid?"

"No, why would I? You'd make a buttload of money." I wrap my arms around my little sister and kiss the top of her head. "But I expect free cleanings twice a year."

"You got it." She nestles into my shoulder. "Love you, Trace."

"Love you, V."

PIREN ALLSTON

"Hey! Get your own." Mason elbows me away from his soft pretzel bites. "What is this, charity week?"

"Mom says you have to share with me." I swoop in and steal one, popping it in my mouth.

"My baby brother is a thieving little bitch, how 'bout I tell Mom that?"

"Go ahead."

"And you know what happens to thieves." He scarfs his last pretzel, crushing the cardboard container in his hand. "Their fingers fall off."

"You know, the first time you told me that, I believed you for, like, two years."

"Seriously?" He rolls his head back. "That's 'cause you're gullible."

"Or maybe it's 'cause you're an asshole."

We amble through the mall's mazelike corridors, whittling away a Saturday afternoon. I'm not sure why we always come to the mall on weekends. We weave around the same stores every time, and it's a town away. But I love my brother, and he loves the mall—probably for the soft pretzel nuggets.

"You know, I used to believe all that stupid shit you told me. Thieves' fingers falling off. Giant killer owl living in my closet. Old Mr. Riley is a serial murderer." I count his lies on my fingers. "Your so-called brotherly wisdom is nonexistent."

"I'm seventeen. You're fourteen." He ruffles my hair. "You'd do well to heed my worldly advice…Hey, it's Ashley! Hey, Ashley!" Mason waves, diverting his course and practically crashing into me.

"Why do you know so many freaking people?" I trudge behind as he approaches an older girl with jet-black hair and a nose ring. She startles and bites her lip.

"She's Steph's friend," Mason says to me over his shoulder.

I crinkle my nose. *How does someone as unfriendly as Stephanie Butler get so damn popular?*

Mason and Ashley chatter about some economics exam, and my eyes glaze over.

"I'll meet you in Cherry's." I point to the nearby knickknack store. My brother ignores me, so I walk across the hall.

Cherry's boasts an extensive assortment of junk that could entertain me for hours. I browse through the magnet display, chuckling at the X-rated slogans. A woman in the magazine aisle gives me a weird look and walks the other way.

Scanning the rack, I double take as a trinket catches my eye. A tiny vampire-fangs keychain dangles off a hooked magnet, practically screaming Trace's name.

Fangs. What better gift for my best friend?

I pluck out the price tag: eight dollars. My entire week's allowance. I fidget the toy in my hands, chomping my forefinger in the plastic teeth.

But it would be the perfect prop for a Fat Head and Fangs adventure…

I rock back and forth for a moment, then swipe the fangs off the display.

Worth it.

I bring the keychain to the checkout line when Mason butts in front of me.

"What're you getting?" He tosses a pack of candy onto the counter, clearly assuming I'll buy it for him.

"Uh, a keychain…and really? After you wouldn't even share your damn pretzel nuggets?" I slide the candy back to him.

He pouts. "Not even for your big bro?"

"Especially not for you. How many snacks do you need, anyway? Pig."

The cashier rings up my purchase, and I dig out my wallet.

Mason flicks the keychain. "What's with the teeth?"

"It's an inside joke." I scratch my neck, not meeting his eyes.

"With Lara?"

"Uh, yeah, Lara."

"That's what you get your Partner?" He raises his brows. "A fang keychain?"

"Yep."

"Weirdo." He grabs his candy and struts over to the sports magazines. I take my bag and head back into the mall.

Plopping down on a bench across from Cherry's, I pull out my headphones. After three songs go by, I check my watch.

Mason better hurry his ass up. Mom will freak if we're late for dinner again.

My knee bounces as I watch the store entrance. Five more minutes pass.

Damn it. He gets distracted by the dumbest stuff in that store.

I pull myself up, ready to drag my brother out by his popped collar, when —

"Piren! Hey!"

I spin around. Lara and her mother wave furiously, speeding toward me from the other end of the mall. My hands clench around my blue plastic bag.

"Hi, Piren!" Mrs. Goodren balances at least half a dozen shopping bags in the crook of her arm.

"Hey, Mrs. Goodren. I love you, Lara Goodren."

"I love you, Piren Allston."

"What're you up to in the mall?" Mrs. Goodren's eyes drift to my bag. "Shopping?"

I force an awkward smile. "Just hanging out with my brother."

Mason emerges from Cherry's, clutching two bags filled with God knows what.

"Hey, Lara, Mrs. Goodren." Mason nods. He turns to me. "You gonna give her your weird little gift?"

I freeze.

"No, uh, not yet. It's…for Christmas."

Lara's face lights up. "For me? I don't have your Christmas gift yet, but you can give that to me now if you want." She reaches for the bag, but I snatch it away.

"No! Uh, it's not wrapped."

Mason scoffs. "Just give it to her. We gotta get going. Mom's gonna kill us."

I crush my purchase to my chest, the keychain suddenly feeling about as heavy as a metal brick. The bag quivers in my shaking hands, and my Partner leans closer, brushing the plastic with her fingers.

No. No no no. Not for you.

"What's inside?" Mrs. Goodren asks, nudging her daughter closer to me. "A surprise?"

Lara practically devours the bag with her eyes.

My brother throws his head back. "Come on, we gotta go."

Damn you, Mason.

Cheeks burning, I thrust the bag to Lara.

Her hungry eyes widen as she digs into it, and I just want to rewind and get my eight dollars back and make this whole awkward situation disappear.

Lara's smile falters when she unveils the keychain. My Partner isn't in the Café Crowd, but the epic Under Five tales of Fat Head and Fangs are widespread knowledge throughout the whole school.

Her shoulders droop. "Thanks."

"You're welcome." I wring my hands, watching the cracked tiles in the floor.

"Teeth?" Mrs. Goodren cocks her head. "What are the teeth for?"

"It's, uh…"

"It's just this thing from school. No big deal." Lara drops my gift back in its bag. "Should we go?" Her eyes glimmer with a hint of pain.

We awkwardly hug good-bye.

The entire ride home, I glower out the window, ignoring my brother's attempts at banter.

The stupid keychain cost eight dollars, and my Partner will just throw it away.

Thanks a lot, Mason.

TRACY BAILEY

Bouncing on my toes, I thrust my signed permission slip into our teacher's waiting hands.

"Oh, phew, Ms. Bailey. Last one in. Was a little nervous you wouldn't be joining us."

"Wouldn't miss this one for the world, Mrs. McDonald." My cheeks ache from grinning, but I don't care.

I line up with the rest of the eighth graders. Piren sidles up to me.

"How'd you finally get your dad to sign?" he whispers.

I cup my hand over my mouth. "Waited till he was plastered. Told him it was the cable bill."

We snicker.

"Field trip day!" Our classmate Alex pumps his fist, plowing into the line and knocking my elbow. "Field trip, field trip!"

I grimace, tapping my foot on the ground.

"We all know what day it is, Mr. Harper," Mrs. McDonald says. "Thank you very much."

"Field trip, field trip!"

"Oh my God, if he does that the entire way to the Lab, I am going to strangle him."

Piren smirks. "He's just showing his excitement."

"I'll give him something to be excited about…"

The teacher ticks off names as we filter onto the bus, one by one.

"Wow, full class," she says as I step on board. "Funny, the eighth grade end-of-year trip always has perfect attendance. Every year."

I beam. "Guess everyone's eager to tour the Lab."

On any other day, kids will fake anything from a scraped knee to a sneeze to manipulate their parents into calling them out sick for class. But on Assignment Lab Day, malaria could strike the town and the entire frigging class would still show up for school.

I sit beside Toni on the bus.

"How do you think they do it?" she asks.

Amanda pops her head over our seat. "Do you think we'll actually get to see the computer?"

"I dunno. That'd be pretty badass, though."

"I read a book about it once." Piren leans in from across the aisle. "Data goes through the main computer, and they Assign your Partner from there."

"Everyone knows that," Alan says. "I want to *see* them do it."

Toni squeals, grabbing my hands as we pull through the gates and into the parking lot. Everyone rises to their feet before the bus screeches to a halt. We shove and elbow, bulldozing through each other to reach the towering metal doors.

I tug Piren's arm as we walk inside. "Bet you a dollar they bring up that stupid Pioneer State thing within the first five minutes."

"You're on."

Our state was one of the first ten in the country to mandate Assigned Partners; the others jumped on the bandwagon soon after, and then it became federal law. Every public building in this whole frigging state feels the need to display this fun fact on a prominent sign.

Lo and behold...

"You're currently residing in one of Assigning's birth states," our bubbly tour guide, Melanie, says. "That's right, we're pioneers of innovation. It all started right here, folks."

"Told you so," I mouth to Piren across the room.

He makes a face at me. I rub my fingers together to show him I expect my payment.

"What you're about to see here today are the tools that make it all possible." Melanie clasps her hands together, brandishing a toothy smile. Behind her, dozens of screens and buttons flash and beep, as if creating the Lab's own theme song. "Now, who can tell me why we need Assigning?"

Sam's hand shoots up. "So people can produce healthy kids."

"Yes, great! What else?"

Amanda pipes up. "I think someone told me, before Partners, people would date a bunch of people, or even marry more than one person and get divorced. Or, like, be with someone and then, like, sneak around with someone else behind their back. You know, before affairs were illegal."

"Bingo!" The guide's eyes light up. "Moral compasses didn't always point due north, if you get what I'm saying. Diseases spread, depression, babies out of wedlock, kids with birth defects, divorce…" She counts the transgressions on her fingers. "It wasn't a very nice place, folks. People couldn't carry the burden of finding the right mate on their own; they needed help. So, that's where we come in, and we have—" she points behind her "—one hundred percent accuracy in our Assigned Partners."

We push in closer to follow her finger, tripping over each other's toes in the packed room. Sure enough, a bright yellow sign boasts:

Assignment Lab: 100% Accuracy!
Assigning Perfect Partners for Over One Hundred Years

Not super modest, but okay.

"Many years ago," Melanie continues, "broken families overwhelmed us. Kids like you didn't have stable homes, because without a married mother and father, kids can't thrive—it's impossible." She pulls out a stack of index cards and reads aloud.

"Between soaring high school dropout rates, teen pregnancy, homosexuality, and rising juvenile crimes, the government had to act. Something had to be done to ensure kids grew up in healthy homes to prevent these travesties. Thus, mandated Partners were created. With a perfect Partner already decided, things like divorce and homosexual behavior became unnecessary." Her eyes flick up from the cards, and she clears her throat before continuing her spiel.

"But that wasn't the only problem. Impoverished people had three, four, five, or even more children, but they couldn't care for them. The growing population led to thousands of people this country couldn't feed—the beginning of overpopulation. Kids grew up in poverty and despair, forcing the government to implement the two-children-per-Partnership law to maintain a stable population."

Sam's hand pops up yet again. "So, is that before the Federal Government was dissolved?"

"Exactly! Yes." She shuffles through her cards and pulls one out. "The national government was dissolved, and power was distributed to local officials — our Mayor, for example, in this town — to enforce the legal system, state by state. As you may have already learned in school, each of the forty-eight states nominates one of its Mayors to attend the annual Council in Kansas City, at which point propositions of change in National Law are brought to a vote. Around the time this system was developed by our Founders, the United States made the decision to close its borders to immigration and emigration, with the understanding that trade and commerce across American borders would remain easy and accessible to and from all countries.

"Some notable countries, such as Russia, Costa Rica, and Germany, have adapted the American system. Some others, like Thailand and England, also recently began discussions of implementing their own Assignment system." She lowers her cards. "And given the chance, I would encourage them to follow through with it. Ever since our country took that leap, let me tell you, it's become a vastly healthier, more positive place. We're lucky to be alive when we are." She hangs her head. "Our ancestors suffered through things we can't even imagine."

My classmates' eyes gloss over as she rambles.

Enough with the frigging history lesson. Let's see some action already.

"Oops, I've lost some of you!" Melanie snaps her fingers. Eyes drift back to the front of the room. "As the Assignment system developed, Ceremonies were implemented to protect the sanctity of this process, serving as a rite of passage. Kids had a new direction for their lives, following a guided relationship timeline. If activities like kissing and fornication are scheduled, there's no need for people to act rashly or on pure emotion. And as a result, teen pregnancy and sexually transmitted diseases have been essentially eradicated. Our ancestors vowed to protect these customs for their children and grandchildren, so humanity could thrive for generations to come."

She takes a deep breath, and her elated expression sinks to melancholy. "But things weren't perfect. Despite the success of the Partnering system, there were some...*reprobates* — " she enunciates the word " — who decided rules were *beneath* them. When a select group of people still chose to act recklessly and promiscuously, a new law was created. Farm and desert land in each state was quarantined from the public, devoted solely to these...*people.* These places were set aside for the uncultured, the criminal, and the rebellious, to live their lives without disrupting civilized society—behind a walled gate. You know our state's section as Lornstown."

Melanie flings out her hand and points to a poster on the wall. A forlorn-looking, tearful woman shivers in the picture, her bony hand clasped around the wrist of a sickly, malnourished little boy. Two dilapidated buildings with smashed windows loom behind her, creating an ominous shadow.

Banishment to Lornstown: Don't Let It Happen to You

"Lornstown is a terrifying place indeed. With rampant disease, starvation, complete disconnection from technology, and some of the highest crime rates in the country, it's earned its reputation for having a 'murder a minute.'" Melanie shudders, as if her own words gave her goose bumps. "But no need to fret. Law-abiding citizens needn't worry."

She taps her computer keyboard, and the screen comes alive. "Darn thing's old as dirt, but it works. Here's how the Assigning process goes. It's simple." Fifty kids snap out of their stupor and huddle closer. "We enter information about the parents, their genetics, the gender of the child, blood type, et cetera, and give the computer time to process. Then, usually before the baby is one year old, we have a Partnership with another baby in the same town. We know very early, but as you all know, it's our little secret until the child is six."

Melanie pulls up a profile on the computer, punching buttons with her stubby fingers. As she types, numbers and names flash onto a square projector screen to our right, like rolling movie credits on crack. The computer beeps and hums as it scans and processes the information. After a few seconds, a photo of a chubby-faced newborn baby boy materializes on the screen.

"See this little guy here?" Melanie jabs her finger at the image. "My nephew, William. Ran his data myself. Can't wait to see which little baby'll be Assigned to him, to give my big brother some grand-children someday."

I squint at the boy's picture, imagining a groom's tuxedo instead of a onesie.

Creepy.

"It's a waiting game now," Melanie continues, "but soon enough, when I open Will's profile, a little girl's face will appear alongside it. Computer does all the thinking for me."

Across the room, Sam scratches his head. Lips parted slightly, he gawks at the screen like it's a magical creature. Every time he sports that dumbfounded expression, my mind jumps to an image of a hairy orangutan. I shoot the stink-eye at the computer.

You. Yeah, you, Computer. You Partnered me with this idiot. Thanks a lot.

The machine beeps and whirs, singing its magical Assigning song. The class watches in awe, absorbing every second of the experience.

What dysfunction could my parents possibly have in their genetics that caused this frigging computer to spew out Sam and me together? Those bastards.

"Let's do a little test to see how well it works, huh?" Melanie strokes her chin. "I'm going to hand out surveys for you to take, to categorize your personality by key traits. Take the survey—by yourself! No sharing answers! We'll run your info into the computer, and you can bet your hat the machine will spit out your Partner's name with yours. You're what, thirteen? Fourteen? Been Partnered for years, but you'll see—your Assigned Partner's still compatible today. Genetics plan everything, folks."

Everyone grabs and pushes until the stack of papers is depleted.

My mouth tightens as I scan the thirty-question survey. The questions are ridiculous. How do I handle being afraid? How often do I cry? Am I an extrovert? What color best describes me?

How the hell is this supposed to prove anything?

I answer the best I can, checking off boxes with my number-two-pencil nub, and hand my survey back to Melanie. The computer scanner sucks up everyone's papers, much to our shared delight.

How will Sam's answers compare to mine? Maybe he'll surprise me…

"Okay, here we go." Melanie studies the jumbling screen. The computer whirs and beeps, as text comes into focus. "Isabella Jaris and Michael Dorney?"

Wow. Trippy.

The Partnership raises their joined hands in the air. Everyone cheers the computer's accuracy.

"I see we have some success. Okay, next! Let's find some Partnerships!" She types into the computer. "Alan Carrey and Antonia Henders?"

Alan high-fives a blushing Toni, as the class breaks into astounded applause.

Eight more couples fly by, all accurate Partnerships. Everyone is transfixed on the projector screen, mesmerized by the whole thing; one-hundred-percent accuracy indeed.

"Okay, okay, last one for today. We're low on time," Melanie says. I suck in a deep breath. "Let's see…Tracy Bailey—" I rise up on my tiptoes "—and Piren Allston."

My heart stops.

What?

Silence. A sharp breath catches in my throat.

No, that's impossible.

I find Piren's unblinking eyes among the horde, jaw hanging from his stunned face. For the first time in this game, the computer's answers elicit no cheers.

"Tracy and Piren? Are you guys Assigned or what?" Melanie scans the crowd. I slink down behind my peers, hiding my reddening cheeks behind my hands.

No no no no no.

Suspicious stares burn into my skin as my classmates' harsh whispers boil like a kettle around me. My heart thuds against my ribs. I can almost feel the rumors starting, draping speculation over me like a dark cloud.

Stop whispering. Stop. Shut up.

I blink back a curtain of warm tears.

Why?

"Um, they're not a Partnership," Amanda says from the front. "Tracy is with Sam Macey. Piren is with Lara Goodren."

I fidget my fingers around my belt, not daring a glance at their accusing faces.

Don't look at Piren.

Don't look at Piren.

Any association with him will condemn me.

Don't look at him.

Melanie glares at the computer, pounding in more numbers.

"Here it is, here it is…Just a glitch, folks. Sorry about that. Right here, see? Sam Macey and Tracy Bailey. Right here. My mistake. Just an error! The Partnership is accurate."

She stumbles into a new topic, drawing attention to another part of the room.

Computer, you frigid bitch. Why do you hate me so?

"Thanks for making me look like an idiot," Sam says, shoving past me. Ragged breaths rip through my lungs, but I don't dare respond.

Piren sweeps up beside me.

"You okay?" he mouths.

I shrug and brush by him to join the rest of the class. Tears cloud my vision, and I suck them back into my brain.

Pull yourself together, damn it!

"And if you look over here…"

Melanie's voice turns to static in my ears.

Stupid Melanie. Stupid Melanie and her stupid effing computer.

My best friend slouches up front, jiggling his restless leg. My gaze softens.

But…what if…

I tighten up, shaking off the thought.

Computers glitch. It happens. That's all it was—a glitch. But who cares? Piren's my best friend, and I don't care who knows it. Of course we're compatible. That's why he's my best friend.

PIREN ALLSTON

Mason's First Kiss Ceremony was yesterday, and I'm still shaking. It was so freaking awful, it's giving me anxiety about my own First Kiss, albeit four years away.

The TV news anchor called it "the worst disaster in a decade." I felt like puking the whole time, so my stomach and I are inclined to agree.

This girl Ashley Wyman caused the commotion. I recognized her as the dark-haired girl who knew Mason at the mall. She's Stephanie's friend, or at least she used to be.

The first hour was fine. Dozens of high school seniors sat poised and ready for their big moment. Five hundred beaming spectators chatted amongst themselves, eagerly awaiting the event to begin. Orange and red leaves clung to branches over our heads, blowing in the cool autumn breeze.

The Mayor gave his drab speech on the sanctity of the Ceremony, and the Master of Ceremonies started announcing couples for their First Kiss. Everything went smooth, until they called Ashley up to kiss her Partner on stage. She went white as a ghost. Seriously, I thought she was going to faint or something. Trembling, she approached her Partner, a lanky kid named Jonny Loris.

"Poor thing, she looks petrified," Mom whispered to Dad beside me.

Right when Ashley was supposed to kiss Jonny, she broke down crying and bolted off the stage. The audience gasped and whispered, unsure what to make of it. That's never happened during a sacred Ceremony before. At least, not in my time.

At first, I thought Ashley got stage fright in front of all those people and cameras, because I could imagine that happening to me. But within minutes, the truth reared its ugly head.

Ashley has been having an affair with a twenty-year-old. The story unraveled as people in the crowd pieced together bits of the screwed-up puzzle. Ashley quivered, hands splayed over her face as accusations flew like poison arrows through the open-air stadium.

Someone recalled spying her at Laney Park one night with a non-Partner; he assumed Ashley and her lover were Assigned and didn't think twice about seeing them together. Another witness swore she saw Ashley *kiss* her lover through a car window last summer. The crowd grew unrulier with each new revelation, pointing and shouting. Ashley rattled with sobs in the corner. With evidence stacked so high against her, her silence solidified her guilt.

Ten minutes into questioning, a woman identified Ashley's lover in the audience. He was tall and pale with dyed-black hair and a sleeve tattoo. Two men jumped into the crowd and dragged him by the scruff of his neck, shoving him to the stage for sentencing.

By this point, the crowd's jeers escalated into an ear-splitting insult soup.

Fists clenched, the Mayor drew his tight mouth up in a thin line.

"I have no words," he said, spitting into the microphone, "for this level of blasphemy. Disrupting a Ceremony is a vile crime, but disrupting it with adultery is reprehensible." His face flushed crimson as he thundered words dripping with venom. The crowd rose to their feet, cheering him on.

The Mayor read aloud Ashley's indiscretions: hand holding with a non-Partner, flirting with a non-Partner, and kissing a non-Partner. Someone in the audience even threw in an accusation of second base, in cruder terms.

Ashley's Partner Jonny swayed at the side of the stage, biting his fingernails. I couldn't tell if he was actually listening to the whole thing or was too shocked to absorb his newfound lonely life. The whole thing sucked. I wasn't even involved, and I wanted to evaporate.

Usually, Banishments attract a handful of spectators. People with nothing better to do flock downtown to ridicule the perpetrators. This time, half the town was present. It's the closest I've seen to a raging mob.

"Go back to your whore house!" a man shouted at Ashley to rumbling applause from the crowd.

"See that boy?" a woman in the next row said to her young son. She pointed to Ashley's non-Partner, whose name no one bothered to learn. "He's a cowardly insect that belongs with that slut."

Mason and Stephanie joined the jeers. I even heard Stephanie call Ashley a bitch, and they were once close friends. My parents whispered together, shaking their heads and glaring at the perpetrators.

I got to my feet with my brother and the rest of the crowd. Everyone pumped their fists in the air as the Mayor signed the paperwork. Usually, he reads the Banishment decree off a scripted sheet of paper, but this time he improvised; he sprinkled in his own attacks and swears against the criminals.

"You!" The Mayor stretched his fingers toward the adulterous couple. "You are unworthy of love. I don't want you in my civilized society, and if I see either of you again, I'll shoot you myself like the animals you are!"

The audience roared with delight.

Four uniformed men rushed the stage, jumping on the perpetrators. Two of them yanked Ashley's arms back, throwing her to the ground. She thrashed her legs, but the men's strength overwhelmed her. The other two men wrestled Ashley's lover, pinning him and pressing his face into the dirt. The audience cheered as the offenders hit the ground.

The Mayor drew his switchblade. He grabbed Ashley's lover by his hair and pried the boy's face upward.

"May this scar be a reminder of the devastating choices you made. May this mark serve as a universal sign of your adultery."

He slashed his blade into the boy's cheek, spattering blood across the stage. The boy grunted as his captors released their grip.

The Mayor strode to the other end of the stage. Crouching beside Ashley, he wiped his bloody blade across her dress before drawing it again.

"May this scar—"

"No!" The scarred boy leapt to Ashley's side. Guards lunged, pinning him to the ground. Blood smeared across his marred cheek as he struggled to break loose, kicking a guard in the shin.

"Restrain him!" the Mayor bellowed.

One of the guards plunged his fist into the boy's stomach. The sputtering boy crumbled into a heap on the stage as the crowd jeered.

"Take him down!" a man shouted.

"Cut the whore!" shouted another.

The Mayor said his lines and marred Ashley's face as she sobbed, tears mingling with blood across her face.

"You are both hereby Banished for life, as of this very moment," he said. "For ruining this Ceremony, I grant you no grace period. You will be escorted to Lornstown immediately, where you will rot for eternity. You are never to pass back through the Lornstown gates into civilization or communicate with any citizen of my town again, under penalty of death." A handful of isolated hoots rang out from the crowd. "Now get the hell out of my town and don't come back." He spit a wad of saliva at their feet.

Ashley fell to her knees, crawling to her mother in the audience. She reached out a quivering hand, but Mrs. Wyman flinched away. Her face contorted in horror.

"You're no child of mine. You're nothing but a dirty slut. A tramp. You're dead to me. I hate you. I wish I never had you." Mrs. Wyman kicked her heeled boot, striking her daughter in the side. The crowd erupted with laughter.

A heavy pit dropped in my stomach.

She cast aside her own blood family.

I glanced at my parents, standing proudly beside my brother and me. My insides churned.

I can't even…

I screamed along with the crowd, shouting with as much force as my lungs could muster. I bellowed until my throat grew raspy and dry. And when I couldn't shout any more, I pumped my fist in the air to the beat of the crowd's angry shrieks.

Guards clapped handcuffs over the couple's wrists, leading them to a waiting shuttle — their last ride through civilization before eternal damnation in Lornstown.

As the guards dragged the criminals away, something struck me. While cuffed, the adulterers touched hands behind their backs. It was only a brush, but it happened. Faces stained with blood and defeat, they stared over the heads of the crowd as they passed. I know it can't be love, but something inside me wants to call it that. When they disappeared behind the tinted windows of the SUV, my fist unclenched and dropped back to my side.

Less than twenty-four hours since the Ceremony, news of Ashley Wyman's adultery infected the entire town. Rumor has it the Wymans locked themselves in their home in shame.

The Burial, when we mourn the adulterers' souls in a fake funeral, is scheduled for Wednesday. After that, they'll be dead to the town. No one will speak of them again.

I feel bad for my brother. By the time the Ceremony resumed, the audience was in disarray. Mason and Stephanie's First Kiss was met with feeble applause. Half the crowd had already dissipated, trailing after Ashley's shuttle to squeeze in final insults. The rest weren't paying attention anymore.

Mason's still fuming from his stolen moment. I listened to his rant on the drive home, but my mind wandered. I replayed the scene in my head: Ashley, reaching for her lover's hand, as they carted her away in shackles. She embraced the suffering and accepted Banishment, all for an adulterous relationship. A faux love, doomed to fail.

How could anybody, Banished forever, torn from their family and society, ever find peace? Is anything worth that kind of pain?

TRACY BAILEY

"You should really treat Sam better," Mom says, taping pink streamers to the wall.

"It's my birthday. Can you not?" I blow a clod of hair off my face. "I treat him fine."

"Well, I'll see about that. I invited him to your birthday party."

"You *what?*" I leap up. "Are you *trying* to inflict pain upon me?"

She narrows her eyes, and I know the conversation is over.

I fall back onto the armchair.

Great. Getting fondled by my stupid Partner is exactly the gift I desired for my fifteenth birthday. Not.

Dad strolls in with a fistful of balloons from the dollar store. "Hey there, birthday girl." He kisses the top of my head. "Can't believe you're almost twenty."

"I'm only fifteen. Sheesh, don't rush it."

"Only five years away." He ties the balloons around the armrest. "But to me you're still that same little bundle we carried home from the hospital." He ruffles my hair. "Same little brown curls, only they've multiplied like wildfire."

"Ugh, Dad…" I knock his hand away and pat down my frizz.

Veronica furiously pounds keys on her cellphone. "Ollie's on his way."

"You invited him to my party?" I throw my head back and groan.

"Aw, come on, Trace." She gives me her best puppy-dog pout. "He likes you!"

"No he doesn't."

She bites her lip.

"Fine." I fling my hands up. "He can come." I suppose he's another one I should treat better, given he's my future brother and all. This frigging event will be less of a party and more a test of my patience.

"Yay!" Veronica crushes me in a hug.

"You know—" I untangle myself from V's arms "—you're quite codependent for a pair of seventh graders."

She shrugs. "I love him."

"You're spending so much time together, you're beginning to mimic each other's mannerisms." Seriously, I've started referring to them in my head as The Wonder Twins.

"That's not true!" She runs her hand over the back of her head.

"That!" I point. "Right there! The head thing! He does that!"

She blushes, whipping her hand back to her side.

My parents enter the room, arm-in-arm. The doorbell rings, and Oliver clomps inside, dragging that hideous saxophone case.

"I thought I'd play you a birthday song," he says.

Oh, great. I get my ears assaulted on my birthday.

Veronica jumps into Oliver's arms, giggling.

"I love you, Oliver Hughes!"

"I love you more, Veronica Bailey!"

"I love you most, Oliver Hughes!"

"I lo—"

"Please. Can you do that elsewhere? Ugh." I shove past them.

My sister is thirteen and has already planned her whole life. It's sickening. Marrying Sam is the furthest thing from my mind, yet here's my sister and her Partner, loudly comparing colored napkins and flatware for their wedding reception. It makes me gag.

I've told Sam there will be zero discussion of our wedding before our Marriage Prep class; even then, I'd prefer zero discussion. As if having him as my effing Partner isn't enough, after graduation, I'll be stuck living with him too. I look forward to it the way I'd look forward to getting all my teeth pulled or getting stabbed in the eye. In fact, put those three events together, and I'll struggle to find the least objectionable option.

Oh, but the fun won't end after cohabitation. Next comes the ginormous, tacky wedding! Thinking about it makes me want to vomit my homemade cake all over the floor and then not clean it up.

I don't know why everybody feels the need to romanticize weddings. Let's call it what it is: another pomp-and-circumstance parade where people ogle at you. Weddings aren't beautiful. They're just an excuse to blow your life savings and flaunt yourself. You re-commit yourself to someone you've already been committed to since before you could walk; it's a pointless, expensive ritual to further fuse me to Sam. Why don't we just read marriage vows at the Assigning Ceremony when we're six? Save time and money later in life.

I grip the cake plate so tight my knuckles turn white.

"Tracy." Mom shakes her head. "Ladies don't scowl, especially on their birthday."

Sam arrives in a hideous, mustard-colored button-down his parents obviously stuffed him in. He tries to pull me into a hug, but I capture him in a handshake instead.

"I love you, Tracy Bailey."

"I love you, Sam Macey."

He thrusts me a poorly-wrapped purple package I presume is my birthday gift. My parents hover over us like hungry seagulls, camera poised to attack. I peel open the gift.

Buried beneath layers of tissue paper rests a pink music box. I open the lid, and it chimes a sweet little tune. It's a cool gift, displaying taste well above Sam's caliber; I'm almost one-hundred-percent sure his mother picked it out.

My mother jabs me in the back. I get the hint to hold my Partner's hand, but I don't want to. I tighten my grasp around my new toy instead. Sam pries my fingers off the gift and entwines them into his. I squirm in an effort to free my hand, but he tightens his grip.

My parents and The Wonder Twins beam with delight. My father whips out his camera and snaps away, capturing the uncomfortable moment forever. My mother tears with joy.

I want to run into the other room and die.

After dinner, I retreat to my bedroom, muttering something about a headache that doesn't actually exist. I'm flipping through a magazine on my bed when the door creaks open. Sam plods in, staring at the carpet.

Way to knock.

"Leave the door open." My jaw tightens. "Mom will get mad."

He shuffles his feet. "I know. I asked your parents; they said I could come up here to see you."

Of course they did. Ugh.

Sam sits on the edge of my bed. I scoot my knees up to my chest to avoid any wandering hands.

"What is it?" I don't bother to hide the thick exasperation in my voice.

"Sorry, I don't wanna bug you." *Too late.* "I know you're not feeling well." He scratches his arm.

And with you in my bedroom, my headache grows more plausible by the second.

I perch my chin on my knees. "It's fine. What's up?"

"I know I haven't been…super nice to you. I mean, I'm sorry if I'm too forward sometimes."

"Sometimes" is the biggest understatement of the century.

When I don't deny it, he continues. "And I don't wanna push you if you aren't ready to be physical. I just…I see everyone else holding hands at school and being all, I dunno, cuddly and stuff at Under Five."

"I'm not big into PDA."

He fidgets. "I know. I just want you to know, I really do care about you. Everyone says how lucky I am, 'cause you're so smart and pretty and all." He picks at a loose thread on my comforter. "I just…I know people say things sometimes. That you're too good to be Partnered with me. That I'm too ugly, or stupid, or…I dunno. And I try to ignore it, but…it hurts."

My shoulders droop. "I'm sorry. I've never heard that."

Thought it maybe, but never heard anyone say it.

"And I mean…I get it. You're the popular, pretty, rich girl, and I'm—" he releases a lofty breath "—me."

"That's not true."

Sam tugs at his sleeve. "Alan Carrey called me a troll the other day. And I just—"

"Alan Carrey's an idiot." I force a half-smile. "You know the computers are accurate."

He rubs his upper arm. "And your birthday gift, I hope you like it. My mom suggested the music box" *—I knew it!—* "but I was the one who picked it out. I listened to a bunch of them, but the song in this one reminded me of you."

"Really?"

"Yeah. I liked the minor key. It's sweet, but kinda powerful too. Beautiful, in a mysterious way."

"I didn't know you knew about music."

"Well, not like Veronica's Partner. I don't play the sax or anything."

I snort. "Thank God."

We share a laugh.

Maybe I'm being too harsh.

I take a deep breath and grab his hand, lacing his fingers with mine.

His face lights up. "Do you think someday you'll want to do that more? In public?"

No.

"Yeah, maybe. Maybe next year or something."

"Awesome. I'll be counting down the days."

We lock eyes, and for a brief moment, my smile feels sincere.

PIREN ALLSTON

Everyone hates gym class. Gym exacerbates mockery of the unco-ordinated, and in a group of awkward ninth-graders, that's almost everybody. I usually skirt past ridicule because I'm pretty good with a ball. Sam, who drops more than he catches, isn't so lucky. He sucks at sports.

At least once a week, Sam loses his temper and has a connip-tion in the middle of gym class. He'll dropkick basketballs, sending them flying; students shriek and duck to avoid getting walloped. Trace nicknamed him "Bounce," because he turns a basketball into a bouncing, orange weapon. She used to drag out the nickname every time our gym teachers inflicted basketball on us, but she's laid off him recently. I think he got her a cool birthday gift or something.

Our teachers must be fed-up with Sam's fits. They've begun of-fering activities that require less hand-eye coordination. For example, last week we were stuck in the weight room, pretending to pump iron. I managed to do a pull-up for the first time in my life. Trace whistled as I dangled from the bar afterward.

"Woot! Super-human strength!" She broke into applause. "Got any tickets to that gun show?"

I dropped to the floor. "Can't buy tickets for these guns, sorry. You wanna try?"

"No way. I'll just hang there like an idiot."

"You mean like I did for the last twenty minutes?" I wiped bead-ing sweat off my forehead.

"Exactly. But I'll still kick your ass on the track later."

Several feet away, Sam grunted beneath the bench-press bar, drip-ping in sweat. Every few seconds, he glanced up at us, nostrils flaring.

Between the weight room and basketball, I didn't think our gym teachers were capable of torturing us further. However, for today's class, their activity choice proves me wrong; we're doing ballroom dance lessons. Joy. The girls squeal and whisper with delight at the news; the guys break out in a collective, long-winded groan.

Our two gym teachers, Mr. and Mrs. Prillowich, are both so annoying, it's no doubt to anyone as to why they're Assigned. Trace calls them the "Prillobitches."

Mr. and Mrs. Prillowich instruct us to line up in Partnerships. Mrs. Prillowich lectures how we should take this seriously, because we'll have to dance at our weddings in a few years.

Gym class is the only place on school property we don't wear uniforms. As one might guess, some people take this freedom to extremes. Toni's sporting tight, hot-pink Spandex shorts today, and a neon yellow tank top that barely hides her boobs. Also predictable, Alan's practically salivating over her. He thinks he's smooth and inconspicuous, pretending to stare at the wall and not Toni's ass. He's not.

Trace is wearing tight pink shorts today too. They do a nice job accentuating her butt.

The Prillowiches strut through the lines of couples. One by one, they position everyone's hands on their Partners for proper dancing.

Lara pulls back her dirty-blond hair, snapping on the red rubber band she keeps around her wrist. She's wearing baggy red shorts and a white soccer-jersey.

"Try not to embarrass me," she says with a wink.

I brush a stray strand of hair off her face. "No promises."

The Prillowiches parade their graceful dance moves as a classical waltz hums from the speakers. They flawlessly dip and twirl around the gym before our stunned eyes. Sliding to a halt, they indicate for us to copy.

Attempting to mimic their cat-like dance, the class tramples each other's toes. Mrs. Prillowich shakes her head as Mr. Prillowich stops the music. They give a brief lecture on paying attention, then they're off again, perfectly waltzing to a dozen violins.

Alan whispers something crude about Mrs. Prillowich, and I burst out laughing.

The Prillowiches whip around, catching me mid-chuckle.

"Enough." Mrs. Prillowich snaps her fingers. "Piren and Lara, down front."

I freeze. The teacher latches onto my arm and tugs me to the center of the room, Lara trailing behind. The class steps back to form a circle around us.

"All right, Piren, Lara. Impress us with your best waltz."

I look to my Partner for guidance, but she shares my empty expression.

Lara deserves a medal for putting up with me; every time I goof-off, she ends up sharing my spotlight of shame.

The violins start, and within two beats, I crush Lara's toes. Pressing her lips together, Mrs. Prillowich rushes over and stops the music. Muffled giggles fill the room. My cheeks burn.

"Okay, okay," Mr. Prillowich says. "Lara, you may be a little tall for this particular waltz…Hmm, we need another girl, just for positioning. Let's see…Ms. Bailey, can you come partner with Mr. Allston for a minute?"

Lara slinks back into the crowd alone, blushing. Sam balls his hands at his sides as his Partner skips over to join me in the center of the gym.

"Thanks for saving me. Sam's cologne reeks," Trace whispers. "I need a gas mask."

Mrs. Prillowich taps her foot, waiting for us to begin.

My hands hover inches from Trace's waist. "How…how do we do this?"

Am I allowed to touch her?

My heart thuds, knee threatening to bounce beneath me.

"Put your hand on her waist, Piren. Tracy, put your hand on his shoulder…I know, it's okay. It's for school…Yes, just like that…Hold your other hands away from your body…That's it…"

The moment Trace's warm body meets my palm, my leg quiets.

"You need to hold your other hands together," Mr. Prillowich says. "Interlock your fingers."

Trace jitters her fingers along my shoulder, avoiding eye contact. After the incident at the Assignment Lab last year, touching Trace with everyone watching feels more awkward than it should.

Stop worrying! It's just Trace. It's not a big deal.

I've never been embarrassed by my friendship with Trace, but I think I'm supposed to be.

Trace clears her throat and grabs my hand, lacing her fingers with mine.

My stomach flips.

"Good," Mrs. Prillowich says. "Now, music."

Silky strings fill the room with a flowing melody. I take a deep breath, and we glide across the gym floor. Trace's long curls wave as we move, flowing behind her like a veil. I don't catch any of her toes, and we're doing it—we're dancing.

The class falls silent, all eyes on us. We float across the rubber-floored room, agile feet brushing the ground in time with the waltz. Our synchronized breathing drowns out the swooning violins and cellos in my ears.

She squeezes my hand, and I squeeze back—some sort of best-friend code only we understand. Trace's face comes alive when she smiles, as if she's laughing with her eyes.

A sharp breath catches in my throat.

A strange feeling rips through my body, twisting and churning as if everything inside me tangles into knots. It's a weird pain, something I've never had before.

We're together only a few seconds when the music dies.

Slowly, I untwine my hand from hers.

"Great job, you two." Mrs. Prillowich's voice snaps my attention back to the present. "Okay, Piren, back with Lara. Tracy, let's see you do those moves with Sam."

I hold Trace's gaze for a moment, but she pulls away.

And the feeling is gone.

TRACY BAILEY

I'm not halfway through the front door when my father slams it shut behind me, yanking me through the threshold.

"Tracy Allison Bailey."

I slide my arms out of my backpack straps. "Dad."

"You are in serious trouble."

"What'd I do?"

"You know what you did."

"What? No, I —"

"Shut up!" He shoves me into the wall. My skull thuds against the barrier.

I honestly don't know what the hell I did this time, but I'm guessing Piren's part of the problem. Could be a late reaction to the Lab incident, could be the more recent dancing incident. Hell, my whole life is a frigging incident. I don't know how he found out, but I'm guessing from some nosy parent. I hate the adults in this town, all overeager for gossip, desperately waiting for someone to fuck up who isn't their own kid.

Neither of the incidents were inherently my fault, so I don't know why I'm in trouble. If anyone deserves blame, it's the Prillowiches, or that frigging Assigning computer.

"Dad, gym wasn't my fault, I just —"

"You're not to see Piren Allston." His growling words slur together. "Ever."

"But he's in my class." I attempt to inch away from him, but he latches his hands around my forearms, holding me in place.

"Then you treat him like any other classmate. Got it?"

"You're drunk." I push past him, but he's not ready to let it go. He rips me back by my collar and throws me to the ground. I wince as my body lands on my arm, crushing it against the tiles.

"Got it?" he repeats.

"Y-Yes, I got it."

"Look at me."

I stare at the ground, water prickling in my eyes.

"I said, look at me!"

Tremoring with rage, he lunges toward me, face inches from mine. The tangy aroma of scotch on his hot breath burns my nose.

"You selfish little bitch. Don't give a shit about your family, huh? Why can't you be normal and not so fucked in the head?" He flicks my cheek. "Well, guess what? You go near that boy again, I'll have him Banished too. Cut his face myself. You get that? Fuck up again, you'll *both* be Banished."

With one final shove, he sweeps from the room, leaving me in a crumbled heap on the floor.

Did he just threaten to Banish my best friend?

PIREN ALLSTON

Every morning, Trace passes my house at seven fifteen sharp. The moment I see her coming, I race outside to join her. We reach the bus stop together by seven thirty. Over the past eight years, she's only been late a handful of times. Her excuses for tardiness become her most hilarious stories. She has a near perfect track record, which is why I'm confused today.

I waited twenty minutes, drumming my fingers along the windowsill, but Trace never came. If I wait any longer, I'll miss the bus.

Maybe she's home sick and forgot to text me.

I trek outside alone, kicking a pebble down the road, into the grate. A hot pink speck catches my eye in the distance.

I squint; it's Trace. My forehead creases.

She left without me? And took the long way?

"Trace?" I chase after her, sneakers clomping against the asphalt. "Trace!"

She doesn't stop or turn around.

"Hey! Trace!" I call louder, but she presses on.

What the hell?

I jog up to her and yank her backpack, tugging her backward in our usual morning greeting.

"Hey, what happened? Your big ugly fangs get caught in your ears? Didn't hear me calling?"

Head down, she dashes ahead. My smile falters. I can't remember the last time I sassed Trace without receiving a witty retort; it's disconcerting. I jump in front, facing her, walking backward in time with her steps.

"Trace, wh —"

A cloth sling binds her arm to her chest. I jolt, stopping dead in my tracks.

"Whoa, Bailey, what happened?"

She dodges around me like I'm a boulder in the road.

What is she doing?

"Stop! Hey!" I pounce in front of her, blocking her getaway. "What the hell's going on?"

She stops walking, but drops her gaze to the ground.

Is this a game?

"W-What the hell happened to your arm? What's going on?"

She balances a shopping bag of schoolbooks in the crook of her slung elbow. That's Trace, never taking care of herself. I reach for her bag, but she pulls away.

Why won't she just talk to me, damn it?

She adjusts her sling, and her plastic water bottle thumps to the ground. I bend to grab it, but when I look up, silent tears stream from her bloodshot eyes, down her wet cheeks.

My leg quivers beneath me.

Is she upset with me? Did I do something wrong?

I rest my hand on her shoulder as she cries. Her body shakes, but she doesn't make a sound. Her silence scares the hell out of me; Trace is never silent, not around me.

"Trace, I —"

"I can't walk to the bus with you anymore." Her voice cracks. "I'm so sorry."

She stretches for her water bottle, but I yank it away. "Why?"

"You're not my Partner. Sam is."

I furrow my brows. "Is that what this is about?"

She bites her lip.

"That's stupid. You don't even like Sam, and I mean, we have, like, three years before you have to live with him, why do you care?"

Something burns in my chest. It's the same burning I got last week when we danced.

"Oh, come on, Piren, you know why. We're not supposed to be friends, not even supposed to talk, but we do, and we're just hurting everyone."

"Your arm…Did Sam do that? 'Cause I'll beat the hell outta him, Trace, Partner or not—"

"No! I tripped down the stairs. Veronica left her shit there, and I fell."

My mouth opens, then closes again.

"Piren. Please. I can't be the friend you want me to be."

"What does that even mean?" A knot clumps in my throat. "You're... my best friend."

Trace blinks, wiping her wet cheek on her sleeve.

"No, I'm not. Lara's your best friend, your only best friend. Weren't you listening to Mr. Wintle back in third grade? I'm your neighbor." She straightens. "You want to borrow a vacuum, come to me. You want friendship, go to her. It's simple." She shrugs my hand off her shoulder. "I gotta go."

She snatches her water bottle and speeds off toward the bus. I can't do anything but watch her leave.

TRACY BAILEY

Piren never goes to the tree house anymore. At least, not when I'm there. I don't blame him. I hurt him pretty bad. I still go sometimes. My parents think I'm out with friends. I don't know what friends they think I have. They took away my only real friend.

I visit the treehouse when I need to be alone, to think and catch my breath. It never lets me down. It's secluded, where no one can bother me.

Sometimes I'll bring a book and curl up for hours till the light fades. Other times, I'll lie against the thick bark, with only birds and my headphones for company. Even when the biting wind whistles through my hair, leaning against the fortress wall calms my racing mind.

After all these years, one stubborn plastic bag remains entangled in a mass of branches; a lone parachute we never retrieved. On blustery days, harsh gusts rattle the plastic, shooting my brain to déjà vu. It tangles me up inside, flooding me with childhood memories. Sometimes I wish I could repress those memories into oblivion.

"Intruders on the west wall! Shoot them down! Pew, pew!"

I make a finger gun with my hand and shoot the parachute. It waves in the breeze, firmly latched to the thick branch.

Sometimes memories feel hard and prickly in your stomach. The treehouse elicits those memories.

I point the finger gun toward my head and pull the trigger. *Pow.*
If only it were real.

PIREN ALLSTON

Trace hasn't talked to me in three weeks.

School sucks. Toni and Trace pass me in the hall. Toni waves, but Trace presses on without a word. I slam my locker shut, knots festering in my chest.

The bus is worse. Every day, I claim a seat near the front, scooting over toward the window. I leave an extra space beside me, just in case. Trace clambers on board, buried beneath her headphones. She strides straight past me and slides into a seat in the back. The moment the bus screeches to a halt at the mouth of our neighborhood, she bolts off alone. I slog home, watching her in the distance as she zips away from me.

For the first week, I tried. Two days after we stopped talking, I glimpsed her from the corner of my eye in the library.

"Hey, Trace!"

She blushed and walked past me like I was a ghost.

Two days later, I plopped my tray down at her cafeteria table. I mustered every fiber of self-control to keep my knee from bouncing as Alan and Toni struck up conversation. Within seconds, Trace excused herself and moved to another table. She could have shot me in the gut, and it would have hurt less.

Now when I see her, I walk the other way. I keep my eyes on the ground and force my legs to move forward. I feel robotic, talking and acting without comprehending.

I'm guessing her family is somehow involved, but I can't know for sure because she won't talk to me. Mr. Bailey threatens Trace with beatings and Banishment all the time, but his threats never broke us in the past. Why is now any different?

For the past three weeks, I've avoided Under Five — to avoid her.

But I awoke this morning with a surge of adrenaline. I'm sick of being snubbed and fed up skirting around her. Why the hell does she get to dictate where I go? At the very least, I deserve a damn explanation for her sudden disinterest in our eight-year friendship. Where does she get the nerve to treat people this way?

Rage boils inside me as I clomp to Under Five after school, ruminating a million unkind things to tell her.

I'm going to ream her out for this. What the hell is her damn problem anyway?

I reach the café doors, and my body freezes. My hand quivers over the door handle.

Maybe this isn't the best idea.

I shuffle my feet.

Just go in!

I take a deep breath and tiptoe through the entrance. I flinch as the dangling bell chimes, announcing my presence to the whole damn restaurant.

Sure enough, Trace and some others huddle around our usual booth in the back. Roars from my boisterous friends echo through the room. My heart threatens to explode in my chest. I close my eyes.

I can do this. Breathe.

Pulse racing, I approach the table, masking my anxiety behind a forced smile.

That's when I see him.

Arm sprawled around Trace's shoulders, Sam slumps back in my old seat. Trace leans into him, nestling her head against his chest. My stomach lurches.

"Hey, guys!" I slide into the booth next to Alan.

Everyone beams and greets me. Everyone except the one who matters.

Trace's laughter dies. She fidgets her hands in her lap, avoiding my gaze.

I clamp my sweaty hand over my bouncing knee.

Stop moving!

Trace's stories aren't causing the commotion today. The table's laughter spawns from Alan, rehashing tales of God knows what. I force a hollow laugh. My eyes drift to my motionless best friend. She laughs along with the crowd. It's unlike her.

I'm there barely five minutes when she gets up to leave, Sam towing faithfully behind.

TRACY BAILEY

I broke down at school today.

Mrs. Pendleton rambled on, but my mind wasn't on Physics. Sam sat beside me, diligently scratching notes.

"As students of scientific research, you have learned that most questions of the universe can be answered with a solid yes or no," our teacher said. "For example, gravity gives weight to physical objects. That statement is irrefutable." She held out her red whiteboard marker pinched between her thumb and forefinger, then released it. It fell to the floor. "There is no subjectivity of what just happened. Gravity pulled the marker down."

I fidgeted my hands in my lap.

"Yet, while science thrives on solid fact, there will always be para-doxes, and paradoxes themselves are contradictory. For example, look at the Irresistible Force Paradox. This paradox poses a question with no simple scientific answer: what happens when an unstoppable force meets an immovable object?" She retrieved the marker and jotted notes on the board. "Will the object crumble under the sheer magnitude of the unstoppable force? Or must the force succumb to the object that refuses to move?"

Resting my cheek on my hand, I tapped my pencil against the desk.

"Stop it," Sam whispered.

"I can't focus."

"Well, don't tap like that. It's annoying."

"I'm just having a bad day."

"Well, now you're making mine bad too."

"Tracy and Sam. First warning." Mrs. Pendleton narrowed her eyes at us. She turned back to the board. "In the end, when we examine the force at work…"

"You happy now?" Sam squeezed his pencil so tight, it snapped in half.

I slunk further down in my chair. "Sorry."

At the other end of the room, Piren ran his thick charcoal pencil across his paper. Most people would think he was studying, but I knew he was doodling in his sketchpad. My lip trembled. He glanced up, and his eyes crinkled at the sides when they met mine.

I looked away, a dry lump knotting in my throat.

I pushed out from my chair and sprinted to the bathroom. I clicked the lock and didn't leave the stall until the period was over.

PIREN ALLSTON

The brakes screech, thrusting me forward in my seat.

"Geez, watch it." I fling my arm out to keep from smashing into Stephanie's headrest in front of me. "Forget seatbelts; I need a straitjacket to stay alive in here."

My brother's Partner flicks her sheet of dark hair behind her shoulders but doesn't acknowledge Mason's crappy driving.

"Sorry, Steph." He puts his hand on her knee in the front seat. "That guy came out of nowhere."

"It's fine." She whips her leg out from under his hand, flashing him a smile.

Mason lays on the gas, then slams the brakes again.

I grab the bottom of my seat as the belt yanks me back. "Seriously?"

"Hey!" He waves his hand back, swatting at my leg. "No backseat driving. This is the last time I drive you home from school."

I rub my temple at the twinge of headache prickling in my brain. "Well, at this rate, you won't have to anyway, because we'll all be dead before we get home."

"Why'd you even want me to drive you, anyway? You like the bus."

"Ew, why?" Stephanie says. "The bus smells like piss."

I rest my cheek against the cold window. "I just needed a break, I guess."

We turn into our neighborhood just as the bus pulls away, depositing Trace on the street. She lumbers ahead in her pink coat, headphones on, arms wrapped around her torso.

Mason rolls down the window. "Hey, neighbor!"

Trace gives him a weak wave. I slink down in my seat.

"It's chilly today," he shouts. "You want a ride?"

I shield my face with my hand. *Just drive.*

"Oh, no thanks," she says. "I'm good."

"Suit yourself."

The car lurches forward.

Stephanie wrinkles her nose. "What a weird girl."

You have no idea.

"Didn't you used to be friends with Tracy?" Mason asks as we pull into our driveway.

I sigh. "Something like that."

TRACY BAILEY

Reliving great memories in your head is a brief vacation from a shitty reality. When I think about my favorite memories, a particularly potent one comes to mind.

We later referred to it as "Fat Head and Fangs' Grand Adventure." It happened last winter, in eighth grade.

When I found Piren after school that day, Lara was screaming at him in the parking lot. He threw his head back as she motioned angrily with her hands. I don't remember the cause of their fight, but it was probably something stupid. I think she was pissed he picked Alan over her to work on a chemistry project or something. Like I said, stupid.

She propped her hands on her hips as he crossed the parking lot toward me. Grumbling, he kicked a stone under a car.

I nudged his arm. "You okay?"

"I don't wanna talk about it."

Piren and I are the only two neighborhood kids in our grade, so we navigate the 157 bus home every day by ourselves. The route begins uptown, stops by the middle school, continues to the high school, rolls downtown, then winds up the hill to our street. Veronica takes the earlier bus with Oliver most days, and Mason drives himself home. The four of us are the only teens in the area, isolating Piren and me alone on a bus with a bunch of adults.

Piren was so flustered that day, he didn't even suggest a milkshake at Under Five. Given his grumpiness, I didn't think twice before following him onto the first bus we saw. He plopped into a seat, smacking his head against the window. I slid in beside him and offered him some Milk Duds. He groaned but extended his hand.

The bus zipped away. Attempting to cheer him up, I spun one of my notorious tales. My goal was to make Piren smile, and within five minutes, his face flushed crimson from laughing too hard. We giggled until our sides ached, oblivious to the world.

It took a solid twenty minutes to realize our blunder. We were on the 297 bus, not the 157. The 297 beelines straight to the edge of town, where it parks until morning. We were prisoners on a one-way trip to the boonies.

I pulled up a map on my phone, and we plotted our course home. The route would take forty-five minutes to reach a place we could transfer to the correct bus.

"Can you believe we did that? Idiots!"

"*We?* I followed you, genius." I shoved his arm.

"Well, I blame Lara. So there."

"Okay, agreed. It's Lara's fault."

An older woman hobbled aboard and took the seat adjacent to us.

"Hey." I poked Piren's arm. "We have an audience." I nodded toward the lady, who stared intently in our direction.

He lowered his voice to a whisper. "Why is she watching us?"

"I don't know. Should we stare back?"

We flashed our eyes toward the woman, and she instantly looked away. We giggled toward the window.

After several minutes, the woman tapped me on the shoulder.

I rotated to face her, tightening my mouth to rein in my laughter. "Hello."

The woman smiled. "You two make a lovely Partnership."

My jaw dropped.

What the fuck?

How does one even respond to that? Maybe it was something we should have anticipated, sitting and joking together on a bus. My heart raced. Luckily, my best friend has an answer for everything.

He slid his arm around me. "Thank you. I think so too!"

"*What?*" I mouthed, craning my neck toward him.

He raised a brow. "*Play along?*"

I smiled coyly in reply.

"Yes, we're very happy together," I said, snuggling into Piren's shoulder. "In fact, we've already begun planning our humongous wedding. I know it's years away, but we're just *so* excited."

"Oh, that's lovely." The woman inched closer to listen. "Tell me about it?"

"Well," Piren said, "Michaela here just *loves* the color purple, so that'll be our theme color. Purple dresses, purple decorations, purple cake, everything purple."

Our new friend clapped her hands together with joy.

I snorted. Purple always has been, and always will be, the ugliest, most vomit-inducing color in the world.

I squeezed Piren's arm. "And Donovan here just *adores* shrimp scampi, so that'll be our dinner dish. Extra shrimp, of course, because he says it just wouldn't be a wedding without seafood."

Piren stifled back a phony gag. He likes seafood as much as I like purple.

We carried on the charade for about twenty minutes. Every detail of our imaginary wedding grew more ridiculous than the last. The old woman ate it up, beaming and clapping as we talked. She was actually pretty adorable.

Right as we were describing our glass elephant chocolate fountain, we reached the woman's destination and bid our good-byes. She said it was lovely to meet us, and she thinks we'll produce beautiful children.

The moment she was out of range, we doubled over ourselves laughing.

Before long, we arrived at the rural neighborhood where we could catch a bus home. We staggered off the bus, and a snowy gust of wind slapped our faces. January's not ideal for standing outside. Street lamps illuminated the dark road with domes of light.

"Bus'll be here in fifteen," Piren said, shivering as he studied the schedule.

Hands in my pockets, I hopped up and down to conserve warmth. "It's so damn cold."

"Hey." He pointed to a coffee shop across the street. "Hot chocolate?"

We pooled together our change, but only had enough for one hot beverage. We got our drink and returned to the arctic outside. Temperatures dropping, we stood amidst a dusting snowfall. Flurries swirled through the air, whooshing to the ground. We sat down on the bus-stop bench, facing each other. Our four hands enveloped the steaming cup.

Teeth chattering, we huddled together, absorbing every possible drop of heat from the cup and each other's frozen fingers. His hands felt nice wrapped over mine. We took turns sipping our scalding cocoa, impersonating our new elderly friend. Piren and I have a habit of creating dozens of inside-jokes, no matter where we go.

Snow fell thicker by the minute, the sticky flakes clinging to our hair. Piren brushed the white powder off my head. I blew a handful of snow in his face.

"How's your hot chocolate, Partner?"

"Great actually. How's yours, Partner?"

We knew the joke couldn't follow us home, but it amused us until our bus arrived.

We eventually made it back to town, bodies stiff, soaked to the bone, but delighted with ourselves. Our wrong-bus debacle was a grand adventure worthy of becoming our best story yet. Although we omitted the Partner joke, the drink sharing, and the hand-touching, "Fat Head and Fangs' Grand Adventure" was a huge hit the next afternoon at Under Five.

Sometimes I wish we could have stayed on that bench in that rural town. Stayed there forever and never looked back.

PIREN ALLSTON

It's December. Trace hasn't spoken to me in three months. Knives plunge through my chest when I think of her, so I force myself not to.

Mom bought Lara a Christmas gift from me. I have no idea what it is; she wrapped it snuggly in a red Christmas bag. She also bought me a corny card to sign. It has a photo of two heart-plastered red stockings on the front, encircled by the words *My Partner is the best, the only one for me, I can't wait to snuggle with her, beneath the Christmas tree.* Probably the last thing that would ever come out of my mouth, but whatever.

For the past hour, I've sat in front of this sappy card, tugging my hair. I haven't the slightest clue what to write inside. I think I've clicked my pen against the table about four thousand times.

> *Merry Christmas, Lara.*
> *From Piren*

I read it again and again. I feel like I should say something more intimate to her, but the words won't come. I'm no good at being romantic. I twirl the pen in my fingers.

> *Dear Lara,*
> *Merry Christmas, ~~Lara.~~*
> *Have a great day.*
> *From Piren*

Mason pounces into the room and yanks the card from my hands. "Hey!"

"Not even gonna write 'love,' little bro?" He ruffles my hair.

I swat him away. "Right. Give me that."

I scribble out "From Piren" and write "Love, Piren." Great, now it looks even worse, because there's pen scribbles all over it. I slap my forehead.

"What'd you get her?" Mason asks.

I paw through the bag. "Um. A sweater, and some earrings. Mom got it. What'd you get Stephanie?"

"A pricey necklace."

"Let me see!"

He carefully pries it from his coat pocket. Pink stones surround a sparkly diamond heart. It's gorgeous, and way beyond my brother's price-bracket.

"Wow, she'll love it."

He beams, lowering the gift back into his pocket.

Stephanie doesn't love anything; she's a big downer. But I lie anyway because I want Mason to be happy. Trace never met Stephanie, but from my stories, she nicknamed my brother's Partner "The Ice Queen."

I spin my pen on the table. "Can I ask you something?"

"What?"

I stop it with my finger. "What do you think of Stephanie?"

"What do you mean?" he scoffs. "What kind of stupid question is that? I love Stephanie; she's my Partner. Don't be an idiot."

"No, I know. I mean, what do you *think* of her? Do you...like her personality?"

He squints. "What about her personality?"

"I dunno, just in general."

"I love Stephanie. She's great. What more do you need to know?"

"Nothing. Sorry."

He rolls his eyes and darts upstairs. For some reason, I caught a hint of insincerity in his voice. Just a hint. A wobble. Something only I would pick up.

In a few months, he'll graduate from high school and move in with The Ice Queen. I guess if she has any unusual quirks, Mason will learn soon enough. He'll have to learn to deal with them. For the rest of his life.

Around eight, Lara shows up at my house to swap gifts.

"I love you, Lara Goodren."

"I love you, Piren Allston."

Mrs. Goodren and my mom exchange pleasantries while my Partner unwraps her present.

"Cool, thanks." Lara holds the purple sweater up to her chest, then refolds it and places it gently back in the bag. She hands me a package wrapped in red and green tissue paper. I tear it open, revealing a brown tie, a history book, and a chick flick.

"Oh…thanks, Lara."

"The man at the store was *convinced* this movie is just perfect for a date night," Mrs. Goodren says, "so we just couldn't resist."

Lara smiles, her new earrings dangling off her lobes like little brass bells.

Mrs. Goodren brandishes an envelope from her pocket. "And as my husband's and my gift for you two. It's a gift certificate to Ford's Seafood, so you can have a *real* date—dinner and a movie."

Lara's eyes light up. "Awesome, Mom! Thanks."

"Thanks, Mrs. Goodren." I take the envelope. "That's very generous of you."

A seafood restaurant? What the hell am I supposed to eat there?

I shake Mrs. Goodren's hand and hug Lara good-bye.

"What a nice family you're marrying into," Mom says.

I nod. She's right; they're lovely. Very proper, very nice.

They just don't know me at all.

TRACY BAILEY

I lie face-down on my bed. My parents scream obscenities at each other downstairs. They've shouted non-stop for two frigging hours. The deafening noise drowns out my blaring music. I didn't know it was physically possible for lungs to work that hard.

What an awesome Christmas Eve.

Some families are the "cuddle and smile around the magical Christmas fireplace!" types. My family is not. I guess I'm luckier than some families where the fighting gets physical. My parents don't punch when they fight, but their words hit hard as fists.

Together forever. Till death do you part.

You work out the problems within your family and shut your trap about it. Bitching and moaning to the world falls on deaf ears.

Sometimes I wonder if my parents would be better separated. If there was a legal way to leave. Maybe they'd be happier alone. Kinder. Better parents.

A slew of F-bombs reverberate up the stairwell, flooding through my closed door. I bury my face in my pillow.

Dad's drunk; Mom is, from the sound of it, "so fucking sick of your drinking!" I'd argue he's drunk in honor of the holiday, but that excuse doesn't cover the rest of the year.

I roll onto my back and clamp my eyes shut. I'm about a notch from obliterating my eardrums under my headphones, but I crank the volume higher. A few tears leak from my eyes, leaving damp patches on my pillow.

This sucks.

Glass shatters downstairs. One of my parents probably threw a dish at the other, as usual. Guess it's another night I'll wait for them to fall asleep and sneak downstairs with the dustpan. I'm not taking anyone to the frigging ER for a glass-shard-speared foot. No way in hell I'm explaining any of this shit to some nosy doctor.

I guess Assigning can't predict rampant alcoholism.

What if Sam becomes an alcoholic? Maybe my father's alcoholic genes Assigned me to someone else with a predisposition. Goose bumps prickle down my arms.

Mom slams into my bedroom door, ripping it open.

"Go to Toni's house!" Her body heaves, her eyes wild and raging. "Spend the night there." Her hair hangs limp, strewn across her sweaty face.

My father screams from downstairs, and Mom twists back around. "Yeah? Say it louder, jackass!" She brushes hair from her eyes.

"Mom, are you okay?"

"Just get the hell out. And call your sister, tell her to stay at Oliver's for the night." The door slams behind her. Her screams echo in the hall. "…And another thing, you wretched son of a bitch…"

I slip out of bed.

Guess I'll be spending Christmas with someone else's family.

Mom feeds into his problem. Between her holiday schnapps, Christmas booze, and fancy wine, she enables him. She brings it home and wonders why it's gone in two days.

Spend the night elsewhere? With pleasure.

I throw a fistful of clothes in a bag and dash downstairs. Silence consumes the house like white noise in the aftermath of a tidal wave. I slip into my heaviest jacket and tiptoe out the backdoor, stepping around my unconscious father—who puked all over the kitchen tiles.

The door slams, and bone-chilling air envelopes me. I wrap my arms around my chest.

I don't have a plan.

I can't go to Toni's place. Her parents pack that frigging house with relatives at Christmas, and I'm not about to spoon with some stranger on the floor. Amanda's too far away.

The Maceys are only a couple miles from here…

I choke out a gag.

No chance in hell.

I can't identify the worse option: Sam's home for Christmas, or my own. They both equally blow. Camping alone in the treehouse would be a viable option, if it wouldn't freeze me into a Tracesicle within hours.

A bitter winter breeze stings my cheeks, blowing my hair across my face. Shivers echo through my core and down my spine. Trudging through ankle-deep snow, I trek through my yard and up to the road. Water seeps into my sneakers, dampening my feet and numbing my toes.

Maybe I'll freeze to death, and it'll be over.

I picture my father, plodding out here tomorrow, finding my frozen, lifeless body. He'd notice my absence when no one cleaned up his drunken mess. He'd probably yell at my rotting corpse for dying and dooming Sam to life alone.

Awesome.

I press my bag to my chest, fighting back a wave of shakes.

Gloves and a hat would have been smart. Apparently I'm as dumb as my stupid parents.

My numb feet traipse forward, forcing me another step. I squint to see through wisps of icy powder in the air. Pudgy inflatable snowmen dapple nearby lawns. Twinkling lights illuminate my neighbors' towering homes, welcoming the Christmas spirit.

My spirit is draped in cobwebs.

Christmas used to mean something else once — something about a deity, before such things were illegal. We learned about it in school. When all other holidays were outlawed, Christmas was allowed to remain as a secular display of lights and gifts because of the positive effect people thought it had on morale. I used to like celebrating, back when my parents actually gave a shit about stuff like this. Now it's just another day in the Bailey household — another cold day.

I stand on my tiptoes to peek in the frosty window of a nearby home. My neighbors are hosting a Christmas party. Smiling people chat inside, snacking on mini sausages and drinking from fancy glasses. They look warm, crowding around a blazing fireplace. I wish I could saunter into that party and make them adopt me. *Hello! My name is Tracy Bailey. I'm fifteen years old, I'm an honor student, and my family sucks. Can I join yours?*

I exhale a foggy breath cloud into the night air.

Oliver's home isn't too far. Maybe I could stay there and wake up with Veronica on Christmas morning, like old times. My stiff fingers fumble the buttons on my cellphone.

"Hello?" she answers.

"Hey, V, how's it going?"

"Tray-Tray! Big sista! How ya hangin?" Her words jumble in a heap.

What the…?

More incoherent slurs emit from the speaker, followed by my sister's unmistakable giggle.

Has Veronica fallen onto the family alcoholism bandwagon?

"V…have you been drinking?"

"What?"

I press the phone to my ear; music blasts in the background amidst a dozen chattering voices. "Have. You. Been. Drinking?"

"Yeah! I'm with Ollie."

My heart sinks. "Look, don't come home tonight, okay?"

"What?" Delighted screams drown her voice, followed by the signature *pop* of a champagne cork.

"Don't come home tonight!"

"Yeah, Ollie! Breaking out the hard stuff!"

"Veronica, are you even listening to me?"

"Sorry, Trace, gotta go."

Click. She's gone.

Howling wind rattles through the trees. I gaze up at the pitch-black sky, and twinkling stars blink down at me.

I'm all alone.

Stinging cold paralyzes my legs, stripping my energy. I drop to the ground in the middle of the road, curling into a ball. The frigid pavement numbs my cheek as I press my face to the cement. Maybe a passing car will take pity and kill me.

No. Get up. Come on.

I hoist my body to a stance and hobble onward.

Maybe I'll spend the whole night walking. Become a living ice sculpture. A thing of beauty.

My frozen body protests every clambering step. I wiggle my chilled toes, but I can't feel them move. My teeth click furiously together in a chattering drumroll. Every joint aches in the raw air as I drag my feet toward an unknown destination.

Delirious, blurred thoughts swirl through my brain. My mind grows fuzzy. Too much cold. Can't think. Can't move.

I have no home. Nowhere to go. Nobody cares. Nobody loves me.

I look up. I'm outside Piren's house.

PIREN ALLSTON

I sprawl over the couch like a corpse, staring at the ceiling. Stale children's Christmas specials play softly on TV, basking the room in a light glow. My eyelids hang heavy, but I don't have the energy to blink.

My parents are at a Christmas party until late. Mason's spending his first Christmas at Stephanie's house. It'll be weird ripping through presents tomorrow morning without him.

The Goodrens invited me to their Christmas Eve dinner tonight, but I made up an excuse. Lara's pissed I declined the offer. She called me "insensitive" or some bullshit. I was only half listening.

My phone buzzes on the coffee table. I fling out a dead arm to grab it: text from Lara. I toss the phone back to the table, message unread, and tug my sweatshirt hood lower over my face.

Caroling snowmen parade across the TV, but my eyes blur. I feel drained, like a vacuum sucked every drop of energy from my body. My left arm dangles lifeless over the side of the couch.

I spring to my feet when I hear a soft scratching at the front door. At ten o'clock. On Christmas Eve.

Who the F…?

I crack it open. Trace tumbles inside, and I barely catch her freezing body before she hits the floor.

"Trace! Are you okay?"

She wobbles on her feet, lips purple, eyes half-closed, torso hanging limp in my arms. Pieces of snow and dirt cling to her hair and jacket.

What the hell? Has she been lying on the ground?

My heart races. Trace hasn't talked to me in three months, and now she's here, half dead.

"Trace? Trace?"

I pat her pink frozen face, but she doesn't make a sound.

"Hey! Hey! Trace! Look at me!"

She murmurs incoherent garble, head drooping onto my shoulder.

"What happened? Trace? Trace! How long were you out there?"

"Piren."

Relief floods my body at the sound of her voice. I pull her close to me, pressing her chest to mine. It's illegal, but I don't care. I close my eyes and rest my chin on her head, inhaling the flowery aroma of her hair. The curly strands tickle my face, and I squeeze her tighter.

She jerks her head back and meets my gaze. Her eyes grow wide, inviting me closer, drawing me in. Her lips part slightly, forming a weak smile.

She looks like she wants to say something, but she doesn't.

She kisses me.

Friendship is certainly the finest balm for the pangs of disappointed love.
❧Jane Austen

SIXTEEN YEARS OLD
PART TWO

PIREN ALLSTON

"You know, separation is best for you both," Dad said, flipping a page in his newspaper as I watched the moving truck pull away.

"Mm-hmm." I pressed my forehead to the window as the Baileys' cars disappeared from view, trailing behind the truck.

It's been a year. My stomach still cramps at the memory.

Trace and I haven't spoken since.

A young family lives in her old home now. Mom whipped up a chocolate welcome-cake when they arrived. She and Mrs. Warren are the best of buddies. They started a neighborhood book club together.

No one knows we kissed. Our parents are the only ones who know about the sleepover, but that's bad enough. They didn't tell Mason, and they sure as hell weren't about to tell Lara.

My parents came home in the middle of the night and found Trace fast asleep on the couch, me in my bed.

Nothing else happened. Thank God nothing else happened. Trace's parents screamed themselves hoarse Christmas day before hauling her off. She cowered beneath them, tears streaming down her face, and all I could do was watch and wait for it to be over.

For a week following "the incident," my dad grilled me: What happened? Did I kiss Trace? Did I have sex with Trace? Nothing, no, and no.

I'm a big damn liar.

I forced my leg not to bounce as Dad interrogated me.

"Piren, if you're lying, they'll Banish you, you know that." His piercing gaze bore into mine. "I can't let that happen to you. I need to know you're telling me the truth."

"I told you, nothing happened."

"If she showed up here and made a move, she'd be the one in trouble, not you." He leaned his elbows on his thighs. "Look at me, come on. Don't be scared to tell me the truth. She'd be the one Banished, not you. Hell, they'd probably consider you a hero for catching her in the act."

"Stop. Nothing happened, okay?"

"Okay. I believe you." He clapped his hand on my shoulder. "Thank you for being honest."

I forced a half-hearted smile, but I couldn't bring myself to look at him.

Trace is my best friend. Even now, even though we don't talk, I still intrinsically consider her as such. I couldn't do that to her.

Then there's another fact—the detail I've never spoken aloud. I don't even think Trace knows. It eats away at me inside, burrowing into my brain, but I can't shake it.

When Trace kissed me, I kissed her back.

I'll take that secret to the grave.

I passed my driver's test last week, on the first try, by the skin of my teeth. Today I'm taking Lara out on an official date, with no parental supervision.

"You wreck my car, I'll kill you." Mason drops the key into my waiting hand.

I scoff. "Please. It's a miracle you haven't totaled it yourself."

"I'm an excellent driver."

"Bullshit."

"That's enough, you two," Mom says. "Piren, what did I tell you about swearing in this house?" She straightens my collar. "You're a smart young man; don't talk like a buffoon."

"Yeah, Piren, stop being such a buffoon."

"At least I know how to drive."

"Okay, really?" Mom steps between us. "Mason, why don't you make yourself useful and shovel the driveway? Your brother has a date."

He groans. "I don't even live here anymore."

"You eat my food, you can shovel my driveway." She tosses him a pair of gloves. "And, Piren, be nice with Mason's BMW. Your father and I are going to get you one next month, but until then, you've got to share."

My eyes grow wide. "I'm getting a car?"

She gives me a half-smile. "It was going to be a surprise for your birthday, but we decided you should have it earlier, for school." She brushes my cheek. "We love you."

I throw my arms around her. "Thank you! This is amazing!"

"But just so we're clear—" she holds my shoulders at arm's length "—that's your seventeenth birthday gift. Just pretend your birthday is a few months early. Think about what color your want."

"He wants pink."

"Shut up." I can't fight the grin off my face. "I want black. It'll be badass."

"Oh my God!" Mom swats at my arm. "What did I just say about the swearing?"

Lara hops into the front seat of Mason's car.

"I love you, Lara Goodren."

"I love you, Piren Allston."

"So…where do you want to go?"

"Hmm…" She taps her fingers to her lips. "How about Under Five?"

My stomach drops. "Oh, I don't know. I haven't really been there lately, not for, like, a year." My leg quivers, making my foot jitter against the brake. "What about that new pizza place?"

"Please? You said you'd take me to Under Five ages ago."

My hands tighten around the steering wheel. "Don't you think it's weird for sophomores to hang out there? It'll be full of twelve-year-olds." The promise of milkshakes entices me, but that place churns up too many damn memories.

Lara pouts out her bottom lip. "Please?"

Inhale. Exhale.

This is a battle I won't win.

"Okay. Let's go."

We slide into a booth, and nostalgia knocks the air from my lungs. A million happy memories dwell within these walls. Now the memories feel like ghosts that haunt the café. I've never been to Under Five without a gaggle of friends, and it's eerie without Trace. It's almost as if I'm in a different restaurant altogether.

"What's your favorite color?" Lara asks as we slurp our black-and-white shakes.

"Blue. What's yours?"

"Purple."

I snort. *The fake purple wedding... That old lady on the bus...*

Lara tilts her head to the side. "What's so funny?"

"Nothing."

"You laughed."

"Sorry."

Silence. My knee jiggles under the table.

"You weren't kidding about the shakes." She chews her straw. "They're the best here."

"Told you so." I reach across the table and give her hand a squeeze.

We lock eyes for a moment before turning attention back to our drinks.

"So, our First Kiss is less than two years away now, huh?" She glances up at me, but darts her eyes back down, spinning her straw through her thick shake.

Sometime senior year, they'll hold the Ceremony. I haven't given it a second thought.

"Oh, right. Weird how soon, huh?"

"Yeah." Her cheeks grow rosy. "What do you think it'll be like?" Her gaze flicks up. "To kiss me?"

To kiss you.

A memory floods my brain; it's Trace, frozen to the core, embracing and kissing me in the doorway.

My first kiss.

My heart leaps.

"You okay?" She cocks her head. "You look distracted."

"Oh, uh, sorry. Right. It'll be fun."

A bemused smile spreads across her face. "Fun?"

"I dunno."

We continue to slurp in silence. I can feel her eyes on me, and it makes me antsy.

"Do you think…we can have our own stories?" she asks.

"What do you mean?"

"Like you did with Tracy Bailey. Nicknames. And we go on adventures, and tell everyone about them."

This café once thrived on our adventure stories.

My chest tightens.

"Oh, um…sure." I twiddle my fingers in my lap. "But you don't really plan adventures; they just happen."

"Well, can ours just happen?"

"Uh…sure, I guess."

It's not the same.

TRACY BAILEY

Last month, I bought some chunky red headphones at a nearby thrift store. They're real old, probably vintage. I feel naked when they're not perched on my head. Mom calls me "anti-social" because I wear them all the frigging time. I don't care; they block out static.

Everyone around me talks in static: buzzing, chattering, speaking, but not saying a damn thing. At school, people open their mouths and emit loud, obnoxious hums. I smile and nod, pretending I give a shit about their mundane gossip. It's exhausting. That's why my headphones are so great; if they're on my head, nobody bothers me. I can listen to music, or I can listen to silence. Either way, I'm by myself, and nobody interrupts. My classmates walk past, bump me, wave, but don't say a word. Sometimes I nod to acknowledge them, but usually I stare ahead, pretending they don't exist. I pretend I'm alone, because I am.

Sometimes I scream thoughts under those headphones. I scream bloody murder in my mind, and nobody bats an eye. Nobody can hear, because the screaming is contained in my head. They don't know I'm screaming, because I force my body to remain expression-less—eyes calm, mouth closed. Screaming in my head all the things I'll never say aloud.

PIREN ALLSTON

Sam is in my geography class. He's kind of a know-it-all, which is ironic, because he knows nothing.

Mr. Jenson jots some notes on the whiteboard. "Okay, who can tell me which continent—"

Sam's hand shoots up.

"—contains the Danakil Desert?"

Sam waves, stretching his arm high above his head.

Alan shoots me an amused grin.

"Anyone else?" Mr. Jenson scans the room and sighs. "Yes, Sam?"

"Africa."

"Correct."

Sam hoots and pumps his fist in the air, his clodhoppers sprawled out on the floor in front of him. I bury my face in my sleeve to avoid bursting. Several kids giggle, imitating Sam's gloats. Mr. Jenson rolls his eyes and returns to the whiteboard.

Sam always does that annoying routine when he gets an answer right. It's stupid, but only half as stupid as when he's wrong. When he's incorrect, he'll fume and pound his fist on the desk. One time, he swiped his arm across the teacher's table and knocked a stack of books to the ground. Sometimes, he'll kick the wall on his way out; the evidence remains in plain sight, a footprint-shaped mark in the plaster. If Trace was in our class, I imagine she'd die laughing and invent some crazy new story about him.

I miss classes with Trace.

The principal's voice crackles over the school-wide intercom.

"Good afternoon, students and staff. I'd like to make a special announcement." The class grows silent. "As you may know, we post each class's top students in every subject at the quarter's end. However, for the first time ever, a sophomore student has crossed the boards, topping English, Geography, and Chemistry. We've never had a single student top his or her class in more than one subject before, so please share my sincere congratulations."

Sam leans forward in his chair, hands pressed to his desk.

"That student," the principal continues, "is Ms. Tracy Bailey."

The class erupts in cheers for our comrade.

Trace works harder than anyone I know. If anyone deserves it, it's her.

I join the applause until my eyes fall on Sam. He hunches over his desk, mouth clamped in a tight line.

My smile falters. *Why is he such a dick?*

The principal praises Trace for a while, then logs off the intercom with a crackle.

"Mr. Macey!" Our teacher throws his hands in the air. "You must be overjoyed. How lucky you must feel to have Ms. Bailey for a Partner."

Sam grunts. "Yeah. She's great."

"I was lucky enough to have her in my class last year, and let me tell you, that young woman is destined for success. You're a lucky one, Sam."

Sam nods. A twisted glint shimmers in his eyes, as if someone sucked the light clean out of them. I don't understand him. His Partner had a great achievement, and he's pissed. Why?

Class ends. Alan and I meander down the hall to Chemistry. Sam shoves past us and kicks a locker with a clang. His boot leaves a dent in the metal.

"Hey!" Alan says.

Sam whirls on us, face flushed. "What?"

"Tell Tracy congrats from us," Alan says, and I nod.

"Why?" Sam snorts. "Doesn't matter anyway. She'll just be my secretary someday."

He spits on the floor and stomps off. His clomping footsteps echo down the hall.

"Nice guy." Alan rolls his eyes. "Computer must really hate Tracy to doom her to life with that douche." He shakes his head. "Makes you wonder, doesn't it?"

Alan fires off into a tirade about Trace's Partner, but the words float straight through me.

She deserves so much better than that.

At lunch, I sneak away to the art room. The dark classroom is deserted, which is perfect.

Taping together four sheets of computer paper, I construct a sloppy banner. I scribble *Congratulations, Tracy!* with nubs of multi-colored pencils and decorate the letters with star stickers. It's not the best, but it's something. I roll it up and stuff it in my bag, stealing a roll of Scotch tape from the teacher's desk.

Darting my eyes around the empty hall, I tiptoe to Trace's locker and tape up my anonymous sign. It's a bit crooked, but I can't risk adjusting it and someone seeing me.

Sorry I can't tell you in person, Trace. I'm so proud of you.

TRACY BAILEY

"I swear, Tracy, you don't care about this family, do you?" Mom crosses her arms.

I tug on my red Converses. "I like the thrift store."

Why does this always have to instigate a frigging fight?

"Does it even occur to you—" she gestures her hands "—that someone might *see* you there?"

"So what?"

"People of means don't buy used clothing." She rubs her forehead. "I don't know why that's so difficult for you to grasp."

"I can buy anything there and guarantee no one else has it. And it's the only good thing about this effing neighborhood. And I happen to like secondhand stuff." I slip on my coat. "Sorry to disappoint you."

She props her hands on her hips. "Tracy Allison—"

"Would you prefer I wear a wig, so your socialite buddies don't recognize me?" I smirk. "Would that be to your liking?"

"You infuriate me. No respect for anyone but yourself."

"At least I *have* self-respect."

"Ugh!"

She throws her hands up and storms from the room, slamming the door behind her.

"If you didn't move us to this wretched house," I shout through the closed door, "I wouldn't have found the thrift shop!" She doesn't respond.

Seriously. I don't have the treehouse anymore, where else am I supposed to go?

Usually I go there to browse, but today I have a special mission.

A few months ago, my sister accompanied me to the thrift store. It was the day I bought my chunky headphones. We perused aisles of old toys and funky jewelry together for over an hour. V appreciates trinkets as much as I do, and I love that about her.

Pawing through a box of assorted headbands and vintage coin purses, Veronica squealed. I turned to find her swooning over a lopsided jade pendant necklace. It was tarnished, and borderline tacky, but her face lit up the moment she tried it on.

She bounded to the counter with her find. However, her smile melted when she learned the price; the thing cost more than her month's allowance. Her eyes grew so glassy, I almost expected tears to start flooding from them. She left the store, pouting and empty-handed.

Today is Veronica's fourteenth birthday, and I have a surprise for her. After we left the store that day, I biked straight back and begged the manager to put the necklace on hold.

It took weeks of babysitting, lawn-mowing, and scrounging for change, but I scraped together the money. I arrive at the thrift store minutes before closing and purchase my sister's birthday gift. The lady wraps it for me, which is awesome, because I wrap presents like a five-year-old.

Panting and sweating from pedaling like a maniac, I bike into our driveway and race inside. The gang's all here to celebrate.

"I love you, Tracy Bailey."

"I love you, Sam Macey."

I grit my teeth as Sam scrawls his name under mine on her birthday card.

"Tracy, you're sweating like a pig." Mom narrows her eyes. I ignore her and dash into the other room to see my sister.

Veronica snuggles in her Partner's lap on the couch. He's got his full winter coat on.

"Take off your jacket, silly. It's hot in here." She tugs at his zipper, but he entwines his fingers with hers, grinning.

"Not yet, love. I'm a little chilly."

Walking over, I stub my toe on Oliver's saxophone, which lies neglected on the floor. I stumble forward, cursing.

"Walk much?" V asks.

I grab my throbbing foot and glare at Oliver. "Stop leaving your sh—"

Sam and my parents enter the room, and I shut up. Mom rests the cake we baked on the coffee table and stabs fourteen yellow candles into the pink fondant. We take our seats around the birthday girl.

"Happy Birthday, V." I pass her my present. Giddy with birthday delight, Veronica rips through the paper and gasps.

"You didn't!" She jumps up and flings her arms around me. "It's the necklace!"

"The very one you tried on."

She squeezes me tighter. "Way too expensive, Trace."

"It'll look great on you."

"Beautiful," Oliver says.

"Lovely," Dad says.

"You have great taste," Mom says.

Veronica slides it around her neck. She poses in the mirror. "How did you afford this?"

"Oh, you know, just saved up some cash here and there. No big deal."

Dad catches my eye and winks.

Maybe I've done something right for once.

"Thank you." Veronica hugs me again. "It's perfect. Best sister ever."

"Glad you like it." I pat her on the back. "Enjoy being fourteen; it only happens once."

"Love you, Trace."

"Love you, V."

"It's from me too," Sam interjects.

I clench my jaw.

"Thanks, Sam." She squeezes his shoulder.

"Our girls are the best," Dad says.

Veronica takes her seat, rubbing her new gem between her fingers.

Oliver drapes his arm over her shoulders. "Guess you should open my gift, then."

"Okay, gimmie!"

He passes her a pink bag smothered in bows and curly pink ribbons. Veronica reaches inside and reveals a white T-shirt. She unfolds it and holds it up for us to see.

"I Love My Partner!" is emblazoned across the front in bright red lettering, surrounded by pink and purple hearts.

"Surprise!" Oliver unzips his jacket to reveal a matching T-shirt.

I snort, coughing soda all over the table. My parents and Sam release a collective "Awww!" at the gift.

Oh, for the love of God. Are you kidding me?

"Ollie!" Veronica tackles him. "I love it!"

"Put it on!"

She tugs it over her head. It hangs to her waist.

"Dad! Take a picture!" Veronica bounces on her toes. The Wonder Twins embrace each other as cameras flash.

"You two look amazing," Mom says.

"Now everyone will know who your Partner is before they even meet you," Dad says.

"We should get shirts like that, Tracy," Sam says.

Over my dead body.

"What do you think, Trace?" V frames the shirt's slogan between her hands. She stares expectantly at me, standing shoulder-to-shoulder with her twin.

"You look like a pair of idiots."

"Tracy!" Mom gasps.

"Well, they *do!*"

Veronica lowers her brows. She opens her mouth, then closes it. Lip trembling, she runs into the hall and slams the door. Oliver follows her, glowering.

"Nice. You just ruined your sister's birthday," Dad says, rushing after them. "Veronica!" he calls in the next room. "Sweetie, your sister's the idiot! Not you!"

Sam hunches his shoulders. "Glad you think showing affection makes you an idiot."

"That's not what I —"

"Tracy," Mom hisses, "can't we have one normal family party?"

I shrug and dig my fork into the cake. They can stomp out like children if they want. More cake for me.

PIREN ALLSTON

I nibble a grilled cheese in the cafeteria while Alan and Travis rehash last night's football game.

"Dude, Bryant dropped the ball. The ref called it."

"Screw you, man. He never lost possession."

"You know what—"

"Piren!" Lara waves, making a beeline for our table. "Hi!"

My friends throw their stuff on their trays.

I groan. "Oh, come on, don't go."

"Sorry, man, you're on your own." Alan speeds away from the table.

Travis shakes his head. "Dude, I just can't take her right now. Sorry." He races after Alan. I release a heavy breath.

Lara plops down beside me. "I love you, Piren Allston."

"I love you, Lara Goodren."

She tucks her napkin into her collar. I prop my cheek against my hand and glance at my watch. Still twenty minutes left of lunch.

Lara slurps her soup with a God-awful sucking sound that makes me shudder.

I bet she purposely slurps like that to annoy me. Or to repel anyone from joining us.

"You know…" I pick at my French fries "…you can sit with me *and* my friends at lunch. You don't need to drive them away."

"Lunch time is our time." She sips from her milk carton. "You know that."

Everyone knows that. You're not exactly shy about it.

"Right."

She pulls out her phone and taps away, clicking her fingernails across the keys.

"Cassidy?" I ask.

"Mm-hmm."

We sit in silence as she texts her friend. Every few moments, her phone erupts in a buzzing hum.

So much for "our time." Sitting with Lara feels a lot like sitting alone. Before I met Trace, I always sat alone at lunch. I was the butt of everyone's jokes. Later in life, everyone knew better than to taunt Tracy Bailey's best friend; if someone pissed her off, they became the punchline in her stories. However, earlier on, roles were different, and I walked the halls with a target on my back.

When you're seven, things begin to filter into categories of "cool" and "uncool." Trace was cool; I was not. I think Trace accumulated her popularity through her humor and bucking authority. Everyone admired her wit.

I, on the other hand, was the wimp. The kid with the shaky leg who'd cried the first day of kindergarten. The pussy.

About a month after Trace and I became friends, Alan's first-grade-boy-gang victimized me at lunch. They spewed insults as I crossed the cafeteria with my tray of food.

"What kind of name is Piren?"

"Peering?"

"Sounds like *peeing*."

My pulse raced as I speed-walked toward Trace's table, laboring to mask my growing anxiety. Alan and the others jumped up and encircled me in the center of the room. The entire student body fell silent at their tables, watching.

"Excuse me," I said, keeping my eyes on the floor.

"Where you going, *Peeing?*" Alan crossed his arms. "Bathroom's that way."

"Hey, *Peeing*," said another boy.

"Go away, *Peeing*."

"Don't pee all over the floor."

My tray quivered in my shaky hands, and my cup tipped over, spilling milk onto my plate and soaking my sandwich. My eyes burned, but I choked back the urge to cry. The boys formed a solid wall, blocking me from Trace's table.

"Look, he's gonna cry!" One of them pointed at me and laughed. "Look at the little *girl!*"

Mason once told me the best way to beat bullies is to ignore them. Mustering every ounce of courage in my body, I pivoted on my heels to find another table.

Classmates whispered and giggled as I hurried by. I saw Lara at a table with a group of girls. I remember thinking I finally found a safe option, but the moment I started toward her, her ears flushed red, and she turned her back. Nobody wanted to sit with the kid named Peeing—even Peeing's own future wife. Heart pounding, I frantically scanned the room for a solution.

Chants of "Peeing!" echoing from all directions, I sped to the outskirts of the cafeteria.

Stumbling over a chair, I collapsed at the lonely, rickety table in the back. My cheeks burned as Alan's cronies roared behind me. I sifted through my soaked lunch, searching for a dry bit of sandwich; milk dampened everything. Blinking back water in my eyes, I inhaled a shaky breath.

Another tray clattered down beside me.

It was Trace. She smiled and sat down.

"Here, you take half." She pulled a large wedge off her dry sandwich, thrusting it to me. Staring at the table, I grunted my thanks. Trace shrugged.

"Shouldn't you be at the *cool* table?" I asked sourly.

She tilted her head to the side and crinkled her forehead. "This *is* the cool table."

Trace proceeded to jabber about her day as if nothing happened.

The jeers silenced the moment Trace sat down.

They never made fun of my name again.

TRACY BAILEY

Our house is a ghost town. I drift past my mom in the hall, but we don't acknowledge each other. She bends at the linen closet, dispensing a stack of towels. Dad lumbers up the stairs. He bumps my mom, and she shifts her position without a word. Two ships passing in the night.

My perfectly-Partnered parents.

After almost two years of residency, this house isn't home. Our new house is stiff and cold, with lots of vacant rooms. I suppose it's perfect for my family, because we can spend days in the same building and never see each other. I walk to the bus stop every morning by myself.

"Where's Veronica?" my father asks.

"Oliver's."

He grumbles and retreats to his room. Mom thrusts me a pile of folded laundry without a word.

On most Saturdays, I blast music in my bedroom, just for noise. For a while, Mom used to rap on my door and scream at me to lower the volume. She doesn't anymore.

Today, I have a different plan.

Our old neighborhood is almost thirty minutes away by car, and there's no direct bus. My heart flutters when I think about my treehouse, waiting for me in the woods. I long to hide away within the walls of my secret solace again. It provokes so many mixed memories of youth.

I follow Mom downstairs. She collapses on the couch, zombie eyes settling on a magazine.

"Can I borrow the car?"

She doesn't look at me. "Where are you going?"

"The library. With Toni."

She flips a page. "Be back by six."

"Thanks."

Home, as I call it. I'm driving home.

I park across the street from my old house. Two little kids run through a sprinkler in the front yard as their mother gardens. The father observes from a lawn chair, smiling.

What a perfect little family.

It must be weird for the house to shelter such a happily-Assigned group of people. The father glances up at me, so I press the gas and keep moving.

I pass the Allstons' home and tap the brakes.

The last time I was here…everything changed.

Lara's VW is parked in the driveway; I recognize it from the school parking lot. Through a crease in the curtain, Piren and Lara stand with Mason and Stephanie, laughing. My chest tightens.

More perfect Partnerships.

Piren squints out the window and double takes. I slam the gas before he can see me.

Parking down the street, I catch the familiar path through Harker's Woods. The overgrown brush scratches my legs along the unkempt trail.

Within minutes, my fortress comes into view in the clearing.

It's still standing and still beautiful.

I climb the rungs, relishing each familiar step.

Leaves and pine-needles overrun the platform, glued to the floor with layers of sap. Howling wind creaks through the boards, as if the treehouse is scorning me for my desertion.

"Well, I'm sorry! Sheesh, don't freak out," I whisper to the rattling treehouse. "It wasn't my fault, I swear. I didn't want to leave."

It creaks in response.

I sink to the floor, filling my lungs to capacity with the bitter aroma of pine. The sappy coating fuses to the butt of my pants. Shivers run down my spine, and I hug my knees. This place feels ghostly, almost haunted. I glimpse initials in the bark and swallow hard.

P.A.+T.B.

Piren and I. This is our tree. But there is no longer an "our."

Not a day passes when I don't feel Piren's absence in my life. He tore out a chunk of my soul when we parted, leaving a gaping hole behind. Best friends aren't meant to be separated. Every day I struggle not to retie all those strings between us.

It's better this way. He's safe. So, why can't I leave it at that?

Wind rattles through the branches, prickling goose bumps down my arms.

Why the hell can't I control my childish need for closeness?

One person shouldn't impact me this way. It's as if a light ignites when he's here, stranding me in darkness when he leaves.

But I hurt him bad. The terrible, awful thing I did is unforgivable. He has to live with our secret adultery forever, and it's my fault.

He hurts because of something I did.

We've been torn apart before—by my parents, by his parents, by some teacher or another. I fought tooth and nail not to lose him, didn't care what anyone said. Want to yell at me for seeing my best friend? Fine, but I'll still see him tomorrow, and you can go screw.

This is different.

I awake in cold sweats, tormented by nightmares of Piren on stage. He cowers as hundreds of strangers spew hurtful words, degrading him. As he quivers, I jump to shield him, but I can't save him. Guards force him to the ground and slice his face. I scream and scream, but they don't stop. They shove him into a tinted van and haul him away forever.

That's not the worst part.

The worst part of this twisted dream is the fact that I caused it. My need for his friendship, and his inability to forget me, condemns him. If they marred his face, I'd hang myself from the branches of this frigging tree.

Piren isn't like other people. He's kind. He's the best person I know. Maybe our scars aren't the kinds that run down your face; maybe our scars are the kinds that form on the inside.

But it's an unruly, tortured bond we share. It's un-severable. It runs thick and deep as the roots of this very tree.

Piren's my stability. He's my constant, my confidant. He's the source of that deep, satisfying laugh that only comes from your best friend. The type of laugh that warms your whole body and makes you forget everything else.

I'm weak.

The former King and Queen of the treehouse reign. Hidden within the bark, our collective child voices chime: all hail the King and Queen!

Maybe I'm weak and horrible, but I can't stay away forever. I'm not strong enough.

Tomorrow is a very special day, and I intend to celebrate.

PIREN ALLSTON

Today is my seventeenth birthday. I've had my car for three months, but my parents still put a big red bow on it when I woke up.

I've spent my entire lunch period alone in the art room, polishing my final project. After meticulously rounding the edges, the oil-painted grapes look ripe enough to pluck off the canvas and eat. This fruit bowl painting is my best work yet. My hand doesn't shake when there's a paintbrush in it. I step back to admire my work.

My Masterpiece.

My chest swells at the shading on the pears and the dark shadow stretching from underneath the bowl.

Only five minutes until fifth period, I sponge the table and unhook the smock from around my neck. My phone buzzes: text from Lara. I take a deep breath and flip it open: *U missed lunch…again. Guess u don't care about spending time together on ur bday.*

I close my eyes.

Inhale. Exhale.

Wrenching my eyes open, I punch out a reply: *Sorry. Had 2 finish project.*

It buzzes a response, but I toss the phone back into my bag unopened. According to my Partner, lunch time is "our time," class time is "our time," after school is "our time," and weekends are "our time." How the hell do I placate her? When is it "my time?" And when was I supposed to finish this damn project? With her lurking over my shoulder?

Knee bouncing against the cabinet, I rinse my pallet in the sink. Anytime I'm in the art room, I think of Trace. Goofing off in third grade art class was the best.

Almost two years ago, she and I parted ways. Sometimes I glimpse her in the distance, in the library or cafeteria, but my sightings are rare. Our high school isn't small and condensed like our elementary and middle schools were. Even after all this time, when she sees me, she turns the other direction.

I wish we had ended our friendship on better terms. Christmas Eve still resonates in my brain: the kiss, sitting by the fire, tucking her in, falling asleep, my parents coming home yelling, her parents yelling, Mr. Bailey dragging Trace off. The moving truck appearing a week later.

Soon after "the incident," I sat hunched on a kitchen chair, my head buried in my arms on the table. My body felt like dead weight. Mason sat across from me, flipping through a comic book and munching on chips. I don't know how long I moped, but Mom took a seat in the other chair. She rested her hand on my shoulder.

"I don't understand." Her words were soft and laced with sadness. "Why Tracy?"

I ignored her.

"All these years, all this duress." She stroked circles on my back with her hand. "There's plenty of boys at school you can be friends with...And Lara, she's crazy about you. Tracy Bailey's a troublemaker." Her voice wobbled slightly. "Why the attachment?"

My dry eyes burned when I blinked. Trace's absence left weights on my limbs, making every movement a physical burden.

Trace is awesome, end of story.

"I dunno," I mumbled.

I didn't have an answer for my mom. Or at least, not an answer she wanted.

"I just wish I could help you." She rubbed her forehead. Early stages of tears glistened in her eyes. "It kills me seeing you so sad."

Mason snorted. "You hang out with Tracy Bailey 'cause she's got more balls than you do."

"Shut up." I flung out my lifeless hand to smack my brother, but couldn't reach.

"She moved; it's not the end of the world. Seriously, when are you gonna grow a pair?"

"Mason! That's enough," Mom snapped. She ushered him out of the kitchen, leaving me to wallow in my misery.

I can't believe it was so long ago.

As the mix of colors rinse off my paintbrushes and swirl into the sink, the answer I should have given my mother hits me: Trace has a carefree ambiance no one can copy. She's one of a kind, a rare masterpiece of a person. She's all the things I'm not.

"Hi."

I jerk my head up. Trace stands in the art room doorway.

My paintbrush slides from my hand and tumbles to the floor. The sight of her paralyzes me, like she shot an icicle down my spine. She steps into the room, not meeting my gaze.

Did she come here to see me? Did she know I was in here?

My eyes follow as she weaves between tables, snaking toward me.

What the hell am I supposed to say? I shouldn't be here. My parents forbade me to talk to her. If anyone sees us together in here, I'm screwed.

I swallow. "Hi, Trace."

A million questions run through my mind. Where do you live? How are you doing? Are you happy? I open my mouth but the words clump and jumble on my tongue. Silence spills out louder and faster than anything I could ever say.

She clears her throat. "How…how are you?"

"I'm good…great, actually." *Am I?* "How 'bout you?"

"Oh…things are good."

"How's the house?"

"It's…really nice." She gives me a weak smile.

Her life is great. Without me.

"Cool."

Knots tangle in my chest, turning my insides to jelly. She's a ghost who's haunted me for years, now rising from the dead.

She's happy. Why do I feel like shit?

"I…Happy Birthday." She darts her eyes to the floor.

"Oh…thanks."

Silence.

"I have a present for you." She picks at her fingernail. "For your birthday."

"You…you do? What is it?"

She's so pretty. Just like she always was.

She runs a hand down the back of her neck. "Well, this is going to sound so stupid. You probably don't remember at all, I mean, you shouldn't, 'cause it's so stupid, but okay, you're going to laugh at me. When we were eight years old, we were in art class, in a room sort of like this, do you remember? Mr. Wintle's class?"

"Yeah, of course I do."

"Well, one day we drew these family portraits, and you drew me in yours…"

I laugh. "Yeah, I remember. Bastard tore mine up in front of everyone."

Trace teeters on her feet. "Well, ha, yeah. I don't know why, but I felt bad that day, like, really bad. I mean, I did instigate it. And I just couldn't let him do that, Piren, because it was just so crappy of him, and so at lunch I came back, and I fished out the pieces—don't worry, the trash just had paper in it, no actual garbage—and I pieced it back together." She rustles through her messenger bag. "Here it is."

Fingers fumbling, she unfolds a crumpled sheet of paper, revealing my Masterpiece. It's ancient and held together by bits of Scotch tape, but I recognize it instantly. The pieces misalign, forming a pathetic, crooked puzzle, but they fit together all the same.

I take the drawing from her and run my finger along the taped seams.

It's just how I remember.

"I know, it's really stupid." She wrings her hands. "I don't know why I never gave it to you before. I mean, it's been, what, nine years since that class? If you're gonna hang it up, you should probably cut off the piece with me on it, 'cause I don't think Lara would like that, and—"

"I can't believe you kept this." *I can't take my eyes off her.* "Thank you."

"Oh, no big." Blush creeps across her freckled cheeks. "I'm glad you like it."

Reach out. Touch her. Hug her. Scream. Grab her. Say something. Anything.

"Well. That's all." She turns away, speeding to the door.

Something twists in my chest. "Wait!"

"Yeah?"

"I…I miss you, Trace. I'm not…good at being away from you."

Her gaze softens. "I miss you too."

Trace's marker-drawn blue eyes pale in comparison to the real thing.

"Let's stop this, this not talking thing." I force past the crack in my voice. "It sucks."

She breathes out a shaky sigh. "We aren't supposed to be friends."

"Tracy." I hold up the mangled drawing. "We were never supposed to be friends."

I want to hug her. I want to scream at her for not contacting me in two years. I want to ask her why she kissed me and why she moved away. I want to know why this time she didn't come back. I want to know if we still have a shot at being friends. If it's too late. If Christmas Eve left wounds that time can't heal.

"Okay, I agree," she says. "Let's not ignore each other anymore."

The moment fizzles at the sound of the bell.

I can't fight the smile off my face the whole rest of the day.

I got the best birthday gift in the world.

TRACY BAILEY

Welcome to the Assigning Ceremony! boasts a bright orange banner. Mom shoves past me. "There she is! Look at my little niece, the star."

My cousin Annabelle twirls, her curled ringlets waving around her chubby face. "Thanks, Auntie Yvonne."

"C'mon, we gotta get seats," my father grumbles. "Ceremony's starting in five."

I scan the chattering crowd and point. "Aunt Gloria, Uncle Roy, and Alton are in the second row. Right there. Look, they saved seats."

We plow through the aisle toward our extended family. Mom pecks her sister on the cheek.

"Gloria, dear, you look lovely."

"I pale in comparison to you, dear Yvonne."

"You flatter me, dear! I feel like an old hag."

I suppose they would be cute siblings if they didn't only talk or see each other at frigging Ceremonies. They always put on a performance that could rival the Ceremony itself.

"What do you think of Annabelle's gown?" Aunt Gloria asks.

"It's divine. Any little boy will be lucky to Partner with her."

"Oh, I know. She's a little princess today."

Everyone oozes excitement. One hundred pristine children giggle and whisper by the stage, pruning themselves like peacocks. They hold postures like miniature adults.

I slide into the row and sit between Aunt Gloria and Sam.

"I love you, Tracy Bailey."

"I love you, Sam Macey."

Veronica and Oliver plop down beside my Partner. Purveyors of fine fashion, The Wonder Twins sport their hideous matching T-shirts. Despite my desperate pleas, they didn't even shield the monstrosities with jackets. Barely seated, they're all over each other, brushing knees and entwining fingers. It makes me want to retch.

Sam rests his hand on my thigh. I keep my arms tight at my sides.

"So, Tracy, your First Kiss is coming up in less than a year, huh?" Aunt Gloria asks.

I nod.

Start the frigging ceremony already.

She leans closer. "You must be so excited."

"We're very excited," Sam says. "It's a big step."

I roll my eyes. *How long did it take you script that answer?*

"It sure is," my aunt continues. "Next big step before your Cohabitation Ceremony, then before you know it, the wedding!"

My stomach drops.

"The wedding's going to be lovely." Three seats down, Mom gestures her hands in the air. "Flowers everywhere, hanging chandeliers, the whole works. Tracy in a big white dress. We're all so unbelievably excited."

So unbelievably excited.

Mom winks at her sister. "You'll have to take notes, soon enough it will be Annabelle's turn. And we get to meet her future groom today!"

"I know. I can't believe it." Aunt Gloria dabs a tissue to her eyes. "Look at me; I'm a wreck. Just imagine me at your wedding, Tracy. I'll need to bring a whole box of Kleenex."

I swallow hard.

She furrows her brows at me. "You're quiet today."

"Sorry. It's just a bit overwhelming for me." I sip my water bottle, purposely un-focusing my eyes.

"Aw, don't feel overwhelmed. It's a great future you've got in store. First Kiss, big wedding...And then, soon enough, you'll be popping out kids!"

I choke, sputtering water everywhere.

"Are you all right?" Sam asks.

"Fine! Fine..." I cough, wiping water off my chin with the back of my hand.

The Ceremony commences. My aunt and uncle assemble their cavalcade of cameras, aimed and poised to attack.

All the little kids amble up to the stage. Annabelle waves at us, and we collectively wave back. She's so cute and young and small—so very innocent.

The moderator starts announcing couples. One-by-one, they exchange awkward *I love you*'s.

"Remember when this was us, baby?" Oliver says to Veronica.

"It was the best day of my life." She swoons.

He whispers something in her ear, and she giggles. They delve into their myopic existence, playing with each other's hands.

Sam pokes my flank. "Remember our Assigning Ceremony?"

I remember you picking your nose.

"Yep." I scrape my chipped black nail polish with my thumb nail. "Sure do."

"Sorry," he says with a smile, "I guess today just brings out the romance in me."

My aunt reaches over me and squeezes my Partner's leg. "Never apologize. It's a beautiful thing to watch a couple so happily in love."

I clench my teeth. *So happily in love.*

Sam beams. "At our wedding—" he brushes a curl of hair behind my ear "—will you wear your hair like you had it the day of our Assigning? It was so cute."

Wow, he's really laying it on thick.

"Oh, uh, okay." I cross my legs.

"And I'm assuming Veronica will be your maid of honor." He wraps his hand around mine. "What color would you like her to wear?"

Are we really having this conversation now?

"Oh, I don't know. It's years away."

"I really like purple."

I snort out a laugh. "Yeah, okay."

Sam's not laughing.

"Oh…you're serious?"

"Yes. You're not?"

I planned a fake purple-themed wedding once…with a fake Partner.

Purple in all my wedding pictures; I gag at the mere thought.

"I hate purple." I crinkle my nose. "It's so…yuck."

"Oh, really? Well, I think it's a nice wedding color."

"Very nice color," Mom says.

"Veronica will look lovely in a purple bridesmaid dress," Dad says.

"Well, I'll get a nice purple dress myself, then." Aunt Gloria says.

"So, we'll do that, then?" Sam asks. It's more of a command than a question.

I force a half-hearted smile. "Whatever you want, Sam."

Piren's face floats through my mind. If he were here, he'd be laughing at this whole exchange. I'd be laughing too if it wasn't my life that's so hilarious.

My parents don't know Piren and I reconnected last month. We talk in secret at school. I can't call or text him, because my dad screens my phone. I won't pretend it's like the good old days, because it's not. We limit our conversations to hallway small talk. Our storytelling days are long over. It's not the same, but he's back in my life, and that fact alone fills me with warmth.

"Annabelle Cohen!"

My cousin leaps up, an eager smile spreading across her round child's face. I can tell she's nervous; she's bouncing like she ingested a heaping mound of sugar.

"…and Brian Bates!"

A twitchy dark-haired boy waddles up to her. His shoulders slump as he approaches his future wife. In some ways, he reminds me of Sam.

"I love you, Annabelle Cohen."

"I love you, Brian Bates."

Cheers erupt in the audience, and cameras flash from every direction.

Those are such big, heavy words on such a small pair of people. How can Annabelle and Brian possibly understand the magnitude of what they've said? Of what they've just promised each other?

All the faces in the crowd blur together in a giant mass, their happy shouts warbling in my ears.

Aunt Gloria pats away joyful tears. Uncle Roy's cameras whir and click, capturing every moment of the occasion forever. Maybe my aunt and uncle will watch the video footage on the eve of their daughter's wedding, a date unofficially scribbled in a calendar years away.

Annabelle and Brian sway awkwardly on stage as if not knowing what to do with their bodies. Strangers stare at them, and they don't know how to respond. All these people came to celebrate their life commitment to each other. To slide imaginary wedding bands on their tiny child fingers.

I want to storm up there and rip my cousin off the stage. Run away. Leave.

"I'm happy too, my love!" Sam says, resting his hand once again on my knee. As if my body is uncharted territory for him to claim.

My muscles tense.

"I have to pee."

I run out of the staged area, into the bathroom, and the tears break free.

PIREN ALLSTON

Lara's parents own a huge saltwater fish tank. The thing takes up an entire wall in their living room. I love watching the little guys swim. Fifteen tropical fish of varying sizes, shapes, and colors float and weave past each other, in and out of a sparkly silver castle in the middle. Sometimes, one fish bumps another fish and reverses directions. I've heard fish memories only last one or two seconds; every time they bump into their tank-mate, it's like meeting a new friend for the first time. I press my face to the glass.

"Lara?"

"Hmm?" She sits beside me, facing the other direction, knitting a hat.

"When we get a house, I want one of these tanks."

"Okay." I can tell she's only half listening to me.

I point through the glass. "Especially these blue ones here, they're the best."

"The tangs?" She doesn't avert her eyes from her knitting.

"Is that what kind they are?"

"Yep."

I've already asked to flip on the TV but was informed this would violate "our time." So, instead, I sit in silence, watching the fish.

Lara's mother rushes into the room. She paces the length of the couch, hands jittering at her sides.

I cock my head, draping my arm around Lara. "What's wrong, Mrs. Goodren?"

"Nothing, it's nothing." She sinks down beside us and buries her face in her hands.

"Mom?" Lara brushes her mother's leg. "You okay?"

At least she's finally paying attention to something other than yarn.

"Lara, come close, I need you near me. This might be tough to hear." Mrs. Goodren takes a deep breath. "Your Uncle Brent is... leaving Aunt Caris."

Lara gasps, clapping her hand to her mouth. Her knitting needles tumble to the floor.

"He's been Banished to Lornstown." Water pools in Mrs. Goodren's eyes. "He met another woman, and they...fornicated."

Lornstown: town for the exiled and the traitors. The only place the Banished can legally go in the entire state without facing execution for trespassing. It's a sad, lonely town, full of loveless people with no hope and no future. Even if traveling there wasn't forbidden, I doubt anyone would dare set foot past the boundary; it's a hotbed of suffering and disease.

"He's in Lornstown?" I tighten my grip on my Partner. "Already?"

"Not yet. He and the horrible other woman, that tramp, are going together." Tears break the barrier and streak down Mrs. Goodren's puffy cheeks. "The Mayor gave them two days to pack."

"What about Aunt Caris?"

"She...she's going to live alone."

Lara's hand tightens over mine like a vice.

Mom says Solitude is one step above Banishment. If your Partner commits adultery, you don't have to leave town or go to Lornstown. You can stay in society, but at a heavy price: you're doomed to a lonely life forever. You're a pariah with no one to love. You're a pitiable cripple without your other half. If you don't already have children, that possibility is gone. If you do already have children, they'll grow up under the shroud of shame, as everyone will know about their Banished parent. In the end, many Solituders voluntarily move to Lornstown, just to be around people again.

"How'd he meet this other woman?" My mouth grows dry.

"I don't know; Caris didn't say. I don't want to know." Mrs. Goodren scrubs her hands through her matted hair. "It'll be in the paper next week. The burial for Brent's soul is next Friday."

My leg jiggles, and I clamp my hand over it. *Not now!*

We mourn the symbolic deaths of the Banished with funerals for their souls. Despite their fate, they have closure. But Solituders die a slow death alone; they're alive, but lifeless.

"I've got to call the rest of the family," Mrs. Goodren says. "She shouldn't have to go through this alone." She strides from the room.

The moment her mother leaves, my Partner breaks down in shuddering tears. My mouth opens, then closes again.

What are you supposed to say when there's nothing to say?

Lara's aunt is doomed to a horrible life, and her uncle is dead to us now. She lost two family members at once. A double whammy, straight to the heart. It's sickening that anyone could do that to their family.

"Don't ever leave me," Lara whispers.

"What? Of course not. I'll never leave you." My words race out in stutters. "You're my Partner. I'm not like Uncle Brent; I know what it means to have a Partner. It's a privilege. I'm not going to give that up." I squeeze her hand.

She sniffles. "Promise?"

"I promise."

She smiles at me, cheeks wet with tears that still rain from her eyes.

"I love you, Piren Allston."

"I love you, Lara Goodren."

"We'll be happy together forever. I know it. I love you so much." She wipes her sleeve across her face, absorbing the remaining tears.

Forever.

TRACY BAILEY

I'm mulling over the fridge for a midnight snack when the backdoor creaks open. I spin around, flicking on the hall light. My sister tiptoes inside, arms outstretched like a tightrope walker, accompanied by the overbearing aroma of alcohol.

She presses her finger to her lips and giggles, slumping up against the wall.

"Very sneaky." I narrow my eyes. "Do Mom and Dad even know you left?"

She smirks. "Nope. They were in bed. I went to Ollie's."

"You're out of control."

"Nuh-uh, I'm invincible!" She thrusts her fist over her head. It sways in the air for a moment before clapping back down at her side.

"You're fifteen, for God's sake." I slam the refrigerator door. "Your drunk ass isn't fooling anyone. Quit the booze."

"Don't be a killjoy." She grabs my shoulders in a feeble attempt at stability. "You should party with us next time."

"Nope, I'm good. I don't want any part in this bullshit." I shirk out of her grasp. "And there shouldn't be a 'next time.'"

I walk away, but she tugs my sleeve. "Don't tell Mom and Dad!"

"I won't, but cut the shit, V. No more."

She holds up her hand. "Promise!"

Three nights later, I'm perched in front of the television when the doorbell rings. My father rushes to answer it, abandoning his third round of scotch on the coffee table. I follow him into the hall.

A cop stands on our doorstep, carting my handcuffed sister. Veronica wobbles back and forth between her feet.

That little promise-breaking liar!

The officer explains that he arrested Veronica for underage intoxication in the Capstone Mall parking lot, a block from Oliver's house.

My father's hands ball into quivering fists at his sides.

"I don't want to catch her drinking underage again." The cop tips his hat.

"Don't worry, officer, you won't." Dad glowers at Veronica.

The policeman scribbles a report and speeds off in his cruiser. His bright flashing lights evoke fluttering curtains from peeping neighbors.

Well, Mom won't be thrilled at that...

The moment the officer leaves, my father erupts.

"Veronica Lynn!"

My sister kicks back her foot against the doorframe. "Whattup, Pop?"

Dad's reddening face tremors. "What the hell is wrong with you?"

"Me?" She jabs him in the chest. "How about your drunk ass?"

"You think this is funny?"

They fly into screaming rages, ripping into each other.

If I wasn't a member of this fucked-up family, I'd find the situation amusing; two people, equally sloshed, slurring and stumbling while bellowing that the other person is an alcoholic.

Veronica shouts in Dad's face, and he roars back, shaking with fury. The stagnant hallway reeks of liquor. Somewhere upstairs, a door slams shut; Mom heard the fight and wanted no part of it.

"You humiliated this whole family! You're not leaving this house for a month!"

"Don't tell me what to do while you're in here guzzling scotch!"

"Don't you dare talk to me that way!"

I step forward. "Okay, guys—"

"You're an asshole!"

Eyes blazing, Dad slaps her across the face.

"Hey!" I barrel forward, launching myself between them. "Leave her alone!"

"You stay out of this!" Dad hurls a sloppy punch, but I duck. His fist shatters against the drywall. "Damn it!"

"I can't, Trace. I'm s-sorry," Veronica stammers, clutching her cheek. "I'm sorry! I'm sorry! I—"

"Shut up!" I hiss at her. I whirl on my father. "Don't you ever hit her again!"

I yank Veronica up by her sleeve. She stumbles and trips over the stairs as I drag her up to my bedroom. I slam the door behind us.

"Trace, I'm sorry. I'm so sorry!"

I shove her up against the wall. "What? You want to be like Dad? Fuck up your life, fuck up your kids? Is that what you want?"

"I'm sorry, I'm sorry, I'm—"

"You should have called me. I would have come get you! Better than the fucking police!"

"I'm sorry, I'm sorry!" Tears stream down her puffy cheeks.

My shoulders relax. *She's apologizing for ruining her own life.*

"Shhh...Veronica...shhh...It's okay..." I pull my sister's body close to mine, wrapping my arms around her. "You didn't know. It's okay."

She sniffles. "I'm sorry."

"I know."

I lead her to my bed and tuck her in under the blankets. "Shhh, get some sleep." I kiss her forehead and plop down at the end of the bed.

"Trace?"

"Yep."

"I love you."

"Love you too, V."

She squeezes my hand. I reach out to stroke her arm.

"Will you stay here?" she asks.

"Yep. Right here."

"Promise?"

"Yep. Get some sleep, drunkie."

My father's hollering continues downstairs, accompanied by thuds and crashes. Mom must have succumbed to curiosity, because her raised voice joins his. I don't care; they won't bother us in my bedroom.

Veronica's eyelids flutter as she drifts into peaceful, drunken sleep.

I'll protect you, V. I promise.

I kiss her cheek and curl up on the floor.

I always will.

Oliver's pissed at Veronica for the arrest. Personally, I don't think his anger is justified; he supplied her with the necessary booze. V's picture cropped up in the Shaming pages this morning, only a day after the arrest, citing her crime as underage drunkenness. It wasn't an affair, so it only occupies one line of the paper. Regardless, my sister saw it and bolted from the room, tearful and blushing. Mom cut out the article and taped it to Veronica's bedroom door.

The page identifies Oliver by name as V's Partner, which could explain why he's so pissed at her. He's ignored my sister all week. She sits at the kitchen table, bloodshot eyes set on her lifeless phone, lying inches away.

"A watched pot never boils." I slouch down beside her, chugging a can of soda, and flick her arm. "Hey. Buck up. Wanna go to the movies?"

Her lip trembles, but she doesn't respond.

"What?" I let my mouth stretch into a grin. "Can't have a little fun without him?"

She blinks, her glassy eyes wet with tears.

Fury wells inside me. *This is my stupid parents' fault: Mom for making Veronica so whiny and codependent, and Dad for making her an alcoholic.*

I rest my hand on her shoulder. "Don't worry. He'll come around." I linger for a moment, then walk away, leaving her to stew in her despair.

PIREN ALLSTON

I sneak into my room and creak the door closed behind me. I press my ear to the wood, but no footsteps patter in the hall. With a deep breath, I open the top drawer of my desk and sift around until I find the crumpled drawing. It's torn and hastily taped together with the precision of an eight-year-old, but my heart flutters when my shaky hands unfold it. *My Masterpiece.*

The picture displays my whole family: my parents, Mason, Stephanie, Lara, Trace, and me. Trace's hand-drawn blue eyes meet mine, captured forever in Magic Marker.

A hard stone drops through my chest as I pluck scissors from the drawer. Positioning them to slice Trace from the group, my hand freezes.

I have to. Trace even told me to do it. What if someone finds it? Cut her out!

I close my eyes.

But if it wasn't for her, this drawing would have been trashed almost a decade ago. She repaired it and saved it all those years. Just for me.

Stick-figure Piren in the picture isn't standing with his parents or brother. He's not side-by-side with his Partner. He's clearly set apart from the others.

He's standing right next to stick figure Trace.

Did eight-year-old Piren know something? Did he feel something?

Heart pounding, I throw the scissors back in the drawer and slam it shut. I refold the uncut drawing and hide it in my desk under a stack of papers.

Did I always feel something?

TRACY BAILEY

It's been two weeks since Veronica's arrest. It's also been two weeks since The Wonder Twins last communicated. So, basically, it's the longest time I've ever gone without being subjected to their gag-inducing phone calls.

When I was the problem child, ignoring my Partner was the worst crime in the Bailey household. For once, I'm not the cause of my parents' chagrin. In fact, tonight I'm doing something ingratiating.

Tonight is my first official date with Sam. I've prolonged the inevitable for years but finally agreed to go. My family better shut the hell up with their problems and appreciate this.

I sit in the kitchen, dabbing on gray eyeliner. Vacant-eyed Veronica wanders in and sits beside me.

"Going on a date like a real lady," Mom says, patting my head. She turns toward V. "Unlike certain others who choose unladylike behaviors…Any idea who that could be?" She smiles sweetly at my sister.

"Mom, come on…" I smear blush across my cheeks. "Give her a break."

Mom huffs. "Honestly, I just —"

The doorbell cuts her off. She floats from the room, primping her hair.

I open the door and can hardly believe my eyes. Hair slicked back, Sam dons black slacks, a white button-down, and an emerald tie. He clenches a bouquet of pricey-looking yellow tulips.

Someone's in rare form tonight. Who are you, and what have you done with my Partner?

Cheeks reddening, he thrusts the flowers toward me.

"I love you, Tracy Bailey."

"I love you, Sam Macey."

I smooth my form-fitting teal dress, shifting the fabric to hide my cleavage. My parents enter the hallway, arm in arm, to greet my Partner. Sam shakes my father's hand and kisses my mother's.

Dad makes us pose for a picture by the door. Also in rare form, he's sober tonight. I'm glad, because I want him to remember I put on a happy face for this date. I'll use it as a bargaining chip next time I fuck up.

Sam entwines his fingers with mine and leads me out to his SUV. We wave to my parents and Veronica as we drive away.

His car smells like shoes.

"It's good we're finally doing this," he says.

"Yeah, I know." I straighten my posture to match the formality of the evening. "Where are we going?"

"I made reservations downtown." He taps his thumbs against the steering wheel. "Real nice place, great reviews."

"Wow. This is…unexpected."

"I wanted to make you happy."

"Well, thanks." I pick at the hem of my dress, keeping my eyes down.

He awkwardly whistles a tune for a few moments, then stops. "You know, we're getting married in only a little over six years, but I feel like I hardly know you at all."

"Yeah, I get that." I twist a loose thread around my finger. "I mean, I understand what you feel."

"Well, okay, how about this. I'll ask you a question, and you ask me one. We have to answer honestly. Sound good?" He steals a quick glance at me. "Everything's fair game."

"Okay. I can do that. You go first."

"Okay…What's your favorite animal?"

"Umm…" I scrunch my mouth to the side. "Dogs, I guess."

"What type of dogs?"

"Uh, probably something like a German Shepherd. Something big."

"That's funny. I pictured you as a yippy, ankle-biter-type dog person."

I wrinkle my nose. *Really, Sam?* "Okay, what's your favorite animal?"

"Nope, no repeating questions."

"Okay, okay, fine. What…umm…what's your best subject in school?"

"Easy. Biology."

"For real?" *My worst subject.*

"Yep. Three years in a row, best subject is science."

"Well, that's pretty cool." I twiddle my fingers.

"What's your dream job?"

"Hmm…" I tap my fingers to my lips. "I think I'd like to be a carpenter."

He chortles. "Carpentry? That's not a *girl's* job."

"Excuse me? That's *anybody's* job."

"I dunno if I want my wife working as a carpenter."

"Well, tough." I clench my jaw.

Ten minutes in and he's already pissing me off. How far away is this effing restaurant?

"Okay, okay." He reaches across the console to squeeze my arm. "I'm sorry."

"Fine. But as your punishment, you have to think of the next question."

"Deal."

We ask each other question after question as the car zips down the freeway. My fidgeting hands grow sweaty in my lap.

Am I supposed to marry someone who knows nothing about me beyond my favorite color?

"Okay…" I shoot him a grin. "Give me a hard one this time."

"Gonna challenge me, eh? Okay, let me think…" He pauses for a moment, eyes focused on the road. "If you could be any age forever, what age would you pick?"

"Wow, good one."

Everyone knows the correct answer is twenty-one; you're an adult but still young. But that's not the answer blaring in my brain. I can vividly picture my perfect age as if it's happening right now. I'm climbing the rungs of the treehouse. There's intruders on the West Wall, but we've prepared parachutes as a strong defense. *I'm happy.*

"Eight. I'd be eight."

He cocks his head. "A little kid? Why?"

"I dunno…Good memories, I guess."

"Okay…such as…"

"Nope, your turn is over. Nice try, though."

He grumbles. "Then, ask me something."

"Okay…" I drum my fingers on my thigh. "What's your favorite food?"

"Uh, probably steak." A sly smile brims across his face. "Guess where we're going tonight? That new steakhouse, Chateau."

"Wow, really? Isn't that place ridiculously expensive?"

He puffs out his chest. "It's our date night; it doesn't matter."

He's trying.

"Well, I can't wait to try it." I rub my arm. "It's your turn, by the way."

He strokes his chin. "Okay, hmm…What's your favorite childhood memory?"

"Oh…uh…I dunno…"

"There has to be something."

I close my eyes. My favorite memory. Chalk drawings. Treehouse. Art class. Walking to the bus. Getting on the wrong bus. Cocoa. They're all my favorite memories.

They all have one person in common.

"I don't want to play anymore."

Sam's smile twitches. "Why not?"

"I just don't."

His hands tighten around the steering wheel. "Come on, I'm trying here."

"I don't want to."

"Why won't you tell me your favorite memory?"

"Because I don't have one."

"You obviously do; you just don't want to tell me."

"Fine! Okay, fine. My favorite memory…I guess it was the day I found this old treehouse with my neighbor. We were little kids… Okay?" I slump against the window to sulk; saying it aloud stung.

The car slows to a stop. "Who was your neighbor?"

"It's not important."

"Tell me."

"None of your damn business."

"Tell me!"

"Piren Allston! Okay? He was my neighbor, and now he's not."

Why not just rip the Band-Aid right off?

"What the hell? Your favorite memory was with *him?*"

"He was my friend!"

"I *know* that! Everyone knows that. You weren't exactly shy about it. How do you think that made *me* feel? Pretty shitty, my Partner always running after some other kid."

I bite my lip. *Maybe he's got a point.*

"I hate that little shit!"

"Sam…"

He flings back his fist and punches the steering wheel with a thud that rattles the whole car. I jump, pulse zipping through my chest.

Sam reaches to touch me, but I recoil. He slams the gas pedal, and the car lurches forward, pressing my back to the seat.

"I'm done here, Sam. Take me home. Now."

"What's going on with you and Piren?" The speed increases.

"Nothing! I lived down the street from him when we were little, okay? We haven't talked in years."

Not seriously, at least.

He slams the brakes, screeching to a halt in the middle of the street. The car thrusts me forward, and I bang my head on the dash.

"Ever since we were Assigned, I've seen it." His voice is venomous and low. "I've seen the way you look at him, and I'm sick of it. I'd like to pummel that asshole."

"There's nothing!" I rub my sore forehead. "I swear to you there's nothing!"

His upper lip curls, baring his teeth. "Get out of the car."

"Excuse me?"

"You heard me. Get out of my car. This date is over."

"We're miles from my house."

"Get out of the fucking car!"

I gape at him. "Wow, and you wonder why I never want to see y—"

His fist lunges and sinks into my headrest, striking two inches from my face.

I freeze. For a half-second, my father glimmers in Sam's eyes.

He leaps back, wide-eyed. "Tracy, I'm sorry. I can't believe that. I'm so sorry, I—"

I wrench open the door, jump out, and run away as fast as my legs can carry. The cold air stings my skin, but I don't care.

I'd rather be anywhere than in that car.

PIREN ALLSTON

The front door flings open, and Dad rushes inside. My parents' hurried voices catch my attention from the other room.

"Police are out looking for her."

"Did they say how it happened?"

"She was out with her Partner and didn't come home."

"The Baileys must be terrified."

I spring upward. *The Baileys?*

"Dad?" I rush into the kitchen. "Mom? What's going on?"

Mom sits at the table, head propped on her hand. Her eyes crinkle when they meet mine. My father paces the room, but stops walking when he sees me.

"Tracy Bailey's missing."

My heart jumps. "What?"

"She went on a date." Dad's eyebrows knit together. "But Sam returned alone."

My arms fall limp at my sides.

"No." The word comes out softer than a whisper.

"Don't worry, honey." Mom rises from her chair and brushes my cheek with her hand. "Cops are everywhere. They'll find her." She smiles, but her hollow tone gives away her insincerity.

"Officer Richards says they never even reached the restaurant." Dad leans against the counter and crosses his arms. "They stopped at a red light, and Tracy bolted. Least, that's what Sam's saying."

Why do I sense a pinch of doubt in Dad's voice?

His phone buzzes, and he answers. "Yeah?...Okay...We'll be right there."

I space out, memories flashing through my brain: Sam pummeling basketballs in gym class, frightening everyone; Tracy showing up at the bus stop with her arm in a sling; Sam threatening us as we walk home.

My mouth runs dry.

Is he capable of hurting her?

Fear courses through my body like hot poison.

My parents pull on their jackets.

"Got to go help them search," Dad says.

"I want to come!"

"No." His brows lower. "Stay here."

His tone makes my stomach turn. It's like they're worried about what they'll find, and they don't want me there to see.

My parents race outside to join the manhunt. Police sirens blaze past our house. I glue my face to the window, pulse rocketing through my chest.

Sam did this.

My hands clench up. Something unhinges in my brain; I can't describe it. Animalistic, uncontrolled rage seeps through my veins. Boiling with fury, I sprint upstairs to my dad's safe. I pound in the code and rip out his handgun. I load the pistol, bring it outside, and toss it on the backseat of my car.

If Sam hurts her, I don't want to beat him. I want to kill him.

TRACY BAILEY

A dull ache burns through my calves with every step, but I can't stop running. I can't go home early from my date and face my parents. What the hell would I even say?

Every few paces, distant car engines rev my ears to hyper-vigilance, prickling fear down my neck.

Is it him? Did he follow me?

I whirl around, but each time, it's an unknown vehicle passing by. I force my stiff body forward, racing down side streets and alleys.

With each step, my overworked heart thumps against my ribcage. Sweat fuses my dress to my body, but my throat sears with dryness. My lungs heave, threatening to collapse from exhaustion as I push myself forward.

Nowhere to go, I keep running.

Maybe Sam drove back to my house and told my parents what happened. Maybe they're all furious, waiting to pounce on me for abandoning our date.

Dread boils in my stomach.

I'll have to face them all eventually.

I dash through the dewy evening air. No destination, but I can't stop.

Sam overreacted. He shouldn't have flipped out.

But he's right. He's always been right. I can't deny it anymore. Not to him, not to myself.

Surged with warming adrenaline, I know where my feet are taking me as I pass the tree line at Harker's Woods. I jog to the treehouse and climb to the top. My feet scale the rungs with perfect agility, as if my body remembers the steps from long ago.

I throw myself onto the platform, gasping for air. Hands on my knees to catch my breath, the engraving greets me at eye level.

Our carved initials still claim the treehouse. No Lara or Sam, just Piren and Trace's friendship, displayed for all who visit. It's a permanent tribute no one can erase, defying all who tried to break us.

Piren Allston is my best friend; no one can change that. They can try to sever our bond, but true friendship is infinite. Together we form an unstoppable force.

I need to solidify it.

I pry out a sharp rock wedged between two floorboards and carve into the bark. Scraping the stone through the wood, I make my forbidden mark, unleashing my prisoner from the dungeon inside.

When the deed is done, I fall back to examine my work. Tears stream from my eyes as I look upon the truth, now carved forever into the side of this tree: our initials are now, and forevermore, encircled by a heart.

I'm free.

PIREN ALLSTON

My body tremors in a sickly, knotted mess as I rev the engine.

At one time, I knew Trace better than anyone. Maybe we've grown apart, but if anyone can find her, it's me.

Demolishing the speed limit, I race to Trace's new neighborhood. Cops and citizens alike swarm the area with flashlights, searching for my best friend. I squint out my window, prowling up and down every possible street.

Come on, Trace. Where are you?

My frantic heart rate skyrockets at every sound. Water clouds my eyes as I scan the dark alley behind a bakery. Nothing.

Please be alive. Somewhere.

I pull to the side of the road and park.

Where the fuck is she?

I press my forehead to the steering wheel and close my eyes.

I wrench my eyes open when it hits me.

Trace isn't here. She wouldn't come here.

This isn't her home.

Gunning the engine, I speed back to my house and screech the car to a halt at the mouth of Harker's Woods. I race to the treehouse, panting for air.

Please be here.

Two rungs at a time, I reach the top.

My heart somersaults.

Trace curls in a ball on the treehouse floor, watching the black night sky.

"Trace! Oh my God, what the hell?" Ragged breaths tear through my words. "Everyone's looking for you! What the fuck are you doing up here alone?"

She meets my gaze, but doesn't speak. An emotion burns behind her eyes, but I can't place it. Her blue dress hugs her body, and I'm struck by how beautiful she is.

I lean against the treehouse wall, face flushed and sweating. Relief floods over me.

She's here, safe and sound, in her little Trace hideaway.

My delirious joy fades into rage.

"You can't do that, Trace! You can't just run away! What the hell were you thinking? Sam's probably terrified. You have no idea how worried I was! I almost…You have no idea what—"

But she gets up, brushes past me, and slips down the ladder without a word.

It is not in the stars to hold our destiny but in ourselves.
❧William Shakespeare

SEVENTEEN YEARS OLD
PART THREE

PIREN ALLSTON

"Are you ready for your big night?" Mom asks. "Or, I guess I should say, big weekend?"

I slide into my tuxedo vest. "I think so."

"Tell me again how you asked her?" She unwraps my black bowtie from the plastic packaging. "I want to tell Grandma."

"Aw, Mom, it's embarrassing."

"It is not! Senior Prom is a huge deal. I remember mine like it was yesterday. Your father was almost an hour late."

"Oh, man, he wasn't."

"He hasn't changed much." She holds the tie up to my chest. "And I love him for it."

"Fine." I give her a crooked smile. "I set a trail of pink daisies leading from her locker to the hallway. Lara followed it, and found me with a painted sign that said 'Prom?' She took a picture. I think she's going to make a whole scrapbook for this weekend."

Mom's face scrunches up. "My son is all grown up." She pats my cheek. "And then tomorrow, your First Kiss Ceremony. In a few years you'll be married—the man of the house. I can't believe it. I remember when you were born."

"Aw, Mom, stop."

"What a nice surprise for the Mayor to arrange the two events together. It'll be really special. Your brother's was in the fall, remember?"

My stomach tightens.

That disaster. How could I forget?

People buzz with excitement all over school for our dual Prom-and-Ceremony weekend, chattering everywhere about the cluster of events. I get all jittery inside when I think about it. The Ceremony may not technically be my first kiss, but it'll be my first legitimate kiss.

Mom swoops in with a comb and brushes a few stray hairs away from my eyes. I tower over her; she has to stretch and stand on her tiptoes to reach my head. Grabbing my forearms, she steps back.

"Nervous?"

"Come on, Mom."

She pulls me into a hug. "Love you."

"Love you too."

I take a deep breath and head to the car, waving good-bye to my parents.

Mr. Goodren answers the door when I arrive, broad smile stretching across his face. Lara emerges from behind him wearing a pink dress. She curled her hair and pulled it back over her head like a princess.

"I love you, Lara Goodren."

"I love you, Piren Allston."

"Wow, you look amazing."

She blushes. "You too."

I lace her fingers with mine, and we head outside. Within minutes, Alan and Toni pull up in the antique car we rented for the evening. They greet us from the front seat.

Climbing into the back, Lara rests her hand on my knee. I place my hand over hers, and our eyes meet. She presses her lips to my ear.

"Thank you," she whispers, "for being the best Partner ever."

TRACY BAILEY

Prom sucks. It's a waste of time and money. Spend the night feigning interest in dancing with Sam? No thanks—I'll pass.

Toni tried to convince me to rent this stupid old car with her and Alan. As if I'd voluntarily spend time with her pig-headed Partner. Let's not blow prom out of proportion; they hang some ninety-nine-cent drugstore streamers on the gym walls. Everyone parades around, pretending it's so magical to be in the same room we sweat in every day.

Big surprise, my parents are forcing me to go. Mom dumps a hideous, black poufy dress on my bed. I groan.

"But, Mom—"

"I don't want to hear it," she snaps. "I'm serious. Not a single complaint, or you're grounded for a year."

"Fine."

"And Sam's picking you up at eight. I coordinated with his mother."

"No! Come on!"

"What did I just say?" Her eyes flash with danger. "You haven't seen that poor boy in four months. You owe him an apology; this is the least you can do. Honestly, I'm ashamed. I still can't believe you left him in the road like that."

"Seriously? Do you have to keep bringing that up?"

"Get dressed. I'm coming back to do your hair in ten minutes."

I collapse onto my bed, sulking.

Tonight better end better than the last time I rode in Sam's stinky car.

My Partner arrives in a hideous olive-green tuxedo. He looks like a leprechaun. It's the first I've seen him up-close since our date disaster. I force my scowl into a painful smile.

"I love you, Tracy Bailey."

"I love you, Sam Macey."

From behind his back, he presents this gaudy purple corsage to me and slips it over my wrist. Dad weaves around us, snapping pictures from every angle. Mom primps me and tugs my hair, trying in vain to make me look pretty. She used about four cans of spray to make my hair behave, and now it feels like plastic on my head. I'm ready to vomit all over the floor.

I link Sam's arm, and we're off.

Don't look at me. Don't talk to me. Just walk.

We climb into his car and slam the doors shut.

He grabs my hand. "Tracy, I'm so, so sorry about that night. I can't believe I did that. I never want to hurt you. I lost control. I—"

"It's fine." I yank my hand away.

"I'll never do it again. I'm so sorry. Please forgive me."

"It's fine. Stop apologizing."

"I don't know how I can ever make it up to you. I'm so—"

"Seriously, will you forget it? Just drive." I glare out the window.

Why does the whole world feel the need to keep dredging up that horrific night?

We drive twenty minutes in silence until we park at the high school. Crowds of formally-dressed teenagers flock to the gym, hands entwined.

Inhale. Exhale. Let's just get this over with.

Sam places his hand on my lower back, and we enter the gym. Gold streamers dangle from the ceiling, sparkling when lit by revolving strobes. The deejay cranks the music, and the bass vibrates through the floor, up my legs. I press my hands to my already aching ears.

I wish I had my chunky red headphones.

The stifling hot air swarms my lungs. A hundred students grind on the gym floor, jerking their sweaty bodies together.

If Sam expects that tonight, he's in for a shock.

He hangs my coat like a good Partner, and goes to fetch drinks.

Toni races over and grabs my arm, squealing with delight. She's wearing a tight, low-cut yellow dress, bright red lipstick, and four-inch heels. The moment she opens her mouth, the bitter stench of vodka stings my nostrils—and the fact that I can identify the type of alcohol by smell is kind of disgusting.

I scrunch my nose, batting my hand to waft away the scent.

"I'm guessing you're not drinking the school fruit punch, then?"

She presses her finger to her lips and giggles, lifting her dress to reveal a bright pink flask strapped to her thigh.

I'm surrounded.

"Really?"

"It's prom; everyone does it." She tugs her dress back down before a teacher sees.

Sam returns and hands me a glass of punch. I doubt it's spiked, but I sniff it anyway.

"Did you see Sophie's dress?" Toni pokes out her tongue. "Ick. She looks like a whore."

"Oh, no, I didn't." *Because I don't give a shit.*

"But Taryn Flagon's dress is amazing." She points across the gym. "It makes her ass look awesome. I'm so jealous. I bet she's totally doing it with Rob tonight."

"That's illegal."

"So? Doesn't mean they're not doing it anyway."

Toni chatters away, rehashing details of our classmates' clothes and speculating who has the potential to wind up pregnant and Banished by the end of the night. I smile and "ooh" when appropriate, commenting how great all the Partnerships look together.

They all look like sweating, horny idiots.

Amanda runs over to join our highly intellectual conversation, dragging Josh by his tux sleeve. Sam smiles and nods, throwing in hollow laughter here and there. He grabs for my hand, but I cross my arms across my chest.

For the first hour, Sam and I chat with various people. Every song, my Partner tries to nudge me to the dance floor, but I shift my body and pretend not to notice. Finally giving up on holding hands, he slides his arm around my shoulders. I cringe.

The blaring music pounds through my aching head. Shirking out of Sam's grasp, I excuse myself from the group, citing a need for fresh air.

I just want tonight to end.

I step outside and lean on the bike rail, inhaling a deep breath. Reverberations from the gym echo in the night air. A cool spring breeze drifts past, rattling the oak leaves on a nearby tree.

Bushes rustle beside me, and I jerk my head up. Piren and Lara tumble out, hand-in-hand, giggling. I jolt.

He catches my eye and stops mid-step. Lara's laugh melts to a frown.

"Hey, guys." I watch their feet.

Piren fidgets. "Hey, Trace."

Lara nods.

"Whatcha up to?" I ask. "Party's inside, not out here in the bushes."

Piren grins. "You wouldn't believe it. We followed Hank the janitor out here. He's supposed to be chaperoning, but he's out back smoking with some of the teachers, and we don't think it's tobacco."

I force a smile. "I'm not surprised."

"If you'll excuse me…" Lara runs her hands down her hot-pink gown, jutting out like a tutu at her hips. "I'm gonna get some food. Piren, you coming?" She flicks a strand of caramel hair behind her ear.

"Um, yeah." He shuffles his feet. "I'll be there in a minute."

Lara's mouth thins to a curt line, but her Partner doesn't budge. She huffs and hurries back inside, leaving Piren and me alone under the stars. Something balls up in my chest. Last time we were alone together, he reamed me out for running away to the treehouse.

Piren puts his hands in his tux pockets and stares up at the dark sky. I fidget, keeping my eyes on the ground.

"Nice night," he says.

"Yep."

He gives me a half-smile. "Didn't think of you as someone who'd come to prom."

"Well…me neither." I tap the bike rack with my foot. "But I'm here."

I miss our friendship before it was awkward.

He tilts his head. "You've got a purple corsage."

"Your visual skills are astounding."

Purple—our little inside joke.

He's got his light hair gelled back, the top button of his white collared shirt undone. My palms grow sweaty around the bike rail, and I tighten my grip.

"You…you look nice…"

"You too."

Nothing's been the same since that Christmas Eve. Was our kiss the catalyst that killed our friendship?

A lump forms in my throat.

"I gotta go."

He grabs my arm. "Wait."

"Yeah?"

"I'm just—" his gaze drifts to the ground "—glad you're all right."

I bunch up the edge of my dress between my fingers.

Does he ever think about that Christmas Eve?

"Oh. Thanks."

This person was my best friend for years, and now we're almost strangers.

The last dance we attended together was gym class, almost four years ago. We waltzed around this very gym, hand-in-hand. It was so long ago, but it could have been yesterday.

It could have been.

I head back inside, but stop dead in my tracks. To my horror, a slow song croons from the deejay's amp. Sam catches my eye and rushes over, sweat seeping through the underarms of his barf-colored shirt.

He grabs my hand and herds me to the dance floor. He slides his arms around my waist, and I plant my hands on his shoulders, pushing back to maximize our distance. Some other girls in the room wrap their arms around their Partners' necks, their eyes swooning with lovesick hypnosis. Their intimacy sends a shudder down my spine, and I stretch my arms further away.

With a sharp tug, Sam pulls my body into his, squeezing me closer. His chest feels damp against mine. I rest my chin on his shoulder to minimize the potential for eye-contact as romantic music drifts over us.

How long is this effing song?

A few feet away, Lara and Piren dance together. She's got her arms all entangled around him. A hard stone drops in my chest.

She rests her head on his shoulder and closes her eyes. He rests his head on hers.

They're so happy together.

He jerks his head up, and our eyes lock from across the room. I clear my throat and avert my gaze back to the floor. I feel like someone shot through my heart with a cannonball.

An eternity later, the song ends. I sprint off the dance floor, dragging Sam by his cuff. Wet stains dapple the front of my dress where we touched.

Gross.

A fast song begins, and grinding recommences on the dance floor.

I guess all that slow-dance romance is short lived.

Sam tugs my arm to dance again, but I twist out of his grasp.

"I have to pee."

Before my Partner can protest, I hurry away to the bathroom. I don't really have to go, but the thought of sharing another intimate dance with Sam makes me want to upchuck.

I lean over the bathroom sink, waiting for the song to end. The bathroom mirror is unforgiving; a forlorn woman stares back at me. With my hair pulled back, my billboard-forehead almost doubles in size. Sweat beads along my hairline. The up-do my mother slaved over for hours is slowly wilting, tugging at my scalp; I want to yank it off my head. Once glued in a hairspray prison, several curly strands broke free and frame my face. My bubblegum pink lipstick wore off. I'm wearing way too much glittery eye shadow. And I look like an idiot in this poufy dress.

With a loud flush, Lara saunters out from the stall behind me. I smile at her through the mirror, but she doesn't acknowledge me. She washes her hands at the next sink.

Lara glows tonight. Dolled up like a pink princess, she's wearing shimmery makeup and lip gloss. Her ballerina dress hugs her figure, highlighting her curves. I'm a fat piece of shit next to her.

Damn it, why does poufy look amazing on her but like a circus tent on me?

Her professionally-curled dirty-blond hairstyle probably took a ridiculous amount of time and money, but it'll straighten back in a few hours. I pat my curly locks with pride.

She catches me watching. "Yes?"

"Sorry. Nothing."

She rolls her eyes and grabs the door handle.

"Hey, Lara."

She pivots. "What?"

"I just…You look pretty."

"Oh. Thanks."

I pick at my black nail polish. "And you and Piren…You make a great Partnership."

"Thank you, Tracy." She sticks out her smug chin. "We really do, don't we?"

I wring my hands. "Go easy on him, okay?"

"Ex*cuse* me?"

"I…I mean, take care of him."

She clenches handfuls of her princess dress in fists.

"That didn't come out right, I just meant—"

"You listen right now." She narrows her eyes. "You are never, ever to comment on me or my relationship, so stay the hell out. Piren doesn't need you, and God knows I don't."

"I just—"

"Maybe instead of remarking on *my* relationship, you should focus more on improving your own—which, from the looks of it, is abysmal."

"Lara, I didn't mean—"

"*I* did."

She strides out the door without another glance.

I take a deep breath and follow after her, back into the ballroom where she disappears into the crowd. Toni runs up with a drink and grabs my hand, gyrating to the music.

"This party rocks." She yells over the bass. Her tipping red Solo cup of spiked punch nearly spills down my front. "I love this song!"

"What?" I shout back, leaning closer.

Piren, Alan, and Travis stand nearby, talking and laughing.

The music dies to silence.

"—but you must have boned Toni by now. Look at her slutty dress!" Travis's deep voice rings out over the silence.

My jaw drops. All eyes in the gym settle on the wide-eyed guys—and Toni.

"Shit," Alan mutters.

Toni's cheeks flush as red as her candy-apple lipstick. But her deer-in-the-headlights face quickly morphs into a tight-lipped glower of pure rage.

Eyes blazing with fury, she rips her arm from my grasp and plows toward the boys. Everyone parts like a retreating tidal wave to let her pass.

"This what you talk about in your spare time, Alan?" Toni snaps. Her Partner frantically shakes his head as she stomps toward him.

"I—"

"And you, jackass!" Toni whirls on Travis. "I know what you say about me. Not that it's any of your business —" she turns to face the spectators "— or anyone else's here —" and back to Travis "— but I am, in fact, a law-abiding virgin. I am *not* a slut."

With one flick of her wrist, she douses Travis in her drink.

"Get a life!" she roars before storming outside.

I clap my hands together in applause that no one joins, and follow her out of the gym.

PIREN ALLSTON

When I arrived home last night, it was after midnight. I could hardly keep my eyes open. After Toni's display, a bunch of people filtered out. On one hand, her freak out was super awkward, but on the other, it cleared out the masses and left plenty of room on the dance floor. Lara and I danced the entire night together, to almost every song. She's an amazing dancer, way better than me. Before I knew it, prom was over. By the last song, only a few Partnerships remained, including us. Lara immortalized the evening in over a hundred pictures.

Today's our First Kiss Ceremony. Lara's so giddy, I don't think she slept last night. She called me at three in the morning. In a groggy haze of sleep, I only half remember the conversation.

My ringtone jerked me out of a REM cycle. I fumbled my hand on my side table in the dark until I found my phone. "Hey…Lara?" My tired voice croaked over the phone.

"Piren. Hi…Did I wake you? I love you, Piren Allston."

"Yeah…it's all right. I love you, Lara Goodren." I scrubbed my hand through my hair, eyelids still heavy with exhaustion. "You okay?"

"I just…Sorry, I shouldn't keep you up. Go back to bed."

"No, it's okay." I sat up, propping my back against my pillow. "What's up?"

"I was just thinking a lot about prom."

Even in a sleepy trance, a smile crept across my face. "Me too. It was a good time."

I could almost hear her smiling through the phone. "You…You're a great dancer."

"Not as good as you."

Silence.

"Are you nervous for tomorrow?" she asked.

"Not really. I'm more excited than nervous."

"Me too." I imagined her blushing, moving a strand of hair behind her ear the way she usually does when she's embarrassed. It's cute.

"I love you, Lara. We should get some sleep."

"Okay…I love you too."

"I'll see you tomorrow. Good night."

"Wait…Piren?"

"Yeah?"

"I'm really glad it's you. I'm really glad you're my Partner."

"Me too."

After we hung up, I drifted back to sleep. Images of Lara looking dazzling in her dress pranced through my mind. But soon the happy thoughts became weird dreams.

In the dream, I leaned in to kiss my Partner at the Ceremony. I closed my eyes, but when I opened them again, it wasn't Lara beside me; it was Trace. Her eyes simultaneously held passion and reservation, reminiscent of our kiss three years ago. I pulled away but couldn't avert my gaze; my eyes saw nothing but hers.

My eyelids popped open seconds before my wailing morning alarm. The dream sucked the oxygen from my lungs.

Maybe Trace was my first kiss, but I can't think of it that way; the memories screw with my emotions. Lara is my Partner, and in six years, she'll be my wife. She's the one I love. My kiss with Trace was the kiss of a friend. She sought comfort that night, and she expressed it physically. End of story.

Lara wears a yellow sundress for the Ceremony. She runs up behind me and squeezes me in a hug.

"I love you, Lara Goodren."

"I love you, Piren Allston."

Her crooked tooth pokes from her mouth as she smiles. We take our assigned seats in the group of yawning high school seniors, still recovering from last night.

The Ceremony commences on time. A woman from the Assignment Lab takes the stage.

"Good morning, participants, and good morning, family and friends," she says into the microphone. "I'm so honored to be your Master of Ceremonies for this beautiful, momentous occasion. How lovely you all look, dressed and ready to begin down a road of physical intimacy. This is, unquestionably, a big step for all of you."

Beside me in the second row, Lara squeezes my hand.

The Master of Ceremonies rambles for fifteen minutes on the importance of cultivating our Partnered relationships and producing healthy kids. Several rows down, Alan's heavy eyelids flutter as he nods off. Toni pokes him in the side, and his head jerks up. She folds her arms back across her chest and doesn't meet her Partner's eyes. Following their argument, Alan ran outside after Toni and Trace, and none of them returned to prom. Lara and I had the fancy car all to ourselves on the ride home. Apparently, Toni is getting suspended for a week for dumping her drink on Travis, which turned out to be spiked. I feel bad for her—that sucks.

The Mayor joins the speaker on stage and starts calling couples. My last name puts us alphabetically fourth in line.

"Piren Allston and Lara Goodren."

We approach the Mayor on stage.

"What do you say?" he asks.

"I love you, Piren Allston."

"I love you, Lara Goodren."

"Good. Go on."

I freeze. Hundreds of spectator stares bear down on us. Cameras flash from all angles, blinding me. My hands quiver at my sides.

Who's supposed to make the first move? What if I miss? What if I look stupid? What if I'm really bad at it?

Lara teeters on her feet for a moment, then leans toward me. I close my eyes and take a deep breath.

Our lips touch, and the crowd disappears.

I could fly. Warmth spreads through my body, all the way down to my toes. My heart speeds ahead, and we soar above the stage. I'm lost in Lara's kiss.

After a few seconds, she pulls away. Cheers erupt from the crowd. A toothy smile spreads across my burning face, elevated to an invincible high.

I open my eyes to scan the audience. Cameras and joyful hollers unfurl at our milestone. Trace catches my eye, her hands entwined with Sam's in the crowd.

Inhale.

I'm plunged into our secret memory. Trace tumbles through my door on Christmas Eve. She's in my arms, shivering and soaked. She's kissing me, and my heart leaps in a way I've only felt once. The world is perfect.

Exhale.

I'm alone on stage with Lara.

In a flash, the memory evaporates, sucking the energy from my body.

Don't go.

But all the happy feelings die with it.

TRACY BAILEY

Our First Kiss was a joke. The Mayor called our names, and Sam practically salivated. I slogged up to the stage, still annoyed with my Partner for his clinginess at prom. Sam's eyes sparkled with a sickening hunger that made me nauseous.

Not wanting his tongue rammed down my throat, I showed him up; I pecked him quick on the mouth and pulled away before he could slip in his slimy appendage. The befuddled audience gaped, wide-eyed and open-mouthed — the world's largest frigging goldfish tank. The crowd broke into feeble applause. I cackled with delight inside as I marched back to my seat.

Ha! I showed them! Force me to kiss this lowlife? I'll give you a show you won't soon forget: not much of a show at all.

Sam drives me home from the Ceremony. He hasn't said a word since we left. Facing the window, I nibble off the remains of my chipping black nail polish.

"Why'd you do that?" he asks, a slight wobble in his voice.

I tighten. "Do what?"

"You didn't…kiss me."

"Yeah I did."

"You know what I mean." He twiddles his thumbs against the steering wheel.

I bite my lip. "Oh, uh…stage fright, I suppose. Sorry."

"Well, it hurt. I felt like you didn't…want to kiss me."

Well, that's the first smart thing he's said all day.

"That's not true at all." I force a smile.

But his fallen face bears a look of sheer defeat. Trampled. Crushed. His eyes glimmer with pain, and it wrecks me with guilt. My smile fades.

Nice going, Tracy.

He's stuck with a crappy Partner forever who won't kiss or touch him. Maybe he's not the best guy, but he's not the worst.

It isn't his fault I'm the way I am.

"Look, Sam, I…" I close my eyes. "Pull over the car."

He does. I take a deep breath.

And then I kiss him. On the side of the road. Full on, tongue in mouth.

You may delay,
but time will not.
❧*Benjamin Franklin*

TWENTY YEARS OLD
PART FOUR

PIREN ALLSTON

ara's a good cook. We have a routine where she cooks and I do the dishes. Evenly distributing housework was an early topic in our Marriage Prep class, and we exceled. I've heard most Partnerships face a major transition cohabitating after high school. For us, it's gone smooth.

Every day after our vocational classes, we come back to our apartment together. It's cozy, which I guess is another word for small. We have two bedrooms until we're married, a kitchen, a bathroom, a living room, and two closets.

Lara perches on one end of the couch, and I collapse on the other. She brandishes her knitting needles to work on her nightly project. I whip out my sketchbook and charcoal, and we sit together in silence. The muted television casts a bluish glow over the room. My Partner clears her throat. Her needles click together, funneling out a stretchy purple scarf.

"Looks good."

"Thanks." She sips a glass of pinot grigio.

After a few hours, Lara dismisses herself to bed, and I do the same.

I brush up against her at the bathroom sink. She shifts a few steps to make room for me. We brush our teeth simultaneously and take our separate rooms.

"I love you, Lara Goodren."

"I love you, Piren Allston."

"Good night."

"Good night."

TRACY BAILEY

I step out of my "Preparation, Accountability, and Organization" vocational classroom for the last time. After two years of post-high-school vocational classes, I'm free. My mind is fried from the excruciating four-hour final exam on the qualities of good employees. Five life-sucking essays. Sixty multiple-choice questions. My hand is still shaking; I wouldn't be surprised if the damn thing fell off my arm.

Toni jumps on me in the hallway. "Dinner party!" Her sing-song voice makes me cringe.

"What dinner party?"

"You, me, Alan, and Amanda. Downtown." She shakes my shoulders. "Class is done, time to party!"

I knock her hands off me. "I don't know. I'm not really in a partying mood. That exam sucked."

"All the more reason to celebrate. Come on, it'll be like old times."

Since high school graduation, I've avoided their company and vapid conversation. But I guess it'd be nice to do something besides studying, for the first time in forever.

I shrug. "Okay, sounds cool."

"Wheee!"

We choose an upscale diner downtown for our celebration. I've been there before with my parents. The food is mediocre, but the atmosphere is retro and awesome.

I slide into a sparkly, red booth beside Amanda. Alan and Toni take the other side. They whisper and flirt with each other behind a wall of their own hands.

"What'd you think of the exam?" Amanda asks.

I tear a chunk off a piece of bread. "It blew."

"Yeah, but do you think you did well, or—"

"I don't know. Can we talk about something else?"

Seriously. Mention the effing exam again, and I'll punch you in the face.

"Yeah, but what did you put for question five?"

Gritting my teeth, I look to Toni for help. She's sitting on Alan's lap, giggling. He kisses the nape of her neck, right there at the frigging dinner table. Toni rests her hands on her Partner's legs, crawling her fingers further up his thigh.

Oh, gross! Get a room!

"I don't know if I got question forty-four right either." Amanda wrings her hands in her lap. "I mean—"

The waiter arrives with my steaming soup. I practically scorch my mouth guzzling it down. Between Amanda's nervous rambling, and Alan and Toni's disgusting PDA, I need a distraction. Why not pain? It burns my throat, but I gulp it anyway.

"Where's Josh tonight?" I ask Amanda.

"Oh, he wasn't feeling great. He's got the stomach bug."

"That's too bad." I slurp another spoonful.

Damn you, Josh. You should share my burden of your Partner's frigging yammering.

"Question eleven, what did you put for question eleven? I mean, I answered B, but then I changed it. I know they tell you to go with your gut and pick your first choice…"

Alan and Toni have progressed to full on making out.

"…but I mean, that was such a hard question, and I just can't—"

I slam my hand on the table.

"Amanda, I have no fucking idea. I can't remember anything about that exam, and frankly, I don't want to."

Amanda falls silent. Toni detaches herself from Alan's lips.

Oops. I need a muzzle.

Cheeks burning, I shove another spoonful of French onion down the hatch.

"What's your problem?" Alan snaps.

"Nothing, sorry…Just tired."

Amanda fiddles with her fork, staring at her plate. She's sensitive, and I have no ability to deal with sensitive. I guess that makes me a horrible person.

Toni taps my arm. "*You okay?*" she mouths.

"*Help,*" I mouth back.

She takes the hint and grabs Amanda's hand. "So, how's your wedding planning going?"

I scarf my meal in silence. Amanda avoids my gaze, facing her body toward Toni and Alan. Two terse hours later, we pay our bill and leave. I'm guessing I won't be invited to future dinner parties.

I arrive home to a pitch-black apartment. I flick on the light.

"Sam?"

He perches in his armchair like a statue, feet planted firmly on the carpet.

Did he sit here in the dark for hours, waiting for me?

"Hi, Sa—"

"Where were you?" He leaps up and charges toward me.

"Excuse me?" I scoff. "Why the hell is that your business?"

"I asked you a question."

"So did I!"

"*Where were you?*"

"I was at dinner, for God's sake!" I throw my hands above my head.

"*With who?*"

"Oh my gosh, no one!" I shove past him. "People from school. Keep your voice down, quit bellowing like an animal."

"Don't turn your back on me, Tracy."

I rip open my bedroom door. "Good night, Sam."

He slams it shut with his fist, blocking my exit.

"Who. Were. You. With?" he seethes.

I don't know why he's pissed. I should be the one pissed that he's so pissed about something so effing menial.

"Alan, Toni, and Amanda. Okay? Can I go to bed now?"

He balls his fists at his sides, face inches from mine. "I was waiting for you for dinner."

"Well, maybe next time you can order in. Chill the fuck out."

"No. There won't be a next time." His voice is cold as ice. "'Cause I'll either be with you at a restaurant, or you'll be here, eating dinner with me. Got it?"

I cross my arms. "You don't tell me who to eat with, Sam."

"I am your Partner."

"Sure, whatever. I'm going to bed."

"I love you, Tracy Bailey."

I spin around. "Do you, Sam? Do you really love Tracy Bailey? 'Cause Tracy Bailey goes out sometimes, Tracy Bailey does things on her own sometimes, and you certainly don't love —"

He yanks my arm back and slaps me across the face.

I recoil with a sharp gasp. My mouth opens, but nothing comes out.

He steps back. "Tracy, I…I'm so sorry…I dunno what happened. I lost my tem —"

I hold up my hand, and he stops.

"I love you, Sam Macey. Good night."

PIREN ALLSTON

"Get the mail," Lara says. "They should be here today!"

I groan. "I don't want to see what they gave me."

"Oh, come on. Whatever you get won't be that bad."

My knee jitters against the table leg. "Did you even read the list of entry-level Placements when we ranked them? They all sucked. The only good job on that entire list was the Assignment Lab." I hold up my index finger. "One job. Out of two hundred."

She kisses my cheek. "Remember what they told us? If you hate what you get, you can go to college after the wedding. Do something else. Okay? It's not set in stone forever."

I clamp my hand over my bouncing leg. "Okay. Fine."

At twenty, we get our Job Placements. With weddings only four years away, making and saving money is crucial; they beat that into our brains during our Vocational classes. After waiting in agony for six months, today we'll learn where we'll work for the next four years.

The mailman delivers two thick envelopes to the Allston-Goodren apartment. Lara's is considerably thinner than mine.

"Why's yours so big?" she asks.

"I don't know."

Lara tears into her packet first. I hover behind as she skims her letter.

"I'm at Webster Printing Press, assembling rubber stamps. Could be worse." She tosses her packet back on the table.

Mindless assembly forty hours a week? That sounds dreadful.

"Cool."

"Open yours!"

I swallow, fiddling with the humongous envelope in my hands.

Her placement sucks. What the hell am I gonna be stuck doing?

I take a deep breath and rip it open, zipping my eyes across the page.

"No way."

Lara peers over my shoulder. "What? Show me."

"I'm at the Assignment Lab!"

"What! Gimme that." She rips the paper from my hands. "This is bullshit. That was my first choice Placement."

"Mine too." I beam. "And Alan's. And Travis's. And just about everyone's, I think."

Lara thrusts the sheet back at me. "So unfair."

"Sorry. I swear, there's only three positions there, I didn't think I'd actually get one." I paw through my packet. "Look, I get a T-shirt!"

I pull out a yellow shirt, proudly parading the "100% Accuracy!" logo, and hold it up to my chest.

Lara pouts. "I didn't get one."

"Sorry...Maybe they'll let you switch?"

"No they won't." She rolls her eyes. "Story of my life."

TRACY BAILEY

I sit beside Sam on the couch, six feet from the glowing TV. My restless hands fidget in my lap. I feel his eyes on me, but I keep mine fixed on the television.

He tiptoes his fingers across the desert of sofa between us. I squirm as he inches closer, crossing my legs to avoid his touch.

He brushes his hand under my chin. "Tracy?"

I keep my face forward. "Yeah?"

"Come here for a second."

"I'm watching something."

"Please?"

"Not n —"

He grabs my face and mashes his lips to mine. My body stiffens, and he jerks away.

"Something wrong?"

"No. Sorry." I force a smile. "Try again."

He kisses me again, twining his fingers in my hair. Queasiness bubbles in my stomach, and it's me who recoils this time, pushing my hand between us. He pulls back.

"Sorry." I dart my eyes to the carpet.

"What's wrong?" Sam hunches his shoulders. "You never wanna kiss me."

I tug at my sleeve. "I dunno. I don't think I like kissing."

It's gross, and weird, and makes me want to hurl.

"How can you not like kissing?"

"It's just...a strange behavior, I suppose."

"Is it me?" His eyes grow wide.

"No!" I bite my thumbnail. "I promise. It's me. I suck at being intimate."

He laces his fingers with mine and plants a kiss on my forehead. "Well, you'll just have to learn, then."

PIREN ALLSTON

Today's my first day of work, and I'm up and showered before my alarm. Hand tight around my spoon, I shovel cereal into my mouth, barely breathing between bites. Lara hobbles into the kitchen, grumbling. My cheeks ache from smiling. I'm probably an asshole for being so excited about my job around her, but I can't help it.

I arrive at the Lab twenty minutes early and stutter incoherently to the receptionist. She directs me to the Orientation Room, where I take a seat at a long table. Tucking my sketchbook under my bag, I spread out my folder of notebook paper and pens. I'm rereading the orientation packet for the twelfth time when the door creaks open.

My heart stops.

Trace enters the room.

Her hair is shorter, and she's gained some weight. She's wearing a tight gray skirt and pink button-down. She looks different; she looks the same. A sharp breath catches in my throat.

I haven't seen her in two years.

My knee bounces under the table.

The last time I saw Trace was high school graduation day. She yanked me into the janitor's closet and gave me a homemade card. I think we both assumed it was our last good-bye. After cohabitation, we knew Sam and Lara wouldn't make it easy to see each other. We wished each other the best, and she gave me a hug. It was a bittersweet farewell, and I haven't seen her since.

Two years and three months later, she's here. In the same damn room.

"Piren!" She throws her arms around me, curls bouncing around her face. My shoulders tense; the last the last time she displayed such unbridled enthusiasm, I had my first kiss.

She pulls back, blushing. "Hi, wow. Sorry."

"Hey, you...Long time no see."

She scratches the back of her neck, keeping her head down.

I guess two years apart can make anyone strangers.

"You're...at the Lab too?"

"Yeah...Pretty lucky, huh?"

"I'd say."

Our exchange is hollow, but I've missed her so much it doesn't matter.

We finish our orientation in two hours. Trace, me, and this girl Pernessa are the only three twenty-year-old Placements at the Lab. Our boss, Clarence, assigns Trace and me to sort questionnaire data from pregnant couples. He gives Pernessa a different task in another room. *We'll be alone.*

Our sorting room is small and cramped. Two chairs sit a foot apart, crowding a small faux-wooden table. Hundreds of packets and papers lie strewn across the surface, waiting to be sorted. Stacked boxes and clutter line the walls, allowing minimal space for movement. I have no doubt as to what happened: the Lab got stuck hosting Placements and allocated us their crappiest space.

"So, our room is a closet, then?" Trace asks. I nod, not meeting her eyes.

We awkwardly climb into our chairs. Our knees brush under the table; I jerk my leg away, heart racing through my chest like a freight train. For several minutes, we read over our respective folder stacks in silence. Trace taps a pen on the table as she scans her first packet. Every half-second, I sneak a sideways glimpse at her.

What does she think about this? Is she happy? Upset?

My shaking hands dampen around the sheet I'm holding. I force my eyes back to my paper and take a deep breath.

Focus.

We work diligently for several minutes.

Out of nowhere, Trace snorts. "You know what's weird?" She throws her pen down. "Everyone on the entire planet kept us apart. Forever. You know, when we were kids. Even in high school."

"Yeah, no kidding." *I mean, her family moved across town to separate us.*

"Seriously, the effort our parents and teachers took, you'd think separating us was their frigging second job. But then, here we are, out of hundreds of Placements, working together at the Lab. Just like that." She snaps her fingers. "Forced to work in a small room alone together, every effing day."

"Guess someone in charge of Placements didn't do their research, huh?"

"Guess not. Slacking on their stalking duties."

We share an awkward laugh.

Trace clears her throat, and we go back to our sorting. We check each folder three times for errors, then drop it into the box of clients ready for Assignment. The job is mindless work, and I'm fairly certain a chimp could do it.

Trace glances at me. I catch her, and she looks away.

She's so pretty.

Her hands are as pale and delicate as the night we shared cocoa in the snow. She's grown into her curvy adult figure, and her skirt hugs her hips. Brown curls dangle around her face, bouncing like coils when she moves.

It doesn't matter how much time passed; it's her. She was my best friend once; she can be my best friend again.

I open my mouth, then close it.

Just talk to her, damn it!

"So, what's your life like now?" I blurt out. "I mean, where do you guys live?"

She picks up another sheet. "We're at The Terrace. You know, those larger apartments on Winthrop Street?"

"Wow, jealous. Didn't our bus always drive by The Terrace?"

"Oh my gosh, yes! Remember we made up that story about those two Partnerships accidentally sharing the apartment?"

"Oh, man, I totally do…The bathroom fight story."

I meet her eyes, and we burst out laughing.

She's so beautiful when she laughs.

"And the Buckley twins. Remember how we wrote them in?"

Her eyes light up. "Plumbers' assistants. And they caused the leak."

"Captain, we have a leak."

"May day!"

We practically fall over the table, heaving for air at the memory of one of our favorite stories. Trace's cheeks flush red.

It's like no time passed. I guess that's the sign someone's meant to be your best friend.

We delve into retellings of our old stories, tripping over each other's sentences, each tale growing more unwieldy than the last. Piles of forgotten papers lay unsorted on the table.

The office door swings open. Our boss pops his head in, lips pressed in a thin line.

"Will you two pipe down already and do some work? We can hear you all the way down the hall."

"Sorry, sir."

"Sorry, sir."

"First day here and already causing me grief." He throws his hands in the air. "I told Kaylee not to hire Partners, nothing ever gets done." He slams the door. A couple stray sheets of paper drift to the ground.

Moment over.

I stare at the floor, heart pounding, not daring to look at her.

Why does every damn stranger assume Trace is my Partner?

Part of me wants to invent another phony wedding story, but it feels inappropriate now.

Trace hands me a questionnaire; I skim it and sort it into a pile.

She hands me another; same thing.

I go to grab another, but my hand brushes hers. She inhales a sharp breath. Something in my chest flutters. I yank my hand away.

This isn't working.

TRACY BAILEY

Veronica comes over to model her prom dress for me. I lay stomach-down on my bed for the show. After ten excruciating minutes, she emerges from the bathroom, decked in a slinky, pink gown.

"How do I look?" she asks, seductively rubbing her hands down her torso.

"Hot." I toss some pretzels in my mouth. "I'll have to beat Oliver off you with a stick."

She spins, showing off the low-cut back. "Good."

"Don't do anything illegal, V."

"Me?" She clasps her hands together. "Never."

"Sure, sure. Wait for your First Kiss, that's all."

My sister studies herself in my mirror. "Wish I had boobs like you." She grabs her chest. "I'm flat as a board."

I scoff. "Don't remind me. If I catch Sam eying my cleavage one more time, I'm gonna pop him in the mouth."

She giggles into her hand. "Really?"

"Yeah, it's bad. I pretend he has a lazy eye so his stares won't creep me out. It's like I talk to him, and he's drooling, staring at my rack."

"Ugh, that's…creepy."

"Tell me about it. I feel like a broken record, reminding him hands off until the wedding."

She leans against my bed. "He's gotten hot, though. Has he been working out?"

"Hot?" I snort out a derisive laugh. "Have you met the guy? He's a jackass."

"He's all muscly now." She flexes her wimpy bicep.

"Correction." I hold up my finger. "He's been lifting weights a lot. But it doesn't help his personality."

Veronica collapses onto the bed beside me. "Tell me honestly." Her lips twitch into a half-smile. "What's it like living with him?"

I roll onto my back. "Actually, not awful. He's tidy."

"Yeah?"

"And he's a good cook."

"That's good, 'cause you suck at cooking."

I munch another pretzel. "I'm just glad he finally has a hobby that doesn't involve blowing up shit on a screen."

"What does he cook?"

"I dunno, anything. He finds new recipes online. Why?"

Her cheeks grow rosy. "I want to learn how to cook for Ollie."

"Oh please." I draw the words out into a long-winded groan. "Should I put a little apron over that sexy dress of yours?"

She sticks out her tongue, whapping me in the stomach with my pillow. "Shut it." She stands up and starts peeling off her dress, exposing her hot pink undies. "You know I just want you to be happy with Sam. You're my big sis, and you're the only one I got."

"Yeah, yeah...Oh, hey, I picked this up for you." I rummage in my bedside drawer and find the dental school flyer I plucked from the Lab's bulletin board.

She takes the pamphlet and cocks her head. "What's this?"

"I know your wedding's still years away, so you won't be able to apply to college for a while, but you should really start looking now to narrow down your options."

"Oh, yeah. Thanks." Veronica bites her lip.

"Something wrong?"

"No." She glues her eyes to the mirror as she slides her shirt back on.

I pull myself up and stand beside her. "Come on, you can tell me. What's wrong?"

She shrugs. "Ollie and I talked about it. He wants to go to business school." She shimmies back into her skinny jeans, not meeting my eyes. "So, I'm probably just going to work for him. You know, take calls and stuff."

I take a deep breath. "V, Ollie's a big boy. He can take his own calls. If you want to go to school, you deserve to —"

"It's cool." Veronica shoots me a toothy smile only I would know is contrived. "I'm excited for it, actually. Working with Ollie every day will be awesome."

"Well, it's your choice. I just want you to be happy." I sink back to the bed just in time to see my sister brushing the pamphlet into the trash. A heavy weight drops in my chest. I guess this means the conversation is over.

"Really, Trace, I'm fine. You're too worried about me." She steals a spritz from my perfume.

"V, I love you. I'm always going to worry."

"I know." She flops onto the bed beside me. "So, how's work?"

Work. We're writing "The Working Chronicles of Fat Head and Fangs." Piren came up with the funniest story the other day...

I cough out a giggling snort and clap my hand over my mouth.

"What's so funny?" She crinkles her forehead.

"I dunno." I look away, but can't fight the smile off my face. "I just really like my job."

PIREN ALLSTON

"If I have to come in here one more time, you're both fired!" Clarence slams the door behind him. Trace and I snicker into our hands.

"How many times is he going to say that?"

"That was probably two hundred."

And as bad as it would be to get in the Shaming Pages and work a menial job until a new Placement opens, I highly doubt Clarence would actually fire us.

"You know—" Trace taps her cheek with her finger "—I think Clarence deserves a role of honor in our stories."

"How about—" I stroke my chin "—Boss Man: World's Greatest Super Villain."

"Killer of fun everywhere…Oh! I almost forgot. Speaking of fun-killers…" She rustles around in her bag and pulls out a plastic container. "Sam-Cookies make a triumphant return."

"Yes!"

She opens the Tupperware, revealing dozens of colorful sugar cookies shaped like zoo animals. My stomach growls as I grab a yellow-iced giraffe.

"Does he know you brought them?"

"Nope. Took them straight from under the nose of the original Killer of Fun himself." She nibbles an elephant trunk. "But I baked them, so they're ours by right. At least, that's my argument, and I'm sticking to it."

I take a bite. "You're the best baker in the world."

She bows in her chair. "Gracias."

Stuffing our faces, we break into our latest saga: Fat Head and Fangs versus the evil Boss Man. Every time we laugh, cookie crumbs shower the table.

TRACY BAILEY

The alarm rings, and I spring to life. I whistle in the shower as I scrub shampoo through my hair, dancing to a beat in my head. Rushing through my routine, I pull on my best work skirt and pink argyle blouse, patting out the wrinkles. I blot on pink lipstick and hot-iron my hair, then step back to examine myself in the mirror.

Sam appears in the hallway as I'm squirting on perfume.

"You look nice," he says through a yawn, eyes still blinking away sleep.

"Thanks."

"You straightened your hair today?"

"Oh, yeah."

He slouches against the wall. "How come the Lab gets to see you all done up and I don't? Wish you tried this hard to look nice for me."

I ignore him, pinning back a clump of strands with a pearly seashell clip.

Sam lumbers into the bathroom, grumbling about the early hour. I'm attempting to dab on mascara without impaling my eye, when... *THUD.*

I dash to the bathroom. My Partner lies in a heap on the floor.

"Fucking bath mat!" He punches the cabinet.

Choking down laughter, I force my best look of concern. "You... okay?"

"Go away." Hand on his ass, he stumbles to a snarling stance.

"Are you—"

"I said get the hell out!" He slams the bathroom door in my face.

What kind of idiot trips over his own effing feet?

Sam's clumsiness inspires a new story, bursting from my seams.

I need to tell Piren. This one's going in the anthology.

The entire car ride to work, I bounce in my seat, embellishing my tale to the perfect degree of hilarity. Practically falling into the doors of the Lab, my stomach aches with laughter as I maintain my composure.

"Hey, Trace." Piren plops his briefcase down on our table.

I take one look at him and explode, collapsing red-faced onto the table. By the time I get my story out, we're laughing so hard we're crying.

PIREN ALLSTON

Lara clanks her plate into the sink. "If this day was any longer, I'd shoot myself."

Here we go, our nightly complaint session.

"Oh, come on." I grab her dirty dishes and start scrubbing. "It's not that bad."

She collapses onto the chair with a huff. "That place is hellish. And all my clothes smell like rubber."

I dry my sudsy hands on a towel. "Stay positive."

"Stop telling me that." She draws her words out into long whines. "I hate my job, I hate the people there, and I hate rubber stamps."

"What about Taylor? Isn't that the coworker you like?"

Lara scoffs. "She's rude."

"Well, there must be something good about it."

"How would you know? You got the best job." She releases a deep moan. "It's not fair."

She hates this, she hates that...Forget Stephanie; my Partner is the damn Ice Queen.

I kneel beside her chair and stroke her hand. "I love you."

"Love you too." Her lips curl downward into a grimace. "But you know, you could be a little more supportive. You work ridiculously late hours, when I need you here."

I work late to avoid this BS!

I grit my teeth. "Sorry. I'll try to leave earlier."

"Promise?"

"Yeah."

"Good."

I force a smile. "It'll get better."

She scowls. "Please."

I wonder if Trace knows half the annoying characters in my stories are Lara.

Then again, I bet some of hers are Sam.

TRACY BAILEY

"Explain this." I drop a thick blue envelope onto our sorting table — addressed in gold lettering to "Ms. Tracy Bailey and Partner."

Please join us in celebrating
the marriage of
Mason Allston and Stephanie Butler

"What, you hate my brother now?"

"No, of course not. He's awesome." I shove Piren's arm. "But I gotta be honest; I didn't think I'd get invited."

"Why not?" He shoves me back. "Did you not grow up four houses down the street?"

Yeah, but your parents hate me.

"Plus," he continues, "I'm Best Man, and you're my best friend. So, clearly, you have to be there."

I grin. "Well, in that case, I wouldn't miss it for the world."

"I'm not going," Sam says, mashing his thumbs on his video game controller.

"What do you mean?" I narrow my eyes. "Why not?"

"Saturday's online multi-player day." His keeps a monotone as he blows the head off a robot.

"Are you kidding me right now? What are you, five?"

"Die, bitch! That's fuckin' right!" Another robot explodes.

I rip the controller from his hands.

"Screw you!" he snaps. "Give it back."

"God forbid you miss a few hours playing a stupid game with a bunch of online idiots you've never even frigging met."

He pounces, tearing his toy from my grasp. "Shut up." He collapses back on the couch, resuming the robot massacre.

I groan. "Come on, going to a wedding alone is pathetic. I don't want to be that one person without a date."

"Then don't go...Die, mother fucker! Grenade to the throat!"

"Ugh!" I throw my hands up and storm from the room.

The day of the event, I try again. I fling open my Partner's bedroom door. It's one in the afternoon, and he's wrapped like a burrito in his bed sheets.

"You coming to the wedding?"

He grunts and rolls over.

"Hey!" I pound my hand on the wall. "Sam!"

He pulls the covers over his head.

"Fine. I'll go alone. See you later."

Everyone can gawk in awe of Tracy Bailey, the grown woman Partnered to a twelve-year-old. Maybe I hate formal events, but I love Piren's family. I'll happily be another notch in their guest-count belt.

Weddings are gaudy events, flaunting over-the-top explosions of wealth and tactless décor. Usually, my parents drag me to garish venues that make me gag. However, Mason's Ceremony venue is, dare I say, lovely.

I push through majestic wooden doors and find myself in a jungle oasis. It's an indoor tropical garden, magically transformed into a grand wedding foyer. Dozens of leafy, flowering plants line the ceiling. Dangling vines drip from the wooden rafters. A waterfall fountain flows behind the Ceremony alter, creating the auditory illusion of a rainforest. Warm dew fills the air, moistening my skin. If I close my eyes, I can almost hear tropical birds screeching. Plenty of potential for Fangs to have adventures in here.

I sit in a pew with my parents, just in time to hear Mom talking off some poor woman's ear about how the wooden rafters make the place look like a "square-dance pit." The orchestra strums to life, thankfully saving me from this conversation.

Stephanie floats down the aisle in a flowing, ivory ball gown. White feathers woven into her espresso-brown hair, she resembles a glamorous bird, suiting the rain-forest theme. Everyone rises as the stunning bride proceeds, glowing with radiance. Mason Allston waits at the end, mouth slightly parted, dark hair combed to one side. Stephanie reaches her groom at the altar, and they join hands.

The Ceremony commences, and my gaze drifts to my best friend. Perched beside Mason, Piren stands up front like a good Best Man. His black tux elongates his already tall physique. I remember when we were the same height, long ago. Now he towers over me. He's no longer a lanky teenager; his broad shoulders frame a perfect triangle over his slim waist. Although his long-sleeved buttoned shirt won't let on, his arms are nicely sculpted; I've noticed when we sort papers. I can't remember the last time his hair was this tidy. Part of me wants to run my fingers through it and make it messy again. The cute little jittery boy who used to race me to the treehouse is now a dashing, grown man — who'd still probably race me to the treehouse.

Mason turns to his Best Man, a slight tremor in his hand. Piren nods and flashes a reassuring smile, passing the ring box to his brother.

Parading happiness on cue, I wonder how Piren's feeling today. He's always found Stephanie kind of a pain, and now she's family! I've never personally met Mason's Partner, but from what Piren's told me, I'm better off. When Piren and Lara get married, Stephanie and Lara can battle for the title of Allston Ice Queen.

My chest tightens.

The short Ceremony wraps with the exchanging of vows, and the ritual "I love you's" with the bride's new last name.

"I love you, Mason Allston."

"I love you, Stephanie Allston."

The perfect Partnership seals their union with a kiss. Four hundred guests politely clap their approval. Here come Mason and Stephanie Allston, joined together forever, just like those mystical puzzle pieces Mrs. Prew yapped about.

I wonder what would happen if I married Sam, but kept my name Tracy Bailey. Maybe I could hyphenate, call myself Tracy Bailey-Macey. It would throw off the whole effing ceremony. I bet nobody would even clap. I can picture our astonished wedding guests, mouths gaping wide like a bunch of stunned trout. Maybe I'd shock some old codgers to death.

My parents and I follow the sea of guests into the next room for the reception.

The Allston and Butler families spared no expense. Like the Ceremony hall, the Reception hall is gorgeous. High wooden ceilings drape over us, adorned with tiny pink and purple lanterns. The tiny lanterns weave around large, black lanterns speckled with white flowers, complementing the jungle Ceremony hall. Dozens of round tables covered in pink satin line the room, surrounding a diamond-shaped dance floor in the center. Glitter-coated white rose petals dapple the tabletops, decorating sets of sparkling white china. Rotating spotlights shine from the floor, illuminating the ballroom in a pink glow.

I find my place card at a table with my parents and people from our old neighborhood. Veronica declined the invite, which is fine by me; I don't need her near an open bar.

The deejay strikes up a romantic melody, and the happy couple glides onto the dance floor. Stephanie twirls like a ballerina, rotating under the arm of her dapper husband.

One by one, wedding guests join the happy couple. Piren and Lara laugh as they spin each other around the ballroom. In their endless quest to humiliate me, my parents also attempt to dance, breaking into a severely outdated routine that leaves me shielding my face. I violently swirl my straw through my soda, clinking ice around the glass. Since Sam isn't here, I'm stuck at the frigging table like an idiot. I could bust a few moves by myself, but I doubt anyone would appreciate that. Piren might.

My elderly former neighbor, Mrs. Riley, is my only companion at our abandoned table. Mrs. Riley's husband passed a few years ago from a heart attack, stranding her dateless today too. She's got her gray hair pulled up in a beehive bun; it quivers slightly when she moves, as if actually housing a nest of bees.

She smiles at me through cherry lipstick. "What a beautiful wedding."

I nod, mesmerized by the dancers.

"I remember my wedding like it was yesterday," she continues. "Music was different then. But the colors and dresses were the same."

"Oh, yeah? I bet it was something, Mrs. Riley."

She clasps her hands together. "What about you, dear? When are you marrying Sam?"

"Oh, I'm only twenty-one." I squirm in my chair. "Three more years."

"Better start planning soon, though." She winks, sipping a flute of champagne.

Yes, wedding planning is at the forefront of my one-track mind. Not.

She reaches across the table and squeezes my arm. "Three years'll fly by, and before you know it, we'll be in a room like this one, celebrating *your* special day."

"Yep." The word feels like a rock dropping into my stomach.

My life is a ticking time-bomb.

Mason dips Stephanie on the dance floor. They float together like a pair of graceful swans. I blur my eyes; the glowing bride morphs into an image of me, draped in white, empty-eyed and spinning on a rotating platform, as if prisoner inside a music box. Mason becomes Sam, suited and stoic, hands on his bride. Puppets on strings, my Partner and I twirl around the dance floor like marionettes, stepping a carefully plotted and perfectly choreographed routine.

I've been committed to Sam fifteen years and lived with him for three, but he might as well be a stranger. Yet there we'll be, three years from now, stars in our own wedding.

"Aren't they lovely?" Mrs. Riley says, watching the couples.

I snap from my daze.

"Oh, the bride and groom? Yeah, they look great together."

She squints at the dance floor. "Well, them, of course, but also the younger brother, the smaller Allston boy, Piren." She tilts her head to the side. "What's his Partner's name? She's lovely."

I swallow hard.

"Lara Goodren."

"Yes, Lara...Well, they're just perfect together."

"Yeah—" my voice cracks "—they are."

My words rip through me as I speak.

What the hell is wrong with me?

As the night progresses, people gradually filter out. Clutching her belly after devouring the steak dinner, Mrs. Riley squeezes my shoulder as she exits the party. In his usual form, Dad is perched at the open bar, butt cemented to a stool. Whatever the Allston-Butler booze tab totals, they can probably thank my father for half.

Mom trolls around the guests, instigating petty small talk with the other socialites. Even from across the room, I spy her exaggerated gasps and phony hand gestures; the usual signs she's fishing for gossip.

Well-dressed Partnerships drift past my lonely table. My legs grow stiff from sitting still.

"Hey, look at the groom," someone shouts. The crowd claps with delight, circling the dance floor.

Standing on my tiptoes, I peer over a dozen heads to watch the spectacle. Mason gyrates in some sort of drunken break-dancing routine in the center of the room, surrounded by amused guests. The deejay flares up a flashing strobe, spotlighting the groom's bizarre moves. I cup my hands to my mouth and cheer, pushing forward for a better view.

Stephanie sulks by the deejay's booth, staring daggers at her husband, radiant smile replaced with a sullen scowl. White feathers drooping in her hair, she presses her hands over her ears.

"Mason!" Stephanie's mouth clearly shouts her Partner's name, but her voice falls silent to the blaring speaker beside her. "Hey!"

I roll my eyes. *Fuck the Ice Queen, Mason. Enjoy your day!*

Shoving to the front of the masses, I join the clapping hordes. Everyone in the rotunda laughs and cheers at the groom's silly dance.

After about five minutes, Stephanie tugs her husband off the stage by his sleeve. Guests dissipate back to their tables. My eyes drift to the corner of the ballroom. Piren and Lara stand off to the side, facing each other. Piren's leg shakes violently beneath him.

He only does that when he's nervous. What the hell did she do to him?

Hands on her hips, Lara glares at him, pigtails dangling around her stone-cold face.

She looks like a nine-year-old.

Hours ago, Mrs. Riley called this brat "lovely." Old bat. What does she know? Hissing like an effing cat, Lara's the antithesis of lovely right now. Veronica looks more mature when she's half-plastered. I sidle over to the cheese and crackers table for a closer view.

Lara thrashes her hands out, pointing around the room as they bicker. Piren retorts, but as he speaks, his Partner gestures her arms back in his face. Whatever he's saying, it's not placating her.

Damn it, I wish I could hear what they're saying…

I meander down the snack table, ears perked, inching closer to the couple. Reaching for a slab of cheddar, I knock a fork to the floor with a clang.

Clumsy idiot!

Lara and Piren glance at me, and I quickly scrub my hand down the back of my neck, keeping my eyes dead-set on the floral centerpiece. A rap song blasts through the speakers, and guests flock back to the dance floor.

Lara stomps off, slamming into Mason's brooding new bride.

My, what a crowd of ladies we have tonight.

Head down, Piren kicks an empty soda bottle along the wall. My shoulders droop.

Why does she have to bring him down like that?

I bite my lip and linger for a moment, but end up walking back to my table. I haven't talked to Piren yet today, and I don't want the first thing I say to him to be, "So, how was your fight with Lara?"

I take my seat with a replenished plate of hors d'oeuvres. Sure enough, Piren plops down beside me.

"Hey, you."

"Hey, stranger." I spread some cheese on a cracker. "Tell your folks this party rocks. Great food."

"Dude, didn't you just eat an enormous filet? I'm stuffed. How are you still eating?"

"Shut up. I'm just grazing," I mumble through my mouthful. "And I've yet to see cake, so I gotta take what I can get."

"Steph said no cake. She's on some weird diet."

"Lame."

"Totally lame." He leans his elbow on the table. "You try the quiche?"

"Stuffed my face with it earlier." I slide another cracker into my mouth. "Big old fangs sunk right in."

"I see you've also managed to find the cheese platter."

"Indeed."

He swipes a piece off my cheddar tower. I hiss at him.

"Hands off the goods, Fat Head."

Piren grins, but his smile fades. He picks at the end of his black tie. "Lara's upset with me."

"Oh?"

I wasn't spying, not me.

He shrugs. "I felt bad. Saw you sitting here, all alone, so I suggested I ask you to dance. You know, a fast song, nothing slow." He wrings his hands in his lap. "Just wanted to be a good host."

The fight was about me?

I keep my eyes down. "So…what happened?"

"Lara said no. That's it. No discussion. Said it was 'inappropriate.'" He steals a cracker, shaking his head. "So, I told her, at our wedding, I don't want guests stuck sitting at the damn tables all night. She got all angry and stormed off."

I snort. "Bit of an overreaction."

"Was it?"

"Yeah, I mean, my baby cousin handles things better than her, apparently."

"Was she right, though?"

"I dunno. I'm here, alone, no Sam, and you don't hear me bitching about it. Guess she couldn't unlock the old ball-and-chain for a five minute dance, huh?"

He raises his brows.

Oops. Perhaps I overstepped a line.

"You don't go anywhere with Sam, though."

"That's not true. I went out for dinner with him last week."

"What'd you get?"

"Pizza."

He shoves my arm. "That doesn't count!"

"Still dinner." I shove him back. "Anyway, would you look at this jungle?" I stretch my hands up toward the decorative ceiling. "Looks like a fine place for an adventure."

"You know, if this were a jungle," he says, "I think I know who'd be the big bad lion preying on all the innocent antelopes."

"The Boss Man?"

"The one and only."

Another story commences, and within minutes we're rolling in laughter. It's like work at the Lab, except I'm in a dress and there's no paperwork to sort. I wish I could say no one breathes down our necks, but I can almost feel my mother's disapproving stare from across the room.

PIREN ALLSTON

Lara hasn't spoken a word since we left the wedding. Her silence is louder than shouting. It's also twice as deadly.

I drum my fingers on the steering wheel. "So…my brother's a pretty good dancer, huh?"

"Mmm."

"Can't believe he's married. Steph and him look good together."

Silence.

"You looked great too." I reach across the console and squeeze her shoulder.

"Sure." She keeps her arms tight at her sides, facing the window in the passenger seat.

I pull over to the side of the road and ram the gear in park.

"Okay, what is this?" I rest my elbow on the wheel and pinch my forehead. "We're having fun, I ask for one dance with an old friend, and now you won't talk. What do you want from me?"

She rotates toward me. "Would you spend more time with me if I gave myself a stupid nickname? Wrote dumb made-up stories about phony adventures?"

My mouth opens, then closes again.

"Or maybe if I'd been mean to Mrs. Henkel when we were kids, I could have been the one doing the show on stage for everyone. Gone to Under Five instead of the bowling alley in middle school. Been all those things you wanted then. Then you'd want me now."

"Lara, what are you talking about?"

"I'm sorry, okay? I'm sorry I'm not that person—that perfect, preppy, laughing-all-the-time, sexy girl you want. I get it, okay? I'm not her."

"What? I love you; I love the person you are."

She grits her teeth. "It's her. Tracy Bailey."

"What about her?"

"You spend more time with her than you spend with me."

"That's not true."

Her brows lower. "At the Lab. At your own brother's wedding. Heck, sometimes I think you work late just to see more Tracy Bailey."

"Stop! That's stupid. You're my Partner." I point to her chest. "You. Not her. You and I are planning our wedding."

"Is that what you want?"

"What?" I reach for her hand, but she yanks it away.

"What if I wasn't your Partner? What if there were no Assignments? What if you had to choose who to marry, like the old days?"

"That's ridiculous. You know that doesn't—"

"Would you pick me?" Her glassy eyes meet mine. "'Cause sometimes I think you wish you were Assigned to her."

I blink. "Lara, that's—"

"Answer the question. If there were no Assignments. Would you still pick me?"

"Of course."

She twists back toward the window, inconspicuously wiping a stray tear from her left eye. My foot jitters on the gas pedal.

Given a choice, would I have picked Lara?

I don't have an answer.

TRACY BAILEY

I pull into The Terrace. My phone vibrates for the zillionth time since I left the wedding. Sixteen missed calls: Mom. I clench the phone in my hand and press my forehead to the steering wheel. My thumb hovers over the redial button for a moment, but I drop the device back into my purse instead.

I take a deep breath and unlock the front door. Sam grabs my arm and yanks me through the threshold. I stumble, steadying myself against the wall.

"I love—"

"Alex Jones said you were hanging on Piren Allston all night."

I rub my arm. "I wasn't 'hanging,' thanks."

"Why do you do this to me?"

"Do *what?*" I flail my hands out. "Hang out with my friend?"

"You make me look like a fool."

"That's not hard."

"Shut up!" He swings his fist, barreling it into the drywall.

"Nice going." I run my finger over the dent. "I'm not explaining to the landlord why this shit is here. And I was not *hanging* on him!"

"Well you were super friendly with him, that's for sure."

"What?" I get up in Sam's face. "Should I have ignored him? At his own brother's wedding? Which, by the way, you *chose* not to attend."

"Shut up!" He balls his fists at his sides, face flushing red. "I'm sick of competing with him for your attention." He whirls around and stomps down the hall. "Done. So done."

I throw my arms up. "I'm *so done* with your temper!"

He slams his bedroom door.

Piren Allston: the one surefire topic to force Sam and me to talk.

PIREN ALLSTON

I tiptoe out of the apartment before Lara's even awake. Her rumbling snores in the next room had me cringing into my pillow all damn night.

I arrive at work two hours early and beat Clarence to the office. I don't care; I just needed to be out of that damn apartment. I can't take another second with her.

Grumbling to myself, I slide into my seat to tackle a stack of to-be-sorted packets. The early-morning janitor runs a growling vacuum in the hall behind me; the noise makes me flinch.

Will someone shut that damn thing off?

My head collapses into my arms. I clench fistfuls of hair in my sweaty hands.

Eight a.m. and this day already blows.

Prying the lidded curtains from my bloodshot eyes, I slug steaming coffee from a Styrofoam cup. It scorches my throat all the way down the pipe. I pick up a packet and wait for the caffeine to seep through my veins.

Folder one: *Parents: Marianne and Roger Corliss. Child: African-American Male. Second trimester. No complications. Parents' blood type: O-positive. Family History of Diabetes.*

I tighten my grip, crinkling the pages.

Sorry, kid.

I slap the packet into the *Ready for Assigning* pile.

By nine a.m., sharp clicks start sounding from the employee time-clock in the hall. Sorted packets lie scattered in stacks in front of me. The diminished to-be-sorted pile lies in a small heap at the other end of the table.

Trace walks in as I'm slamming the final papers into their piles. I mumble out a greeting.

"Whoa, there. Easy, killer." Her mouth curls into a grin. "I have a present for you."

I blink my overtired eyes. "What? Why?"

"I found it. And it made me think of you."

She tosses something at me, and I catch it midair. It's a rubber toy shaped like a plump man with bulging green eyes.

"Squeeze it." She bounces on her toes. "Squeeze the body!"

I wrap my hand around its rubbery mass and squeeze. The head engorges, popping the eyes out with a squeak.

Trace claps with delight. "It was made for you, Fat Head."

I couldn't stop the smile if I wanted to.

Bad day cured.

TRACY BAILEY

I rush home from work and dump my bags on the floor.

Five fifteen sharp. He can't balk at that.

Draping my coat over a hanger, I peek into the living room. Sam stoops over the coffee table, surrounded by slabs of wood and various tools. A kitchen chair lies upside down on the rug, prepped for surgery. Ah, yes, one of my Partner's many household projects. Sam squints, twisting a screwdriver into the chair's splintery underbelly. I clear my throat, and he jerks up.

"I love you, Sam Macey."

"I love you, Tracy Bailey."

"Whatcha makin'?" I crouch down beside him.

He grunts, returning his focus to the tools. "Trying to fix this damn wobbling chair."

I rock on my heels, shifting my weight back and forth. "So, how was work?"

"Fine." He tightens the bolt, tongue clasped in his teeth in concentration.

I grab a wooden piece and rotate it in my fingers. "Anything… fun at the office?"

"No." He rips the wood from my hands and tosses it back into the pile. "We don't all get to goof around the Lab all day. Some of us have real jobs."

Oh, like mopping piss off the floor at the doctor's office?

"Right."

He still hasn't gotten over the fact that *I* got *his* first choice Placement.

I squat in silence while he screws and tightens various knobs and pieces. I'm not sure he knows what the hell he's doing. What's with the random pieces of wood to fix a damn chair? And since when does a wobbly leg require a hammer? But that doesn't stop him. He doesn't give me another glance.

"Okay—" I stand, brushing a stray wood shaving off my leg "—I'm gonna go."

"There's something for you on the table. My mom dropped it off."

I swing into the kitchen to find a thick pink book waiting for me.

Ten Thousand Baby Names.

My stomach drops.

"I highlighted my favorite ones," Sam calls from the living room.

I pinch the book between my thumb and forefinger, holding it two feet from my body as I trudge back to the other room.

"You know we're like, four years from needing this, right?"

He drops his screwdriver into the toolbox with a clang. "Yeah, but I wanna start trying immediately, on our wedding night. I wanna be prepared."

My teeth clench so tight they might shatter. "Don't you think it's a little soon?"

"Nope." He grabs his hammer, haphazardly positioning a nail over the chair leg.

"But—"

He starts hammering, driving the nail into the wood with four hard whacks and drowning out any further conversation.

I scurry back to the kitchen and open the first page to find a yellow sticky note:

I prefer Dominique for a girl and Rafael for a boy.

Let's discuss. Xoxo - Mrs. Cassandra Macey

The book falls onto the table with a thud. Hands up, I back away slowly.

PIREN ALLSTON

I lie on the couch, immersed in my drawing. Lara hovers nearby.

"I think we should start a new tradition," she says, pressing her fingers to her mouth in concentration.

I flip to a clean page in my sketchbook and trace a charcoal circle. "Like what?"

"I was thinking…game nights. Like, we can invite other couples over, hold board game competitions, what do you think?"

"Oh, uh…sure, I guess."

She leans over me and pushes my open book down onto my chest. "We need to be more social. I love you, but seriously."

She kisses my cheek, then sinks down into the armchair. Black charcoal marks now dapple my white button-down.

I release a deep breath. "Okay. When do you want to do it?"

She flips through her cellphone calendar. "How about Tuesday night?"

"Okay."

She frowns. "Why aren't you more excited about this?"

"I am! It's just, board games aren't really my thing."

Her frown melts into a scowl. "I'm listening for better ideas."

"It's fine. Board games it is."

"Who should we invite?"

"Oh, um, I don't know." I drag my charcoal in a straight line down the center of the circle. "Who do you want to invite?"

Somehow I'm guessing "Trace and Sam" isn't an acceptable answer.

"I was thinking Toni Henders and Alan Carrey."

"Sure."

"But you've got to invite them."

My head falls back to the couch cushion. "Why me?" The words come out whinier than intended. "It's your idea."

"Oh, come on." She rises from the chair. "I hardly know them. Just call and invite them. Tuesday at seven. I'll buy wine and snacks."

I rub my forehead. "Fine."

I sit in a circle with Lara, Alan, and Toni. Alan drapes himself over his Partner like a throw rug. Toni absentmindedly twirls a finger through her hair, thumbing over her cellphone.

Lara bounces with delight as she arranges Monopoly pieces on the board.

"You're up!" She tosses Toni the dice. Eyes on her phone screen, Toni fumbles, and the cubes fall to the floor. Lara scrambles to retrieve them. "Here you go."

Twenty minutes in, I'm pretty sure everyone except Lara is bored.

Toni's thumbs click across her cellphone keys; every few seconds, her phone glows and buzzes with a new message. Alan's droopy eyes focus directly on Toni's chest. Each time she looks up, he pretends to scratch his head and gaze at the ceiling. I carefully observe the duo for new story fodder.

Lara stares intently at the game.

"Ooh, Alan!" She claps her hands together. "You can buy Atlantic Ave. Damn it, I wanted that one. I'm totally getting Marvin Gardens before you, though." She plops her terrier piece across the board. "Ha!"

"You got drinks?" Alan asks, through a moaning yawn.

"Um, yeah…Hang on." I start to stand, but Lara bounds up and dashes to the kitchen before I can move.

Alan arches his brows at me. I fidget my game piece in my hands.

My Partner returns with two full glasses and hands them to our friends.

"Some vino for our guests." She pats me on the head. "Piren, honey, would you mind taking your turn? You've got to pay attention to these things." She ruffles my hair.

"Sure." My ears burn.

Alan slugs his white wine in two gulps, then nuzzles into Toni's neck. She giggles and squirms away, her own wine threatening to spill over her glass onto our carpet.

Lara tugs my sweatshirt hood hanging down my back. "You could have offered them something when they arrived," she hisses in my ear.

This is your game night, not mine.

"Sorry."

She pats my hand. "It's okay, just remember for next time."

"Whose turn is it?" I ask.

"Oh my gosh, I knew it." Lara huffs. "You weren't even paying attention."

Toni rubs her upper arm, keeping her eyes on the floor. Alan pointedly focuses on the wall.

"Ugh...Piren." Lara shakes her head. "What am I supposed to do with you?"

What did I do?

I grit my teeth. "Can I talk to you in the kitchen, Lara?"

She nods and puts on a smile. "Stay put, folks. We'll be right back."

Lara follows me into the kitchen. She releases a lofty sigh. "What?"

"Why'd you snap at me?"

"Why? 'Cause you made me look like a horrible hostess. And besides, they're *your* friends, not mine."

"You invited them."

"*You* invited them."

"'Cause *you* made me!"

"Well, I want us to have friends! We need to do *something* social. It's like you don't even care."

"Well, sorry!" I throw my hands up. "Sometimes when I get home, I just want to relax."

"Yeah? Tired from all that work you do with Tracy Bailey?"

My arms clap back down at my sides. "Why do you always have to bring her into this?"

"You spend more time with her than you spend with me."

"Will you stop?"

"You do! I'm so damn fed up! She gets your attention and sends you home to me exhausted!"

"But—"

"You always have another excuse to spend time with her, and I can't even get five minutes with—"

"—Come on, Trace, I—"

Shit.

I catch my blunder mid-sentence, but it's too late. Lara's stung expression speaks louder than any of her harsh words.

"Lara…"

She tears from the kitchen and back to the living room. I fall over my feet trying to catch up.

"Well, I hope you two had a lovely—"

We stop in our tracks. Alan and Toni are gone.

"Do you think they heard us fighting?" Lara whispers.

I run my hands through my hair. "I think the whole block heard us."

TRACY BAILEY

"Congratulations." Clarence pokes his head into our office. "You survived a whole year here without driving me to insanity. Come to the break room at lunch for cake…That's an order." He gives us a wink before leaving us alone to sort.

I suppose our boss deserves a medal for tolerating our antics all year and not firing us after our thousandth warning.

"A whole year, huh?" I pass Piren some papers.

"Crazy."

"So, what do you think?" I thumb through a stack. "Work at the Lab all you hoped and dreamed it would be when you filled out that Placement thing?"

"Oh, so much more. After all, where would —" he squints at the sheet in his hands "—little Kimberly Arsenal be without my genius sorting?"

I shove his arm. "Better off, that's where."

He sticks out his tongue at me, and I return the gesture.

We gather in the break room at lunch for the celebration. Pernessa, the Placement Third Wheel, slouches on a seat in the corner, texting.

"*100% Accuracy!*" adorns our cake in puffy orange icing.

"You'd think they'd put *our* names on it." Piren jabs his finger into the frosting. "'Cause, you know, this party *is* to celebrate us, right?"

"You'd think. But you're not Boss Man."

About twenty other Assignment Lab employees crowd around the small table. Clearly, they came for the free food; I don't think any of them know Piren, Pernessa, or me by name. I recognize a beady-eyed man who referred to me as "Trudy" the other day.

"Cake?" Piren slices into the dessert. "It's your favorite color."

He rotates the plate, revealing the cake's spongy purple innards.

I stab my fork into it. "My favorite."

We demolish our dessert and settle back at our station for another afternoon of hard work.

By the time seven o'clock rolls around, spotlights from streetlamps dapple the dark parking lot. We volunteered to stay an extra couple hours to wrap up the day, but we probably owe about four hundred extra hours for all our time spent screwing around.

The bitter wind bites our faces as we exit the Lab. As always, Piren parked beside me—we like to say our cars are best friends too. However, they're quite the mismatched pair; his sleek sports car overshadows the rusting lump I lovingly refer to as "The Shitmobile." Our two cars sit alone in a pavement desert. At this late hour, the parking lot is practically empty. Aside from our cars, the only other vehicular residents are Clarence's beat-up station wagon and another car isolated in the furthest dark corner of the lot.

"Kinda creepy this late, huh?" he asks.

"Yeah, The Shitmobile's pretty menacing in the dark."

He smirks. "You wish."

"I do indeed."

We say good night and climb into our cars.

I rub my numb hands together to fight the frigid winter air and ram the key into the ignition.

Cla-cla-cla-cla…

Unamused by the cold, The Shitmobile grumbles and struggles, but doesn't roar to life.

"Are you frigging kidding me?" Shivers rattle through my body. "Come on…"

Stubborn as hell, it revs and moans. My teeth chatter as I curse the car in my head for not starting—or heating.

"Come *on!*" I slap the steering wheel. "Really?"

"*Eh-eh-eh-eh,*" The Shitmobile responds, emitting freakish grunts from its engine.

"Ugh." I slam the back of my head against my seat in frustration.

What the hell do I do now? Wait for Clarence or whoever owns that creepy car in the corner to come outside? Great.

My breath clouds against the rearview mirror.

I jump as Piren taps my car window, tottering back and forth on his feet. I crank the window down a crack.

"Hey, stranger," he says. "Mighty chilly out, need a lift?"

I bat my eyelashes. "Oh, happy day! A strange man has come to rescue me."

"Did The Shitmobile finally die?"

"No." I sigh, patting the dashboard like it's a dog. "Just seriously ill."

He sticks his head in the window. "This thing is ancient. Probably can't handle the cold."

"Hey now!" I press my hand over my heart. "The Shitmobile doesn't appreciate being insulted."

"You can ask it how it felt to transport dinosaurs back in its childhood."

"You know, you're opening your mouth, and all this bullshit keeps pouring out."

"Yeah, yeah. Well, it's probably too late to tow it." He hops up and down on his toes, rubbing his gloved hands together. "Am I driving you home, or are you going to sit there and mope all night?"

"Mope. Definitely."

"Nope. Out." He opens my car door, pointing to his car in the next spot. "Get in the car, punk."

"You kidnapping me?"

He gives me a sideways smile. "Yep. You and your big fangs."

I click my keys from the obstinate ignition. "Good."

We slide into the cushy leather seats of his snazzy car, and I crank up the heat dial.

"What are you, a lizard?" he says. "It's like ten thousand degrees in here."

"Shut up. It's nice in here." I hover my face by the dash's vent, basking in the wafting warmth.

"Well, if you want to make it home in one piece, turn that inferno down before I fall asleep at the wheel."

Piren's car smells like Piren. I inhale, breathing in the aroma of coffee and cinnamon mingled with the smoky scent of leather.

"The Shitmobile finally ready to be laid to rest?" he asks.

"No way. I can resurrect it. There's another year of life there, I swear."

"Didn't you say that about a year ago?"

"Unimportant."

His car rumbles as he puts it in gear; the cold is no match for a spiffy engine.

"This could be an awesome story," he says. "A helpful stranger, a damsel in distress?"

"One chilly, chilly night."

"A stubborn car that eats its victims alive."

He meets my gaze, and I crack up. "This one's a keeper. I foresee it being our best story yet."

We pull out of the parking lot. We're about to turn, when Piren slams on the brakes, lurching me forward. The seatbelt digs into my stomach, knocking the air from my lungs.

"Geez, watch it!"

He spins toward me in his seat, eyes glimmering with excitement. "You know what would be crazy?"

I rub my seatbelt-sliced midsection. "Not dying in a fiery car wreck?"

"Remember that time we took that wrong bus after school?" He practically bounces in his seat. "There was that old lady?"

"Of course. One of Fat Head and Fangs' proudest moments."

"We got cocoa at that café? And it was snowing and cold, like tonight?"

"Yeah." I inconspicuously raise the heat two notches. "You almost froze your balls off."

"Wanna go back to that café? See if it's still there?"

My heart jumps.

Sam will flip if I'm late. I bite my lip. *I'll need to rehearse a good excuse.*

A devious smile stretches across my face. "Let's do it."

Piren grins and slams the gas.

"Whoosh!" I thrust my hand forward. "Superhero car."

"You're so weird."

"Oh yeah? You're my best friend. What's that say about you?"

We drive for over an hour, making turn after turn into the maze of the outer edges of town. Piren cannot for the life of him find the street that will lead us back to the café. I don't even know if we're going the right direction, but my ribs ache from laughing.

"Some chauffeur you are," I say after Piren's sixteenth illegal U-turn.

"Oh, Ms. Bailey? You think you could do better?"

"I think anyone could do better. Your brother could do better, and he's the worst driver I've ever seen."

"Comparing me to Mason." He clicks his tongue. "That's low. Should we just follow the bus route?"

"I don't know how to find the frigging bus route."

"Can you check your phone?"

And deal with Sam's texts surely piling up? Nope.

"Nope, too lazy, and I don't want the battery to die."

"Well, see, you're not much of a navigator yourself!"

My heart flutters, filling my chest with a floating lightness. Life settles back behind my eyes, dusting away the cobwebs.

Piren spins the wheel in a sharp right turn, and centrifugal force knocks me into his shoulder. My chest tightens. I dart my eyes to the window.

Ebony sky surrounds us in a protective shield. Silver stars twinkle above our heads, welcoming us into the night. I feel…*happy.*

Why does that feel so foreign?

Another hour flies by, but it might as well have been a minute.

"Tell me another one!" Piren begs.

"You've depleted my story stash. I'm all out."

"Pleeeeease?"

"Well, since you asked so nicely…You wouldn't believe what my mom said the other—"

My phone vibrates in my coat pocket, tickling my leg.

"Geez, hang on." I pry it out.

Seven missed calls: Sam. The smile melts from my face.

"Something wrong?" Piren asks.

"What? Oh…no…"

An ache digs through my stomach as my Partner's name flashes across the screen.

I should at least text him so he knows I'm not lying dead in a ditch…but, eh…

Swallowing down the guilt, I tuck my phone back in my pocket.

"Anyway, she was all like—" I straighten my spine to match my mother's terse posture "'— *Tracy, you need to be a proper lady. Sitting with your legs wide open is* not *for ladies!*'" I gesture my hands in the air.

My best friend snorts beside me.

"'*I swear, Tracy,*'" I continue my impersonation, "'*sometimes I think you do these things just to annoy me.*' Bingo, Mother."

Piren's face burns crimson as he roars with laughter.

Thank you, thank you very much. I'll be here all week.

I hold up my hand. "Oh, and sometimes, she irons her pajamas."

"Oh, man, she doesn't."

"She does."

"That's ridiculous."

"That's my mother. Ridiculous doesn't even begin to cover it."

He shakes his head. "Your family is...something else."

"Tell me about it. And this one time, she *cried* because she got a food stain...on her oven mitt."

"No way!"

"Yep."

"Literally cried?"

"Literally cried."

He gasps for air.

"You think that's funny? You should hear my dad! '*I swear, Tracy, why can't we trade you for a proper daughter?*'" I mimic his drunken slurs, lowering my voice an octave for effect. "'*I love you, but I love scotch more! Guzzle guzzle guzzle.*'"

Piren chokes laughing, swerving the car across the double yellow. I steady the wheel as he collects himself. I hold my breath to rein in my giggles, but it's hopeless.

Mid-laugh, a sharp pain strikes me in the heart.

These laughable stories are my life. But I'm laughing anyway. And it hurts.

The thought is almost too silly to be true, but I can't shake it. It sucks the laughter from my lungs.

"It's funny, though." I smile to the window. "When you spend your life hearing how horrible you are...you start to believe it."

Piren's grin fades to a twitching line across his face. "What?"

Damn it. Did I say that aloud?

"Uh, nothing, just joking." I force a phony chortle. "Anyway, my mom—"

"No." He furrows his brows. "What do you mean?"

"Nothing. Forget it."

"They're just silly, Trace. Don't listen to your fam—"

"I don't."

Silence.

Stars and streetlamps sail past outside, shining dim domes of light through the enveloping darkness. I run my fingers along the edge of the window.

Soon, tonight will end, and I'll be back to my normal life. That laughable, painful, meaningless life.

Why does my life feel so stifling? Is life supposed to feel like that?

"Sometimes…I don't know who they want me to be." The words slip out softer than a whisper.

"What do you mean?" Piren's forehead wrinkles. "Just be yourself."

"Being myself—" I give a derisive snort "—is what gets me beaten up."

Piren lets out a deep breath, his gaze focused on the road ahead. His fingers tighten around the steering wheel.

I exhale. "Sorry. I—"

"If they don't see how great you are, Trace, they're idiots. You're the best person I ever met."

His words catch me off guard. "Oh, well—"

"I…I like you the way you are."

"Thanks." I hide my flushed cheek behind my hand.

Lamp posts hypnotize me, rhythmically floating by. Piren clicks on the right blinker, and we make another turn into oblivion.

"Do you know where you're going yet?" I ask in a fickle attempt to re-lighten the mood. "Or are we still hopelessly lost?"

"Nope. Still lost."

"Ha…good."

Words stick in my throat, as if hanging from the tip of my tongue, threatening to fall. There's something on my mind I can't say to anyone else. I take a deep breath.

"Remember when we were kids—" I pick at the hem of my coat "—and that tight-ass lady talked about Assignments, and she made that cheesy metaphor that your Partner is a puzzle piece?"

"Oh, of course, how could I forget?"

"Well…this is going to sound so stupid—" I bunch up the edge of my shirt, peeking out from under my jacket "—but, do you believe what she said?"

He arches a brow. "That everyone has a puzzle piece in their Partner, or something dumb like that?"

"Something like that."

"Oh, I dunno…I thought it was just a stupid seminar. Only slightly better than the guy with the masturbation story. I never gave it much thought."

"She said you can only fit with one other puzzle piece, your Partner, and no one else."

"Yeah, I remember."

I release the fabric and wipe my moist hands across my skirt. "Do you think it's true?"

He lifts his right shoulder in a half-shrug. "Your sister and Oliver seem pretty happy."

"Do they?"

"They're perfect together. Clarence could make them poster children for the Lab."

I snort. "Maybe on the outside. On the inside, Veronica's a hot mess. Oliver is…well, Oliver. Great match on paper, I suppose—both equally impulsive and clingy. Self-concerned. Maybe they're too similar, but stuck together forever, and that's why their lives are so screwed up. Happy together till they drink themselves into a stupor."

Piren pulls off the road and parks the car.

"Okay. What's this about, Trace? You seem…sad."

"I dunno." I rub my upper arm. "It's been on my mind."

"Well, I guess I think of it differently. I guess maybe I'm a puzzle piece, and then maybe Lara's a puzzle piece that fits with me. But there are other pieces in my life too. There's Mason, there's you, my other friends, my parents, my job, my artwork, our adventure stories, all kinds of stuff. I'd hope my life wasn't just made up of two pieces." He jabs my arm. "Sounds like a boring life."

"But…I don't know…" I wring my hands. "What if I'm one puzzle piece, and Sam's one puzzle piece…but we don't exactly fit together? Like I'm an orange one, and he's a blue one."

Piren gives me a half-smile.

"Or maybe there's still a piece missing. Maybe Sam and I together are a jigsaw puzzle that's supposed to be complete, but it's not, because it's missing a piece or two."

He stares outside into the dark abyss. "Maybe you need to make it fit."

"How, though?"

"I guess you just assume your Partner will eventually fit with you." His voice holds a low monotone. "Maybe it takes time."

"Maybe."

Piren closes his eyes. "But I…I get it." His monotone falters.

"You do?"

He doesn't respond.

"Sorry," I mumble. "I didn't mean to totally depress everything. I'm a frigging idiot like that sometimes."

"Hey." He rests his hand on my arm. "That's my best friend you're talking about."

"That's my line." My hand brushes his, and a sharp breath catches in my throat.

Our eyes meet.

He leans closer. "Hey…Trace…"

I swallow. "Yeah?"

BZZT. BZZT…

He jerks his hand off my arm. I fumble to silence the vibrating phone in my pocket. I'm guessing it's another message from Sam, but I don't bother to check.

"You're popular," Piren says with a shaky laugh.

The dashboard clock flashes 12:00 a.m. One dim light pricks through the darkness outside.

"Piren. You won't believe this. Look." I point out the window. It's the café.

PIREN ALLSTON

I can't stop looking at her.
Can she tell?
I'm all jittery inside.
What's wrong with me?

TRACY BAILEY

I rush through the café entrance as the barista slides the sign from *Open* to *Closed*. He huffs, but steps aside to let us in.

"We're closing; you gotta take your order to go," he says.

We nod, bounding to the counter. Upside-down chairs stack on red tables over a freshly-mopped checkered floor.

I breathe deeply, allowing the smooth aroma of coffee beans to fill my nose.

This place hasn't changed.

The smell invokes a surge of memories. Seven years ago, we pooled our change for one hot beverage. That was the same year I humiliated myself in Under Five when I couldn't pay for my own frigging milkshake. Now, Piren and I both have jobs and can each afford our own cocoa.

We pay for our drinks and step outside, and the barista bolts the door. I bob up and down to conserve warmth in the bitter air.

"Hey." Piren nods to the left. "Isn't that where we sat last time?"

Coated in a thin dusting of powdery snow, the bus stop bench loyally waits. I close my eyes and can almost feel my best friend's hands engulfing mine around a steaming cup.

I can't believe we actually found this place again.

"What do you say?" He motions his hands toward the bench. "For old times' sake?"

We plop down, our cocoas threatening to spill over the sides of our foam cups.

I sip my drink. "This cocoa is mad hot."

"You were just complaining about how cold you are!"

"Well, it's two extremes."

"*You're* too extreme."

"Psh!"

"Some adventure, huh?"

"Can you believe we actually found it?"

"No! It looks the same."

"This is crazy."

"I know, right?"

"Have you ever brought Lara here?"

"I don't love Lara."

Stop.

PIREN ALLSTON

Holy shit.

"What?" Trace's jaw drops. She sets her cup down on the bench. "Wait…no!"

"You can't just say stuff like that!" She jumps from the bench, flailing her arms. "Of course you frigging love Lara!"

"I know! I do!"

"Shit like that gets you a one way ticket to Lornstown!"

"I know! I love Lara. I love her!"

"You better!"

"I do!"

"Good!"

"Good!"

She rubs her forehead.

I lean back on the bench, left leg jiggling like a gelatinous mass.

Nice going. Way to fuck up the night.

My ragged breath rips like razors through my lungs.

What the hell is wrong with me? Why the hell did I say that? And why to Trace?

Trace sits back down beside me and stretches her legs out into the snow, gazing pensively up at the sky. Nausea swirls in my belly. I rest my head in my hands, elbows on my knees, grasping my hair in fists.

I can't look at her.

After a silent eternity, Trace nudges my arm with her elbow.

"To us." She holds up her cocoa in a toast. "To the best friend I've ever had."

I weakly raise my own cup. "To us."

We gulp our final sips.

"Let's go home." She brushes the hair from my eyes with her frozen fingers. "It's late."

A thousand fluttering insects crawl through my chest. I thrust my hands in my pockets and stand up.

Inhale. Exhale.

"Great adventure," she says.

"It was."

Our eyes lock for a moment. Then she turns back toward my car.

TRACY BAILEY

I press my cheek against the cool glass, fogging the window with every breath. Telephone poles fly by outside, blurring in and out of focus through my drooping eyelids. A heavy stone settles in my stomach.

Piren's an idiot. I can't let him talk like that. I won't let them mar his face.

"Do you...want to talk?" he asks.

I can't.

I clamp my eyes shut, letting the seatbelt constrict my rising and falling chest.

"...or not..."

Did he mean it?

PIREN ALLSTON

Trace's face hides behind a curtain of hair in the seat beside me.

She's pretending to sleep. Why the hell won't she talk to me?

My hands grow restless around the steering wheel.

Breathe.

The headlights prick two tunnels of light ahead, illuminating the deserted road to Trace's apartment. A lonely stoplight flashes red, and I gently tap the brake, slowing to a stop.

Saying good-bye to someone you want to spend every minute with is the worst damn feeling in the world.

My motionless best friend curls away from me. The window grows foggy and damp as she breathes.

My best friend. My Trace.

She's so lovely. So peaceful.

I want to touch her. I want to feel her warmth.

I stretch my trembling hand toward her and something flickers inside me. Inches from brushing her shoulder, I snap my arm back. A lump sticks in my throat as I force my eyes shut, wrapping my fingers back around the steering wheel.

Pull it together.

"Hey." I nudge her leg. "You awake? We're…back."

Eyes down, she withdraws her face from the window. "Yeah."

I park beneath a dim street lamp in The Terrace lot.

"That your place?" I point toward the nearest apartment. Trace nods, shuffling back into her jacket. Overgrown bushes suffocate the front door. Moonlight basks her porch in a ghostly glow, illuminating paint-chipped rails. The place is eerily still, almost haunted. Lifeless. It doesn't feel like a home that would be inhabited by Trace.

Curtains flutter in the window, and Sam's face pops into view.

He waited up for her?

I can't make out his expression; he's too far away. Something in my chest jolts.

Not safe.

"Good night," she mutters, opening the car door.

"Trace." I throw my arm out in front of her. "Wait."

She glances up at me, her eyes swollen and pink.

I swallow hard. *Has she been crying?*

"Never mind." I slowly withdraw my arm, focusing on the crease in my sweatshirt. "See you tomorrow. Good night."

She smiles downward. "Night."

Please be okay.

TRACY BAILEY

It's after one in the morning. I take a deep breath and push open the front door. Glimmering moonlight shines in the threshold of our dark apartment, basking the entrance in elongated shadows; they stretch from beneath my feet, into the hall. The spookiness sends a chill down my back.

Something's wrong.

My body freezes in the doorway, legs tingling with the urge to run back outside.

Don't be a baby; just go in, for God's sake. This is your home!

Pulse charging through my chest, I force my feet into the smothering darkness. My hands twitch at my sides, alert and ready to deflect an attack.

No one's here.

I fumble with the switch, flipping on the hall light.

"Sam?"

Where is he?

I swoop around the corner, tensing my arms.

Nothing.

"Sam?" I flick on the kitchen light. "You in here?"

Nothing.

"Sam?" I call up the stairs.

Hairs prickle on the back of my neck.

He's here. Somewhere. Waiting.

A single light shimmers down the hall, beckoning me closer. I creep toward it, heart jackhammering in my chest.

I press my back to the wall outside the living room. Shaking hands splayed to guard my face, I leap inside.

Sam leans back in his armchair. Calm. Peaceful.

Creepy.

His fingers lie still on the edge of the armrests.

Why the hell is he so calm? Isn't this the part where he freaks out?

"Hi, Sam." I creak open the closet door and drape my coat over a hanger. "You startled me. I thought you'd be sleeping."

He doesn't budge. "I love you, Tracy Bailey."

"I love you, Sam Macey." There's no light in his eyes.

I kick off my shoes, not turning my back on him.

"Late night?"

"Yep." I pull off my scarf, laboring to hide my quaky hands. "Lot of sorting."

"I saw Allston's car. Why didn't you drive yourself home?"

"Car died at the Lab. Need to get it towed tomorrow, I guess."

"You could have called me."

"Sorry. Didn't want to bother you." I keep my chest squared to him.

"Tracy." His brows crease in an expression sickeningly akin to my father's. "It's one thirty in the morning. Don't you check your phone?"

"It was on silent. I'm sorry."

"Well, don't do it again. I was worried sick. I'll drive you to work tomorrow." He remains poised, feet planted on the floor, hands on the chair.

I watch him through the corner of my eyes. "Okay."

"You should get some rest," he says with the slightest hint of amusement. "Don't want you falling asleep on the job tomorrow." His fingers twitter on the armrest, but he doesn't move.

"Sure."

"Good night."

"Good night."

I exit the living room, then break into a run in the hall. I race to my bedroom, shut the door, and lean my back up against it. Chest heaving, I catch my breath, pressing my ear to the door, waiting for ominous clomping footsteps on the other side.

Nothing.

My pulse slows to a normal rate, and I collapse on my bed, keeping my eyes on the doorknob. After a few minutes, I slide under the covers.

Nothing.

He didn't do anything to me.

That was weird.

PIREN ALLSTON

I tiptoe into my apartment. Lara slouches over the kitchen table, rubbing her bloodshot eyes. Knitting needles lie scattered around her, intermingled with spools of multicolored yarn. She jerks her head up.

"I love you, Lara Goodren."

"I love you, Piren Allston." She jumps from the chair and puts her hands on her hips. "Where the hell were you?"

"Had to work late."

"It's two in the morning."

"I'm sorry. It was a long—"

"Were you with Tracy?"

"Yes! We were at work together all day! Happy?"

If she could shoot knives from her eyes, I'd be dead. I force my droopy eyelids open, bracing myself for interrogation.

Her lips form an icy line. "I—I ju—How cou—You—Ugh!"

She shakes her head and stomps off. Her bedroom door slams in the distance, disseminating floating dust from the counter.

I lean against the fridge and close my eyes.

Churning pain writhes through my stomach. It won't go away.

It hasn't stopped since I started this job.

TRACY BAILEY

I tossed all night, waiting for my bedroom door to fly open at any second.

It didn't.

I hardly slept three hours. By the time I finally succumbed to sleep, light peeked through the blinds, basking my bedroom in the soft glow of morning.

Nightmares of Piren's Banishment tormented me as I drifted through cycles of consciousness. His marred face swam through my dreams, mingled with visions of Sam, bludgeoning my best friend to death. Every few minutes, I rocketed upward, tangled in sweaty sheets.

I finally awaken to the harsh chime of my morning alarm. Blinking away a sleepy haze, I rub my stinging eyes. Pillow lines form craterous indents across my cheek. Lovely.

I cloak myself in my bathrobe and stumble into the kitchen in a groggy daze. When my toes brush the cold tile floor, I stop dead in my tracks.

What the…?

Sam bends over the stove, fully dressed and showered, sautéing eggs. Sizzling bacon crackles in a pan, permeating a mouth-watering, smoky aroma through the room. I cautiously step closer to observe the full scene as he gallivants around the kitchen.

Isn't he tired? What is he, a vampire or something?

"There's a plate for you on the table," he says with a wink.

Sure enough, a full breakfast waits on my placemat, complete with a folded cloth napkin.

"Um…thanks?"

What the hell?

I plop down in my seat, too tired to mask the perplexity in my sideways expression.

"I love you, Tracy Bailey."

"I love you, Sam Macey."

He floats back to the stove as if dancing on a cloud. As he cooks, he hums a cheery tune, flipping fried eggs in the air on his spatula. I scrunch up my face, too exhausted to lift my weak limbs.

Is this just a continuation of my bizarre dreams?

"You look lovely this morning," he says, kissing the top of my head, "as usual." He places a glass of orange juice on a coaster beside me.

I glance at him through the corner of my eye. "Thanks."

Sam never calls me lovely. And I'm in my ratty bathrobe. And I smell like hell.

"Can you drive me to work today?" I paw at the napkin in my lap. "Or should I take the bus?"

"I'm driving; don't you worry." He rubs his hands together and takes a seat opposite me, delving into his own heaping breakfast.

I try to return his smile, but all I can muster is a wide-eyed gape.

Is he cutting me a break? Did an alien ship kidnap my Partner in the night and replace him with a clone?

I finish my eggs, shower, and throw on my work clothes without incident. I go to brush my teeth, and Sam vacates the sink without an argument. My alien-invasion theory grows more plausible by the second.

He kisses my cheek and hands me my coat, still humming his cheery breakfast-cooking tune.

I climb into Sam's car. He's got the radio on, but immediately flips it off when I sit down.

I wrinkle my nose. *It always smells funny in here.*

He starts the engine. "I hope you enjoyed your breakfast."

"I did, thanks." I can't wipe the dumbfounded look off my face.

"I left a message at Chuck's auto. They're gonna tow your car and take a look at it this afternoon."

"Oh, cool…Thanks." I buckle my seatbelt. "One less thing I have to deal with today."

My Partner's giddy humming progresses to full-blown whistling.

I toss my purse in the backseat. "Why so jovial?"

He grins. "Gonna spend the whole day with my Partner."

"What?" I pinch the lever beneath me, thrusting the car seat forward.

Sam turns left out of the parking lot. The Lab is to the right.

I squint out the window. "Where are we going?"

"Work. Surprise!"

"What do you mean?" My forehead crinkles. "You're going the wrong way."

"Thought I'd surprise you, but you're too quick." He roughly ruffles my hair. "My little former-top-sophomore-student Partner still has her wits about her."

I knock his hand away. "What the hell are you talking about?"

"You're working with me now. A spot opened at Doc's office, and they've offered it to you — Partner Priority."

"Wait, what? I work at the Assignment Lab."

"Not anymore. I stopped by your office last night, met with your boss. Told him you had an opportunity to work with your Partner, and he couldn't have been happier."

I gape. "What?"

He didn't. There's no possible way. He can't.

"I thought it'd be a good chance for us to spend more time together."

"What? No..."

"It'll be fun." He squeezes my knee. "You'll see. I'll train you myself."

"You...you were that creepy car in the parking lot?" My eyes narrow. "What the hell is wrong with you?"

"You didn't come home. I came to check on you."

"To spy on me!"

He smirks. "Well, now I won't have to. You'll be working with me all the time."

"You...you can't do this." My voice quavers. "That's my job."

"You're my Partner. You belong with me." He chuckles. "You didn't expect to have that job forever, did you?"

"You can't do this! You can't make my decisions for me!"

"Well, I made this one for you. I'll get you some scrubs when we get to the office."

"I'll just go back tomorrow and get my job back."

He snorts. "Really? You think the Assignment Lab is gonna pull someone away from their Partner? Go ahead. Try."

"Stop the car. Right now."

"You'll like it at Doc's, I promise."

"I'm not going."

"Yes, you are."

"You can't make me."

"It's already done."

"No!" I pound my fist on the window. "Damn it, let me out!"

He pulls over, his white knuckles vicelike around the wheel.

"Your duty is to me!" he bellows.

"Fuck you!"

"Hey!"

I strike out to slap him, but he catches my wrist.

"No more of this shit with Piren Allston. No more!" He shoves my arm back to my chest. "You're with me. You are my Partner. End of discussion."

"No! Let me go." I unbuckle, but he thuds his arm across my stomach, knocking the wind from my lungs.

"You are with me!" His eyes flash with venom.

I lash out and strike him hard as I can on the shoulder. He grabs my hand and twists it backward.

"Hit me again, and you'll regret it."

My eyes well with water.

Hell. I'm in hell.

"Pull yourself together," he says through gritted teeth. "I don't wanna see this attitude when we get to work."

The engine roars. I scramble for the door handle, but he slams the gas, rocketing over the speed limit. I reach for the window, but he clicks the child locks, trapping me inside.

I'm a prisoner. This isn't real. I'm dreaming.

My pulse thumps wildly through me in a sickly surge of adrenaline.

I could jump out. I could end it right now, a million miles per hour on the highway.

I cling to the door, tears prickling behind my eyes.

Together forever. Till death do us part.

I'll wake up with Sam. I'll spend my days with Sam. I'll fall asleep with Sam. My life will eternally entwine with his.

My heart sinks into the pit of my chest, plummeting hatred into the depths of my soul. I hate Sam. I hate him with a burning fire that rips through my very being.

I close my eyes, welcoming the warm tears now seeping down my face.

I didn't even get to tell Piren good-bye.

PIREN ALLSTON

I plow through the Lab doors.

I have to see her.

Rushing into the sorting room, I screech to a halt. A blond girl sits in Trace's chair, thumbing through folders, carefully examining each one. Something bristles in my chest.

Where's Trace?

The girl nods at me without meeting my eyes, thin white headphones clasped over her ears. My heart stops.

Something happened.

I sprint back down the hall, bulldozing into Clarence's office. He startles behind his desk, setting down his steaming coffee.

"Piren, what's—"

"Clarence…where's…Tracy?" I lean on my knees, panting.

"Her Partner stopped in yesterday." He shrugs. "Said she wanted to switch to the medical field."

"No…" I run my fingers through my hair. "No. No…"

"Are you okay?"

"No…"

"They don't usually allow Placement switches this late, but I guess 'cause they're Partners, they made an exception. Plus, the waitlist for a job here was long enough, we found a replacement within hours. Her name's Sarah. She got here early and has been hard at work. You'll train her up and ready this week."

No.

"'Bout time." Clarence chuckles. "I was so sick of the two of you, running your yaps instead of doing your damn jobs. But Tracy's with her Partner now; that's what really matters…"

He continues, but his words crackle like static in my ears. My pounding heart thrums in my ears, drowning out every other noise.

No more Trace at work. No more Trace at all.

My eyes blur, and the edges of the room go out of focus.

No more fun. No more stories. My life consists of work and Lara.

Sharp breaths suck the oxygen from my brain.

I feel sick.

"Piren, are you okay?"

I bolt from Clarence's office, race to the parking lot, jump in my car, and bury my face in my hands. Heaving for air, I surrender to sobs.

It's over.

We are never so defenseless
against suffering as when
we love.
•Sigmund Freud

TWENTY-THREE YEARS OLD
PART FIVE

TRACY BAILEY

For the first six months at Dr. Patel's office, I wanted to die. I came home every day after work, locked myself in my room, and clenched a steak knife in my fist. I pressed the blade to my neck, longing to sink it into my throat and end everything in a pool of red salvation.

It got better.

The beginning sucked. I didn't think bosses stricter than Clarence existed, but that was before I met Ivanna. Her shrill barks followed me down every corridor.

"Tracy! Clean that up."

"Tracy! Faster. Come on."

"Tracy! Get your fat ass up. Patient in four-ten needs fresh sheets. Hustle."

I'd lock myself in the employees' bathroom and cry into my scrubs.

"Ivanna's fine; you're too sensitive," Sam would say. "Lighten up."

It was hell. But I adapted.

After two years diligently mopping people's shit, I follow Doc around like a sheep, soaking up every last drop of his medical knowledge.

"I'm impressed, Ms. Bailey." Dr. Patel pulls off his rubber gloves. "You didn't even flinch when the bleeding started. Better than most Placements we get here."

"Thanks!"

"Only your third time assisting day surgery, and I don't know how I ever operated without you." He claps his hand on my shoulder. "Good work."

My cheeks burn. "Well, I mean, it doesn't take rocket science to pass you tools."

"Tell that to my last assistant." He squirts sanitizer on his hands.

"I would, but didn't he run out screaming?"

"Indeed."

Five months from today, a week after my twenty-fourth birthday, I will marry Sam.

Mom and Veronica spend their weekends at Sam's and my apartment, helping me plan final details. We never run out of things to do; there's food to taste, decorations to order, dresses to buy.

"Fireworks!" my sister squeals. "You need them. After the reception."

I scratch out notes on my Wedding Planning pad. "For the last time, V, no fireworks."

"But they're so romantic!"

"It isn't a hoedown."

"I wanna kiss Ollie under the fireworks."

"So, do it at your own wedding."

"Aw, come on Trace—"

"I said no."

She sticks out her tongue at me. I flip her off.

"Rude," she scoffs, tapping her thumbs across her cellphone. I absentmindedly look through a wedding catalog, slumping over on my arm.

"Did you hear?" Veronica asks, her eyes glued to her screen. "Lara Goodren and Piren Allston's wedding date was just confirmed. Six months to the day after yours."

I clench my jaw. "Fascinating."

"What? Their date? How is that fascinating?"

"No…these candles. Look." I open a random page and point.

She raises her brows. "There's nothing interesting about these candles, Trace."

"Well, there's nothing interesting about their wedding date, V!"

"Sheesh, okay."

Her long fingernails *click-click-click* across her cellphone keyboard.

My body tenses. "That noise is grating my nerves. Who are you texting?"

She doesn't look up. "Ollie."

I swoop in and pluck the phone from her hands.

"Hey!"

"You're spending your entire life with this kid. Do you need to spend every second *now* with him too?"

She juts out her bottom lip. "I love him."

"Your life can include other things besides Oliver."

"Give it back." She draws her words into whiny syllables. "Come on."

"Fine." I roll my eyes, thrusting the phone back into her hands. "Just cool it on the tapping."

PIREN ALLSTON

I drop a hefty pile of mail on the kitchen table, scattering colorful envelopes everywhere. Lara sifts through it.

"Ugh, another one? How many flipping people were in our graduating class, anyway?" She rips open a thick green envelope and dumps out the contents. "You know, they don't warn you how flipping expensive it is to be twenty-four. You have to buy gifts for all these people. Well, here's another fifty bucks down the hole. Raymond and Alyssa. Didn't even like them, and here we go, celebrating their wedding. Ugh."

She tosses the Save-the-Date back onto the table and grabs another. As her eyes scan the invitation, her lips thin to a narrow line. She slides it toward me.

"*Join us for Tracy and Sam's big day!*" proclaim vibrant orange letters across a cloud-dappled sky background. My chest tightens.

The date is sooner than I expected. I should be happy for them, and I am! It's just weird because I haven't heard from Trace since she quit the Lab two years ago; no texts, no calls, no run-ins, nothing, and now here's this damn invitation in the mail.

My eyes glaze over, fixed on the parchment paper lying two feet away on the table.

Lara struts toward the counter and uncorks a bottle of merlot. "We have to go to that," she says with a huff.

"We can just send a gift."

"Absolutely not." She tips the bottle into her waiting glass. "I want everyone at our wedding, and no one's gonna come if we miss everyone else's."

"I don't wanna go."

"Excuse me?"

"It's stupid."

"It's not!" She anchors her right hand on her hip, her left hand gripping the stem of her glass. "Don't say that. You should be excited about our wedding."

"I'm excited about ours. Do I need to share that excitement about everyone else's?"

"Well, a little enthusiasm about something would be nice. Seriously, you haven't had one nice thing to say to me — to anyone! — for, like, two years now!"

"I'm sorry! What do you want from me?"

"I want you to cut it out! The attitude! I'm so sick of this!"

She storms from the room with her wine. I don't follow her.

TRACY BAILEY

I park in my parents' driveway and press my forehead to the steering wheel.

First time home in five years.

Mom nagged me forever to clear out the last of my belongings, so here I am. The Shitmobile rattles as I slam its door.

Yeah? You're not happy here either, then.

Veronica's silver sports car sits by the garage. Dad bought it brand new from the luxury dealership downtown. My sister lives with Oliver but comes home a lot. She likes pilfering goodies from Dad's liquor cabinet.

"Mom! Dad! I'm here!" I call up the stairs. "V?" I shout. "Mom? Dad?"

No one answers.

I'm being ignored. Feels good to be home!

I clamber upstairs to my old teenage bedroom. Dust coats the dresser and lamps in a gray blanket. My bookshelf remains fossilized, as if frozen in time, each item tilted and stacked exactly as I left it. Fingerprint smudges still speckle the rectangular window.

The old house was home, but this place never was.

I sink down on my childhood bed.

It's as foreign and lonely in here as it was the day we moved in.

I close my eyes.

We moved here…because—

Something thuds loudly downstairs.

I jump up and spring to the platform. Veronica lies in a heap at the bottom of the stairs, convulsing with sobs.

"V! Veronica!"

I trip over my feet, flying down the stairs to her side.

"Are you okay? Hey!"

Vomit stains streak down her shirt. Chunky liquid drips off her chin, dribbling to the floor. The hoppy scent of beer swirls through my nostrils.

Are you effing kidding me?

"I'm so tired…" Her eyelids flutter.

I grit my teeth. "Okay, let's get you to the couch to lie down." I attempt to position my arms around her. "Do you want me to call Oliver, or —"

She tugs my collar. "Trace!"

"Yes?" I exhale a heavy breath. "You got puke on the floor."

"I'm bad. I did it. I did something."

"Veronica." I give her shoulders a slight shake. "What did you do?"

"I — I — I — I —"

"Okay, I'm going to get you some water, because you're not making any sense."

She yanks my head down. "I slept with Oliver."

"You *what?*" I leap up.

"I did. Two days ago." Her eyes cloud with tears. "I was drunk, Tracy. I was drunk."

"You're still drunk! Right now!"

"No…I'm…not," she says between heaves. "Don't tell Ollie I told you."

"Veronica —"

"Stop yelling at me!"

I clench my fists to rein in the urge to scream. "Are you looking to get Banished? Want me to drive you to the Mayor's office myself? How could you ever —"

Her ear-splitting wail cuts me off. I rub my pinched forehead.

Great, now I'm the bad guy.

"Veronica…shh…Veronica. It's okay…shh…It's okay. Listen to me. You're getting married in a few years, but you can't — you *cannot* — do that. Do you understand? No one can know, okay? You can't tell anyone else, V…Shh…It's okay…I won't tell…"

I pull her vomit-smeared body into my arms and press my face into her hair, inhaling the honey scent of her shampoo.

I won't be here to pick her up every frigging time this happens.

I rock my sister in my lap, embracing her as she cries.

I'm her mother, as always. I'm protecting her, as always. I'm keeping her safe, as always. But still, I'm helpless, because I can't help her. She sobs and sobs, and I just sit here like an idiot and let her wail. Sit here like a useless mass, laboring to stay calm and supportive. I'm powerless. Watching her cry is all I can do. I don't have a shoulder to cry on.

An hour passes before Oliver finally decides to grace us with his presence. I've cradled my sister's head in my lap for the past hour, and what has he done? Been M.I.A., that's what. He rings the bell, and I tense my muscles, mustering every bit of self-control not to unleash my rage.

"Hey, Tracy."

I glower back at him.

Nice of you to join us, jackass.

My sister was a normal, intelligent person before he introduced her to alcohol. She was a good kid. Oliver and his martini-slugging family threw her down a black hole. If she pulls herself up, he'll always be right there to drag her back down.

Oliver saunters through the door and tracks mud on the carpet. I count my breaths in my head, squeezing my hands into tight balls. Arms stiff at my side, I follow him to the landing.

"V, Oliver's here. He's gonna take you home now, okay?"

"Ollie?" she groans, her cheeks puffy and red.

"It's okay, Tracy." Oliver crouches beside us. "I've got her."

How can you be so frigging calm and expressionless, you son of a bitch? You illegally fucked my sister—when she was drunk! It boils my blood!

I give him a curt nod.

Shifting Veronica's weight between Oliver and me, we clumsily drag her to her feet. As we lift, Oliver's face crosses into my line of vision.

I haven't seen my sister's Partner in a few years, and he's aged. He chopped his long, unwieldy hair to a slick crew-cut. For the first time in forever, he's not lugging that hideous saxophone case. With a lion-like yawn, he steadies my sister in his arms.

What the hell happened to him? He looks...different.

"This is going too far." I shake my head. "This drinking has to stop."

And if you prematurely fuck my sister again, I'll rip your fucking face off.

I brace myself for his whining, arrogant reply. The blame, the denial, the blah blah blah "pay attention to me" bullshit. Then I'll have two babies to watch. He better be careful he doesn't talk his way to a black eye.

He meets my gaze. "You're right. I screwed up. You shouldn't have to deal with this. I'm so sorry."

I blink. "You are?"

"Yeah, she needs help. I know she does; I see it." He takes a deep, quavering breath. "And I know it's probably my fault."

"Oh, you think?" My words blurt out snarky and nasty, and I don't care.

"I'm sorry. She has a problem." He sighs. "And I do too. I'm gonna get help. I'm gonna fix it."

My rigid arms relax at my sides.

Oliver? Taking responsibility?

"Come on, Veronica. Let's get you home." He drapes V's arm over his shoulders. "I'm gonna make sure she eats something the moment we get back."

I nod.

Who is this person, and what has he done with Oliver Hughes?

Maybe holding down a job thrust him into maturity. Or maybe he just grew out of his dumbassery.

Oliver watches V carefully, embracing her for balance as we lead her out the front door. His gaze is deep and vast as an ocean, unveiling his emotions to the world. I can see it plainly in his eyes: he loves her.

"You gonna be okay?" he asks.

"Yep." I brush a hair strand off my sister's face as we buckle her into Oliver's car. "Take care of her, all right?"

"Of course."

He starts his car, and I head back toward the house.

I lean against the doorframe, fiddling with my fingers, studying The Wonder Twins as they drive off. When the car disappears beyond the horizon, I trek back inside to clean her puke before my parents catch wind of the mess.

Next time she's drunk, I'm gonna haul her ass to a frigging toilet.

I moisten a wad of paper towels and dig out the baking soda from under the sink. Crawling on all-fours, I scrub the crap out of the carpet fibers.

Elbow sore and aching, I pull back into a kneeling position to examine the stain. The carpet on the platform has returned to its original off-white, with a slight dark patch in the middle.

Good enough.

I wipe the sweaty film off my forehead with the back of my hand, letting the dirty paper towels float to the floor.

Mom steps down the stairs. "What's all this mess?"

Nice to see you too, Mom.

"Nothing. Spilled some Pepsi. Just cleaning it up."

She scowls. "I keep this place in decent order, and you come home and mess it up."

"Okay, Mom."

"I still see a brown mark." She steps around me. "I want it gone."

I reach for the worn paper towel. "I'm on it. Sorry."

She disappears into the other room, and I slump back against the wall.

Some people are self-sufficient; I've always considered myself one of those people. My sister is a different kind of person; she relies on others.

I always knew I couldn't fall down, not even for a moment. If I fell, no one would catch me—not my parents, not Veronica, not Sam. I learned to pick myself up. I keep myself safe and hold myself in my own arms. I am my own savior. For my entire almost-twenty-four years, this has held true.

Except...once...

My heart contracts at the memory I've tried so long to repress. I close my eyes.

Nine years ago. Snow on the ground. A chill in the air. Christmas lights sparkling from every rooftop.

One person who was different. One person who cared for me on a night I couldn't take care of myself.

Piren Allston.

After I kissed him in his parents' doorway and committed the blasphemous crime, I gaped at my best friend. Realization of my action dawned on me like an ominous shroud of mingled guilt and fear. My mouth ran dry as a terrifying thought played through my brain on repeat: *What have I done?*

I expected him to hit me. Punch me. Call the police. Offer to cut me himself. I would have deserved it all.

After three months of not talking to him, of ignoring him, of pretending not to hear when he called my name, I had the nerve to show up at his house. I had the gall to come crawling back in my time of need, seeking comfort, seeking friendship, after I denied him both for so long. That's why I expected him to throw me down, scream at me, send me back out into the cold — because that's all I wanted to do to myself that night. I hated myself. I was a horrible, awful friend, and in that one kiss, I became a horrible, awful human being.

But Piren is not a horrible, awful human being. He has a heart of gold and a friendship I never deserved.

"I'll go," I said, frozen in the doorway, eyes prickling with tears.

"No!" His voice cracked. "Stay." He grabbed my arms. "Please… stay."

I can't. I should go. I shouldn't be here. My brain buzzed with a thousand different apologies and excuses, but the words wouldn't form in my mouth.

I swallowed, and a whisper seeped out. "Okay."

My heart raced at light speed, a pattering drum roll in my chest. He took my hand and led me to his parents' living room. We plopped down on his leather couch, cross-legged, facing each other like a couple of kindergarteners. He wrapped a Christmas quilt around my shoulders.

"Your hands are like ice," he said, squeezing my frozen fingers in his hands.

My eyes drifted to the television, glowing softly in the background. "I love this show."

"With the cartoon snowmen?" He grinned. "You would."

Teeth chattering with residual cold, I wrapped the blanket tighter around my body.

"Here." He ripped off his sweatshirt. "Put this on."

We sat for hours, my hands in his, talking about everything and nothing all at once. It was like no time at all had passed. When my eyelids grew heavy, he tucked me in, under layers of blankets.

"After midnight." He brushed hair off my forehead with his hand. "Merry Christmas."

"Merry—" I let out a roaring yawn "—Christmas."

As I succumbed to sleep, one single thought settled in my brain: *Safe. I feel safe.*

I committed a crime when I kissed him; he committed a crime when he kept me. If anyone learned what he did for me, he'd have been Banished within hours. He risked everything, just to protect me. He shouldn't have been kind to me. He shouldn't have cared if I froze to death. Hell, he shouldn't have cared for me at all that night. But he did.

Reliving the memory in my head simultaneously churns my stomach and puts me at ease.

I can't talk to him again. Can't be his friend again. Can't hurt him again.

It's my turn to protect him. If I'm in his life, I'll only hurt him.

And he deserves so much better than that.

PIREN ALLSTON

Work sucks. I applied for a Placement transfer seven times, but no one takes me seriously. Lara insists she can get me a job at the printing plant, and I tell her I can't stand the smell of rubber stamps, but really I can't stand being around her. Whenever I see her I feel angry.

I come home from work, and she's there, sitting on the damn couch, not saying anything, not doing anything, just sitting. Staring. Useless. Boring. Nothing. It sickens me. We have nothing together. Nothing.

TRACY BAILEY

Toni grabs my arm. "Please come!"

"I don't know." I pry her vicelike grip off me. "Bachelorette parties aren't really my thing."

"Come on; it'll be fun," she pleads. "I'll be trashed the whole time."

"Well, that doesn't surprise me."

She puckers her lips. "How can you say no to this face?"

"Easily."

"Pleeeeease?"

I know her tricks. The real question is not "will you attend my bachelorette party?" but rather "will you be my designated driver?"

"I don't know…"

My phone vibrates in my back pocket, and I startle. One new text message: Sam.

Ryan coming over 4 multi-player tonight.

I release a winded groan. Last time Sam and his stupid friend Ryan joined video game forces, I fell asleep to the sounds of digital gunshots and screaming curse words. It took me two weeks to remove a beer stain from our white couch.

Great.

I shove my phone back in my pocket. "Fine. I'll come."

Toni squeals and throws her arms around me.

"It'll be so much fun," she says. "You'll see!"

"Sure."

Four hours later, we arrive at a dive bar called Chevy's. It smells exactly as dank as I expected when I laid eyes on the water-logged awning outside.

Eight girls attend, several of whom I haven't seen in years. It's a big, unwanted, high school reunion. The girls I don't know are from the deli where Toni has her Placement.

Within forty minutes, everyone's tipsy and blathering about how their wedding plans are better than everyone else's. I'm perched on a bar stool in the corner, swirling my bendy straw around in my Sprite. I prop my head up with my hand.

One of Toni's work friends shrieks at the other end of the bar. I jerk my head up. Several girls giggle around a table, taking turns modeling a baseball cap they stole off a drunk guy's head.

Ew! I crinkle my nose. *Apparently hygiene goes out the window when you're trashed.*

"Hey!" I lunge toward them. "Don't touch that!"

I rip the hat from the girl's hands and plop it back down on the man's head. He nibbles a plate of buffalo wings, orange sauce dripping off his fingers.

"Aw, this bitch is a killjoy," he says, taking a long sip from his beer.

I point at him. "Shut up." I turn my finger toward Toni's friend. "That's nasty, don't do that."

She flips me her middle finger. I sneer at her and return the gesture. The others howl and jeer, slurring something incoherent about sobriety being "for bitches."

"Yeah? Keep talking, you can drive your own drunk asses home." I stride back to my corner of the bar.

Story of my life, I'm babysitting drunks. If one of them pukes, I'm not cleaning it up.

An hour passes, and the overall sobriety of the room steadily declines. Some of the girls disappear outside, while others prop each other up and engage in semi-coherent conversations.

"Tracy! Shots!" Toni slides one down the bar to me.

I fling out my hand, stopping the glass mid-slide before it shatters into the wall.

"No thanks. I don't drink."

"Sure you do. Everybody drinks." She wobbles in place, beer bottle in one hand, shot glass in the other.

"No, they don't. If it's all the same, I'll just watch."

"Whee!" She knocks her shot back in a single swoop.

"How many was that? New personal record?"

"I dunno. I'm trashed," she slurs, dropping her empty glass onto the bar with a clank. I'm guessing she's about one shot away from a head injury.

"No kidding. I noticed you were double fisting. Take a seat."

I pull her butt down onto the nearest stool. She snatches my undrunk shot and shoots it back herself, spilling her beer all over the counter in the process.

Typical. I go home, I get drunks. I come out, I get drunks. I'm surrounded.

"I'm marrying Alan," she says, a smile spreading across her flushed face.

I steady her tipping beer glass. "Yes, next week. First one in our class. I can't wait."

"Meee too!" Her squeaky voice reaches a new decibel.

"Yes…Why don't I get you some water…"

"And then is yooouuur wedding!" She steadies herself against the counter. "And then…Amanda's…and then…Lara's!"

I swallow hard. "Yep."

"Lara's a big bitch, though," she says. "Going to her cousin's wedding over mine."

"The nerve," I mumble.

"I looove weddings, Tracy. Don't you?" She links my arm, her stool rocking onto two legs.

"Sure." I grab her elbow to stabilize her.

"We're getting married," she says through a hiccup.

Yeah, thanks, I heard you the first twelve times.

Her "Bride-To-Be" tiara tilts over her forehead, obscuring her eyes. She reaches out to push it back onto her head but completely misses and snorts out drunken laughter. "Your wedding's soon too. Gotta get you one of these crowns."

A gust of rage shoots through me.

I'm sick of doing this. It's insanity. My whole life is insane.

Lara and Piren's stupid little wedding is in a few stupid months. I'm going to have to sit there and watch and be just so utterly *thrilled* for them.

"But they're such a *lovely couple!*" I say, mimicking Mrs. Riley.

Toni's forehead creases. "Who?"

My mind goes blank. *Ummm…*

"You and Alan."

"Ohhh, wheee!" She downs another shot. "Barkeep, hit me up! Vodka, stat!" Her voice grows simultaneously raspier and louder with each beverage. "Last night out for this girl!"

I highly doubt that.

The bartender slides two shot glasses down the bar to us. One stops inches from my hand, sloshing clear liquid over the side.

It's right in front of me. Right there in my miserable existence. It cures everyone else's misery, why not mine?

Fuck it.

I tighten my hand around the glass and slurp down the shot.

And then a second.

And then a third.

"Go Tracy, go!" Toni hollers. "Yeah!"

The liquid burns flowing down my throat, but I don't care. I love it all.

One hour and eight shots later, the edges of the room blur together into a dizzying glob. Warmth floods my body straight down to my toes. I can't stop giggling.

"I'm gonna drink you under the table, bitch." Toni shoots back tequila.

Only semi-cogent, I lean on the trashed bride-to-be and break into a string of hiccups. "Your tits are…falling…out of your top." I squint my eyes to steady the spinning bar. "You whore."

"Tequila, good sir!" Toni pounds her fist on the counter. She doesn't bother to adjust her shirt.

The bartender slides two more shots to us. We knock them back.

"Tell me a secret," Toni says, gripping my elbows.

"I hate purple," I say a little louder than intended.

"Shhh!" the barkeep hisses.

We cover our mouths and snicker.

"You tell me one."

She giggles, pulling my ear to her lips. "I fucked Alan. Twice. And we aren't married."

"What! No!"

Maybe a good, illegal, pre-wedding fuck is common these days. Plus, it's Toni and Alan. I suppose it's shocking they waited this long.

"I know, shhh." Her pink cheeks redden at her confession.

We down another shot. It singes my throat and burns all the way into my belly, and I savor it. I want to drown in the wonderful amber liquid. I could fly home.

"I could fly home!" I announce, flapping my arms.

Toni roars with laughter, nearly toppling to the floor. "So much for being my DD, you drunk slut."

The barkeep shakes his head and strides to the other end of the bar, leaving us alone.

"I've got a secret," I whisper. "I hate my family."

"What!" She giggles into her hands. "I'm gonna Banish your crazy ass."

"They're crazy cuckoo." I dance around on my stool.

"You can't hate your family, Tracy. No no no. That shit's bad."

"I love my sister. That's. It."

It's illegal, and I don't care. Toni committed an equally offensive crime. We're both sinners.

"Veronica and I…How'd we end up in this fucked up family? How?" I wrap my arm around Toni's shoulders. "They all suck. This world sucks."

"I'm tired."

"Stop moving. You have five heads."

Vision crossed, the room glides by as I veer into my friend's side.

My drunk homecoming will shock Sam. For some sick reason, I can see him enjoying it.

"Sleepy time, Tracy…" Toni leans closer to me, then collapses face-down in my lap. Her legs dangle off the stool. Dozens of empty seats and tables surround us.

Where the hell did everyone go?

I stroke my friend's hair, fighting to force open my heavy eyelids. Liquor seeps through my bloodstream, submerging my body in a peaceful haze.

I shift in my seat, and nausea swirls in my stomach. I press my fingers to my lips until the wave passes.

"Ten minutes, ladies," the bartender says wiping a rag down the counter. I ask him to call us a taxi and hand him my credit card to settle the tab. He disappears into the back room to make the call, leaving my drunk friend and me alone at the bar. My buzz unleashes a thought that torments my sober brain.

"Secrets...? You want secrets, Toni? I've got one for you..." My words slur in a drunken jumble. Unconscious in my lap, Toni's dead to the world.

"I love Piren Allston," I whisper to nobody. Then I puke all over the clean bar.

PIREN ALLSTON

Red Xs on the kitchen calendar greet me when I open the fridge. My eyes catch the date, and a stone drops in the hollow pit of my stomach.

Trace's wedding is in two weeks.

The date snuck up on me. I haven't bought them a gift. What do you buy your estranged best friend to celebrate the happiest day of her life? Cash? A toaster? I don't know what they want or need, because I don't know her anymore.

I lie corpselike on the couch, my face buried behind a book I'm not reading. My eyelids hang low, blurring the words on the page.

Lara twists her fingers through her hair, compulsively dusting the same spot on the coffee table. Every few seconds, her eyes dart toward me, then immediately back to the table. We haven't spoken in hours.

She tried her usual slew of "what's wrong?" and "let's talk!" but I can't do anything except stare silently at the pages that might as well be blank. I have no energy to speak.

Lara puts down her duster and cuddles up to me on the couch. She nestles into my arm, but I can't bring myself to drape it over her. My weak limbs lie still at my sides.

She clears her throat. "I talked to my mom; she knows this woman Kasey who could play violin for our processional. I asked if we could hear a sample, 'cause I heard she's good, and…"

Lara chatters on and on and blah blah blah. I don't give a shit.

I press the book to my nose. Lara slides closer.

"…And she's got a good résumé, and I think…"

I clench my teeth, letting her words float straight through my body.

She's insufferable. All she does is complain and fixate over stupid details of our stupid wedding. I swear, she hasn't said one damn thing this whole month not involving some mundane detail of the occasion.

I don't even hear her anymore. When she talks in that whiny voice, I want to blow my brains out.

"…And I know she's young, but Mom says she's been taking classes since she was four, and she'll give us a discount of—"

"I'm going out."

I spring to my feet. I have no idea why I said that. I have nowhere to go, but the words fell out of my mouth before I could stop them.

"What?" Lara leaps off the couch and puts her hands on her hips. "Piren, this is our night in. We've got wedding stuff to do. You know that. Honestly, if you just—"

I blaze past her and out the door. No coat, barely got my shoes on, but I'm out.

I expect her to rush after me, screaming, but she doesn't. A dull ache splinters through my brain as I climb into my car. I press my throbbing forehead to the steering wheel.

What the hell is wrong with me?

I straighten up and glimpse my reflection in the rearview. Bags the size of walnuts droop underneath my bloodshot eyes.

I look like shit.

I drive with no destination in mind and wind up at the entrance to my parents' neighborhood. The place rips me open like an old wound. I tap the gas and press forward, because why not twist the damn knife a little deeper?

Lights glimmer from my parents' house. Maybe I should stop in, but I don't want to explain why I'm alone tonight.

Ghosts of my childhood linger here, in the form of Trace's and my tiny bodies, scribbling across my parents' driveway in a carefree world. The images fade, replaced by visions of the morose, adult version of myself, alone.

Life was so uncomplicated back then.

I park by the forest and hike through Harker's Woods. Stiff grass and pointy twigs scrape up against my jeans as I traipse down the overgrown path. The familiar scent of sap and bark drifts through my nostrils, pouring calmness into my body.

I can breathe here.

As the crisp evening air darkens, sunlight fades into the horizon. The growing gibbous moon lights my path, as if beckoning me to hide away amongst the trees. Pushing through a mound of mangled underbrush, I step into the familiar clearing.

Frozen in time, my sanctuary waits. Each board exactly as I remember, the treehouse balances on the same thick branches. It's as if an image plucked straight from my childhood memories traveled through time and materialized in my adult world.

I was a king here once. An explorer. A pirate. Anything I wanted to be.

With her.

I run my fingers across the rough bark, in and out of every crevice, until I find the ladder. Rushed with adrenaline, I climb the familiar rungs, reaching the top in record time. I hoist myself onto the empty platform, and my heart swells. The last time I was here, the joy of finding Trace alive, shivering at the top, almost reduced me to tears. This time, I'm alone.

Stars twinkle above, offering their comfort as I stare into the abyss.

I wish I could sprawl out under a blanket and fall asleep to the sound of crickets.

I sink to the floor and lie back against the boards, inhaling the oaky aroma. Neglected for years, pine needles overrun the treehouse floor, crusted with sap and leaves. I grab a handful of invading twigs and toss them over the side of the fortress.

"Protect the west wall! Psshhh." My inner child cackles with delight.

Trace and I carved our initials here once. King and Queen of the castle, we needed to mark it as our own. As if drawn by an invisible magnet, my eyes instantly find the spot.

A jagged heart encircles our initials.

I jolt back. A shallow breath catches in my throat.

Trace is the only person who knows about this place. She's the only one who could have done this.

My fingers graze the carved message, and a feeling I can't describe washes over me like a tidal wave.

Trace.

TRACY BAILEY

Sam left for his bachelor party hours ago, boasting his elaborate plans for inebriation. He thinks I'm at my bachelorette party, but I lied. I planned a better party for myself tonight, the kind where I'm the only guest. Plus, after Toni and Alan's overcrowded wedding last night, I need a break from people.

In two weeks, I'll be Mrs. Tracy Macey. A few weeks later, the pregnancy questions will arise: Are you pregnant? Have you been trying? Aren't you so excited for Baby Macey?

It makes my skin crawl.

It's late by the time I arrive at Harker's Woods for my private soiree. I relish being swallowed whole by the dark forest as I step past the tree line. There's a certain invincibility about being invisible.

Sam mocked me for wearing a thick gray jacket in the middle of summer. He said I should dress better for my big party. Who does he think he is, my mother? He thinks I'm at a bar. Honestly, the fact that he even bought that lame excuse flaunts his stupidity. When do I ever freely go to a bar? Especially after the raging hangover following Toni's party last week — no thanks.

Little does Sam know, I plan to spend the night lying alone on the treehouse floor, and I want to be toasty enough to last for hours. Hence, the many layers of clothing.

I amble down the dark walkway, holding my cellphone at arm's-length for light; the green glow illuminates my path. Piney scent bites my nose, sparking my brain to déjà vu. My footsteps crunch and crackle against leaves and underbrush beneath my feet.

My shoe catches on a protruding root, and I trip, stumbling into the clearing. Catching myself mid-tumble, I lay eyes upon my fortress of solitude, and the world freezes.

Home.

I race up the ladder like a child, scaling the mighty fortress. Even as an adult, this treehouse enchants me. I wriggle into the fort.

I'm not alone.

Piren whirls around. My stomach lurches.

No. I can't see you. Not tonight. Not two weeks before my wedding.

"Trace."

My breath hitches in my throat. I leap toward the ladder, but he grabs my sleeve, and I don't fight him.

I shouldn't be here. We shouldn't be here together.

"Trace. This." He points. I follow his finger to our carved initials.

Fuck. My heart stops. *He knows.*

"Did you do this?"

I look from the graffiti to my best friend.

No. No no no.

"Trace. Did you do this?"

My heart hammers in my chest.

I could deny it. Would he believe me?

"Trace. Look me in the eyes. Please. Tell me the truth. Did. You. Do. This?"

His brown eyes catch mine—the same eyes I remember from childhood, from dancing in the gym, from cocoa in the café, from sorting in the Lab. It's Piren. My Piren.

He knows me better than anyone. He'll know. He already knows. I can't lie to him, not to my best friend.

I inhale a shaky breath, filling my lungs to capacity. Slowly, I force my head to nod.

He exhales a wavering gust of air. With one swift motion, he pulls me into an embrace. It's just like nine years ago, in his parents' doorway, when we were freshmen. Before it all went to shit. My body tightens in his arms. I squeeze my eyes shut, burrowing my face into his sweatshirt.

No. We can't. It's not right.

His warmth seeps through my jacket, prickling goose bumps down my neck. Burning water stings my eyes, breaking the dam and flowing down my cheeks.

I can't.

My stiff arms grow limp as rubber, and I entwine them around my best friend, pressing our bodies together. His comforting familiarity smothers my senses, drawing me in. It's a forbidden hug, but I can't pull away. Not yet.

This is wrong. I'm weak. Piren is my vice.

This is our place, the place we hid as children, wishing our days together never died. Maybe the best days of my life happened long ago, and I'm destined to spend the remainder of my miserable years fondly remembering my childhood. Maybe untapped feelings are ghosts, doomed to haunt me until I die, surrounded by my Partner and my family, but still alone.

This is insane. We're two betrothed individuals, completely committed to our Partners. Yet here we stand, together, unable to sever a friendship never intended to be.

I'm nauseous. I don't want to be here. I'm prolonging the inevitable gash in my heart.

I don't know who I am. I don't know what I am. It isn't supposed to be like this. Why couldn't I have fallen hopelessly in love with Sam and forgotten about Piren? Why couldn't I have been normal and not such a fuck-up?

I step back, pushing my best friend away.

I can't hurt him again.

He scrunches his forehead, parting his lips slightly. "Trace…"

"I'll go."

Before he can protest, I'm halfway down the ladder.

"Trace!"

I'll go straight to the Mayor's office and take the blame. I'll throw myself on his desk and beseech him to spare my friend. I've endangered Piren's safety for the last time.

"Trace! Wait!"

I hit the ground running.

"Trace!"

I sprint toward the forest full-speed, but he races after me and bounds in front, stopping me in my tracks. Damn him and his long legs. Hands on his knees, he catches his breath four feet away.

"Trace...what if...oh God, this is so stupid..." He throws his hands behind his head and meets my eyes. "What if...what if there were no Assignments?"

"Piren...What—"

"If there were no Assignments, no Partners, no Ceremonies, if there never were. What would that have meant for us?"

I freeze. I'm completely lost in his eyes.

"No Partners, Trace. No Lara, no Sam." He steps toward me. "What would have happened between us?"

Stop. I can't.

"Would we have been friends?" Another step closer. "Or something else?"

"What do you—"

"No." He grabs my arms. "You know what I mean. If I was never betrothed to Lara. If you'd never been with Sam."

"That's impossible, Piren, because things are the way they are, and—"

"No. I didn't ask that. Answer the damn question."

"I—"

He kisses me before I can speak. My heart rockets into the stratosphere. Every part of me floods with warmth. I succumb to him, allowing my lips to move with his. My dizzying mind whirls into a haze as I taste my best friend. I entwine my fingers in his soft hair, pulling him closer, savoring every second.

Seventeen years built up, seventeen years my best friend. Seventeen years of memories, of thoughts, of everything my heart never put into words, spins into a million feelings at once, rushing through my body.

All the things I never felt with Sam.

PIREN ALLSTON

Oh my God, I kissed Trace.
Shit.
What the fuck was I thinking?
Leave. I should leave.
I can't. I can't leave her anymore.

TRACY BAILEY

An hour passed since we kissed in the moonlight. Maybe two. Time passes, but we remain. We lie on the floor of our treehouse, my head on his chest, his hand in mine, my thumb drawing circles on his palm. Our feet dangle off the side of our haven, into the darkness below.

His scent overwhelms my senses as I inhale, clinging to every last drop of this moment. It's the same scent that always meant my best friend was here.

Piren watches the stars, but I watch him, studying every freckle on his cheek. I snuggle closer, burrowing into the nook under his arm. Warm breeze drifts over us, blowing my hair over his face.

"Trace?"

I brush my curls off his eyes. "Hmm?"

"We could do it."

"Do what?"

"Run away. Go to Lornstown."

Wait, what?

That's the not the answer I expected.

"What?" I prop myself up on my elbow. "No. That's crazy."

"Why?" He sits up. "Why is it crazy?"

Why? How could that suggestion ever not *be crazy?*

"Why? Because us, Piren! Our families, our Partners. Lornstown isn't habitable. It's hell; it's for criminals. That's why." I trace my finger down his cheek. "No."

"We could be together."

No. He can't go to Lornstown. He can't ruin his life for me. I won't let my nightmares come to fruition. No.

"Absolutely not."

"Why?"

"It's irrational. Crazy."

"Maybe it is! Maybe it is crazy!" He raises his voice. "It's completely and totally crazy! But that's what this always was, Trace! That's what we always were. Crazy."

"N—"

"Our friendship was crazy. That time you showed up at my house nine years ago and kissed me, that was crazy! And I think about that all the damn time!"

"You…you do?"

"Yes! Every second of every damn day. Every second I'm with Lara. Every damn second. I try to focus on something else, anything else, and I can't. Just like I couldn't crop you out of that drawing. Just like I couldn't send you away Christmas Eve. Just like I came here tonight. It's absolutely insane, completely and totally crazy. But that's us."

"I won't see your face marred," I whisper. "Not because of me."

"Tell me, Trace. Tell me you don't feel the same way, and we'll go our separate ways. You can go home to Sam and pretend tonight never happened. I'll respect that. But if you tell me there's a chance, an inkling, even the slightest most miniscule possibility that maybe, just maybe, you could feel the same way…then we owe it to each other to try. Just to try. See for ourselves."

"But—"

"I let you go too many times, Trace. I can't do it anymore."

I leap to my feet. He jumps up beside me.

No. This is a bad effing idea.

I need to voice a rebuttal, to save him from making the worst mistake of his life. This is crazy. My wedding is in two weeks—to a different man. A man I'm supposed to love forever. And here's this other man, my best friend, telling me all these things he's not supposed to say. Things we're not supposed to feel.

But his words shoot through my body like a poison arrow, filling my core with venomous longing. A bull's-eye to the heart.

"Trace…please…Say something…"

I swallow down the sticky lump growing in my throat. "I can't see you hurt."

He gives me a half-smile. "You don't need to protect me. I know what I want." He kisses my cheek. "I want you." My heart flutters.

This is right. I could step off this treehouse and float...

No!

"Tell me you'll do it, Trace, tell me we'll go. We can go tomorrow in secret, just try for a night, and if we hate it, if it's awful, we come right back home and never speak of it again. I promise. Just one night, and then we make a decision. Nothing permanent until then. No pressure, I promise."

"Upheaving your life isn't a decision to be so frigging rash about."

"Rash? You think this is rash? God, Trace, come on. I've known you my entire life for freak's sake."

"You'd throw it away. Just like that." I glance sideways at him. "Your parents. Your brother. Your friends. Your fancy car. Your...Lara."

He nods quickly, his eyes fixed on mine.

Great. You'll get your face slashed and then change your mind, and you won't be able to come back, and it'll be my frigging fault.

"No." I furrow my brows. "I don't believe you."

"I'd do it, Trace! I swear I would! What the hell more can I do to prove that to you? I...I need you."

This is a bad fucking decision, but I can't fight it.

I don't want to fight it.

I close my eyes.

"Okay."

My heart lightens as the word slips from my mouth. He pulls me into his arms, a huge smile spreading across his face. I giggle into his sleeve.

"So, let's do it," he says. "Let's go to Lornstown."

PIREN ALLSTON

Saying good-bye to Trace leaves a vile, visceral taste in my mouth. Knots twist in my stomach as I watch her drive away, even though I'll see her again in the morning.

We solidified our plan before we parted, standing in the moon's shadow of our treehouse.

"No one can know about this," she said, wringing her hands. "I mean, traveling to Lornstown? It isn't exactly a beach resort."

"I won't tell anyone."

"I know."

I held my hand up, and she pressed her palm to mine. Her chest rose and fell with uneven breaths.

"Nervous?" I asked.

"No."

"I don't buy it. You're fidgeting."

"Sorry." She thrust her quivering hands to her sides. I caught one and laced her fingers with mine.

"What are you afraid of?" I asked. "Being caught? That they'll Banish you for spending the night in Lornstown?"

"Not exactly." She bit her lip.

"Then what?"

She brushed my cheek with her fingertips. "I like your face."

I laughed. "Well, I like yours."

"No, I mean, I like your face. I don't want it scarred."

"What?" I grinned. "Not gonna like me anymore if they cut me?"

"Don't even go there."

I rested my hand on her trembling arm. "It'll be fine; you'll see. We'll be together, and we'll never want to come home. It won't even be an issue. Don't worry."

She gave me a weak smile. "I hope you're right."

We stood in silence under the stars, holding each other's hands.

"Are *you* scared?" She squeezed my hand.

"No…" I smiled sheepishly. "Maybe a little, yeah."

"Me too. You need to promise me you won't tell anyone about this. I need to know we'll have the choice. If it sucks, we can come home, and no one will ever know about any of—"

"—I already promised—"

"We won't make any final decisions till we spend the night there. Sunday morning, we'll decide if we actually want to stay in Lornstown, but if we don't, we come straight home. Can't come home if someone found out and we're already Banished."

"I promise. It's your choice. If you hate it there, hate being with me, we'll come straight back home."

"It's *our* choice," she said. "And I won't hate being with you."

"Well, then, we won't have a problem!"

She sighed. "We'll see."

"You better not chicken out," I said with a wink.

"You either!" She shoved my arm.

"I won't."

She cocked her head. "How do you know?"

"Well…I guess…years ago, at my brother's First Kiss, this girl Ashley caused a big mess."

"I remember reading about that."

"Yeah, you and your trashy newspaper clippings."

"They're not trashy!"

"Yeah, yeah. I hated seeing them Banish her, 'cause to me, Banishment meant pain was all she had. It sucked. She withstood hell, but she left hand-in-hand with the other man—the man I thought ruined her whole damn life. I never got it before. Spent years wishing things went different for her. I guess…I don't pity her anymore. Because I understand."

"Understand what?"

"Why she did it."

Trace shuffled her feet. "And what if we decide to stay? Then what?"

"Then we'll stay." I shrugged. "It'll be great."

"And our weddings?"

I smirked. "Your parents might lose a few deposits."

"Oh, they'll be devastated." She gave me a lopsided grin. "About the money, of course. Not about me running away. 'Where has that little bitch run off to? Ladies attend their weddings! Goodness gracious!'" She flipped her hair in an exaggerated display.

"Two years apart and you're still the weirdest person I know."

"And yet you wanna run away with me. Who's weird now?"

We shared a nervous laugh.

"So, you'd really do it," she said. "Leave your family. Go to Lornstown. For me."

"I would indeed."

"Sounds like a poor life choice." She tightened her hand around mine. "You can back out, you know."

"Stop that." I kissed her forehead. "I'm going. End of discussion."

Her eyes ignited, sparkling in the moonlight. She kissed me under the stars, and the whole world disintegrated as we said good night.

I drive home, flooded with a million thoughts.

Maybe the odds of an un-Assigned couple succeeding are slim, but it doesn't matter. I'll live in Lornstown with Trace a thousand years before I live one more day here without her. Tonight can't fly fast enough before I see my best friend again.

I zip through the front door of my apartment and almost smash into Lara.

"I love you, Piren Allston."

"I love you, Lara Goodren."

The hollow words float off my tongue. I'm an actor reciting lines in a meaningless script, going through motions until tomorrow.

Lara lingers by the kitchen as I pour myself a glass of water. My hands shake so bad I can't hold a damn thing still, and water sloshes onto the counter. I slug it back in two gulps.

The sooner I sleep, the sooner I wake, the sooner I meet Trace at the train station.

"Night," I mutter, putting my glass in the sink.

Lara grabs my collar and hungrily presses her lips to mine. Nothing flutters inside me. I try to kiss her back, but the movement won't come.

She pulls back. "Is something wrong?"

"What? No! Sorry, just tired."

She tilts her head. "Where've you been?"

Her high voice feigns innocence, but her question comes laced with poison.

"Went to my parents' house, just checking in."

"Why didn't you bring me?"

"Oh, sorry." I tug my sleeve. "It was just a quick visit."

"You were gone awhile."

"Sorry. Guess I lost track of time."

"Right…" She watches me through the corners of her narrowing eyes. "I bought some decorations, to fill our new place after the wedding."

"Oh…cool."

"They're in the bathroom."

She beckons me to follow her into the hall. A pile of smoothened pebbles fill a purple basket on the bathroom sink, each one adorned with a word: *Love, Honesty,* and *Fun* glare at me from the top.

"They're inspiration stones," Lara says, rubbing *Honesty* between her fingers, "to bring good energy into our home."

"Cool."

"You hate them."

"I don't!"

She tosses the rock back into the collection with a clack. "I want to visit my parents tomorrow, and I want you to come. I haven't seen them in ages."

"Oh, well, um, I was actually planning…uh—" my knee jiggles beneath me "—to stay with Alan this weekend. Toni isn't feeling good, and he needs help keeping the place clean."

It's a flat lie, but "going to Lornstown with Trace" won't go any better.

"Oh…okay." She scrunches her mouth to the side. "Well, I'll come too, then. Keep Toni company."

I scratch my neck, not meeting her eyes. "I was actually planning on some guy time with my friend, you know? Watch some football, drink some beer…"

"Won't Toni be there?"

"Well, yeah, but she's really sick, completely bed ridden."

Lara crosses her arms. "What does she have?"

Um… "The stomach flu."

"Isn't that super contagious? Maybe you shouldn't go. I don't need you getting sick; we've got tons of weddings in the next month."

"I know! Don't worry, I'll be careful."

She squints.

She doesn't buy it.

"Okay, I'm beat. Good night, Lara!" I push past her and shut my door before she can interrogate me further.

Tomorrow is all that matters.

TRACY BAILEY

I creep into my dark apartment, creaking the door shut behind me. My brain reels from the evening, clouding my senses.

So, that's what it's like to make out with my best friend: amazing.

Maybe I'm a shitty, weak person for dooming him to Lornstown, but it was his idea, so it's okay.

Right?

I step into the hall.

Sam pounces from the darkness. "Boo!"

I jump back, heart plunging into my throat. He roars with laughter.

Asshole.

"You know I hate that, Sam!"

You insufferable, small-peckered prick. Who the hell gets joy from scaring people?

I catch my breath, hand over my heart. He slumps over onto me. Lips pressed together, I maneuver out from under his arm.

"I love you, Tracy Bailey."

"I love you, Sam Macey."

"You're back early."

"Ditto."

I hang my coat. I mean, I wasn't expecting him to have some wild bachelor party, crawling through dive bars with his brother, but still.

He reeks of liquor. I hold my breath and walk past him.

"How was your bachelorette party?"

What?

Oh, right, my alibi for sitting in the treehouse with Piren. If only he knew…

"Fun. Toni got wasted." It's plausible. "How was your bachelor party?"

"Awesome."

"Good."

He saunters toward me, wrapping his muscly arms around my waist. His grip is sweatier and tighter than Piren's. He leans in to kiss me, but I turn my cheek, and he presses his sweaty lips to my face instead.

Not in this lifetime, Sam.

"So...wife-to-be?"

Silence. *Oh, he's addressing me?*

"Oh. What?"

He smirks. "Wanna fool around?"

"*Excuse* me?" I shove him away.

"You heard me." He winks. "Come on, babe, the wedding's in two weeks. We don't have to go all the way..."

He reaches for my breast, but I swat him away.

Horny bastard.

"You're drunk. You know I hate alcohol."

"Come on, babe, what do you say?"

"I say good night, Sam."

I yank open my bedroom door, but he rams it shut again.

"Stop it. I'm going to bed." I clench my jaw. "Alone."

He holds his hand over the door. "What's the password?"

"Seriously, move."

"You have to say the password."

"Fine." I grit my teeth. "What's the frigging password?"

He grabs my hand and presses it to his crotch, hard and bulging. I yank my hand away at light speed and slap him so hard across the face.

"We aren't married; you don't touch me!"

He sneers, holding his hand to his reddening cheek.

"Not yet," he growls. "We aren't married yet. But soon enough. Go to bed. Soon as we're married, I don't want this bullshit."

Don't worry, Sam.

I slam my bedroom door.

After tomorrow, you won't get any bullshit from me anymore.

PIREN ALLSTON

I bolt up at the crack of dawn and speed through my morning routine, whistling to myself in the shower. I throw two changes of clothes in a backpack and zip into the hall.

"I love you, Piren Allston," Lara mumbles, emerging from her bedroom cave.

I prance through the kitchen, rehashing last night's beautiful details in my head.

"Hey!" She stomps toward me. "I said I love you, Piren Allston!"

"I love you, Lara Goodren!" It comes out sarcastic, but I don't bother to correct myself.

"You're happy this morning." She crosses her arms. "What's so great about seeing Alan and Toni?"

"Can't talk. Gotta run!" I peck her on the cheek and race out the door before she can protest.

I park in a vacant lot several miles away and pull out my cellphone map to plot our course. Lornstown is clearly marked, encircled with a bright red line labeled "KEEP OUT."

Ironically, venturing a visit to Lornstown is punishable by Banishment there permanently. No one goes unless they're Banished… or choose to run away.

We'll travel to the last stop on the train, switch buses twice, then plod a mile or so by foot. There's no direct public transportation to the cut-off town.

I can't risk anyone seeing my car parked overnight at the train station, so I leave it in the vacant lot and board the bus. I tug a red baseball cap over my head, covering my identifying blond hair.

This is it.

I'm at the station twenty-minutes early, but Trace beat me here. She sits cross-legged on a bench in the back of the station, with sunglasses over her eyes and a black wool hat—completely wrong for the summer—hiding her distinguishable curly hair. It's a strong disguise, but I'd recognize my best friend anywhere.

My heart lurches when I see her, and I quicken my pace. She beams, but keeps her hands in her lap. A balloon swells inside me with each step. I sit down on the bench, leaving several feet of space between us.

For the first time ever, I have twenty-four hours with Trace. Just Trace.

"Hey, stranger," she says slightly louder than a whisper. "Ready to write the story Fangs and Fat Head go to Lornstown?"

"Should have written it a long time ago."

She smiles into her hand, her cheeks blushing rosy.

People amble by on their way to the tracks. Each time a new person passes, my pulse races until I mentally confirm it's a stranger.

Two minutes.

My leg jitters as my furiously blinking eyes scan the station. Trace inhales short, uneven breaths, tapping her fingers along the bench. I slide my hand over and brush hers. She recoils, but I catch the hint of a smile on her face.

After a damn eternity, a harsh whistle blows, announcing our train's arrival.

We climb aboard, and Trace clambers to the back, claiming seats far from prying eyes.

I plop down two seats away, leaving an empty seat between us. My hands grow sweaty in my lap. The conductor inspects our tickets, then returns to his place at the front.

The train whistle screams, and we're off.

We glance up and down the aisle, peeking into every nearby row of seats, but see no familiar faces. I close my eyes and release the heavy breath I didn't realize I was holding.

We're safe.

Strangers will see us together and assume we're Partners. Just a perfectly acceptable couple, riding the train. Nothing unusual to see here, folks!

I slide into the empty seat between us, and Trace lights up.

"Candy?" She pours some chocolate drops into my hand. "I stole it from Sam's stash."

I can't stop smiling. I feel like I'm going to explode out of my skin.

This is the best day of my life.

"Where'd you tell Lara you were going?" she asks.

"Alan's." I toss the candy into my mouth. "Where'd you tell Sam?"

She grins. "I'm so glad you asked. The drunken idiot was passed out in his own piss when I woke up. I stepped over him on my way out."

"You didn't tell him you were going away overnight?" I shove her arm. "Possibly forever?"

"Left a note on the table. He'd flip if I didn't, and then blow up my phone with stalker texts all night."

I click my tongue. "'Bounce' still has a temper, huh? Didn't he outgrow that crap after high school?"

"You'd think, but sadly my Partner is a twelve-year-old. I wrote that I'm sleeping over V and Oliver's. He'll never think to call and check; he hates my sister. He'll never admit it, but I know he does." She nudges me with her elbow. "Maybe when he wakes up and cleans up after himself, he'll see the note."

"You landed a winner."

"Oh, I know." She drops another candy into her mouth. "And get this. He tried to fuck me last night..."

I raise my brows.

"...but I slapped him."

"Ha!" I jab her leg. "Good. You're too good for that loser."

"Hey, I've always thought that. But you know what they say, 'One-hundred-percent accuracy! We know best!'" She mocks a near-perfect impression of Clarence.

She meets my eyes. I love her eyes.

"No, they don't..." I squeeze her hand. "They don't know best..."

How anyone could Partner me with Lara before Trace is insane.

I have to keep reminding myself that before yesterday, we hadn't seen each other in almost two years. We might as well be eight again, embarking on another adventure together.

Trace rests her head on my shoulder. "What do you think it's like?" She tiptoes her fingers up and down my leg. "Lornstown."

"I guess we're gonna find out, right?"

"I mean, do you think it's as bad as the horror stories?"

"Erm...I hope not?"

"Maybe it's not so bad?" Her statement comes out like a question. "Maybe the stories are blown out of proportion?"

"Maybe." My leg jiggles against the seat in front of us.

"Miserable, mopey people everywhere? That's like our high school. Can't be worse than that, right?"

My knee progresses to full-blown bouncing. "What's the scariest Lornstown story you ever heard?"

"Hmm..." She scrunches her mouth to the side. "The 'murder a minute' thing is pretty scary. But I'm not sure how possible that is, or the whole town would be dead."

"I've heard they've got lots of creepy diseases."

Trace nods. "My dad calls them sex diseases."

"Well, remind me not to bone any locals."

"Noted."

Her hair tickles my face. I lean in and kiss her cheek.

"Piren, there's one thing."

"What?"

"I don't wanna see any kids. We see them coming; we walk the other way. Okay?"

"Okay...why?"

"I can't...handle...sick kids. It's too sad." She shudders. "I mean, I don't want to sound like an ass, but I just...can't take it. All the scars and deformities and stuff they have there. Okay?"

I press my forehead to hers. "Okay."

She laces her fingers with mine. Fields and houses zip by as we chug along, closer and closer to our potential new home.

I close my eyes, fighting back the growing nausea in my stomach.

What if Lornstown is really as bad as everyone says? Can I doom myself to life with only pariahs and criminals for company? Can I be happy knowing all my friends and family back home hate me and think I'm a horrible person? Can I handle calling Mason and my parents to inform them they'll never see me again? Can I commit to being Banished and never look back?

Trace leans her warm body into me, her chest rising and falling as she breathes. Her hair smells like honey and mint. She consumes my senses, roping me in.

I can. I can commit to that life.

TRACY BAILEY

One long train ride and two buses later, we're trekking through grass as tall as my waist. It brushes up against my shins, making them itch like hell, but I don't care.

We swing our entwined hands as we walk. My heart's all feathery inside, like it could float right out of my body and up to the sky. It reminds me of that light-headed dizziness after all those frigging tequila shots, as if my best friend manages to intoxicate me merely with his presence. I can't look at him without beaming, like some swoony, lovesick kid—Oh God, I'm becoming Veronica!—but I relish it.

We've started a new adventure story called "Fat Head and Fangs Go to Lornstown." I add a sentence, then he adds another, weaving a twisted tale of shenanigans. If they have pens and paper in Lornstown, this one's going in the anthology.

We tackle the mangy trail step by step, stumbling every few feet over rocks and debris. Protruding tree roots trip us as we trudge along. Every time one of us flounders over the terrain, we break down in paralyzing laughter.

I try to keep Piren laughing so we don't ruminate. With each step, a pit grows in my stomach. Neither of us mentions Lornstown, and I won't be the one to start, because it makes my stomach cramp. I have no idea what to expect. I've heard the stories, but never seen a picture; I mean, the Banished can't exactly come home to show slides.

In all my wildest, craziest dreams of where my life would lead, I never once thought I'd end up in Lornstown. Why would I? You get your Partner, you love your Partner, and unless you're a horrible person, you marry your Partner and stay with them forever. It's simple.

Maybe in an alternate universe, I'd be Partnered with Piren. I'd be home with Veronica right now, gleefully comparing wedding notes and trying on poufy dresses. I'd be normal. It's a nice delusion, but it's a pipe dream. Lornstown or not, I have Piren now, and I'll take what I can get.

We hike past abandoned barns and dried farm land, surrounded by seas of tall, grassy plains. Neglected corn fields line the road, overgrown with weeds. The summer breeze blows a faded barn door to our left; it swings and thuds against the side of a paint-chipped silo. I inhale the smooth scent of wheat and grass, savoring the aroma.

"I'd say this is our boldest adventure yet," Piren says.

"Agreed."

"How will we know when we're there? Do you think it's marked? Will they send out the welcoming committee?"

"Oh, a parade, I'm sure." I squeeze his hand. "Are you sure we're going the right direction?"

"Yes! No faith in your best friend."

"Well, that's what you said two years ago, when you totally butchered directions to the café."

"Hey, now, I checked the map this time."

The further we walk, the more decrepit the buildings and farm houses become. Some have holes the size of boulders in their roofs. Maybe this was once a functional farming town, but I'm guessing the inhabitants dissipated to distance themselves from Lornstown.

The breeze whispers through the wheat fields around us. To my right, a thick oak tree splits into two hefty trunks.

That would be a perfect treehouse tree. Maybe this won't be so bad…

As the sky dampens with evening dew, we approach a vast wooden wall, stretching at least twenty feet high. It sprawls left to right, as far as the eye can see. We cautiously step closer, tightening our grip on each other's hands. Yellow posts marked with warnings dapple the ground.

FORBIDDEN — DO NOT CROSS BOUNDARY LINE

Perched atop a dandelion-infested hill, a rickety wooden archway divides the wall, creating a slim opening barely wide enough to pass through. The arch boasts a two-foot wooden sign with white painted lettering.

LORNSTOWN
POPULATION 28,151

"Population's smaller than I thought," I say. "Also, I was expecting guards, but I guess the town itself is deterrent enough."

Piren fidgets. "So…this is it?"

"Guess so."

"Do we…go under it?"

I take a deep breath. Everything behind the wall, beyond that arch, is Lornstown. This is it—passing through the barrier into the forbidden world. A living horror movie awaits on the other side.

I unlink from Piren's grasp and step toward it.

"No." He grabs my arm. "Together."

Heart thudding in my chest, I take my best friend's hand.

"You ready?"

"Let's go."

Holding my breath, I squeeze him tight, and we step under the arch.

I don't know what I was expecting to happen, but nothing does.

A sprawling hillside presents itself to us, draped in the darkening shroud of night. My shoulders tighten as my body prickles into hyper-vigilance.

We're in criminal territory now. Someone could come out and stab us at any moment.

Piren's face drains of all color. His eyes flick side to side, scanning the hill. My arms grow ridged, clamped tight at my sides. Below our feet stretches a dirt road, leading down the mound, probably to the village. I squint ahead, but thickening nighttime darkness blinds me. Piren clicks his cellphone, emitting a dull light.

"Where do we go?" I ask. "Should we head down there?"

"I don't like how dark it's getting."

"Hey!" booms a voice.

We whirl around, jerking our fists up. A burly, unshaven, sweatshirt-clad man stands before us, Banishment scar etched across his cheek—the first reprobate. My pulse rockets through my chest.

Does he plan to rob us? Rape us? Kill us?

I gulp.

A jovial smile blooms across his round face. "Welcome to Lornstown, the walled city!"

I jump at the depth of his voice. My eyes flash from my quivering best friend, to the stranger, and back.

"I'm Michael, but everyone calls me Mikey. So glad to meet you folks!"

He thrusts out a grubby hand. Keeping my eyes locked on him, I shake it. His firm grip leaves a dirty film on my fingers.

"And what do they call you?" He's got one silver-crowned tooth on the bottom and a gap between his top front teeth. "You kids got names?"

Piren's hand trembles beside me. I reach out to steady it.

"Aw, I don't bite," Mikey says. "Well, not hard anyway. Promise." He winks.

Mikey's hiking boots are caked in several layers of mud. His green eyes glimmer, even in the setting sunlight. My tense arms relax. In a weird way, I trust him.

"Tracy Bailey."

"Piren Allston."

He gives us a sly smile. "Those fake names?"

I gape.

Shit. Maybe we should have given fake names.

"Ha! I'm only kidding. Come on, don't be shy. You look starved half to death."

Our new friend presses ahead down the path, beckoning us to follow. Piren signals me with his hands.

"*What do we do?*" he mouths.

I freeze. "*I don't know,*" I mouth back.

Above our heads, stars twinkle, offering their reassuring light. They're probably the same stars we watched together yesterday, from the treehouse floor, wrapped in each other's arms. A warm calm settles over me; I feel like we're going to be okay.

I tug Piren's hand with a squeeze, and we follow Mikey down the hill.

Pebbles crunch beneath our feet when we reach the main road below. A few street lamps dangling from wooden posts light the way, illuminating the stretch of gravel. Two women stride past us with a nod, their hands entwined together at their sides. My gaze follows them as they pass.

Huh?

The dirt road is devoid of vehicles, and layered with bulging bumps and rocks. It's only slightly less treacherous than the path from the bus. Log cabins line the street on both sides, lights flickering in almost every window. Curtains flutter as we trek by, hiding peeping faces. Each cabin is constructed of thick tree trunks plastered in green moss—overgrown treehouses.

Do people live in these?

"So, what's your story?" Mikey asks. "You know, why're you here? Are you two Banished or—"

"No." *Let's not rush things.*

"We chose to come," Piren says. "We ran away."

"Yeah?" Mikey says. "Thought so. Didn't think I saw scars on your pretty faces." He spins around. "I take it your Assigned Partners didn't work for you, huh?"

Piren tightens his grip on my hand.

What's safe to say to this stranger?

"Eh, it's okay. You two look like you've seen a ghost. Anyway, I'll tell you 'bout me. Been here six years, married to Lilian. You'll meet her eventually. Anyway, city Assigned me to this girl, Karen Otis. Now, Karen's a fine woman, really she was..."

"This dude is crazy," I whisper.

"Crazy awesome," Piren says.

"Now, Karen's mother kept telling her, she should—"

Shouts burst from our left, and I leap a foot in the air.

"Geez, you two are jumpy." Mikey halts beside the door of the noisy building.

"What...what was that yelling?"

Mikey chuckles. "Probably one of Ed's dirty jokes. He's a rowdy one. You'll see. My apologies in advance if he's too much; that guy's got no filter."

He indicates toward the door. A brown hanging sign above our heads advertises this building as "The Lighthouse Restaurant."

Mikey yanks open the door, unleashing an explosion of laughter from inside that practically bowls me over. He walks in.

We step through the entrance after him, squeezing together to keep our grip on each other. Piren's hand is sweaty and hot from holding mine so long, but I don't care.

People pack The Lighthouse wall-to-wall. Some stand off to the side, but most huddle around a bulky, wooden table in the center of the room, cackling.

"Hey, everybody! Look who I found!" Mikey thunders, waving his arms. "It's Piren and Tracy, from the city!"

Two hundred eyes flash to us. The room falls silent. A fork clinks against a plate.

I inhale a shaky breath, offering the crowd a weak wave. "Hi."

Everyone leaps to their feet, erupting in applause. People clap and stomp, whistling, smiling and happy. Dozens of healthy, normal people, cheer for *us*.

My mouth hangs open.

This is not what we expected. This is not what we expected at all.

PIREN ALLSTON

The crowd thrusts us to the center of the room, into folds of people. Men and women of all ages, races, and sizes pat us on the back and cheer, proclaiming variations of "Welcome to Lornstown!" While some faces bear the slash of Banishment, others are clean, unmarred faces of runaways. Misfits. Outsiders. They swarm us, pushing and shoving to shake our hands.

Trace beams beside me, her cheeks growing pink as she greets everyone.

Is this real?

A pale older woman with wispy white hair and a floral dress hobbles up to the table. Her crooked nametag identifies her as Loretta. She slides a tray of salami sandwiches down the table to us. Trace pounces, stuffing one in her mouth. Stomach grumbling, I follow.

Mikey climbs up on a chair and raises his hands. The commotion dies to silence, all eyes descending on Trace and me.

"Um…thanks everyone. This is…very nice," Trace says, her mouth bulging with food. I nod in agreement.

"So, who are ya'll?" a guy in the back shouts. "Runaways? Adulterers? What?"

Trace scarfs the remainder of her sandwich in one bite. "Well, this is my best friend—" she nudges me with her elbow, mid-gulp "—since age seven."

I cringe at her public use of the words, waiting for someone to excoriate her.

But they don't.

Aw's and sympathetic pouts fill the room, as if everyone holds some sort of mutual understanding. My ears burn, but I can't fight my growing smile.

"One of *those* stories, eh?" Loretta saunters over.

"One of what stories?"

The crowd parts to let her through. "Honey, it's the biggest reason we see a new face around here. Falling for the wrong person—or as I call it, the *right* person." She brushes my cheek with her fingertips. "Let me tell you, honey, you ain't weird. It happens all the time."

The room explodes with cheers. Hands thump us on the back.

"It does?"

"Sure thing." Loretta collects our empty plate. "Someone's not happy with their Partner, loves someone else, wants their best friend instead...You're no different. When you love someone, *really* love someone—" she takes my hand in her wrinkly fingers and presses it to Trace's "—nothing else matters. And that's how it should be."

Several people nod. Trace laces her fingers into mine, and as if jolted with electricity, I sense our shared thought: *they understand.*

The room buzzes with a hundred voices aimed at Trace and me. Some people want updates on family in town they haven't seen in years. Others want to congratulate us on "making the move." After several rounds of meet-and-greets, everyone settles around the table. Loretta pushes Trace and me into seats at the head.

One by one, the Lornstowners share their stories.

Bill and Pasha met at work. They chose to leave their Assigned Partners within days, embracing their Banishment. They call their Banishment scars "Battle Scars."

Lauren ran away from home and her abusive Partner. She now owns a small construction business and lives happily here by herself.

Constance felt smothered by her family and wanted to make her own decisions. She ran away a month before her Assigned wedding and fell in love with Albert, who left for similar reasons.

Mark didn't exactly want to be Assigned to a woman; he was Banished for this and now lives with his husband, Erich, and their adopted baby daughter.

Tom's Partner died in a freak accident two months before their wedding. Wanting kids, and dreading solitude, he ran away to start a new life. He settled in Lornstown and is expecting his first child with his wife, Olivya.

Janet was Assigned to Kevin's brother, but wanted Kevin instead. They were Banished together when the affair was discovered.

Eloise and her Partner, Martin, were Banished when Eloise became pregnant before their wedding. They live together in Lornstown with their three children.

Partners Wren and Carmen were married with two children, but became pregnant with a third child. When forced to choose abortion or exile, they chose exile. They now have five kids.

As each person talks, the balloon in my chest expands, threatening to pop from the excitement inside. Each person is different, but somehow the same. Each person, estranged from the herd, found acceptance among the outcasts. We belong here as easily as everyone else.

A familiar woman strides through the restaurant. I whip my head to the left in a double take. Long black hair waves down her back, flowing freely as she walks. A bearded man carrying two mugs leans in to kiss her cheek.

It's an older, pregnant, still beautiful Ashley Wyman. Scarred but glowing, she clutches the hand of the same man she wanted long ago. He whispers something in her ear, patting her engorged belly.

They're still together. It's possible.

TRACY BAILEY

These people are…crazy? Maybe. But I don't care. Maybe I'm crazy. Maybe Piren's crazy. Maybe we're all a little bit crazy, but maybe that's what happens when you're with that one person who makes you feel all jumbled inside.

No one cares Piren isn't my Partner. No one castigates me for abandoning Sam. No one calls me a slut for holding Piren's hand. No one harasses me to plan my stupid wedding. And for the first time in forever, I'm in a room full of people, yet there's no one I want to strangle.

I lean against my best friend at the table and bury my face in his sweatshirt. He wraps his arms tighter around me. I close my eyes and inhale his cinnamon scent, enveloping my senses.

Freedom. This is freedom.

Constance plops down next to me. Her floor-length, wavy brown dress brushes the wooden floor. Long, black braids flop against her back as she moves. Her unscarred face is free of makeup, aside from cherry lipstick, which accentuates her most striking feature: her shiny white teeth and unwavering smile.

"So, I bet you both have a lot of questions," she says, chewing a wad of gum.

My cheeks ache from grinning all night, but I can't stop. "Right now I'm just overwhelmed. You're all so nice."

"Well, thanks," she says. "You sound so surprised."

"Oh, I uh…"

"Ha! I'm joking. I know, I know, the *miserable Lornstowners,* right?" She gestures around the room with her hand. "We're out here all alone, drowning in our own depression. Ha!" She slaps her thigh. "Tracy, right?"

I nod. She blows a gum bubble until it bursts, then sucks it back into her mouth.

"Tracy, I mean, we of all people know it's not easy being Banished. We try to make this a second home for everyone who comes our way, regardless of who you love or who you are."

"That's…really cool."

"Yeah, I know, right? See Casey over there?" She nods toward the corner of the room. "Tiny redhead with the green shirt?"

I nod.

"Came here last week. That's her boyfriend, Todd. Poor things nearly wet themselves when they met dear old Mikey."

I cock my head. "What's a 'boyfriend?'"

"Wow. Just, wow. You really are a lost little lamb." She pats my arm. "Boyfriend, girlfriend, whatever, it's a word for someone you want to be with. Not married, just *with*."

"Like a lover?"

"Ha! That's great. Yeah, I guess you could call it that."

Piren leans in. "Will you be my girlfriend, Trace?"

"Sure, but only if you'll be my boyfriend."

"I don't know. You're kind of a pain in the ass." He strokes his chin as if deep in thought. "But you do bring me chocolate, so I guess it's a deal."

"Well, I get the worse end of the deal. I mean, I have a boyfriend who drives like a crazy person." I shove his arm and turn back to Constance. "You're not scarred, not Banished, so you must not be trapped behind the walls, then? You can leave whenever you want?"

She shrugs. "I could, I guess. I'd have to explain where I was the past twelve years, and I don't think they'd like my answer. Haven't ventured a trip past the walls since I came." She wads up her gum in a tissue. "Plus, I don't care to. Those people are prudes."

"Tell me about it." I shake my head. "How do you guys get food? And medicine? I mean, aren't you disconnected from everything?"

"We're self-sustainable with food — grow it all ourselves. Sometimes we make trades to passing travelers, if they don't know we're Lornstowners. I mean, passersby see a nice guy on the side of the road selling fruit, and boom! Easy trade for some aspirin."

"Wait, the road? All the way back by the bus stop? So, people do venture outside the wall?"

She smirks. "Not supposed to, but they do. Only way to make trades with travelers. We gotta send unscarred people, of course.

They're the only ones who can pass through the wall without fear of instant identification. Otherwise it blows the whole thing."

"But what if someone sees them leave Lornstown?"

She shoots me a sideways smile. "No one's been caught yet. They're sneaky."

Sneaky, huh? I could do that job. Sounds fun.

"What about medical care?" Piren leans over my shoulder. "Like, doctors? Dentists?"

"What, you think they all fell in love with their Partners too?" She snorts. "Please, we've got more doctors here than we know what to do with. They're kind of a nuisance, actually. Think they know everything about everything."

"What about Internet?"

"Well, the town cuts us off from theirs, but we wouldn't want that censored BS anyway. We've got some people working on developing a Lornstown network. I'd say it'll be up within the next few months."

My eyes drift to the silver device on the table beside her. "And phones?"

"Same thing, really." She picks up her cell and rotates it in her hands. "The town blocks our area code, to keep any of our phones from reaching people back home. And when someone's reported as a runaway, their line is cut off too. It won't even work to check the time." She thrusts her phone in my face. "But look! Magic! We have our own phones we—gasp—make ourselves!"

I arch a brow. "I see that."

"Better than the shitty town ones, if you ask me. We text and call each other all the time." She nods at a guy across the table, whose fingers zip across his phone screen faster than Veronica's. "Some people, a little too much."

I twirl a ringlet of hair around my finger. "Where do you all live?"

"Cabins. Didn't you see them on your way to The Lighthouse? We keep some empty ones for new people, so you guys can live there a few months while you settle. Quit doubting us!" She pokes my arm. "We've got it all right here: schools, doctors, stores, restaurants, everything. Self-maintained and proud of it. Who needs some stuffy town anyway?"

Loretta slides a beer across the table to Constance.

"Thanks, Etta!" Constance takes a sip, and yanks my hand out of Piren's. "Want to meet my son? He's only four."

"Oh…umm…"

"Evan!"

Footsteps patter against the floorboards. A small figure races into the room, screeching to a halt beside us, the top of his head barely visible over the tabletop. My heart rate accelerates to an alarming zip. I cup my hand around my eyes, obscuring my view.

"*Don't let him over here,*" I mouth to Piren. "*I don't do sick kids.*"

"*What?*" His forehead creases. "*You okay?*"

"Evan, say hi to your new friend Tracy!" Constance says. The boy tugs my sleeve.

I rub my hands down my pant legs. Clenching my jaw, I rotate down to greet the boy.

Dark hair curled atop his chubby face, his hazel-brown eyes blink up at me. He shares the same dimpled smile as his mother, with a large gap from a missing baby tooth.

"Hi," he says, covering his blushing face behind plump fingers.

This isn't possible.

"Hi, Evan." The words slip out in a breathy whisper. "He's…healthy."

"What?" Constance scrunches her face. "Oh, you can't really believe all that garbage, do you? Please! Evan's fit as any Partner-produced child; I'd stake my life on it." She gulps a swig of beer and returns her attention to her son.

I slink down in my seat, cheeks burning.

Well, I'll be damned. What a cute kid.

"Do they have weddings here, Constance?" Piren asks.

I raise my eyebrows.

"I'm just curious! I mean, they have everything else here…"

"All the time," Constance says. "Please, we love weddings. Mine was crazy. Big open party out in the field, it was the best. We celebrated all night, dancing under the stars."

"Age twenty-four, right?" I ask, staring at the table.

"What?" She tilts her head. "Honey, I got married at thirty-two. Anna over there, she's sixty-one, never been married. Man, you're both sheep. Welcome to freedom, friends." She lifts her drink to us in a toast.

My mouth opens, then closes again.

Constance's wedding sounds *perfect.* If I ever someday marry here, it's exactly what I want — not some over-the-top wealth festival everyone drags me to back home. Definitely not the shit-show people expect from Sam and me in two weeks.

Could Lornstown be my reprieve?

Constance butters a roll for her son. Piren engages Evan in conversation beside me, asking all about his friends and preschool, to which the boy animatedly responds. My fidgety hands grow quiet in my lap. Their voices fade. My eyes blur, conjuring images in my mind.

Piren talks to a different little boy — one with his blond hair and my curls. My best friend is old and gray beside me, in a treehouse cabin on the side of the dirt road. We're sharing stories at The Lighthouse and laughing with Constance and Mikey. I spin with Piren under the stars, in a simple white farmer's dress, among a handful of cheery friends. I can see myself wanting all those normal things I didn't want before. I can see myself being normal.

But maybe I was always normal. ·

PIREN ALLSTON

Two guys and a girl bustle to the front of the room, hauling keyboards and guitars.

Mikey whips out a fiddle, strumming a chord as he passes us. Half the restaurant gets to their feet, pushing tables to the sides of the wooden-plank floor to form an empty space in the middle. After a few minutes tuning squeaky notes, the band breaks into music, and peppy beats fill the restaurant. One by one, people rise to their feet, crowding to the center of the room to dance. Some of the drunker individuals caterwaul along with the music.

Trace grabs my hand and yanks me to the dance floor.

"I don't know this song!" I shout over the crowd.

"Me neither!" she shouts back. "Just go with it!"

I wrap my arms around her waist, pressing our bodies together. Tightly-packed dancers spin and laugh around us, whirling with the music. Several people thump on tables, adding percussion to the array of instruments. The floor rumbles under a hundred stomping feet.

Trace meets my eyes, and we're off, galloping around the room with the others. Maybe we look silly together, her being a good eight inches shorter than me, but we're as swift as anyone else. And in this crowd, I doubt anyone cares.

"Hey, Piren!" Trace shouts over the music. I twirl her under my arm, and her thick hair whips past my face.

"Yeah?"

"Remember when we had to do this in front of the whole gym class?"

"And everyone thought it was so weird?"

"I remember thinking, I would never, ever, ever need to know how to do this stupid dance! And now I'm doing it! I'm dancing with you!"

"Yes!"

She throws her arms in the air and spins. We dance and whirl until our heads grow dizzy and our ribs ache from laughing. Gasping for air, we collapse into giggles, sweat beading on our foreheads.

"You guys are on fire," a woman says, gleefully waltzing past us. Trace gives her an embellished curtsy.

"Let's slow it down a bit, folks," Mikey croons over the microphone.

The band decelerates, strumming into a romantic melody. The restaurant's yellow lights dim to a soft, flickering blue. Trace reaches up and slides her arms around my neck. I crane my neck down and touch my forehead to hers. Our feet glide side to side, and we sway together. Her lips part slightly.

"Piren?"

I swallow. "Yeah?"

She kisses me in the middle of the restaurant, in front of a hundred people. My heart leaps. She entangles her fingers in my hair, and the whole world disappears.

TRACY BAILEY

I want to kiss Piren again. I want to keep dancing and rocking in his arms, but it's almost one in the morning, and yawning Lornstowners filter out of The Lighthouse one by one. They say their good-byes and head home, wherever *home* may be.

I catch Piren's eye. "Should we go?"

"Go where?"

"Oops. I don't know."

"Guess we didn't plan this one through, huh?"

"Nope." A stifling yawn rips through my body. "Typical."

The last group of rowdy restaurant-goers empties into the street, their hollers and laughter echoing into the night air. A bus boy in a yellow apron sponges crumbs off the big table.

"Well, I guess we could camp outside?"

"Yeah, that wouldn't be too bad—"

"All righty, folks." Loretta hobbles toward us. "Now, I assume y'all are staying here tonight? At the Inn?"

Piren thrusts his hands in his pockets and stares at the ground.

I fidget with my fingers. "Oh, um…we don't really, um, have a lot of money with us."

"It's fine, dears. You aren't putting anyone out."

"Are you sure?" I bite my lip.

"Of course." She pats her wrinkly hand to my cheek. "Follow me."

We tiptoe after her, into the kitchen, and up a set of rickety wooden stairs in the back. The floorboards creak with each step.

"All righty, you two." Loretta's eyelids droop. "Bathroom's down the hall. Extra blankets in the closet. Do you want two bedrooms or one?"

My eyes widen.

How the fuck do I answer that?

We're not married. But when we move to Lornstown officially, won't we share a room anyway? What if I say I want one bedroom, and the suggestion completely disgusts him? Would he bolt back to town without me? Would Loretta think I'm some kind of pervert? Will they laugh at me? What do I say?

"One," Piren says.

I raise my brows; he shrugs. We both suppress a giggle.

"All righty. Room three, right here. In you go. I'm in the next building if you need anything, dears. Good night."

She shuts the door. We are alone.

PIREN ALLSTON

One bedroom? What was I thinking? Did I totally freak her out?

One king-sized bed sits in the middle of the room like an elephant, draped in a fuzzy red comforter. Two plump white pillows perch at the head. Trace pulls down the cream-colored sheets, not meeting my eyes.

My left knee itches with the desire to bounce, but I force it still. Trace hasn't said a word since Loretta left. The mattress squeaks as she slumps down on the edge of the bed.

She smiles. I smile back. We dart our eyes away.

All I want to do is crawl into that cozy-looking bed with her.

Is that all I want to do?

"I...I'm gonna put my pajamas on." She rises from the bed. "Look over there."

I turn toward the wall to the sounds of ruffling fabric and zippers behind me.

I wonder what I would see if I turned around...

Something twists in my stomach. I shift my eyes to the wooden plank floor.

I'm in the same room with a non-Partner. Alone. She's naked. I'm not married.

This is so weird.

Rebelling is fun.

"I'm going to put mine on too," I say. "So, no peeking from your side either."

"Mm-hmm."

Keeping my back to Trace, I slip out of my clothes and slide on my plaid pajama pants. Trace stays silent, rustling in her bag behind me.

What's on her mind? Is she upset? Happy? Nervous? Excited?

"Trace?"

"Mmm?"

"Is this…all right?"

"Ha! I was waiting for that question…Yeah, it is."

"Are you sure?"

"Yeah."

"I can…sleep on the floor if you want."

"No, it's cool. I promise."

"Okay." I stretch my arms over my head, pulling on a white T-shirt.

"So…weird to think we could live here soon, huh?"

"Yeah…" I twiddle my fingers. "I can see us here, though. You know, happy."

"Me too."

Silence.

"You know, I feel a little betrayed, in a way," I say.

"What do you mean?"

"They made Lornstown sound so shitty, and it was just a big lie. A farce."

"Yeah, I know, right? Kinda makes you wonder…" She trails off.

"Wonder what?"

"If the whole Assignment system is a sham."

I shuffle my feet in the corner. A warm night breeze drifts through the open porthole window. I close my eyes and inhale. There's something familiar about this place.

It reminds me of the treehouse.

"Piren?"

"Yep?"

"Are you nervous?"

"About what?"

She doesn't answer immediately.

"This. This whole thing. Making our choice."

"Nope. Are you? Nervous, I mean."

"No," she says. "Actually, I'm kind of surprised how not-nervous I am."

"Me too."

Trace is quiet again for a long moment.

"When did you know?" she asks.

"Know what?"

"Know…about us. How you…felt about me."

"Oh, wow…I guess…I guess I've always sorta known. I just never *knew*, you know? Never admitted it."

"Me too."

"I mean there was this one time…" I run my finger down the wall. "You'll never remember it."

"Try me."

"I'd just turned thirteen. We were sitting in the school library, and I don't know. You just…looked at me. And I felt something. I wanted…I wanted to kiss you."

"Really?"

"Yeah. What about you? A specific moment?"

"Oh, gosh," she says. "There were so many."

"Ha! Really?"

"Yeah, like, dozens. I think…that time at the Assignment Lab. The field trip."

"You mean, the most awkward moment of my life?"

She snorts. "Yeah. Exactly. I mean, I think I always had the feelings, but when she called our names together…I don't know…I guess I started questioning everything. All the 'What if's,' you know?"

"Yeah."

We share a jittery laugh.

"Can I turn around now?"

"Yeah. Turn around."

I step back from the wall.

My breath hitches in my throat.

Trace stands before me, blushing and barefoot, draped in a silky pink nightgown. She wrings her clasped hands, smiling shyly. I swallow hard, unable to take my eyes off her.

"So…should we get into bed?" she asks.

"Okay."

Neither of us moves.

Do I get into bed first? Do I touch her? Do I leave space between us?

Coming to Lornstown was bad enough, but jumping into bed with Trace will seal the deal. This sin betrays everything. Once I do this, there's no going back. My old life is over.

We face each other, separated by a mattress desert. Warm blankets lie open in the neutral zone, inviting us to a tantalizing crime.

My leg jitters. *No.* I clamp my hand over my knee. *Stop.*

I take a deep breath and crawl into bed. She follows.

I lie stiff on my back, staring at the ceiling, blanket pulled up to my waist. We lie in silence, as far apart as two bodies on a king-sized bed could possibly be. The heat from her body seeps through the sheets.

Maybe once, I've thought about this moment, wondered what it would be like, to lie beside her. Now we're here, together, in a surreal fantasy world.

My hands dampen, clamped in tight fists over the sheets. Trace's leg brushes mine under the covers, and she jerks away. Our ragged breathing mingles with the soft hum of crickets outside.

She rolls onto her side to face me, resting her cheek on her hands.

"Hi," she whispers.

"Hi."

Her electrifying gaze churns my stomach, and I brush a curly hair strand from her face. Freckles glitter in her eyes, like a solar system of stars, pulling me closer with the gravitational force of the sun. She strokes my cheek, and I inhale a sharp breath.

I can't go back.

I kiss her lightly on the mouth. She tilts her face closer and presses her lips harder to mine. I caress the back of her neck, relishing her warmth beneath my fingers. The world spins out of focus as her body sways into mine. She runs her hand down my back, and my whole body comes alive.

TRACY BAILEY

I inhale, and all I smell is Piren; all I taste is his sultry breath. I shudder as his tongue caresses mine, evoking an airy moan from deep inside. He tangles his fingers through my hair, and our limbs entwine beneath the sheets.

He rolls on top, kissing me deeply, setting my body on fire. I wrap my arms around his neck and press my body to his. His racing heartbeats thump against my chest. My body tingles as he kisses my neck, trailing his lips across my collar bone. Our chests rise and fall together.

"Trace." He pulls back.

"Yeah?"

"Is this…okay?"

I lock my lips to his in response. Our dueling tongues ignite my entire body with magnetic longing. I run my hand up his shirt, brushing against his bare skin. Goose bumps prickle along his trim chest as I caress him. I savor every moment, fusing my lips to his.

His hard mound grows as he thrusts his body against mine. I slide my hand under the sheets, skimming my fingers over his hardening groin. Pressure pounds through my chest; a sweet melody stirs in my belly, yearning for him. Our bodies writhe beautifully together, awakening something deep inside me.

I shove him to the bed, rolling on top, grinding into him. My body thrums with desire, lost in his gaze as we kiss. He trails his fingers up to my chest, caressing me over the silky fabric.

I tug my nightgown over my head, releasing my breasts. Piren rips off his nightshirt and tosses it to the floor. I shimmy my panties down my legs and kick them off.

Naked and vulnerable, I lean back, straddling my best friend. My cheeks grow warm as he meets my eyes.

He's looking at me. Looking at my whole body.

"Trace, you're...you're so beautiful."

I want him on me, in me. I want him to consume my entire world, breathing in the lust that has become my air.

I place my hand over his, leading it up to my bare breast. His breathing deepens. I dismount him and yank his pajama pants down to his ankles.

"Are you sure about this?"

I take a deep breath. "I'm sure."

I press his palm to my lips and kiss it.

"I want you, Trace. I want all of you."

We join as one body, and everything sparks with color.

PIREN ALLSTON

I fall on top of Trace in a pile of sweaty flesh. Chest heaving, I roll onto my back beside her. Our feet tangle in a heap of blankets at the end of the bed. I prop myself up on my elbow. My best friend lies beside me on the rumpled sheets, her cheeks flushed, eyes closed, hand over her heart. My eyes linger on her body, studying her every curve.

She's so beautiful.

Her stomach rises and falls in perfect rhythm, hair flowing onto the pillow in billowy wisps of curls.

It's Trace. My Trace. My best friend. Here. With me.

Her eyes flutter open.

I give her a sideways grin. "Well?"

She smiles up at me. "Hi."

"Hi."

I lace my fingers with hers and fall back to the pillow. She rests her head on my shoulder, nestling closer, draping my chest in a wave of her hair. I wrap my arm around her, holding her body tightly to mine.

This is where I'm meant to be. With her.

I kiss the top of her head. She traces her finger in circles around my bare chest. My eyes drift closed.

It's seamless. Effortless. Being with Trace feels like home.

Home.

I wrench my eyes open.

Lara.

Lara's alone.

If I stay here, she'll be alone forever.

Lara will be doomed to solitude, and it's my fault. She's annoying, but does she deserve that? Does anyone?

Stop it!

An onslaught of knots pang my stomach.

My mind flashes to a vision of my Partner, alone on our couch with her knitting needles, in a dark apartment meant for two. My parents bought us that furniture to share. To use in our married home.

I swallow down a hard lump.

My parents. I dishonored them. They'll cower in our house in shame like the Wymans did. All those nasty things Mrs. Wyman said to her daughter will apply to me. Will my own mother wish I'd never been born? Will my father tell his friends I died, rather than bear the shame? Will they shred my baby pictures, the way Mr. Wintle tore my family portrait? Will Mason blacken out my face on pictures of his wedding party? Will everyone gossip about the Allstons' horrible douchebag son who forced his family into a humiliation-ridden isolation? My mother's a sweet woman who cares for me no matter what. And this is how I repay her? What kind of sick fuck does that to his family?

"Piren?"

I jolt. "Hmm?"

"Let's build one of those cabins."

Don't fuck this up! You're with Trace.

I shake away the protruding images in my head. "Which ones?"

"The ones we passed on the way here. The Lornstown cabins." She speaks in a dreamlike voice, soft and peaceful.

"Okay."

I rotate in bed to face her, but my leg fidgets under the covers.

"No, I mean, let's build a special one," she says, "a treehouse cabin."

"Oh, sure." I look away.

"Sure?" She rests her hand on my arm.

"Yeah, I...I love that idea."

"You *love* it?"

"Yeah."

She runs her fingers through my hair. "Something wrong?"

"Nope."

I'm not sure what else to say.

"Promise we'll do it, okay?" she asks.

"I promise."

Promises.

I made a promise to Lara once. I promised I'd never leave her.

My chest tightens.

I broke that promise.

TRACY BAILEY

We awake naked, tangled in a sea of blankets and each other. As if our bodies synced in the night, I open my eyes a mere moment before Piren. I roll onto my elbow and gaze down at him.

"Morning, boyfriend." It's a struggle to conceal my growing grin.

"Morning," he grunts.

Today's the day we make the decision.

"Sleep well?" I ask.

"Yeah."

"Did you…wake up with anything on your mind?"

"Not really."

Damn it.

"Oh."

Will Piren say something to solidify our plans? Something about our treehouse cabin or dancing at The Lighthouse? Something to show he's made a decision? Has he made a decision?

My heart somersaults in my chest.

Say something!

He doesn't speak, so I do. "So…should we shower?"

"Okay."

I untangle myself from the sheets and lean over the bed, waiting for him to follow.

It'd be fun to wash my hot boyfriend in the shower…

He stares straight ahead, not meeting my eyes.

"So—"

I'm interrupted by the buzz of a cell phone. I expect it to be mine, as usual, but it isn't.

Piren's telephone vibrates, buried in a pile clothes in the corner. He leaps from the bed to answer it, and the bundle of sheets tumbles to the floor.

Interesting, I didn't even know we got cell service out here.

He presses the phone to his ear. "Hey, Mom."

I slip on my nightgown for cover and indicate I'm heading to the bathroom to shower. He nods, turning his back to me.

I scratch my arm. *Odd.*

The hall closet is packed with fluffy white towels. I grab one and head to the bathroom.

He'll join me when he's done. He only gets a few more chances to talk to his mom, what am I so upset about?

Just chill out, Tracy! Stop worrying! Last night was amazing.

Scrubbing shampoo through my hair, I let the warm water cascade down my body.

Do I love him? Does un-Assigned love even exist?

Can we survive here? Forever?

Will Veronica be all right with Oliver?

Loretta's voice chimes in my brain: *When you love someone, nothing else matters.*

A soapy smile bursts across my dripping face as the bar soap thuds to the shower floor.

Everything will be all right.

As if a million puzzle pieces slide together, my decision erupts from the fog inside me. I want to scream at the top of my lungs. I want to shout my decision from the rooftops: *I choose Piren! I choose Lornstown! I choose Banishment, and I don't care!*

Laughter overcomes me. Crazy, convulsing, bubbling laughter, as if someone shot a confetti cannon through my heart.

My decision is simple, and it is made: I vote we move to Lornstown, permanently. If Piren won't admit it first, I will.

I pat myself dry and wrap my hair in the towel. I saunter through the hall in my nightgown and back into the bedroom, dancing to an imaginary beat.

I take a deep breath.

"Piren, I—"

"We've got to go back. Mason's in the hospital."

PIREN ALLSTON

Mason was in a car crash. He's in critical condition in the ER back home. Mom talked and talked, but I just froze. I couldn't breathe, couldn't think. Couldn't hear a single damn thing she said.

"I abandoned him," I whisper to the air.

"You didn't…" Trace says.

"My own brother. My blood." The words choke in my throat. "I wasn't there."

She pats my shoulder, but I pull away.

What have I done?

A stranger at Mason's First Kiss Ceremony said Ashley Wyman's lover was an insect. A coward. A snake.

Is that me now? Am I the cowardly, traitorous insect?

I collapse on the edge of the bed, head in my hands.

It's too much. Too fast.

I'll never be there for Mason again. I'll never meet my future niece or nephew. I'll never help my parents grow old, or even see them again. They could grow sick, or die, and I wouldn't even fucking know. They'll spit on my tombstone, erected as a permanent tribute to my deceitfulness, my dishonor. Mom will cry herself to sleep at night knowing her own son is an evil, deserting piece of shit.

Tears streak down my cheeks; I let them fall, dripping down my face and into the sheets. Trace rests her hand on my back, but my body tenses at her touch.

Stop looking at me that way.

Tremors tear through my body, shaking my core with intermittent sobs.

This is my fault.

What if Lara was the one in an accident? Aren't I supposed to love and protect her? Does she deserve to be alone forever because I selfishly desire the wrong person? She didn't ask to be stuck with me, and yet here I am, jilting the poor girl.

Cramps dig through my stomach.

I made a promise to Lara. Does that mean nothing to me?

TRACY BAILEY

I shimmy into my jeans and a shirt, but Piren's already out the door. I throw my stuff in my bag and race after him. He speeds down the stairs and into the deserted street. The morning sun peeks over the horizon, barely a sliver in the sky.

I reach for his hand, but he rips it away and hurries onward, practically jogging up the hill toward the arch. I struggle to keep up, mouth drying with each panting breath.

"Piren! Hey! What the hell? Wait up!"

He doesn't answer.

"Stop! Hey!"

We blaze under the arch, through the wall, back onto the rocky trail. He dashes several paces in front of me, agilely slaloming around protruding rocks and roots. My lungs burn as I push them past my limit, but I press on, closing the gap between us.

"Wait! Slow down! Piren! We never said good-bye to Loretta! Mikey, Constance, no one!"

His pace quickens. I trip and stumble over the terrain, wincing as sticks and roots scratch my ankles.

"Wait up! Hey!"

He doesn't falter, but strides ahead as if I'm invisible.

What the hell? What'd I do?

"Shouldn't we tell them to hold a room for us...tonight? They don't...know our plan." I pant. "Piren?"

He presses further ahead, further away from me.

What's wrong? Did we go too far? Was it me? Did I move too quick?

We jump onto the first morning bus seconds before it pulls away. I collapse onto the seat beside him, shallow breaths ripping through my sore throat.

He faces the window, knee bouncing against the seat.

We don't speak.

An hour later, we're on the train. Piren hasn't said two words to me since we left Lornstown.

"Are you okay?" I rest my hand on his leg. "Will you say something? Talk to me?"

Blurry fields zip past as the train chugs onward, carting us back to town. I reach for his hand, but he recoils.

"Piren, are you—"

"What's Veronica supposed to do without you?"

My forehead wrinkles. "She's fine; she has Oliver. She's a big girl. I mean, I can't protect her forever. What are you insinuating?"

"Listen." He closes his eyes, inhaling a deep breath. "Oh God, this is so hard."

"Wh…what? What is?" I touch his arm.

"I…I…can't do it. I just can't. I know you want me to move here, and part of me wants that too, but I have my family. My whole life is back home."

"Where did this come from?"

"Mason was in a car accident." His voice cracks. "And I wasn't fucking there."

"That's not your fault."

"But it *is* my fault. And I can't do that to them." His words blurt out harsh and assertive; the blunt voice of the man beside me is not the calming voice of my best friend.

"But, Piren—"

"No. He could've died."

"Piren, I—"

"Trace. Listen." He grabs my hand, but this time I retract. "Our childhood was the best time I ever had, up until this weekend. But it was childhood."

"Don't do this." *Don't hurt me.*

"This decision, this stupid, rash decision to come here was childish. And I know it was my idea, my fucking fault."

"Stop."

"I promised Lara I wouldn't leave her, and I'm accountable for that promise, Trace."

"Stop."

"What I had with you, I mean, I wouldn't trade those memories for anything. You're amazing. Last night was incredible, and I'll never forget that. But I have responsibilities."

"Stop."

"And so do you, to your family, to Veronica, to Sam —"

"Stop."

"I don't want a memorial people spit on. I can't do —"

"*Stop!*"

He meets my gaze. "A part of me will always be linked to you." He blinks back water welling in his eyes. "But we need to move on."

No. I can't absorb.

"We didn't think this through, Trace. It was an impulse. Didn't think about what we were really doing, who we'd hurt. I need to go home. I need to be with my family, with Lara."

My lungs contract, crushing my chest under the weight of his words that pierce my heart like a knife.

How could he?

The churning sorrow in my stomach morphs into hot rage, searing through my veins.

He wants to hurt me? Fine. I can hurt him too.

"Tracy, I —"

"So, this whole weekend was meaningless to you."

"No, Trace! That's not…I just…"

"You fuck me and leave me, huh? Wham-bam-thank-you-Tracy? That what I am to you? A good fuck?" I snort, curling my lips into a sneer. "Oh, wait, a practice fuck. You used me. That it, *best friend?*"

"No, I swear, you don't under —"

"No, I get it. It's crystal clear." Tears cloud my vision, and I don't care.

"Tracy, this choice we made to come here yesterday, it was a bad choice."

He called this a choice.

"No." My body stiffens. "Don't you fucking dare."

"I—"

"Shut up." The words taste bitter on my tongue. "It may have been what you call a *bad choice.* Maybe it was. Maybe it was a stupid fucking choice. But it was a choice. I haven't made a choice about a damn thing in my entire fucking life, and I'll be damned if I'm about to regret this one."

"Trace, I—"

"You are just like all the others. Just another scumbag asshole."

"Trace—"

"Fuck you, Piren. I hate you. I wish I never even met you."

"Trace, please."

"I wish my mom never dragged me to your stupid house. I wish none of these past seventeen years ever happened."

"Trace—"

"I hate you!" I jump into the aisle. Several passengers jerk their heads.

Piren flinches, his eyes growing wide with pain. I watch him squirm, fighting back the growing agony inside.

I hope you hurt.

"I hate you," I repeat, softer than a whisper. Stinging water streams down my face, but I don't care; I open the floodgates and let it rain.

His mouth hangs open. "Trace…"

The train squeaks to a stop halfway in town, several miles from home. I bolt off, into the humid summer air.

He hasn't followed. I'm alone.

For the rest of my life, I'm alone.

It's over.

Wherever you go,
go with all your heart.
♥Confucius

TWENTY-FOUR YEARS OLD
PART SIX

PIREN ALLSTON

Thirteen days ago, I said good-bye to Trace. Her parting words struck me like a machete to the jugular, but I did the right thing. I made a promise to Lara long ago, and I don't break promises. Not to my family. Not to my Partner.

I come home from work, and Lara's on the couch, knitting.

"I love you, Lara Goodren."

"I love you, Piren Allston."

She flips on the TV, and I flop down beside her.

"Hey. Mason's being discharged tomorrow. I'm going to his place for dinner. You want to come?"

"Mmm." She keeps her glazed eyes fixed straight ahead, her fingers nimbly working through a scarf.

"Did you hear me?"

"Mmm."

"So, I take it as a no?"

She doesn't respond.

This is how it's supposed to be. This is who I'm supposed to love.

Five hours later, we retreat to bed. This is our pattern. This is my life now.

I can go through the motions. I can pretend.

I arrive at Mason's dripping in sweat from the sweltering summer air. My brother limps over on his crutches to answer the door.

"Welcome to our humble abode," he mumbles, crutches clicking as he walks.

"Nice stilts. How you feeling, cripple?"

He grumbles, hobbling into the kitchen. "Been better."

Last time I visited this place, my brother was a newlywed. The cold silence inside sends a shiver down my spine. Lined in gray-papered walls, the house permeates an eerie stillness akin to a cemetery.

I take a seat in the living room. My leg bounces against the gray armchair to the beat of the ticking pendulum clock.

Tick. Tock. Tick. Tock.

"How's your leg?" I call into the kitchen.

Pans clatter. "Gone to shit."

"Sorry."

Tick. Tock. Tick. Tock.

"You want help with dinner? You probably shouldn't be lifting—"

"Nah, I'm good. Just hang out in there for a bit."

My feet grow antsy, planted on the gray carpet. After an eternity, a tantalizing savory aroma wafts into the room. Mason sets heaping plates of prime rib and beans on the table.

"Steph! Food!"

Stephanie emerges from their bedroom cave and slogs to the table. She passes me without a glance, sinking into her chair with a grimace. I take my seat, keeping my eyes on my plate.

Tick. Tock. Tick. Tock.

Mason slumps over, his head wrapped in a thick bandage, shoveling forkfuls into his mouth. His wife rests her cheek on her hand, pushing beans around her plate with her utensils. She releases a lofty sigh.

Tick. Tock. Tick. Tock.

"Pass the salt?" Mason asks. Stephanie hands it down to him. Forks scrape against my brother's fine china.

"So, uh, kinda warm out today, huh?" I ask.

Mason grunts. Stephanie gives a curt nod.

I nudge my brother. "You see the beard on that dude who wheeled you out to the car? He looked like a wooly mammoth."

"Yeah." Mason's lids hang heavy over corpse-like eyes. Blank. Completely defeated, but not by the accident.

Awkward.

I stuff a spoonful of beans into my mouth, crossing my legs to thwart the shakes.

This guy isn't my brother. Where's the kid who made me laugh? Who tormented me with bad advice?

He reaches for his cup with the passion of a vacant shell. It's as if someone sucked the life from his eyes.

He might as well be a stranger.

Gray walls envelope us, suffocating me under a veil of gray silence. I inhale gray. I exhale gray.

This whole damn house is gray. It even feels gray. How can they live like this?

It's hot outside, but this house is stone cold. I cross my arms over my chest to fight the shivering gray chills.

Tick. Tock. Tick. Tock.

Someone talk. Please. Anyone.

Stephanie pushes back from the table, chair legs screeching against the tiles.

She pats her mouth with her gray napkin. "Excuse me."

She struts from the kitchen, abandoning the remains of her half-finished meal. Moments later, somewhere in the house, a door thuds shut.

Mason sprinkles salt onto his meat and chomps a large bite.

I squint, craning my neck toward The Ice Queen's path. "Is she... okay?"

"What do you mean?"

"She's just so...quiet."

His mouth bulges with food. "Yeah, so?"

"Is she always this quiet?"

"Yep. Always." His monotone doesn't falter.

People live here, but they don't live.

I fiddle my napkin in my lap. My stomach churns.

Mason and Stephanie: perfect Partners, together forever.

Just like Lara and me, together forever.

Lara and I sit in silence in a cold gray house.

Tick. Tock. Tick. Tock.

Following a monotonous routine for years.

Tick. Tock. Tick. Tock.

We exist until we die.

Tick. Tock. Tick. Tock.

Is this me? Is this my future? Am I destined to be a ghost in my own home? Will I go crazy from the silence? Will a ticking metronome clock be all that separates me from insanity? Will my desires simplify to merely craving another person's voice?

Tick. Tock. Tick. Tock.

"Hey," Mason says. I jerk my head up. "Isn't our old neighbor Tracy Bailey's wedding the day after tomorrow?"

My chest tightens.

"Oh, yeah. That." I force a smile. "I'll be there."

And it will be the death of me.

TRACY BAILEY

"Four hundred twenty-four guests," my mother says, thumbing through RSVPs in the front seat. "That's at least a few dozen more than the Byers' girl's wedding."

"Did you include the Martins?" Dad asks. "Got their reply yesterday."

"Oh, no, I didn't. Four more. Excellent," she says. "That's three hundred sixteen for the filet, and one hundred twelve for the trout. I'll submit that to the caterer tonight."

I gaze out the car window, eyes half-closed, as the world passes outside. My hands lie limp in my lap.

"Tracy—" Mom cranes her neck toward the back seat "—for a young woman on the eve of her wedding, you could try to be a little more cheerful." Her nose crinkles. "And for God's sake, put on some mascara before we go inside. You look horrible."

I am a ghost. I am not real.

"You know," Dad says, "your mother and I spent a lotta fuckin' money on this event. It wouldn't kill you to smile."

I am invisible. You cannot hurt me.

"That's why I insisted on the corset dress," Mom says. "Cost an arm and a leg, but it'll suck her in so she can't slouch. Soon as we get to the seamstress, I'm going to make it quite clear: taut and snug. That's what I want to see." She tugs at her shirt sleeve. "I swear, Tracy, sometimes I wonder if you're really my child."

My father chuckles. I press my cheek against the window.

"The dress hurts my ribs," I say in a robotic mutter. "I can't breathe in it."

"Well, maybe you shouldn't eat so much junk food, then." Mom straightens her posture in her seat. "We got the plus-size dress against my better judgment, but I'm not letting it hang loose like a tent. And really, most people can't afford designer wedding gowns. You should be grateful you have parents with means."

My father snorts. "She's not fuckin' grateful. Look at her…Sam's problem now."

Sam's problem now. I am Sam's problem.

"Regardless," Mom says as she touches his arm, "the wedding will be flawless. A perfect occasion. I told the florist not to skimp on the flowers. I want to feel smothered by calla lilies." She gestures her hands into the air.

I exhale a heavy breath.

The guests will have a grand time.

The seamstress stuffs me into my dress. She nimbly laces up the corset back, yanking at the strings. Each tug clamps my chest, forcing air from my lungs. Mom paces around me, squinting.

"That sequin is off, lower than the others," she says. "I want it fixed."

The seamstress approaches, pins clasped between her teeth. "Hold still, dear. I've got to pin it."

My lifeless arms hang limp at my sides.

I've been still for almost two weeks now.

"There! Look how beautiful you are," the seamstress says, leading me to the floor-length mirror. My lip quivers at the lifeless person, draped in glossy white fabric, staring back at me.

"What a beautiful bride," Mom says, clapping her hands. "You and Sam will be so happy together."

"Sure."

Happiness is a farce. It only ends in pain.

My parents pull up in front of my apartment.

"We really don't have to stop here," I say in a monotone. "We can just go back to the house."

"Five minutes." Mom studies herself in the rearview. "You need to kiss your Partner one last time before the wedding. Bad luck not to."

"Hurry up." Dad waves his hand in dismissal. "I've got stuff to do."

More like stuff to drink.

I trudge inside and hardly recognize the bare walls. Stacked boxes of my possessions lie strewn across the apartment floor, waiting to be hauled to our married home.

"Hey, babe." Sam pushes a box to the side. "I love you, Tracy Bailey. My almost wife."

"I love you, Sam Macey." The automatic words fall out as if spoken by a machine.

"I got these for you." He hands me a bouquet of white calla lilies. "Thanks."

He yanks me toward him like a ragdoll, smashing his lips to mine. My body tenses in his vicelike arms. He tugs my hair, jabbing his tongue into my mouth, forcing it to the back of my throat. I flinch, and he jerks his head back.

"Something wrong?" He caresses my cheek with his thumb. "Kissing works better when your Partner isn't a dead fish." He pecks me on the cheek.

My body won't let me laugh. "Sorry. I'm just out of it today."

He squeezes me tighter in a hug. Invisible barbells weigh me down, and my muscles can't muster the strength to reciprocate his passion.

Piren is with Lara. I am with Sam. All is right with the world.

Maybe love is what kills us, and Assigning saves us. Maybe a numb, blank existence of fake emotion trumps the pain of loss.

"I can't wait for tomorrow." Sam gives me one final peck on the lips. "Next time I see you, we'll be getting married."

"I know." A stone drops in my stomach. "See you then."

PIREN ALLSTON

Feet propped against the coffee table, I sprawl on the couch with a book. My eyes scan the same two lines again and again, a wordy record on endless replay. My head pounds as if a thousand armies wage war in my brain.

Love. I tell Lara I love her. What the hell does that even mean? Have I overused it to the point where it's just as damn meaningless as any mundane word?

My leg jiggles against the coffee table, thumping on the wood.

What if the one you're supposed to be with, and the one you want to be with, are two different people? My entire life was mapped out for me before I was born. Is my only choice to silently follow the course already plotted? To blindly accept my future and walk that trail until I die? To smile and pretend everything is okay and I'm happy and in love with my Partner when I'm spiraling downward and drowning in my own loneliness? I'm drowning, like in my childhood nightmares. Only this isn't a nightmare; I can't wake up from this life.

Trace's smile flashes through my head, shooting a lightning-sharp pain through my chest.

I hurt her. I hurt my best friend. And for what?

I slam the book down on the coffee table and throw my head back.

What the hell am I supposed to do?

Lara ambles into the room and scowls. She rushes over and heaves my feet off the coffee table.

"Can you not do that?" she snaps. "It's not your personal footrest. This furniture wasn't cheap. Your parents didn't buy it for us so you can scuff it up." She sweeps back down the hall. Somewhere in the distant corridors of our home, a door bangs.

Forever.

The inflating balloon bursts inside me, spewing a million pieces that fall into place.

I know what to do.

TRACY BAILEY

I sit at my parents' kitchen table, cheek drooping against my hand, sorting place cards for the seating chart. Chunky headphones smother my ears with the same silence that consumes me inside.

My parents went downtown to mingle. I'm sure they're enjoying trolling around greeting everyone, busy being the center of attention. They're the parents of tomorrow's bride!

Hooray! I don't give a fuck.

I count eight guest name cards and stack them together on the table. Then another. Count, stack. Count, stack. I stack the cards randomly, because I don't care. They can sit in the hall. They can sit home. I just don't care.

The door slams, and Veronica walks in. "Hey, Trace. Excited for tomorrow?"

"Sure." Count, stack.

She hovers by the stove. "You okay?"

I nod, not meeting her eyes.

"I'm going out with Ollie. You want to come?"

I throw my current stack onto the table. "Why? So I can *get trashed? Get wasted?* Isn't that what you kids do with your time?"

Her forehead creases. "We're just going to the movies."

"Gotcha. Have fun." The words snap from my mouth.

V rubs her hand down my back, and I bristle.

"Trace, talk to me. Something's up; I know you."

"What's there to talk about?" I flare out my fingers. "Tomorrow is the wedding of the year! Fun fun. Let's all get trashed. I'll go shot for shot with you tomorrow. Kick your skinny ass."

"What has gotten into you?" She walks around the table, brows lowered, forcing herself into my line of vision.

"Nothing. Sorry." Count, stack. "I'm in a mood."

"I can see that."

"You go have fun with Oliver. I have wedding stuff to do here." Count, stack.

She examines my latest pile. "The Murphys can't sit with the O'Fallons. They don't get along at all."

"Awesome. Maybe we'll have a wedding brawl. Mom will get her little panties in a bunch."

V snorts. "You're so weird, Trace."

I shrug.

"Well, if you're not coming, I gotta go." She heads toward the door. "Text me if you need anything. I don't want you to be so sad, especially for tomorrow."

"Oh, right, I forgot." I slam the cards down, scattering piles across the table. "You're in that contingent who wants me to be just so utterly *happy with Sam.*" I bat my eyelashes at her.

She pauses by the door.

"No." Her gaze softens. "I just want you to be happy."

PIREN ALLSTON

Gunning my car, I race to the Ceremony Hall. A wedding begins there in twenty minutes, a wedding starring my best friend. I'm not wearing a customary full suit. I will not be attending any wedding.

I am going to rescue Tracy Bailey.

TRACY BAILEY

Sam stayed in our empty apartment alone last night. I slept in my teenage bedroom. I sat still for hours in the dark, letting time wash over me. As the second-hand clicked, my even breaths rose and fell like a ticking time-bomb. The clock struck midnight, and I closed my eyes.

It's the happiest day of my life.

Mom ties me into my wedding dress, sucking breath from my lungs with each tug. The gown explodes at my sides, suffocating me in an eruption of white lace. It consumes half the space in the cramped dressing room.

"There, that's my bride," she says.

My listless arms dangle from my slouching shoulders. I inhale, and the corset digs into my ribs, pressing against my stomach.

Mom paces around me, pruning pieces of hair and loose threads from my dress, thrusting them into Veronica's waiting hands.

"Smile." She pats my cheek. "You look like a zombie." She pushes in front of me to the mirror and starts dabbing on lipstick. My tired facial muscles won't budge.

Veronica shifts from one foot to the other, smoothing her purple bridesmaid dress.

"Don't just stand there." Mom snaps her fingers. "Get your sister's flowers."

Head lowered, V trudges from the room. I slump down on a pink seat. The bones of my dress constrict like a boa.

The makeup lady comes and slathers some paint on my face. I stare straight ahead as she dollops mascara and shadow over my eyes. My mother purses her lips, pointing to places on my face that aren't covered enough.

"Do you have any drops for her eyes?" she asks the woman. "They're so red, you'd think she's back here smoking."

"Sorry, Mrs. Bailey, I don't carry eye drops."

"No?" Mom grabs my chin, yanking my face toward her. "Well, just layer the mascara on a bit thicker then."

Veronica reenters the room and hands me my bouquet. Purple and white flowers burst from a silver ribbon, radiating springtime. I let it fall into my lap, sprinkling petals to the floor.

"Tracy!" Mom hisses. "Be careful with those."

"They're flowers. They're fine."

The makeup lady packs her trunk and leaves. Mom slips her a fifty-dollar bill. "For your trouble," she tells the woman. "I'm sorry she's so difficult."

My tuxedo-clad father wobbles into the dressing room, releasing a roaring belch into the air. He smashes into the makeup stand, knocking brushes to the floor.

Let's commence the Bailey Family Circus.

"You're drunk?" Mom's eyes blaze with fire. "Today? Really?"

He sways on his feet. "Just…buzzed." He leans too far, and a tiny glass vial slides from his pocket and shatters on the ground. Liquor explodes onto the carpet, soaking my waiting veil. Veronica gasps. Mom shrieks and slaps him on the arm.

I run my fingers across my bourbon-stained veil. Liquid seeps onto the edge of my dress, slowly infecting the lace like a disease.

Mom's face flushes crimson. "How can you do this to me on my daughter's wedding day?"

"Shut up!" Dad stumbles into the wall.

Mom jumps up in his face, screaming. Veronica presses her trembling hands over her ears and slips outside. Dad swings his arm, crashing into the makeup table. Glass vases and canisters smash to the floor, sprinkling powders and liquids everywhere.

Mom's face contorts into a snarl. She grabs the hairdryer and flings it at him, shattering it against the wall. Dad throws out his bumbling arms and storms from the room. Mom follows after him, shouting obscenities that echo in the hall.

The door slams behind them with a boom. My chest rises and falls, stretching against the corset, drowning the silence with my sharp breaths.

My family left a tidal wave of destruction in their wake. Scattered items litter the floor. Stains and colors dapple the carpet.

I press my hands to my cramped stomach. My body is a prisoner in a white, puffy, glittering cell. Floor-length mirrors wall the dressing room; my pallid face stares back at me from a million angles. Hair drawn up like a princess, eyes layered in sparkly purple shadow and thick black mascara, I don't recognize myself.

These are my last moments of being Tracy Bailey. My last moments of being me.

My throat burns with a thousand angry lumps. The weak and wilting woman in the mirror gazes back, dead-eyed and cold. I want to smash her into a million pieces.

I jump at the *tat-tat-tat* I hear behind me and twist toward the window. Piren stares back at me through the glass. I unhinge the locks, and he topples inside.

Here I am, in my expensive wedding gown, suffocating in layer upon layer of tulle and bows, hair done up like a celebrity, face painted like a porcelain doll, reeking of liquor. And here he is, sweatshirt and jeans. Hair uncombed. Shirt untucked. Smelling like Piren.

I dart my eyes to the floor, ribs aching with every sharp breath. My palms grow sweaty at my sides, and I wipe them along the edge of my dress.

"What happened in here?" He scans the disaster that is my dressing room. "A hurricane?"

Someone beats on the door.

"Go away!" I shout. The knocking ceases. I whirl on Piren. "What do you want?"

"Trace, please, just hear me out."

I open my mouth, but words won't come.

"Five minutes!" my coordinator screams through the door.

"Okay!"

"Trace. Please. I need to…God, you're so beautiful." He takes a deep breath. "I need to say something."

I keep my eyes looking at anything but him.

"I…I've done a lot of stupid shit in my life. But the stupidest, the worst, the most ridiculous thing I've ever done—" he throws his hands behind his head "—was letting you go. Watching you walk off that train."

His arms fall back to his sides. "I get why people go to Lornstown. It's a sacrifice; no one's saying it isn't. It's giving up everything. But it's also gaining everything. It's understanding what you have to gain. I love my family — I do! — But you... What I have with you is unlike anything else in the world, Trace."

I stare at a scuff mark on the wall, fighting back tears prickling behind my eyes.

"Don't marry him. You can walk away. You can. You don't have to do it. You're my Partner, Trace — my real Partner."

Partner. What a stupid word.

"Trace... I'm so sorry."

I shake my head. "I'm sorry too. Those things I said on the train, I... I didn't mean any of it. I don't hate you." A knot twists in my chest. "I'm sorry."

I touch my eye to stop the seeping trail of water. Black moisture stains my fingers, mascara mingling with tears across my cheek.

Piren holds up his palm, and I press my hand to his. He gives me a half-smile, and in his eyes is the same little boy who scurried through the woods with me growing up. The same little boy I couldn't ever let go.

Maybe I don't have a family. Maybe I have no one to love.

I swallow hard.

But he does.

Because no matter what we have, no matter what we are, this place will never change. Being together will always be a crime. There will never be a time when he can truly be happy with me, because being with me will always mean leaving so much behind.

Our unstoppable force has met its immovable object.

When you really love someone, nothing else matters.

I love him.

I love him with every fiber of my heart.

I love him absolutely and completely.

I love him.

And so I'll let him go.

"Trace —"

"I can't do this anymore. It's too much, to see you, to be around you... this friendship, this, whatever it is..." I force the words past the choke in my throat. "I can't be your friend anymore. It's over. This is good-bye."

The venomous words rip through my body. The words I was too selfish to speak before. The words I should have said in that janitor's closet on graduation day and every day since. Makeup-tainted tears drip into the folds of my ivory dress.

Water pools in my best friend's eyes. His pain rips a hole in my heart. I reach out my hand, longing to comfort him one last time.

I sigh. "Piren, I—"

"I love you, Tracy Bailey."

My arm falls back to my side. I clamp my eyes shut.

"I can't."

With two swift steps, I exit the room.

I plod into the long hall, tripping over my train. My parents stand stoic by the doorway, waiting arm-in-arm beside my coordinator. Mom presses her lips together when she sees me blotting my eyes. Dad shakes his head with a disapproving frown. I stare ahead, back straight, shoulders poised, bouquet clasped between my shaking hands.

Veronica steps to my side.

"*You okay?*" she mouths, rubbing my arm. I nod.

The Ceremony doors clang open, revealing an endless aisle lined with benches and the backs of four hundred twenty-four heads.

My coordinator nods to someone I can't see, disappearing into the Ceremony Hall. Processional music strums to life, filling the room with romantic ambiance. My parents smile and step forward, gliding through the doorway. They float up the aisle, waving to their spectators.

Veronica proceeds after them, leaving me alone in the hall. My heart thuds like a hammer in my chest.

I'm next.

Music blares as fifteen violins ring out a melody akin to my funeral toll. I tighten my dampening grip around the flower stems, elbows clenched at my sides.

Soft footsteps patter behind me.

Perfectly framed in the doorway of my dressing room is him, my Piren Allston, my best friend. The man I love. The man who protects me. Who loves me. Who should have been the one waiting for me at the end of this aisle. The man I just banished from my life forever.

We stand eight feet apart in silence. I take a deep breath.

This is for you.

My legs move like wooden stilts. I pass through the doorway, step by step, down the aisle. Music grows louder, echoing through the rotunda as I progress through the Ceremony Hall.

Hundreds of people rise around me, surrounding me with blank, empty faces. Cameras flash from every angle, capturing every minute of the show. Everyone I've ever known is here, and they're all strangers, standing to watch me process down the aisle, the audience at my big performance.

I pass my parents and sister in the front row. Sam puffs his tuxedo-clad chest by the altar, dark hair slicked back in a shiny wave.

Sam takes my hands. Everybody sits.

My thudding heart drowns the preacher's words in my ears. He indicates to my Partner.

"I love you, Tracy Macey," Sam says, beaming.

Four hundred hot stares bear down on me. My fingers constrict around the quivering bouquet in my hands. I blink back a threatening veil of tears and inhale a shaky breath.

"I love you…Sam Macey."

We are married. Too soon, we are married.

PIREN ALLSTON

My swollen eyes sting as I slam my apartment door. Tears flow like a river down my face, and I don't even care.

She did it. She actually did it.

I throw my body against the bathroom sink, heaving for air. The mirror taunts me, hovering on the wall as a clear reminder of who I am: the Partner of Lara Goodren, and nothing to Tracy Bailey.

Look at you, you piece of shit. You fucked everything up.

Lara's inspiration stones mock me from her ugly purple basket. The *Love* rock gloats, boasting manufactured romance, inscribed into the stone by a faceless factory.

Fuck you.

I swipe the rock from the basket and hurl it at the mirror, shattering the glass into a million pieces.

I collapse in a quivering heap on the couch, head in my hands.

The front door swings open. Lara stomps into the room in a pink evening dress.

"You didn't come." Her shrill voice grates into my ears. "You left me alone like an idiot. Your parents asked where the hell you were, and I didn't have an answer for them."

She walks into the hall and gasps.

"Holy shit, what is all this glass on the floor? What the hell happened to our mirror?" She rushes back to the living room, hands on her hips, glowering. "Were you *crying?*"

I don't respond.

She huffs and storms off to her bedroom. Several minutes later, she emerges, flopping onto the armchair beside the couch. She drops something on the coffee table with a clatter.

It's the fang keychain I bought as a teenager. I snort and pick up the trinket, rolling my eyes.

"You kept it."

"It was the first gift you ever bought me yourself."

I slump back on the couch, stretching my legs under the coffee table.

"But it wasn't meant for me," she says, "was it?"

I stare straight ahead.

"Was it, Piren?"

Pause.

"No."

She chuckles and shakes her head. "Boy, was I an idiot back then. Clean up the glass."

She rises from the chair, collects her coat, and walks out the door without another word.

I understand the purpose of Assigning now. It isn't to be happy; it's to be compatible. To reproduce, to raise children…to get Assigned, and reproduce. It's all a cycle of going through the motions. It is a life, without living.

If you want to be happy, be.
❧Leo Tolstoy

TWENTY-FOUR YEARS OLD
PART SEVEN

TRACY BAILEY

Sam and I had sex on our wedding night. And three times a week since the wedding, six weeks ago. Just like we're supposed to. I lie still, and he does what he needs to do. He grunts and thrusts, and I stay there until he's done. I lie back and take it, because that's what you do with your Partner. You deal with it. You suck it up and let them.

Nausea swells inside me, through my stomach and up my esophagus.

I jump out of bed and sprint to the bathroom. Collapsing on the linoleum, I fall to my knees at the toilet. Gags rip through my body in waves as chunks spew into the bowl. I pull away and wipe my mouth, shaking.

Sam stumbles into the bathroom, rubbing his eyes. "Third time this week. That's it. You're going to the doctor."

"No! I —"

Another load rockets up from my stomach, spilling into the toilet in a retching mess.

Sam raises his eyebrows.

"Fine." I shudder on the floor. "You drive; I'll go."

I shiver on a cold bench, wrapped in a medical robe at Dr. Patel's office. Sam hovers over me, pacing, as we wait for the doctor to return. Doc took several vials of my blood, and probably enough urine to fill a gas tank. I run my thumb over the white bandage in the crook of my elbow.

The door squeaks open, and Dr. Patel steps inside.

"Well?" Sam leans closer.

The doctor flips through pages on his clipboard.

"Well," he says, "I've got some great news. Tracy, you're pregnant."

Sam slaps his hand to his mouth.

"Congratulations, Macey family." The doctors shakes my husband's hand. "You're going to have a new member."

A weak smile spreads across my face. I rub my hand over my stomach, and my heart swells.

My sweet, little baby swims inside me.

Warmth spreads all the way down to my toes.

Dr. Patel hands me some vitamins and breaks into a spiel about nutrition. Sam nods, stroking his chin with one hand, embracing me with the other.

Love. My entire being engorges with love for this little bean in my belly.

I cradle my stomach in my hands. He or she dwells inside, waiting to meet me.

Little Rafael or Dominique.

I slide my arm around Sam's waist, cuddling into his side. He kisses the top of my head.

"How far along is she, Doc?" Sam asks, patting my belly.

"Well, judging by her urine test," Dr. Patel scans his notes, "I would say definitely eight weeks along."

My heart stops.

No. It can't be. That doesn't add up.

Sam's smile fades.

I gulp.

This is it. I'll be Banished forever, alone, with my bastard child.

Sam's eye twitches. "Are you...Are you sure?"

"Clear as day, right here in the tests, Mr. Macey."

My Partner's grip tightens around my arms. "Thank you, doctor. We can't wait to start planning."

We climb into Sam's car, but he doesn't speak. The engine roars to life.

Is he going to drive me straight to the Mayor's office?

I tap my fingers on my thighs, watching him from the corner of my eye. His knuckles grow white around the steering wheel.

"Sam—"

"Who did you fuck, you filthy whore?"

I stare at the ground.

"I said, who did you fuck?"

"No one. Just you."

I rest my hands over my stomach.

It's okay. I'll keep you safe.

We zip down the highway, obliterating the speed limit.

"Sam...please slow down..."

The speedometer reads ninety.

"Sam!"

Ninety-five.

"You think I'm an idiot?" he mutters.

I keep my head down.

"You disgust me. You don't deserve to breathe."

"Sam—"

"Shut your trap, or I'll shut it for you."

I pat my stomach.

Go to sleep, little one. I'll protect you.

He speeds into our driveway and slams on the brakes with a ghostly screech. I grip the bottom of my seat as the car thrusts me forward.

Sam grabs me by the hair and yanks me out of the car. I stumble over my feet as he drags me up the driveway.

"Ow! Sam! Stop!" I flail out my leg to kick him, but it doesn't reach.

Someone, come outside. See us. Help me. Anyone.

"Stop! Help!"

My screams echo, but no faces appear. He tightens his grip, ripping clots of hair from my skull. I wince, water welling in my eyes.

He shoves me through the door and throws me to the ground. I spring my arms out, shielding my stomach from the fall. The rug slices my hands, and shiny burns streak across my palms.

Sam rips open the liquor cabinet and shoves a bottle of scotch under my nose.

"Drink it."

"No. I'm pregnant."

"It's a bastard." He showers me with spit. "Drink it now and kill that piece of shit inside."

I spread my hands over my belly. "No."

"Shut up!" He swings his arm back and slaps me across the face. "Or I'll pour it down your slut throat."

He grabs my chin, but I yank my face away.

"I'm going to fuck you tonight." He slugs from the bottle. "And you're gonna give me a real child."

My heart hammers in my chest.

"But that's what you like, isn't it?" he says. "I bet you begged some guy to fuck you. Ran to the first one you saw, hiked your skirt up, made him ravage you like the whore you are."

"Just Banish me. I'll go. I'll take the blame my —"

"Shut it!" He tilts the bottle, spilling liquor down my face. "You think I'll let them Banish you so some guy in Lornstown can fuck you? You'd like that, wouldn't you? Stupid bitch. If I can't have you, nobody can."

I rip the bottle from his hands and hurl it against the wall where it shatters, raining shards and scotch over our heads. I roll to the side, shielding my belly from the glass.

"You're gonna protect that *thing?*"

I shove him with all my strength and bolt from the room. With heavy footsteps plodding behind me, I sprint to the bathroom and slam the door, ramming the lock.

Chest heaving, I fumble the buttons on my cell phone, back against the door, and dial 9-1-1.

I hear ringing through the phone as the doorknob jiggles. "Tracy… I know you're there…"

Come on. Why won't someone answer the phone?

The knob shakes under my Partner's grip. "Tracy, open the fucking door!"

The ringing continues.

Come on!

"Hello, nine-one-one dispatcher, this is Susan —"

"My name is Tracy Bailey Macey. I live at four-fifty-one Elm. My husband —"

With an explosive *bam!* Sam's fist plunges through the wood. I shriek into the receiver.

"Help! Please!"

He bursts inside, rips the phone from my hands, and flings it into the toilet.

"You called the cops, you fucking whore?"

I shove past him into the kitchen, but he grabs my shirt and throws me to the floor.

Before I can move, he's straddling me, slamming my head into the cabinet by the stove. His fingers wrap around my throat, throttling me into the edge of the sharp wood, slicing the back of my neck. I flail out my arm and punch his cheek.

"Stupid bitch." He springs to his feet and flings his booted foot into my side. I curl into a ball with a yelp, pain searing through my flank. "Look what you made me do." He spits on the floor.

Warm blood trickles down my neck. I brush the cut, and my fingers stain red. He glares down at me, sickly fire raging in his eyes.

"Clean yourself up," he says, "and come into the bedroom."

Shallow breaths rip through my lungs.

Plan. I need a plan.

"I said, get up. I'm gonna fuck you. Right now."

I splay my fingers over my stomach.

Something. Anything.

"Get up!" His fists quake at his sides. "I love you, Tracy Macey."

My pulse speeds through my body like a freight train.

"I said, I love you, Tracy Macey!" His brows lower. "Tell me you love me, you bitch!" He slaps me across the face. "Say it!"

Zapped of energy, I lie motionless on the cold tiles. An upturned chair lies beside us, my husband's latest unfinished project. A hammer and assorted nails scatter across the floor around it, waiting for a repair that will never come.

Sam's sweat-beaded face hovers inches from mine, menacing and threatening, ready to strike.

My father bears down on me, hurling insults and fists at my meek child's body. Laughing at me. Calling me weak. I cower in the corner and take it.

Adrenaline shoots through my veins.

No. He won't hurt me anymore. Won't hurt us.

I prop myself on my elbows, wincing. "My name…" I say in a barely audible whisper, "…is not Tracy Macey. It never was. It never will be."

"Fuck you!" He slaps me again. "Tell me you love me!"

"Oh, Sam. You're an idiot."

He leans closer, eyes wild and brimming with insanity. "What did you call me?"

Keep him talking.

I force a smirk. "Love is such a strong word, isn't it?"

He glowers, narrowing his eyes into slits.

"But in this town," I continue, "we pass it around like dinner rolls." Strength builds behind my words. "You know what, *Partner?* I've only ever really truly loved three people in my entire life: Veronica. Piren. And my baby in my belly."

"You little slut, you're my Partner. You belong to me."

"No." I shake my throbbing head. "I'm not a slut. And I'm definitely not yours."

His reddening face tremors with rage, but I don't care. I stare straight into his eyes.

"I *don't* love you, Sam Macey. I've *never* loved you, Sam Macey. And I. Never. Fucking. Will."

A pulsing vein in his forehead bulges, threatening to pop out of his skin. "You love that thing in your stomach more than you love me." His lips curl into a sick, demented grin. "If I have to cut it out of you, I will." He draws a switchblade from his pocket.

No.

My heart pounds in my ears. I scoot back, all strength draining from my body.

"Don't do this." I quaver. "You're not a killer."

He inches closer, and I scramble backward on my raw hands.

"Sam…please…" My voice cracks. "Don't do something you'll regret."

"You're scared, huh?" He twirls the blade in his fingers. "You should be."

He lunges, but my fingers wrap around the hammer—his hammer—which I send flying top speed toward his face, through his temple. It smashes into his skull with an earsplitting crack.

He drops to the floor.

And just like that, I am a widow.

PIREN ALLSTON

Two hours ago, a police officer rang my doorbell. My heart lurched, as if my body knew why he was there. Lara peeked over my shoulder.

"Are you Piren Allston?" he asked, flashing his badge.

I nodded.

"My name is Officer Edwards, and I'm here to ask you a few questions about the death of Samuel Ryan Macey."

Lara gasped, clapping her hand to her mouth. My jaw dropped. *What the fuck? Sam is dead?*

Lara's frightened eyes fell on me. I focused on a button on the officer's uniform. My stomach churned in a sickly stew.

Trace.

I swallowed hard. "What…happened?"

"May I come in?"

We stepped back from the door to let him pass. Lara led the officer to our living room, where he sat down on the edge of our couch. I sat in the armchair across the room. Lara leaned against the wall, arms crossed.

"What happened?" I asked again.

"Where were you this evenin'?" the officer asked.

"Here." I trembled. "What hap—"

"Can you verify that?"

"He was." Lara rubbed her forehead. "He was here all night."

The officer jotted in his notepad. Elbows on my knees, head in my hands, I sat at his mercy. My throat burned as I choked out answers to his questions.

"A source tells me you're close to Mrs. Macey?"

"No." My insides clenched. "Not anymore."

Brows furrowed, he scribbled more notes. After an hour interrogation, he stood to leave.

"Officer." I jumped up. "Wait."

He halted mid-step.

"Please." I furiously blinked my swollen eyes. "What happened?"

He took a deep breath. "We think there was a domestic scuffle. Got the call, swarmed the home, but it was too late. Chief found his body on the kitchen floor, blood everywhere. Our CSI team thinks it was a mix of his blood…and hers."

No.

I inhaled, but breath wouldn't fill my lungs. He reached for the door, but I grabbed his arm.

"Tracy Bailey," I said. "Where is she?"

"Mrs. *Macey?* She's gone. Nowhere to be found. Called the station, screamed some incoherent garble, then the line went dead." He scrubbed his hand down his face. "We have…theories. We suspect a murder-suicide combo. Classic case. Probably went somewhere to off herself after killing the poor guy."

Murder-suicide. The words shot me in the chest.

"Murderin' whore. Who in their right mind kills their own Partner?" He shook his head. "I don't understand some people. We've got people out now, searchin' for her. Personally, I'm hopin' she already did herself in. Better than if they catch her alive. I hate hostin' executions. Bad for morale on the force."

Execution.

"G'night." He tipped his cap and strutted outside, leaving us alone in the kitchen.

Trace.

Lara spun toward me. "Did you have something to do with this?"

"No, I swear!"

"Good." She uncorked a bottle of white wine and tossed the cork into the sink. "You know, for all that shit Tracy Bailey caused me in my life…" She slugged back a swig, straight from the bottle, then wiped her mouth on her sleeve. Her face contorted into a sick grin. "I hope they catch her."

"You don't mean that."

"Oh, don't I?" She flicked her hair behind her shoulder, proceeding down the hall toward her room, bottle in hand.

My heart raced.

This is my only chance.

I took a deep breath.

"Lara! Wait!"

That was two hours ago. A lot has happened.

I race down the dark streets on foot because they took my car. My heart thumps louder each time my sneakers hit the pavement, but I can't slow down. I don't have much time.

If she's alive, I've only got twenty-four hours to find her. If she's not...

Blood trickles down my face, but I don't feel it like they want me to. I wipe it away and keep running. My pulse races through my skin as I jog to our old neighborhood, pushing my cramping lungs with each step. It's miles away, but it doesn't matter.

I'll find her.

I did something. Something big. For her. For us. For myself.

I left Lara Goodren.

TRACY BAILEY

After one quick stop, I park Sam's car at the tallest bridge in town. It's secluded and ghostlike, only one lane wide. Two dim street lights illuminate the green, rusty posts, creating elongated shadows in the night. Howling wind rustles through the sloppy ponytail I tied as a hasty disguise.

Sirens blaze in the distance, probably looking for me. They'll never look here — at least, not until it's too late. I won't give them the satisfaction of killing me.

Mustering every ounce of strength in my broken body, I climb the maintenance ladder to the top. I used to drive over this bridge sometimes, and I always had a perverse curiosity about this service ladder. I've always wanted to climb it.

Every inch of my body screams, fingers stiff with dried blood. Bruised and broken, I press on.

The plan must be carried out. All the way to the bitter end.

I reach the top and cling to a rusty pole. One hundred feet below, icy white rapids rush in sickening gushes. I close my eyes, heart pounding. My jagged breaths slice through my lungs.

Don't be afraid. I pat my belly. *It'll be over soon.*

I kick my shoe over the edge, into the dark abyss.

Something for them to find, when they can't find my body.

I remove the first layer of my three coats and drape it from the beam above. It sways in the wind, but stays in place.

Piren, wherever you are, I love you. I hope you find my note. And I hope you don't hate me.

I clench my fingers around the rungs of the bridge, close my eyes, and lean my body over the edge.

This is good-bye.

PIREN ALLSTON

The Mayor gave me twenty-four hours to pack before the Lornstown shuttle whisks me away. I ran to his office to confess my crime immediately after leaving Lara. I caught him just as he was putting on his coat. His guards pinned me to the desk and cut my face, right then and there. I didn't even feel it.

They confiscated my car; legally, it's now Lara's.

My Partner screamed till her face turned purple. She called me a thousand ugly names and hurled a shoe at me; it bounced off the doorframe as I dashed outside. Her echoing wails followed me a block, but she didn't.

My family doesn't know what I've done, but they will soon. I sent them a letter explaining why I did it. I hope they receive it before the newspaper prints the story and desecrates me. At least they'll hear my side.

I don't expect them to forgive me. They'll probably hate me until they die. Regardless, I love them, and that will never change. I can't force myself to stop loving them simply because I am not with them; that's not how love works. Love is not a light switch you can flip on and off as you please. It's not something you can manufacture or create. It's not a decision you can make. You can't destroy it with a law, or beat it out with fists. It swarms you when you least expect it, and grabs hold of you.

I didn't choose to fall for Tracy Bailey. But I did.

I know her better than anyone in the world, which is why I know where to go. There is only one place in the whole world to find my best friend.

Face dripping in blood and sweat, I race through Harker's Woods and into the clearing. My feet catch and trip over the rungs as I throw myself to the treehouse floor, panting.

My heart stops.

She's not here.

That's when I find the note.

I have found the one
whom my soul loves.
❤ Song of Solomon 3:4

TWENTY-FOUR YEARS OLD
PART EIGHT

TRACY BAILEY

No, I didn't kill myself.

Maybe there was a time I wanted to end my life. Wanted to stop the pain. Wanted to jump off a bridge into the rushing rapids and hurl myself into final peace. But something changed that night. The night he almost killed me and my baby.

I've always been a survivor. I'm good at surviving. I survived twenty-four years of life, waiting for something to happen. I allowed myself to survive, but not to live.

As Sam throttled me, my survival instinct slipped away. The one thin string inside me, the single thread forcing me to hang on, snapped.

But as if my child fueled me with strength, as if my little unborn baby saved my life, something inside me shifted. It was a hunger, a deep down desire to *live*. Because surviving, going through the motions of a meaningless existence, isn't living.

Standing on the bridge, my life flashed before my eyes; it was all cold and dark. When I left that blood-stained jacket on the post, I left my old life with it.

I didn't die. I said good-bye to Tracy Bailey.

Every piece of evidence I planted — the coat, the shoe, Sam's abandoned car by the bridge — will point the cops to my suicide. The frantic phone call probably helped.

My parents, my friends, and my sister will believe it. I'm a Partner-murderer now; no one can know I'm alive. I couldn't risk anyone tracing me to Lornstown; they needed to believe my death. My parents will mourn, but they will return to their old lives. Veronica will ache, and picturing her bereaved face clenches me inside. But I can't protect her; she must do that for herself. In the end, I know she'll find peace and happiness, and so must I. In this town, being a murderer is less of a taint than loving the wrong person. In their eyes, I committed the worst sin before ever laying eyes on that hammer.

I'm on my second bus now, after a long, five a.m. train. Hair tucked under my hood, I mask my drooping eyes in thick sunglasses. Two layered jackets conceal my bleeding body.

I'm going to Lornstown.

No. I pat my stomach. *We're going to Lornstown.*

We're going home.

I don't expect Piren to leave Lara and find me, not after all we've been through. After all we've done to each other. But I do expect him to find the note. At news of my suicide, he'll come to the treehouse for answers, I know he will. He knows me well enough to go there, and I know him well enough to know that.

He's a father, and he doesn't even know. Maybe he never will.

And someday, if he wants to come find me, I'll be here. I'll wait for him. I'll build a home for us—our own Lornstown cabin treehouse. I'll build it with my own hands, and add to it over time. I'll raise our child the best I can—without a Ceremony in sight. I can see my baby running through The Lighthouse with Evan, causing all sorts of mischief. I'm proud already.

Maybe someday Piren will come. Maybe today, maybe in a year, maybe in a hundred years, but I will be here waiting. Being with him in Lornstown was my fondest memory, and I'll hold it forever. If he never comes to Lornstown, if I never see his face again, I'll still revel in knowing that for those few short hours, he was mine.

The note I left in the treehouse was short:

I'll cya under the arch.

And I intend to go to that arch as often as I can.

I'll see a doctor in Lornstown to fix my broken body. Fix what I hastily bandaged together with whatever I could find, because I'm worth fixing. Piren thinks so, and he's my best friend, so I'm inclined to believe him. Plus, I need to be healthy—I'm a mother now.

The doors slide open, and I've arrived at that quaint farming town, at the mouth of my treacherous hike. I hoist my bag over the seats and jump off the bus. I take a deep breath.

Here we go. You ready?

The arduous hike wrecks my torn muscles, but within a few hours, the sprawling Lornstown wall peeks from the horizon, and I quicken my step. Stumbling and panting, I reach the arch at the top of the hill.

That's when I see him. Framed in the archway, face marred, hair matted, caked in dirt, my best friend waits. My legs freeze, heart jumping into my throat.

I can't breathe, can't think. All I can do is gape.

"You know, for a great adventurer—" he steps toward me "—you suck at disguise. I could tell it was you a mile away."

It's Piren. My best friend. My missing puzzle piece.

"How...how did you get here?"

"Oh, a limo," he says. "The Lornstown shuttle."

"How long have you been standing there?"

"An hour or two. I dunno." He sprouts a half-smile.

My stomach knots with a tangled mess of emotion.

Don't you dare cry.

"But you...Lara..."

"No." He steps closer. "It's over."

I brush his scar with my finger, crimson blood cemented across his cheek.

"You're Banished." The word cracks in my mouth.

"I am."

"They caught you. Because of me?"

"No. I turned myself in. I made the choice."

"And you...you'll stay here?" I ask. "With me?"

"Always. Forever. I promise."

Maybe when love is the unstoppable force, there is no object it can't move. And maybe when it reaches that immovable object, that single thing standing in its way, it will find a way around. It will find a way to live.

I take a deep breath. "I have to tell you something." I press my hands to my belly. "I'm pregnant."

His lip quivers. He darts his eyes to my stomach and back up to my face.

"Is it...?"

"Yours." I meet his eyes. "Are you upset?"

He reaches out a trembling hand and presses it over mine.

"No way," he says. "I just...I don't believe it."

"Believe it."

"Trace, I missed you, I —"

I throw my arms around his neck, locking his lips to mine. My heart bounds.

It's not forbidden anymore.

As we kiss, my lips curl into a giggly smile. He pulls away.

"What's so funny?"

"I'm just…happy."

His toothy grin expands across his face. "To our new lives?"

"The best adventure yet."

He takes my hand, and we pass under the arch together.

"I love you, Tracy Bailey."

"I love you, Piren Allston."

And I always will.

Acknowledgments

I'd like to acknowledge everyone at Omnific Publishing for believing in me and this story from the beginning. I couldn't have done it without the help of the Omnific staff, especially Elizabeth Harper, Colleen Wagner, Jennifer Haren, Micha Stone, and Lisa O'Hara. Also to Omnific's partner, Gallery Books (Simon & Schuster).

I would like to especially thank editor extraordinaire, Sean Riley, for putting up with my emails at all hours of the day and night, and for believing in my vision for *Missing Pieces*. Thank you for everything!

I'd like to thank Carrie Fenn, my first CP, and the amazing Christina de Henry Tessan at Girl Friday Productions for helping me develop this story. Also, Molly Dean Stevens and Jamie Howard, for being so supportive and amazing.

Steve Shannon, for taking my author photos and helping me design my website, and my wonderfully talented cousin Elizabeth Siegel for designing my banner.

I couldn't have done it without the support of my amazing family, especially my parents, Jessica and Paul Tate, and my grandmother, Elizabeth Ross.

My eleventh-grade English teacher, Joann McGlynn, who encouraged me to pursue my dreams—your words stuck with me, even a decade later.

To my in-laws—Vincent F., Michele, Catherine, Ryan, Gabriella, Alexander, Brianna—for supporting not only my book, but their son/ brother/ uncle's decision to marry a writer!

Everyone in the Tate/ Ross/ Bombardier/ Servello families, Diane Pion, and all those who might as well be family—especially Aunt Robin and Uncle Larry, and the Dame School Group.

My wonderful husband, Vincent, for wrangling my sloppy first drafts and proof reading *Missing Pieces* more times than I can count.

Also, for being so unconditionally supportive of my writing and giving me the chance to follow my dreams — I love you!

Kate Smith — thank you for all your authorly guidance over the past few years, and for blurbing my book!

To the St. Louis Writer's Guild, especially the Write Pack Radio team and Thursday table — Jamie, Jennifer, David, Melanie, Brad, Kathleen, Teresa, Matt, Emma, Fedora, Peter, and everyone else — I'm so grateful to you for welcoming this NH girl into the fold.

The three friends I've known since the dawn of time: Kristina Rieger, Caitlin Clark, and Jill Schaffer — thank you for being there all these years. Bekah Mar-Tang — thanks for putting up with all my freak-out texts while I wrote this book. Kirsten Cowan — for being all around awesome. Finally, to Brendan Bly, Alexis Carr, Monica Craver, Amy Debevoise, Audrey Desbiens, Katie Gill, Chris Kinnier, Amy & Eric Lousararian, Paige MacDougall, Brett Roell, Caitlin Stevenson, Lydia Timmons, Sarah Winters, and Molly Wyant. Thank you for believing in me. Your support means the world.

ABOUT THE AUTHOR

A proud New Hampshire native, Meredith Tate lives in St. Louis with her husband, Vincent. Meredith has a master's degree in social work from the University of New Hampshire and is a licensed certified social worker. She is a contributor to the St. Louis Writer's Guild's *Write Pack Radio Show* every Sunday afternoon. When she's not writing, Meredith enjoys traveling to new places, playing the piano, befriending wild geese, and spending time with family and friends. Much like her characters, she's always up for another adventure.

← ⋯ →New Adult Romance← ⋯ →

Three Daves by Nicki Elson
Streamline by Jennifer Lane
The Shades series: *Shades of Atlantis* & *Shades of Avalon* by Carol Oates
The Heart series: *Beside Your Heart, Disclosure of the Heart* & *Forever Your Heart*
by Mary Whitney
Romancing the Bookworm by Kate Evangelista
Flirting with Chaos by Kenya Wright
The Vice, Virtue & Video series: *Revealed, Captured, Desired* & *Devoted*
by Bianca Giovanni
Granton University series: *Loving Lies* by Linda Kage
Missing Pieces by Meredith Tate

← ⋯ →Paranormal Romance← ⋯ →

The Light series: *Seers of Light, Whisper of Light* & *Circle of Light* by Jennifer DeLucy
The Hanaford Park series: *Eve of Samhain* & *Pleasures Untold* by Lisa Sanchez
Immortal Awakening by KC Randall
The Seraphim series: *Crushed Seraphim* & *Bittersweet Seraphim* by Debra Anastasia
The Guardian's Wild Child by Feather Stone
Grave Refrain by Sarah M. Glover
The Divinity series: *Divinity* & *Entity* by Patricia Leever
The Blood Vine series: *Blood Vine, Blood Entangled* & *Blood Reunited*
by Amber Belldene
Divine Temptation by Nicki Elson
The Dead Rapture series: *Love in the Time of the Dead, Love at the End of Days* &
Love Starts with Z by Tera Shanley
The Hidden Races series: *Incandescent* (book 1) by M.V. Freeman
Something Wicked by Carol Oates

← ⋯ →Romantic Suspense← ⋯ →

Whirlwind by Robin DeJarnett
The CONduct series: *With Good Behavior, Bad Behavior* & *On Best Behavior*
by Jennifer Lane
Indivisible by Jessica McQuinn
Between the Lies by Alison Oburia
Blind Man's Bargain by Tracy Winegar

← ⋯ →Erotic Romance← ⋯ →

The Keyhole series: *Becoming sage* (book 1) by Kasi Alexander
The Keyhole series: *Saving sunni* (book 2) by Kasi & Reggie Alexander
The Winemaker's Dinner: *Appetizers* & *Entrée* by Dr. Ivan Rusilko & Everly Drummond
The Winemaker's Dinner: *Dessert* by Dr. Ivan Rusilko
Client N° 5 by Joy Fulcher
The Enclave series: *Closer and Closer* (book 1) by Jenna Barton

Historical Romance

Cat O' Nine Tails by Patricia Leever
Burning Embers by Hannah Fielding
Seven for a Secret by Rumer Haven

Anthologies

A Valentine Anthology including short stories by
Alice Clayton ("With a Double Oven"),
Jennifer DeLucy ("Magnus of Pfelt, Conquering Viking Lord"),
Nicki Elson ("I Don't Do Valentine's Day"),
Jessica McQuinn ("Better Than One Dead Rose and a Monkey Card"),
Victoria Michaels ("Home to Jackson"), and
Alison Oburia ("The Bridge")

Taking Liberties including an introduction by Tiffany Reisz and short stories by
Mina Vaughn ("John Hancock-Blocked"),
Linda Cunningham ("A Boston Marriage"),
Joy Fulcher ("Tea for Two"),
KC Holly ("The British Are Coming!"),
Kimberly Jensen & Scott Stark ("E. Pluribus Threesome"), and
Vivian Rider ("M'Lady's Secret Service")

Sets

The Heart Series Box Set (*Beside Your Heart, Disclosure of the Heart* &
Forever Your Heart) by Mary Whitney
The CONduct Series Box Set (*With Good Behavior, Bad Behavior* &
On Best Behavior) by Jennifer Lane
The Light Series Box Set (*Seers of Light, Whisper of Light, Circle of Light* &
Glimpse of Light) by Jennifer DeLucy
The Blood Vine Series Box Set (*Blood Vine, Blood Entangled, Blood Reunited* &
Blood Eternal) by Amber Belldene

Singles, Novellas & Special Editions

It's Only Kinky the First Time (A Keyhole series single) by Kasi Alexander
Learning the Ropes (A Keyhole series single) by Kasi & Reggie Alexander
The Winemaker's Dinner: RSVP by Dr. Ivan Rusilko
The Winemaker's Dinner: No Reservations by Everly Drummond
Big Guns by Jessica McQuinn
Concessions by Robin DeJarnett
Starstruck by Lisa Sanchez
New Flame by BJ Thornton
Shackled by Debra Anastasia

Swim Recruit by Jennifer Lane
Sway by Nicki Elson
Full Speed Ahead by Susan Kaye Quinn
The Second Sunrise by Hannah Downing
The Summer Prince by Carol Oates
Whatever it Takes by Sarah M. Glover
Clarity (A *Divinity* prequel single) by Patricia Leever
A Christmas Wish (A *Cocktails & Dreams* single) by Autumn Markus
Late Night with Andres by Debra Anastasia
Poughkeepsie (enhanced iPad app collector's edition) by Debra Anastasia
Poughkeepsie (audio book edition) by Debra Anastasia
Blood Eternal (A Blood Vine series single, epilogue to series) by Amber Belldene
Carnaval de Amor (*The Winemaker's Dinner*, Spanish edition)
by Dr. Ivan Rusilko & Everly Drummond

coming soon from
OMNIFIC PUBLISHING

Chronicles of Midvalen: *Command the Tides* (book 1) by Wren Handman
The Hidden Races series: *Illumination* (book 2) by M.V. Freeman
The WORDS series: *The Record of My Heart* (novella 3.5) by Georgina Guthrie
The Counterfeit by Tracy Winegar
The Embrace series: *Entwined* (book 3) by Cherie Colyer
The Adventures of Clarissa Hardy by Chloe Gillis
The Ground Rules by Roya Carmen
Trouble Me by Beck Anderson

CPSIA information can be obtained
at www.ICGtesting.com
Printed in the USA
FFOW02n0701030315
11506FF